Cat [...] oon
books as a teenager, and now that she's writing them

[...] every boo[...] is a new adven[...] Cathy lives in
London. Her three daughters—Charlotte, Olivia and
Emma—have always been, and continue to be, the
greatest inspirations in her life.

Growing up near the beach, **Annie West** spent lots
of time observing tall, burnished lifeguards—early
research! Now she spends her days fantasising about
gorgeous men and their love-lives. Annie has been a
reader all her life. She also loves travel, long walks,
good company and great food. You can contact her at
annie@annie-west.com or via PO Box 1041, Warners
Bay, NSW 2282, Australia.

THE HOUSEKEEPER'S INVITATION TO ITALY

CATHY WILLIAMS

REUNITED BY THE GREEK'S BABY

ANNIE WEST

MILLS & BOON

First published in Great Britain 2023
by Mills & Boon, an imprint of HarperCollins*Publishers* Ltd,
1 London Bridge Street, London, SE1 9GF

www.harpercollins.co.uk

HarperCollins*Publishers*
Macken House, 39/40 Mayor Street Upper,
Dublin 1, D01 C9W8, Ireland

The Housekeeper's Invitation to Italy © 2023 Cathy Williams

Reunited by the Greek's Baby © 2023 Annie West

ISBN: 978-0-263-30664-4

02/23

Printed and Bound in Spain using 100% Renewable Electricity
at CPI Black Print, Barcelona

THE HOUSEKEEPER'S INVITATION TO ITALY

CATHY WILLIAMS

MILLS & BOON

To my supportive and loving daughters

CHAPTER ONE

THE BUILDING WASN'T quite what Sophie had been expecting. Although now that she was standing outside the impressive Georgian edifice she had to concede that she had just rushed to assume the obvious.

Arrogant billionaire…shiny over-the-top offices. The sort of place that announced in no uncertain terms that its occupant was not a man to be messed with because he was bigger, stronger and richer than you.

Buffeted by a brutal winter wind, and noting that it was already dark at a little after five-thirty in the afternoon, she remained hesitantly staring at the building.

It was an impeccably groomed four-storeyed town house, fronted by black railings and a shallow flight of steps that led up to a black door. In all respects it was identical to all the other town houses in this uber-prestigious crescent in the heart of London. From Bentleys to Teslas, every single car parked was high-end. There was a hush about the place which made her think that if she hung around for too long, staring and frowning and dithering, wondering whether she had done the right thing or not, then someone would materialise out of thin air and escort her right back to the busy streets a stone's throw away. Possibly by the scruff of her neck.

Galvanised by the prospect of that, Sophie hurried across the completely empty road, up the bank of steps, and realised that the gleaming brass knocker was just there for show—because there was a discreet panel of buttons to the side and a speakerphone.

Just for a few seconds, she took time out to contemplate where she was and why.

She'd had a long and uncomfortable journey from raw and wintry Yorkshire down to London—a journey undertaken with the sort of subterfuge she personally loathed, and with an outcome that was far from predictable. She had a message to be relayed under cover of darkness, because Leonard-White had expressly banned her from contacting his son, and what sort of reception was she going to get? Having gone against the wishes of her boss to uneasily follow what her inner voice had told her?

She had no idea, because Alessio Rossi-White, from everything she had seen of him, was a forbidding and terrifyingly remote law unto himself.

Sophie pressed the buzzer, and the nerves which she had been keeping at bay leapt out from their hiding places and her heart began to beat faster. The disembodied voice on the other end was a woman's, clipped and well-modulated, and it told her that, no, unless an appointment had been made, there was absolutely no chance that she would be allowed in.

'I'm afraid,' the woman said, without a trace of regret in her voice, 'that Mr Rossi-White is only in the city for a few days, and his calendar is far too packed for him to see *anyone* at all, whatever the circumstances. Of course,' she added, 'if you would like to make an appointment...'

'I've spent hours getting here...'

The cut-glass accent dropped a few shades down from cool to positively glacial. 'Perhaps you should have checked first to find out whether Mr Rossi-White was available? Now, if you don't mind, I have calls waiting—'

'I *do* mind, actually,' Sophie interjected, before the next sound she heard could be the sound of a disconnected intercom. However unpleasant this task was, she was here for a reason, and she wasn't going to be deterred by a receptionist, however cut-glass the accent happened to be.

She had dealt with bigger, weightier setbacks in her life than an overprotective receptionist behind a closed door. The bottom line was that she wasn't leaving until she saw Alessio Rossi-White and told him about his father.

'I *beg* your pardon!'

'This is personal,' Sophie said shortly, unwilling to divulge anything further to someone whose business it most certainly wasn't. 'If you really want to refuse me entry, then be my guest. But I can assure you that there'll be hell to pay when Alessio finds out that I've been turned away.'

She noted the momentary hesitation at the other end of the speakerphone and quietly breathed a sigh of relief. Of course she should have done precisely as the woman advised and alerted Alessio to the fact that she was travelling to London to see him, but it had all been all so hurried and so hush-hush. She'd known he would be in London because, in her typically formal manner, his PA always uploaded his movements to his father's email on a weekly basis. Just in case. To her knowledge, Leonard had never once used the information to contact his son.

So, yes, she'd known where to pin him down, but still... it had been a time of anxiety, during which she had barely stopped to catch her breath as revelation after revelation had crawled out of the woodwork, sending her into a tailspin. It went so beyond her brief to be here that she seemed to have lost sight of her job title completely—but what else could she do? She was incredibly fond of Leonard, and the thought of the uncertainty and stress he had carried around with him for months...was still carrying... had propelled her into this unfamiliar territory. She was paid way over the odds for her work, and with that, she accepted, came unfamiliar territory—even if this category of 'unfamiliar' was something she hadn't banked on ever having to deal with.

'I'll see what I can do. Might I have your name?'

'Sophie Court.'

Would he even recognise the name?

'You can tell him that I work for his father.'

'Please hold the line.'

It took Alessio a couple of seconds to register the name, but it fell into place as soon as he was told that the woman was his father's nurse/companion.

Or maybe it was companion/nurse. It was a distinction that had never really been clarified.

His father had had a stroke two years ago—or, as he had impatiently brushed it off as, *'A silly health scare... nothing to worry about...no need to tramp all the way to Yorkshire... I might be old but I'm not completely decrepit yet...* But did he really need someone to look after him on a daily basis?

The last time Alessio had visited—which had been months previously—the old man had seemed his usual self. Scowling...impatient...and disinclined to do or say anything that went beyond the absolute minimum on the politeness scale. There had certainly been no touching confidences of any kind—not that there ever was. When it came to their quarterly duty visits, punctuated with dry, superficial telephone exchanges, he and his father had cornered the market.

Alessio had long given up debating the normality of this situation. It was what it was. If his was a life of hard edges, a place where regret and nostalgia no longer existed, then it was because bitter experience had shaped him, and he had grown to see those hard edges as symbols of an inner strength that had made him the hugely successful and powerful man he was.

Sophie Court... He'd forgotten the woman even existed. She had certainly never been in evidence on the last few occasions he had visited his father's estate.

But here she was, and she couldn't have come at a worse time, because his inbox was overburdened with things waiting to be addressed. Several meetings were banked up, and he had an overseas conference call in under an hour with three CEOs in three different time zones.

Whatever she had come to say, she would have to say it quickly, succinctly, and without any embellishments.

Time, after all, was money.

In truth, he couldn't begin to think what might require a visit from the woman, and he buzzed her up and settled back in his chair, fully prepared to dispatch her if she didn't cut to the chase in time for him to complete what remained of his already long day on schedule.

She wasn't kept waiting. For that, Sophie was relieved. Because the less time she had to think about what she had to say, the less leeway it gave her nerves to spiral away in the wrong direction.

The truth was that she could handle pretty much whatever life chose to throw at her. She was twenty-nine years old now, and from the age of fifteen, when her father had died, she had been the one to pick up the pieces, in charge of the household, with all her youthful dreams snatched away by grim, unforgiving reality.

A kid sister, five years younger, to be protected... A mother who had retreated into her own depressed world, barely able to function and certainly not able to keep things together, to be supported... And a scattering of relatives who had clucked with sympathy whilst shutting all their doors when it came to actually helping out on any kind of practical level.

Money had been scarce, and she'd had to learn fast how to run a household efficiently, with minimum resources, and how to claim what benefits could be claimed just so that they could all survive.

She had studied hard, made sure Addy kept her head down, and nursed her mother through months and years of bewildered misery. If lessons had been learnt the biggest, for Sophie, had been to avoid the recklessness of becoming so dependent on one person that your world fell apart when that person was removed from it.

Her mother had loved too much. That would never be Sophie's downfall.

Her years at school had been a grinding mix of studying hard and working at whatever after-school jobs she could pick up so that there was a little extra cash coming in. There had been a mortgage to maintain, bills to be paid, and the juggling act involved to keep all the balls in the air had made her grow up at the speed of light. There had been no time to enjoy her adolescence. Too much had been going on.

Her dream of becoming a doctor had bitten the dust but, that said, she had found joy in the nursing career she had fallen back on, and even more in working for Leonard. Because hers was far more than a simple nursing job, and it paid so well that for the first time in her life she was able to save a bit, whilst helping out her mother and her sister.

Life had been tough, but she had handled it.

Alessio Rossi-White, though…

No, he was an entity she couldn't handle. He did something to her—made the hairs on the back of her neck stand on end and sent her nervous system into disturbing freefall. She had met him only a handful of times since she had started working for his father two years ago, and she had known instantly that she would always make sure that her days off coincided with his visits.

He was cold, arrogant and dismissive. He came for the barest minimum of time and always, *always* managed to give the impression that he had better things to do. On every level, he was the most objectionable man she had ever met in her life. She didn't think he had addressed her directly once, on any of the occasions when they had met, and with his father he was cool, guarded, and so chillingly formal that he made her shiver. From opposite ends of the table they would sit and exchange information with such a lack of warmth that it was little wonder his father had absolutely prohibited her from telling his son about his ongoing problems.

She had taken matters into her own hands because she had seen no choice, but even so, she still wondered whether she was doing the right thing.

Standing outside the pristine Georgian town house had been sufficiently daunting, but inside it was even more so. Pale marble and burnished wood were complemented by a discreet scattering of exotic plants in strategic places. The desk behind which sat the woman whose mission had been to get rid of her was a masterpiece of dull chrome and highly glossed very smooth wood, and the paintings on the walls were all abstracts which looked as expensive as everything else.

There were no raised voices from above...no sounds of ringing phones and no clattering of urgent footsteps. If vast wealth could have a sound, then this soft hush was it.

Sophie was tempted to turn tail and flee, but instead she smiled politely at the immaculately groomed thirty-something blonde before briefly taking a seat by the window.

So this was what money looked like, she thought. His Leonard's estate was huge and sprawling and grand, but inside it had remained unchanged over the years, with dated furnishings and an air of fast-fading elegance. It was a once-grand house quietly collecting dust from the lack of money being spent on it. This space, though…

She knew that it was just one of Alessio's offices and the smallest, specifically used by his massively profitable elitist hedge fund team. His other huge offices were in Rome, Lisbon and Zurich, and from there the many tentacles of all his other concerns were managed.

She was channelled into a glass elevator which whizzed her up three floors to the top and disgorged her into an area that looked more like an office, insofar as there were desks separated by wood and glass partitions, and people sitting behind those desks surrounded by screens and working with the sort of quiet, frowning concentration that seemed to indicate huge sums of money being handled.

They barely glanced at her as she walked past them.

At the very end of the open-plan space were a handful of private offices, and Alessio's was right at the end. Only when she was standing outside, hand poised to knock on the streamlined highly polished walnut door which was slightly ajar, did she feel that flutter of butterflies in her tummy once again, and this time it had nothing to do with the conversation waiting to be had. This time it had to do with the fact of *seeing* him.

It had been a while. She revived all the reasons why she disliked the man, but her stomach clenched as she was called in to an outer office by his PA, who was expecting her. She was relieved of her coat and scarf and woolly hat, and was aware of murmured pleasantries, but all she could focus on was the solid door dividing this outer office from Alessio's inner sanctum.

Did the smartly dressed PA even know who she was? Her manner was crisp, but uber polite, and Sophie assumed that, given the reach of Alessio's power, if he'd allowed her entry within his hallowed walls, then that was sufficient to ensure all due respect from every single one of his employees, whether they knew who she was or not.

He owned them all, didn't he? From what Sophie had glimpsed of the man in the past, his attitude was that of someone who owned everyone around him and really didn't mind them knowing.

She breathed in deeply, waiting for the imposing door in front of which she was standing to be opened, her heart beating in her chest like a sledgehammer as her head was suddenly filled with visions of the man she was about to confront.

Tall...olive-skinned...with raven-dark hair and even darker eyes. He was the embodiment of physical perfection, as beautiful and as cold as any marble statue ever sculpted. Every line of his half-Italian ancestry was imprinted in the aggressive, sinful perfection of his features.

Sophie had seen pictures of Isabella Rossi, his mother, who had died many years previously, and had been rendered speechless by her outrageous sultry beauty, every gene of which she had passed down to Alessio, her only child.

Everything single thing around her...the streamlined dove-grey furniture...the pale silk rug on the blonde wooden floor...the cream leather sofa tucked against the wall...faded away as that connecting door was gently pushed open and there he was, sprawled behind a desk the size of a single bed, hands folded behind his head, waiting.

There was only mild curiosity on his face as he looked at Sophie, who stood, hovering, in the centre of his massive office as the door behind her was closed.

The woman specialised in the art of fading into the background, Alessio mused. Grey trousers, grey jumper, a long dark cardigan and an over-the-shoulder bag that might have held the kitchen sink. She had short-cropped fair hair and brown eyes, and in defiance of nearly every woman he had ever met seemed to have only a passing acquaintance with make-up. And yet there was still something about her that defied the faded image she seemed intent on conveying.

He continued to stare at her in silence, vaguely trying to work out what it was about her that didn't conform to the uninspired standard she clearly wanted to set, before abruptly sitting forward, slapping the desk with both hands and nodding to the wide black leather chair in front of it.

'No need to stand by the door as if waiting for divine inspiration, Miss Court. Have a seat and tell me what you're doing here. Tea? Coffee? Something a bit more spirited?'

He glanced at his watch before rising to his feet and strolling towards the window to briefly peer outside at bleak, grey, wintry London, before spinning round to face her. He perched against the window ledge and shoved his hands in the pockets of his trousers, while she slid into the chair opposite his desk and tucked her hair neatly behind her ears.

'No, thanks.'

'Well…? I would while away some more time on pleasantries, but I'm afraid I have a lot to do…'

'Maybe I'll have a cup of coffee after all,' Sophie said. 'It's been a long trip getting here.'

She realised that she actually needed a few pleasantries before launching into what she had to say. She needed to swim in the shallows for a bit before diving into the deep end.

She looked around her, taking in her surroundings. The building might be Georgian, but it had been refurbished to a dizzyingly modern standard, with muted colours and pale chairs and cream wooden shutters at the windows.

'I didn't expect you to work in a place like this,' she heard herself say, and blushed when he raised his eyebrows in question and he lazily strolled back towards his desk. He sat, pushing the chair at an angle so that he could tilt it back, his long legs stretched to the side and crossed at the ankles. A dangerous predator at rest.

'A place like what?'

Sophie shrugged and steeled herself to meet the jet-black eyes lazily pinned to her face. 'I suppose I expected something more modern. Glass and steel.'

Hard edges for a hard man.

'This part of my business portfolio deals exclusively with hedge funds. My clients enjoy privacy, and that's exactly what they get in this postcode. I'm surprised to see you here, Sophie, but I can only assume that this has something to do with my father?'

His eyes didn't leave her face for a single second as he buzzed through to his PA and asked for a pot of coffee.

'Or are you here for some other reason?'

'No.'

What other reason could she possibly have had for visiting this guy?

'I am here about your dad... I wish I could put this another way, but Leonard had another stroke a couple of weeks ago,' she said bluntly.

She noted the way he suddenly stilled, the way his eyes narrowed and the guarded mantle that dropped over him like a powerful protective shield.

'That's impossible.'

'What do you mean?'

'I would have known.'

Coffee was brought in, but Sophie barely noticed because she was riveted by his dark, dark eyes, which were now as hard and as cold as the frozen wastes of Siberia.

She knew so much about this man—largely through all the articles his father had tucked away about him over the years, and from the pages of the memoirs he faithfully dictated every evening, just before his dinner was served. Whether she liked it or not, she knew where he worked, and what he did, and all about the fortune he had single-handedly amassed from the springboard of his mother's inheritance, bequeathed to him when she'd died many years previously.

She knew that he was some kind of financial genius. She also knew that he was a guy who played as hard as he worked. She had seen the carefully cut-out glossy pictures of him captured by paparazzi, with a series of gorgeous tiny little blondes on his arm, usually smiling and gazing up at him with adoring eyes. She knew that none of them ever stayed the course.

Now, she shivered and wondered what it was that drew all those women to him. Surely, however rich and beautiful the man was, no one could ever really be attracted to someone as chillingly cold as he was? Money talked, but surely it didn't talk *that* much?

Looking at him now, mesmerised against her will, Sophie tried and failed to imagine him laughing or crying or showing any emotion. Certainly, on the few occasions when she'd seen him with his father, none had been in evidence.

She thought of Leonard and those meticulously and lovingly collected articles about his son and she hardened inside—because Alessio had certainly never repaid his father's devotion with any show of affection…none that she'd ever witnessed at any rate.

'How?' she asked flatly. 'How would you have known when you never visit?'

'I beg your pardon?'

This was the first time Sophie had ever really spoken to Alessio, aside from polite utterances in the company of his father, after which she had faded away into the role of practically invisible carer, there to do a job and not contribute to the conversation. Now she felt as though there was a dam inside her, waiting to burst.

She had survived years of having to make herself heard by people in positions of authority, which, in the beginning, as a shy, gawky teenager, had been alien to her. Her sister had always been the bubbly, outgoing one, who captured attention because she was so small and pretty, with her blonde hair and baby blue eyes. But circumstances had foisted a personality upon Sophie that had become ingrained. She had learned to stick up for herself and to have a voice, and she saw no reason why she shouldn't exercise that voice now. Because after all Alessio, for all his money and power, wasn't the one who paid her salary, was he?

She uneasily wondered how many more pay-cheques would be coming her way, all things considered, and then decided that that was all the more reason to tell this arrogant, odious guy exactly what she thought.

If she'd read him correctly, then he was the sort of man rarely confronted by people who spoke their mind.

'The last time you came to see your father was over five months ago.'

'Do I detect a note of criticism in your voice, Miss Court?'

'I think it's amazing that you seem surprised by what I've come to say. I think it's even more amazing that you actually expect to be in the loop when it comes to your father's day-to-day life when you're hardly around.'

'I don't believe I'm hearing this!'

'I'm only being honest.'

'And remind me when I asked for your honesty?' he gritted in a voice that could freeze water, as he stared at her with grim disbelief. 'I don't believe I've ever heard you mutter more than two words at a stretch, and yet you've suddenly decided to show up here uninvited and give me the benefit of your opinions.'

Sophie flushed and met his coldly discouraging gaze head-on and with silence.

'So,' he continued icily, 'returning to the matter at hand. My father's had another stroke. When exactly did this happen, and why is this the first time I'm hearing about it?'

His dark eyes were boring into her and they never left her face—even when the door was gently opened and his PA reminded him that he was due somewhere in under half an hour as she depositing a coffee pot on his desk. He dismissed her with a couple of words and a wave of his hand, and informed her that he was not to be disturbed until he said otherwise.

He clicked his tongue impatiently when Sophie didn't immediately fill in the silence and answer his questions.

'You have a duty of care to my father,' he informed her acidly, 'and part of that duty entails informing me of all matters pertaining to his health.'

'He forbade me from doing so,' Sophie returned bluntly, and then felt awful at the sight of the dark flush that spread across his sharp cheekbones.

She'd toughened up over the years because she'd had to, but since when had she lost the ability to empathise? Alessio might rub her the wrong way, and he might have little or no time for his father, but was it really in her remit to pass judgement on anyone? To be needlessly forthright? She'd struck a nerve, and if she could have swallowed those words back then she would have.

She might have needed strength to deal with what Fate had thrown at her, but she had also needed patience, understanding and love, and she'd always had those in abundance.

Those were the very qualities that had seen her look out for her younger sister, support her in her endeavours to become an actress, even though, personally, Sophie could not have thought of a less sensible road to travel down. They were also the qualities that had guided her through her darkest moments, when her mother had been a lost soul, unable to cope after her husband's sudden death.

Both were settled now, but being tough had only been part of the answer when it had come to handling their adversities, so where had her sense of sympathy gone?

'I'm sorry,' she said quietly. 'I shouldn't have said that.'

'Because it's not true?'

'It was a tactless way of putting it and I can see that I've hurt you.'

Alessio stiffened. *Hurt?* He was incapable of being hurt. He had been hurt in the past—hurt by the death of his beloved mother, hurt by the indifference of his father towards him in the aftermath of that death. Dealing with those past hurts had toughened him...made him impregnable. His lips thinned in affront that the woman sitting opposite him might actually think herself capable of hurting him by anything she said.

He felt as though he might be seeing Sophie Court for the very first time, because on those other occasions she had been as quiet as a mouse, head bowed, voice subdued when he'd addressed her, with none of the fire on display now.

For the first time in a long time, he was discovering what it felt like to be in the presence of the unexpected. She might be dressed like a maiden aunt, but she certainly wasn't behaving like one, and he narrowed his eyes and looked at her...*really* looked at her.

Tall, slender, she had skin as pale as alabaster and a wary expression in her brown eyes that spoke of a contained personality.

Why was she so contained? And how was it that someone still in her twenties was willing to take on the full-time role of looking after an old, cantankerous man?

A sudden wave of curiosity threatened to steal a march, and he brought it firmly back to heel.

'Don't worry about my feelings, Miss Court,' he said with exaggerated politeness. 'I've always found that I'm perfectly capable of handling them myself. So my father would rather I did not know of his stroke? He's proud and likes to think he's infallible. Sadly, he's not. What has his consultant said?'

He decided to refrain from telling her that not only should she have immediately told him what had happened, but should also have ensured that he was kept in the loop by his father's consultant.

'Well?' he prompted, when he was greeted with silence.

He felt the stirrings of disquiet. So much water had flowed under that bridge, so many doors had been shut over the years, and yet the thought of losing his father was oddly unsettling. Was it because there had been so many issues that had never been addressed by either of them?

His heart picked up pace and he suddenly sprang to his feet to pace the room, walking jerkily to the window and staring out at the private circular courtyard, which was lit enough for him to make out the exquisite landscaping, the hedges and overhanging trees, the vague shapes of the benches where his employees could choose to relax whenever they wanted.

'Is he in a critical condition?' Alessio demanded, raking his fingers through his hair as he spun round to face her.

'He was in hospital for two nights. He's back home now.'

Alessio breathed a sigh of relief. 'Then why this reticence on the subject? You should know that the last time my father had a stroke he waved aside my offers to go to Glenn House, so he has form when it comes to making sure his pride takes precedence over everything.'

Looking at him, Sophie was startled at the bitterness that had crept into his voice. Was he even aware of it?

'The consultant said that the stroke was very likely caused by stress.'

'What has my father got to be stressed about?' Alessio asked, his voice genuinely puzzled.

'He's been having financial worries.'

'I would know if that were true. We don't talk a great deal, but we do cover the financial markets. He would have said something. No. You must be mistaken.' He sighed. 'This is not the right place to be having a conversation of this nature.'

'It doesn't matter where we are,' Sophie told him. 'I'll just say what I've come to say and then I'll leave.'

'It's nearly six-thirty. Have you eaten today at all? What time did you leave Harrogate?'

He was talking and walking, and Sophie watched in consternation as he began putting on his jacket and then opened a concealed door that faded into the polished walnut panels to extract a coat.

'I know a wine bar not a million miles away. We can go there. I think I might need a drink for this particular conversation.'

'What about your work? Your meetings?'

Did she *want* to carry on chatting in a wine bar? She was uncomfortable with the idea of that. Maybe even a little panicked, although she wasn't entirely sure why.

She could understand why he might find it constricting to have an intensely personal conversation with interruptions from his PA and his computer reminding him that there was still work to be done, even though in most normal offices the stampede for the exit would have already begun. It was late, and yet there were no signs that anyone was getting ready to leave. She figured that making money didn't keep nine-to-five hours. A bit like nursing.

'I'm the boss,' he said neutrally, coming to stand directly in front of her, his towering six-foot-three swamping her senses and bringing her out in a fine nervous perspiration. 'The buck stops with me. If I want to cancel meetings, I can do it. The position of tycoon,' he said, with wry self-mockery, 'comes with little perks like that.'

Just like that, Sophie felt her breath leave her in a whoosh and she glanced away quickly, although she could feel the heat in her face as he continued to look at her for a few more seconds before moving away.

She stood up, but her mind was all over the place as she reached for her bag. She'd come with a prepared speech, and all she could think was that she'd somehow been swept away on an unexpected riptide that had not at all been part of her plan.

In no corner of her mind had she anticipated being ushered into a chauffeur-driven Bentley, staring out from behind privacy glass at pedestrians scurrying across packed pavements, and then being swept into a wine bar that was the last word in understated monochrome luxury, with black leather sofas and stark wooden floors and concrete effect walls.

For the whole of the trip Alessio had been on his phone, sometimes switching languages, making sure that his work was covered in his unplanned absence from the office.

It had been a relief, because it had given her time to get her scattered thoughts in order and to remind herself that this was, in essence, a business conversation. Nothing she couldn't handle.

You can do this, and before you know it, it'll be another day...

It was the mantra she had repeated to herself so many times through the years, as her adolescence had slipped away between her fingers, lost in the business of growing up too fast.

She repeated it now, as she perched on the edge of the plush leather sofa, but even so she still tensed when he leaned towards her from his chair opposite, dwarfing the thin glass table separating them, and said in a low, driven undertone, 'So, Miss Court, here we are. Time to talk to me about everything that's been going on with my father. You have my undivided attention…'

CHAPTER TWO

UP CLOSE TO HER, as he was now, Alessio absently noted that she had the most unusual eyes—almond-shaped and nut-brown and fringed with very long, dark lashes, dramatic against the smooth pallor of her skin. His eyes drifted to the stern, no-nonsense cropped hair. He was so accustomed to women advertising their assets that this particular woman's strenuous efforts to disguise what she had under her drab, unrevealing clothes roused a flare of curiosity.

Just briefly.

'Well?' he prompted. 'You've decided that a character assassination is in order, so the very least you could do now is tell me what exactly I've been assassinated for. You've told me that my father's stroke may have been caused by stress, and you've followed that up with hints about money problems he's been having. Money problems I know nothing about because, of course, I am the son who doesn't give a damn. So I think a little more enlightenment is in order, don't you?'

He sat back when a waiter approached, but instead of taking the menus extended he ordered tapas, leaving the selection up to the chef, and a bottle of Chablis. Not once did his eyes leave her face.

'Or,' he drawled, as she chewed her lip and met his un-wavering dark gaze with silence, 'have you got more criticisms of me stashed up your sleeve before you cut to the chase and get down to providing me with a little proof to back up what you're saying? Please…' he waved his arms expansively '…don't let good manners stand in the way of home truths.'

Sophie was sorely tempted to tell him that, yes, she had lots more criticism stashed up her sleeve, but instead she snapped out of her dazed silence and pursed her lips.

'The two things are connected,' she said quietly. 'Your father's health and the fact that he has financial problems. He didn't want you to know about either of them, but I felt I had no choice but to tell you because his bank manager paid a visit to the house while he was in hospital and confided in me that most of the company holdings are in the red. I don't know the exact details, but I gather a loan was taken out against the company some years ago and repayment is now being demanded—except there's nothing to pay it back with because the company has been losing money for years. I think Mr Ellis would have contacted you directly, but he's always been under strict instructions that all financial matters are to be kept private and under no circumstances are you to be asked to intervene. I think the only reason he spoke to me was because he felt he had no choice.'

'He felt he had *no choice*? I don't believe I'm hearing this…' Alessio muttered under his breath. 'What the hell has the old fool been getting up to up to behind my back?'

'Don't say that,' Sophie returned, stricken. 'He's proud. Many people his age are. He admires you so much and he doesn't want you to find out that he's made mistakes and… I don't know…trusted people to do a job which they haven't done…'

Alessio laughed humourlessly. 'I suggest you stick to the script, Miss Court, and not go off-piste with yet more personal observations that bear no resemblance to reality. It's outrageous that Ellis didn't come to me first.'

'I suppose client confidentiality…'

'And yet you're here, despite my father forbidding you to get in touch with me.'

'I care about him very much, and I don't think he can survive the collapse of his company.'

'I'll need to get full details of whatever mess my father has got himself into. And Ellis should start scouring the job columns, because when I'm through with him he'll realise just how misjudged his loyalties have been.'

'How can you be so unsympathetic?' Sophie gasped, as impulse got the better of common sense.

'If you think this is the sound of me being unsympathetic, then stick around and you'll find out what it *really* sounds like when my patience snaps,' Alessio grated. 'I'm being practical. Ellis is a bank manager. He's in charge of money matters. He's not there for hand-wringing and misplaced loyalties. When it comes to bankruptcy, all's fair in love and war. The man should not have thought twice about coming to me. Who else can sort out my father's financial problems? Magic fairies with chequebooks? If I'd known about these money problems earlier, they would have been sorted by now.'

They were interrupted by the arrival of food, but for a couple of seconds Sophie was barely aware of the dishes being placed on the table in front of them because she was one hundred per cent mesmerised by the eyes pinned to her face. The man was hypnotic and terrifying in equal measure.

'I don't know all the ins and outs…'

'You know enough, and I'm guessing that if you think it's drastic enough to bring yourself out of hiding to confront me here, then chances are it's even worse than you imagine.'

'I haven't been in hiding.'

'I can't think of the last time I set eyes on you when I was at my father's house.'

'I… I like to leave you both to…to bond. You don't need me hovering in the background, dishing out Leonard's tablets and telling him what he can and can't eat…'

'You'd be surprised. It might make a refreshing variation on our usual line of conversation, which would appear to be even more superficial than I thought possible if he's been keeping all of this from me. But enough of that. First and foremost, do *you* need help.'

'Help…?'

'On a practical level. Someone to assist with my father's recovery now he's at home. I realise you're a qualified nurse, but there might be issues with physically helping my father to move around that you might find tricky on your own.'

Sophie was impressed by his immediate grasp of what might be necessary. He was being practical, and she realised that in a strange way that was just what she needed, because her emotions had been running wild for the past few days. Focusing on the more pedestrian stuff would calm her, and having someone else alongside her in doing that would be even more calming, even if the 'someone' in question was Alessio.

There was also concern in his voice. She could *sense* it. And yet on the surface anyone would think that he was dealing with a business matter, without the intrusion of any emotions muddying the water. She'd presented him with a problem and he was finding ways to deal with it, because he was solution-orientated.

'No…' She paused, then added with heartfelt honesty, 'But thanks for asking and I mean that.' She half smiled and belatedly began to pick at the tapas, because she was ravenous. 'You'd be surprised how strong you need to be when you're a nurse. There's a lot of lifting involved, but we're all trained in how to do it in the most efficient and least damaging way possible.'

'What else do you do?' Alessio asked abruptly, and Sophie looked at him with surprise.

'What do you mean?'

'You're…how old?'

'Twenty-nine,' she said awkwardly.

'You're twenty-nine years old and yet you're content to work full-time for my father. He hasn't needed round-the-clock care for all these years, surely. So, that being the case, what do you *do*? You're young. Don't you find the work lacking in stimulation?'

Sophie stiffened. His voice was genuinely curious, and that was what made it all the more insulting.

Twenty-nine years old and willing to spend most of her days with an old man. An old and very interesting man, but an old man all the same. And she had more than sufficient time off, and saw her nursing friends as often as she could, catching them when they weren't on awkward shifts…having a laugh with them and watching from the sidelines as they all began to get involved in serious relationships.

That was a world she was not tempted to enter. She'd seen what love could do. She wasn't her mother—of course not. She hoped she had more inner strength. But who knew? She couldn't bear to think about losing herself in anyone to the point where she became so reliant on them that if they were snatched away her life would collapse into pieces.

Was that being wise and cautious? Or had she become accustomed to running scared? She didn't know. Maybe she would go there one day, but it would be with someone who was more of a friend…someone who wouldn't get to her enough to topple her world if things didn't work out.

Was she content to work for an old man because, sub-consciously, it prevented her from tackling the real world and dipping her toes into the unpredictable business of dating? Her last boyfriend had been a nice guy, but they had broken up years previously. He had wanted more than she was capable of giving. Was that to be her destiny?

It didn't scare her. Never finding true love didn't scare her. Finding it and losing it did.

Still, those mildly curious eyes on her were unsettling.

'Is it any less stimulating than working behind a computer in an office?' she retorted sharply, her bristles up.

She was uncomfortably aware that she'd thought nothing of telling him what she thought of him, and yet now she was resentful and defensive because he was repaying the favour. He'd struck a nerve without even realising it.

'I… I'm not held prisoner at your father's house,' she expanded, talking into a silence that was getting on her nerves. 'I see a lot of my friends who are in the nursing profession.'

'And you don't miss being out there with them?'

Sophie paused, but only fractionally. 'They're rushed off their feet all the time,' she said truthfully. 'They work shifts and they don't get paid enough.'

'You *are* extremely well-compensated,' Alessio murmured, tilting his head to one side and pushing his plate away with one finger, so that he could relax back in his chair. 'Money means a lot to you?' He leaned forward again, voice low, eyes coolly assessing. 'Underneath the care and concern, have you come here to tell me about my father's financial situation because you fear you could lose your job if there's no money to pay you?'

'No!' She felt the sting of colour in her cheeks.

But wasn't the money more or less essential? She was paid a small fortune compared to all her friends, and that money disappeared down the drain. She helped her sister out, because acting jobs were few and far between and the temp work Addy did so that she could go to auditions at the drop of a hat didn't pay very much. And of course there was her mother…now living in Somerset with the family home sold. But there was still a mortgage, and someone had to pay it. Thank goodness it was small.

'Where are you staying?' he queried in an abrupt change of subject.

Sophie blinked and stared at him in silence for a few seconds, before naming a cheap chain hotel in a reasonably seedy part of South-west London.

'It's all I could afford,' she blurted out when he frowned, which only made his frown deepen.

'Surely not? I don't believe that. Like I said, I happen to know how much you're paid.'

'How do you know that?'

'I insisted on handling the matter and paying the salary. I wanted to make sure my father didn't decide to get rid of you on the spur of the moment.'

'I wasn't aware…'

'Why would you be? I recognised at the time that he needed help after his first stroke. He insisted on choosing the right candidate himself, and I wanted to make sure that whoever got the job would be paid enough that he or she would think twice about leaving. My father, I imagine, isn't the easiest of people to handle.'

'He's a pussycat,' Sophie inserted absently, dwelling on what he had said about being responsible for her paycheque and wishing she hadn't been so quick to speak her mind when she'd confronted him.

'Come again?'

'I had no idea you paid me.'

'Pussycat?'

'We get on like a house on fire—which is why I'm still with him, I guess. He does need some help…reminders with his diet and his medication, and making sure he does appropriate levels of exercise every day…but it's also about companionship. He all but gave up work when he had his stroke…his confidence took a knocking and he delegated everything to his CEOs. He needs companionship, even though he would never say it in so many words. And aside from my expected list of duties on the medical side of things I've also started helping him collate material for his memoirs… I drive him to places as well. He enjoys his chess club on a Wednesday, and every so often he has friends over, and is very particular about what gets served for supper…'

Listening to her, seeing the way her features softened, Alessio felt as though he was being given a glimpse of a world he knew nothing about.

Since when had his irascible, overbearing, prickly and difficult father ever been described as a *pussycat*?

And hadn't he always scorned people who played chess? Played games of any description?

Alessio could remember trundling down to his father's study, chess board under his arm, and knocking on the door behind which he had retreated following the death of his wife. Alessio had been ten at the time, and with his mother only gone a handful of weeks the loneliness of his bedroom had become too much.

But his father didn't play games. That much Alessio remembered very clearly. He didn't play games and he had no time for a child whose bedroom was too lonely or whose heart had suddenly been torn out.

Alessio had shrugged and left.

'So my money,' he drawled now, shutting the door on memories that had no place in the present, 'is at least well spent. Which brings me back to why you can't afford anywhere more salubrious to stay—especially when you could have charged it to my father's account. Or were you afraid that he might spot your destination and have a hissy fit if he suspected you might be trundling down here to see me? No matter. You'll be pleased to hear that your contract continues to be safe.'

He called for the bill with a barely-there nod of his head.

'If I'm to intervene in my father's affairs, then he's going to have to find out that you've told me what's going on.'

'I know,' Sophie said jaggedly. 'You might want me to carry on there, but that won't be up to you if your father decides he can't trust me.'

'And what would you do should that be the outcome?' Alessio asked, his dark eyes watchful and his long, lush lashes shielding his expression.

Sophie shrugged her narrow shoulders, but she looked awkward, and a tinge of pink touched her cheeks. 'I'll do what I've always done. I'll manage.'

'You'll do what you've always done…?' he murmured.

'Don't we all?' Sophie added quickly.

Alessio looked at her steadily. In the space of a couple of hours his life had been turned on its head. From a standpoint of historical non-involvement with his father, he was now looking at a completely different picture. He would naturally have to step in and find out what the hell had been going on with his father's financial affairs, and the old man wasn't going to like that. He would also have to protect this woman who looked as though the skies had fallen in.

She needed the money. Why? And what had she meant when she'd said that she would do what she'd always done and 'manage' if she lost her job? He had no idea, and in the wider scheme of things he didn't care. It was just a miracle that someone existed who described his father as a *pussycat*.

If his father was in trouble on both fronts, with his health and with his finances, and if she was right in reporting what the consultant had said about stress being the root of his stroke, then Alessio couldn't afford to add to the stress levels.

Along with this analytical dissection of the situation Alessio felt a thread of ancient hurt trickle through him—the same hurt he had felt as a child, when his juvenile overtures after his mother's death had been met with cold rejection. Hurt that he had not been told of momentous things happening in his father's life.

He gritted his teeth and dismissed that passing weakness.

'I'll make sure to be discreet in my enquiries. I'll get to the bottom of whatever's been going on, but my theory is mismanagement. From the little I glimpsed of my father's holdings ten years ago, it's run along the lines of a gentlemen's club—which might have worked back in the day, but doesn't cut it in this day and age.'

'Can I ask you something?'

'Would it deter you if I said *no*?' Alessio asked coolly, yet with a trace of amusement in his voice.

'How is it that you never took an interest in your father's company?'

The question lodged between them like a rock hurled into still waters. Her eyes were clear and curious, her head tilted to one side.

Alessio realised that he was in the presence of a woman who breached all boundaries. She had asked him an intensely personal question without any hint of an agenda behind the asking. She wasn't trying to get close to him. She wasn't trying to forge any kind of intimate connection by enticing confidences. She was curious and that was the end of it.

He wondered if that was why he said, surprising himself, 'My father and I…we've had a difficult relationship. My mother died when I was very young. Just ten. Things were rocky. By the time I hit twenty-one and finished my university career at Oxford, I knew that I was going to make my own way in the world without the help of my father. Fortuitously, my mother brought her own personal fortune to my parents' marriage, and much of it remained intact when she died. It was passed on to me. I suppose you could say that I had a head start when it came to getting my career going. A head start that completely bypassed my father, which suited me.'

Sophie, listening intently, nodded. 'It's good to be independent,' she murmured. 'It's good not to rely on anyone for anything.'

'You're more than welcome to ditch the cheap motel and stay at my place,' Alessio volunteered, appreciating the brevity of her response and startled by his unexpected foray into touchy-feely sharing, which was a gene he'd thought he had been born without.

But she shook her head without hesitation. 'I'm fine. Can you tell me…what happens now?'

'I'll call Ellis first thing tomorrow—and don't worry, I'll make sure no feathers are ruffled in the process. I'll get the loan that's outstanding paid off, and then I'll get my team to examine the accounts of his company in forensic detail. I'll weed out the dross, replace it with people who know that they'll be answering to me, and set things back on the straight and narrow.'

'And all of this without your father finding out what's going on?'

'Nothing is beyond the wit of man.'

'How can you achieve all that when you don't really talk to your father, Mr…er… Rossi-White?'

'I think, given the circumstances, we can dispense

with the formal titles, don't you, Sophie? You can all me Alessio.'

He paused. For all the time she had been working for his father, he realised that he knew precious little about her, and it was ironic that his newly born voyage of discovery into her thoughts had kicked off by her revealing the fact that she didn't approve of him and didn't like him very much—if at all.

'Well, all things considered, it seems that I'll have to have a conversation with him now, doesn't it?' A dark flush delineated his sharp cheekbones and he shifted in the chair.

'Let's hope the sudden shock of that doesn't cause another stroke...' she said at once.

Their eyes met and Alessio burst out laughing. The laughter soon died, but his dark eyes remained on her face and he knew there was amused appreciation in them.

'Is that why you don't like me?' he drawled. 'Because you think I'm to blame for the distance that exists between me and my father?'

Just like that the atmosphere shifted.

And that was what raced through Sophie's head as she stared at him, mesmerised by the depths of his dark eyes. Some tiny voice inside was telling her that this drowning feeling carried a thread of danger.

Drowning was always about a loss of control, and she'd been there and experienced it enough to know that she was never going to return to that place again. She'd felt the panicked confusion of circumstances running away with her, pulling her in directions she couldn't handle.

She'd known real fear for her future, for her sister's future, as she'd swum in the turbulent waters of social services and GPs and school governors in the wake of her father's death, when her mother had retreated into herself with no interest in anything outside. For weeks and months treading water had become a way of life, and even when at last her mother had shaken herself out of her stupor she had still been too depressed to really engage in all sorts of small, daily decisions. Little by little she had come to, had re-entered the world, and she had never stopped apologising for leaving her daughter to handle everything on her own when she'd been just a child, too young for the responsibility. But by then Sophie had grown up, and she had seen the ugly side of losing control and what it could do to a person.

So now…

No…this drowning feeling wasn't good, but surely there was nothing to fear? This was just some silly reaction to a guy—nothing that could have any impact on her life.

Alessio got under her skin for a lot of reasons, and she had to concede that the way he looked had something to do with her reaction. She might have her head very firmly screwed on, but she was still a woman, after all, and for all his faults he was an extremely beautiful man. Who wouldn't shiver in the presence of physical perfection?

Honestly, what was there to worry about just because she was a little unsettled by those fabulous dark eyes and that exquisite bone structure? She was beyond temptation on that front—of that she was one hundred per cent sure.

Self-control regained, she said, matter-of-factly, 'I don't have any feelings for you one way or the other, and it's not something I've given much thought to.'

'Is that right?' Alessio mused with cool neutrality, eyebrows raised. 'There have been times when I've thought that you might have been actively avoiding me by making sure you weren't around on the occasions I came to see my father… That's probably a wild flight of imagination on my part…' He paused and then carried on, in the same musing, thoughtful voice, 'Although let's not forget you *did* have a lot to say on the matter when you confronted me earlier this evening…'

Sophie pursed her lips, but remained silent until he shrugged and sat back.

'No matter. All finished here? Dessert? A stiff drink for the road? No?' He signalled for the bill and looked at her from under lush lashes. 'You may have got away with scuttling out of sight like a timid little crab whenever I've been to visit before…but things are going to be a little different for a while…'

Sophie resented his phraseology, but she couldn't take issue with it because the wretched man was spot-on.

'How so?' she asked.

'Well, once I've started the business of finding out what's been going on with my father's holdings I'm going to have to be on site, to make sure everything is being done my way. I don't see any choice in the matter. His head office is based in Harrogate and I'm going to want to oversee what happens there.'

'What…? Why?'

'Like I said, there will be a need to clear the dross, and very often dross doesn't particularly like to be cleared. It's something I won't be able to delegate—at least not at ground zero. Aside from which…' He hesitated and flushed. 'My father and I may not have seen eye to eye on a range of things over the years, and he may rant and rail against my being there and seeing him when he's weak, but he's still my flesh and blood. And this time I intend to make sure his pride doesn't get in the way of my presence.'

He grimaced.

'You might have to warn him of my impending arrival, though. Like you say, the shock of an unexpected visit might spark another stroke…'

'I will. Okay…'

'Tell him that I phoned you to find out how he was because I'd heard on the grapevine that there might be problems with his company. The world of business can be small, and I am exceptionally high-profile. A lot of people know who I am and who my father is. It would only have taken one concerned voice to propel me to Harrogate… Feel free to tell him that I bullied the truth out of you about his stroke. He'll buy that easily enough.'

'Because he thinks you're a bully?' Sophie asked.

'Like I said,' Alessio drawled, 'we've had our differences over the years. He can be stubborn, and sometimes the only way to trump stubborn is to go one step further and be even more stubborn. My father may think he's tough as old boots, but he ain't seen nothing yet. I have some things to finalise here, but first thing tomorrow I'll get my people to start going through my father's accounts. I'll be up on Saturday, which will give you two days to brace him for the inevitable. If you don't think that you're up to the task, you can always give me a call…you have my number. I can always think of something to absolve you of the duty. Because you might find that my *pussycat* father can turn very easily into a roaring lion if he thinks you haven't done what he's asked you to do.'

Sophie met his gaze steadily. 'It may not be a great job, breaking the news to your dad that I've told you about his health issues, but you don't have to worry that I'm going to run scared. I won't.' She set her jaw at a stubborn angle, remembering a past stuffed with doing uncomfortable things. 'Believe me, I've dealt with my fair share of uncomfortable and unpleasant tasks.'

She blinked, smiled, smoothing away the sharp edges of what she had just said. because confiding in anyone about her past wasn't something she usually did.

'It'll be fine. Deep down, I'm sure he'll be really thrilled to see you.'

Alessio gave nothing away as he looked at her for a few seconds, digesting what she had just said. He thought absently that there was no way he would bet a buck on, that because the last thing his father was going to be thrilled by was his son's arrival on the scene with a suitcase packed for more than just a brief overnight stay.

You couldn't teach an old dog new tricks, and that particular old dog had learnt the trick of making sure that he, Alessio, knew just where his place was in the grand scheme of things.

Mostly, though, his mind was preoccupied with those 'uncomfortable and unpleasant' tasks Sophie had mentioned. Had she known how transparent her face had been when she'd said that? Whatever had been flitting through her head had cast a shadow over her features. Maybe things to do with work? Nursing would have brought her into close contact with a lot of uncomfortable and unpleasant tasks... But somehow he'd got the impression that that passing remark harked back to something that was a lot more personal.

What? Never one to delve into the quagmire of other people's psychological motivations—because what was the point of that?—Alessio couldn't stop another sudden flare of curiosity about the woman sitting opposite him, so calm on the surface. And yet beneath that surface the promise of turbulence swirled...

Turbulence and passion. Didn't the two go hand in hand?

He banked down whatever obscure wild imaginings were trying to worm their way to the surface of his thoughts, but he couldn't resist a second look at her face. Alessio was accustomed to women who kept nothing hidden from him. They flung themselves at him. They wanted him to be curious about them...to want to get to know them. They were specialists in the art of using their womanly wiles to get what they wanted. They pouted and flirted, ever keen to engage his attention and hold it.

But this woman…

She had spent so long fading into the background, or else being completely missing in action, that he had somehow failed to notice just how flawlessly smooth her skin was and how alluring the depth of her cool, intelligent brown eyes.

'At any rate,' he said smoothly, 'you know where to find me. You have my personal number—the one I gave you some time ago for emergency use. Use it.'

Bill paid, he stood up, and she hurriedly followed suit. His eyes drifted over her once again in casual inspection.

She was very slender. Tall and willowy. That much he could make out under the formidably dull clothes. She was wearing workmanlike flat shoes, and in them she was only a few inches shorter than him. He usually went out with small, voluptuous blondes, so it made a change to be with a woman almost at eye level with him.

But then he quickly reminded himself that this wasn't a date and he wasn't going out with the woman.

'How are you getting back to your motel?' asked Alessio.

'It's a *hotel*,' Sophie corrected, as their coats were brought and she manoeuvred herself into hers. 'Motels… motels are things in horror movies.'

She said this in an attempt to squash her previous unguarded remark about not being able to afford anything pricey. Her personal life wasn't open for perusal, so why should he know about her money issues?

Alessio shot her a curling smile. 'A sense of humour? I like it. That's a side of you that's been kept under wraps… Feel free to bring it out of hiding whenever you want while I'm around.'

Sophie blushed, momentarily lost for words. Because this man and being light-hearted weren't things that went together in her head.

Before she could come up with a suitable response, he said, with a return to cool gravity, 'I'll probably be there for a week, depending on how things go. You'll need to put whatever issues you have with me on the back burner.'

'I have no issues with you.'

'Whether you do or don't is immaterial.' Alessio shrugged his response. 'The key thing at this stage is my father's recovery and sorting out his business problems. When those two things are dealt with…well, life will return to normal and you can…' he raised his brows and met her eyes steadily '…return to hiding from me whenever I show up. In the meanwhile, for the sake of my father, we pretend that everything is as it should be between the two of us. Agreed?'

Sophie hesitated, but only for a split-second. Alessio in close proximity for a week? But he would be occupied in dealing with all manner of things, and she would be as well. Their paths would probably cross for the barest amount of time. Could she deal with that for the sake of Leonard? Of course she could. Like Alessio said, once things were sorted he'd be off, and her life would resume where it had left off.

She nodded. 'Agreed.'

CHAPTER THREE

'YOU'RE LATE.'

That wasn't what Sophie had meant to say. What she had meant to say was: *You're a little later than expected and your father has retired to bed. He tires easily these days.*

Unfortunately, she had had an hour and a half to stew in her own frazzled nerves, and by the time the doorbell had rung, she'd been wired. She'd been wired since her trip to London.

Nothing had prepared her for meeting Alessio face to face. Yes, she'd been in his presence before, when he'd blown in from London on one of his whirlwind visits, bringing with him a sense of high-voltage energy, restless impatience and those critical dark eyes that had made her cringe. On such occasions, before she'd resorted to taking her days off in advance of his arrivals, it had been easy to mumble some pleasantries and fade into the background. As he had remorselessly pointed out when she had gone to see him.

But up close and personal with him, she had felt her nerves go into free fall. He was so much more compelling than she had given him credit for. So much more devastatingly impressive. So much more downright scary.

Those fabulous dark eyes had mesmerised her. His deep, velvety voice had wrapped around her in a stranglehold that had turned her brain to mush and left her feeling hot and bothered. By nature, she was cool, calm and collected. She had learned from a young age that common sense trumped emotion when it came to getting things done, and those lessons had stayed with her...had become part of her DNA. So it had been alarming to discover how easily all her cool could be shot to smithereens by a guy she had successfully managed to avoid for over two years.

Even more alarming had been the way her heart had beat faster in his presence, and the way her mind had started playing tricks on her, conjuring up all sorts of thoughts of Alessio as a man and not just as someone objectionable she was being forced to do business with.

There was no place in her life for such foolishness. Really, Sophie had no time for flights of fancy. Until now, they hadn't even been on her radar. Her teenage years had passed by in a fog of duty and obligation and responsibility. When all her friends had been having their adolescent flights of fancy, she had been way too focused on the nitty-gritty of taking care of her mother to follow their lead.

It had never bothered her.

In fact, hadn't she felt just a tiny bit smug when those flights of fancy had so often ended up crashing and burning?

So her meeting with Alessio had left her feeling on edge, and more so as the time of his arrival had got closer and closer.

'Damn boy could at least have the common decency to show up on time if he's to lecture to me about my business problems!' Leonard had bellowed, as he'd made his way up to his bedroom on the stairlift which had been installed two years previously.

'Traffic...' Sophie had murmured soothingly.

Which had met with a predictable, *'Pah! Traffic, schmaffic.'*

She hadn't ventured further into dangerous terrain by prolonging the conversation. The less stress Leonard had the better, and he had been on tenterhooks ever since she had broached the conversation about Alessio coming to discuss his financial situation.

It had been a blessing that he hadn't been more incandescent when she'd told him that his son had found out about his money woes and had informed her that he would be visiting so that he could discuss the situation.

She had tiptoed around the issue with the agility of someone avoiding landmines, and she had shrewdly guessed that Leonard might be privately relieved to have everything out in the open, pride or no pride.

But since Leonard had been settled in bed, tablets taken and hot drink duly brought up, Sophie had had plenty of time to fulminate.

Now, staring at Alessio, she felt all the dispassionate responses she had rehearsed vanish under a blizzard of anger.

Against the bitter wintry darkness outside, with the raw cold of Yorkshire at its most brutal and a freezing blast of ice-cold wind tousling his hair, the man still managed to look unfairly sexy.

He was wearing a beige cashmere coat and a black scarf and, from what she could see as she blinked into the grim black night outside, dark jeans and some kind of dark jumper.

'It's only a little after nine-thirty.' Alessio brushed past her, divesting himself of his coat and scarf before turning to look at her as she slammed the front door shut against the freezing cold. 'I had no idea lights went out here at sunset.'

Sophie folded her arms, her whole body rigid with pent-up tension, already frustrated with herself for the way she was reacting to him.

'Your father retires early to bed now.'

'How early?'

'By eight he's flagging.'

'I spoke to his consultant and got a briefing on all his health issues,' Alessio said, heading towards the kitchen.

Sophie pelted behind him.

The house was enormous. They went past several rooms, most unused and all decorated in a style that had once been elegant but now seemed stuffy and overdone. The kitchen, though, which was the heart of the place—especially since Leonard had had his stroke—was warm and inviting, with a comfortable arrangement of sofas at one end, where French doors opened out onto the extensive gardens at the back. Right now those acres of land were shrouded in darkness.

'You were right,' said Alessio. 'The less stress he has, the better. And as an aside, I had some urgent business to conclude—hence my slightly late arrival.' He looked at her and shoved his hands in the pockets of his jeans. 'There was no need to wait up. I do actually have a key to the house, even if I don't always choose to use it.'

'I… I'm always up at this hour, Mr…er… Alessio. I was just disappointed because your father was…'

'Sorry to have missed me? I'm not buying it.' Alessio's eyebrows shot up. 'Now, I haven't eaten since this morning…' He glanced around the kitchen, and then made a slower and more thorough visual tour of his surroundings. 'If you stick around while I get myself something to eat, we can outline how this week is going to progress.'

Sophie didn't have to say anything, because it was clear that he'd assumed she would fall in line with his plans.

He began rummaging in the fridge, frowning, half bent over as he searched and sifted through the contents.

'What are you looking for?' Sophie asked politely.

Alessio glanced across at her for a couple of seconds,

then resumed his search. 'Something interesting that can be stuck between two slices of bread.'

Sophie clicked her tongue impatiently and padded towards the cupboards. Then she nodded for him to sit down.

'I'll make something,' she said. 'If you'd turned up on time, you could have had dinner when we did.'

'Where did you put the leftovers?'

'In the bin. On your father's instructions.'

Alessio burst out laughing. 'Yes, that sounds about right. So, tell me… What was his response when you spun your merry little yarn about me finding out through the grapevine that his business was in trouble? Told him that I contacted you to elicit information rather than confront him directly? Or does the food being chucked in the bin say it all?'

'He was upset.' Sophie began making a ragout of tomatoes and vegetables. She was a good cook. She'd had years to get it right. 'But…' She turned to Alessio thoughtfully, running her hand through her short fair hair, spiking it up 'But I think, deep down, his ranting and railing hid a certain amount of relief. He's been carrying the burden on his shoulders alone, and that's not an easy thing to do.'

'No…' Alessio sat at the kitchen table, swivelling one of the heavy wooden chairs to face her so that he could stretch out his long legs. 'And my father is not known for his ability to bear burdens alone for very long.'

'What does that mean?'

Alessio looked at her in silence for a moment. Leonard? Coping with burdens on his own? What a joke.

He breathed in sharply, accosted by a blast from the past. A memory of that very moment when he'd been told that his father was remarrying.

Three months after his mother had died he had been dispatched off to boarding school, and six months after he'd gone there he'd been called in to the principal's office and told that he would be given two days' leave so that he could attend his father's wedding.

Alessio could remember the surge of shock and hatred that had flowed through him like toxic lava when he'd been told that.

His beloved mother had barely been buried and his father was remarrying. He had been old enough to reach conclusions he had never voiced. Had his father been having an affair all along? His mother had died in a car accident. What had she been driving away from? He had thought them to have been in love…happily married. Yes, his father had always been taciturn, and his mother a ray of joyful sunshine, filled with the sort of Italian *joie de vivre* that could light up a room. But had there been cracks he hadn't seen?

Certainly his father had changed after her death, had withdrawn into himself, but had he simply withdrawn because of guilt? Because he hadn't been able to face his own son in the knowledge that he'd been fooling around behind his wife's back?

Alessio had duly returned home to witness his father tying the knot with a woman nearly half his age.

His bitterness had been a solid lump inside him that had never shifted.

His father had never carried the burden of his beautiful wife's death. Life had moved on for him faster than a speeding bullet.

Marriage number two had ended a year and a half later in a long, acrimonious and costly divorce. It was never mentioned now. Alessio could only remember a blonde with a taste for jewellery and living the high life who had come and gone in the blink of an eye. It was just something else that was never mentioned between them.

And then the years had rolled by in ever-increasing silence until here they were now.

'It means nothing,' he drawled, vaulting upright and strolling over to where she was stirring something in a frying pan. 'Whatever it is you're concocting smells very tempting.'

Sophie stiffened as she felt him peer over her shoulder. His breath was warm against her neck and she wanted to rub the sensation away.

She had asked a simple question and yet he had changed the subject effortlessly. He was a man with a lot of *Do Not Trespass* signs posted around himself, and she wondered what lay behind those signs and then quickly reminded herself that it was none of her business.

'If you'd like to sit down...' She edged away just enough to escape his suffocating nearness, which addled her wits. 'I'll bring your food to you.'

'I'm not my father,' Alessio murmured softly. 'I'm more than capable of getting a plate for myself, and some cutlery, and dishing out my own food.'

Rattled by the tingling racing up and down her spine, Sophie stood back, leaning against the counter, and said testily, 'But can you cook the food that goes on the plate?'

Their eyes met and she reddened.

Alessio burst out laughing. For a few seconds his dark eyes roved over her burning face, before he sat down, nodding at the chair opposite him in an invitation for her to sit.

'No, I can't,' he said, and helped himself to the tomato and basil and herb sauce, dumping it over the pasta she had boiled and tossed in olive oil. 'Why deprive a decent chef of earning a living?'

'You *never* cook anything for yourself?'

Sophie sat. There was a cup of tepid tea in front of her, which she had been drinking before. She fetched them both some water and then, when he asked her whether there was any wine, poured a glass for him.

'I never drink on my own,' Alessio said.

'I don't drink on duty...'

'You're not on duty now.'

It feels like duty, Sophie thought. Or something else. Something that made her pulses leap and her cool mind suddenly begin to unravel...something that was just enough to make her nervous.

But she wasn't going to let him see that.

For one thing, she was the woman in charge of his dad and, whatever issues he and Alessio had between them, it was important that she gave the impression of being some-one capable and professional. How much confidence in her abilities would Alessio have if she was flustered and tongue-tied around him?

She duly poured herself a small glass and took a sip. 'So you eat out all the time?'

'You look shocked,' he said.

'Doesn't it get a little boring?'

'I have a personal chef who cooks for me when I'm at my place.'

'You're spoilt.'

'The more I'm with you, the more you surprise me.'

'Please don't ask me where I've been hiding,' Sophie said, realising with a start that the glass of wine was nearly gone, even though she couldn't remember having any. 'I do a job. I wouldn't be here if it weren't for...for what's happening with your dad just now.'

'That was excellent.' Alessio pushed the empty plate to one side and refilled their glasses.

And seeing that simple gesture Sophie realised just how much in control he was. He started conversations when he chose to. He bypassed what he had no intention of sharing. And he was brazen when it came to prying into other people's motivations.

She had seen all the articles his father had cut out and saved over the years. Even now that online search engines had made knowledge accessible at the flick of a button, Leonard still ferreted out the most flattering and had them printed into hard copy so that he could keep them.

Every article was glowing in its praise for this guy who ruled the financial world. Every gossip column was stuffed with pictures of him somewhere, doing something important, with someone very beautiful on his arm.

He was clearly a man who played as hard as he worked.

But there was nothing that ever gave the slightest indication of what sort of man he really was on the inside.

His private thoughts and opinions on anything other than business deals were nowhere to be found.

Sophie didn't want to expend energy in thinking about the guy, because she was here to do a job and so was he. She ignored the compliment about the food and looked at him steadily until he smiled…a slow, curling smile that seemed to acknowledge every single little thought that had been running through her head.

It was disconcerting.

'Have you managed to get your accountants to look at the books?'

'They've begun,' Alessio said. 'My father's finances were decimated after his divorce, which I assume you know about, but since then it's just been the usual series of misjudged investments, an adherence to old technology and too many dinosaurs in top positions who haven't make the sort of brave decisions they should have along the way. A company run like a gentlemen's club will always end up going down the drain because in this day and age there's no room for companies like that. Have you met any of my father's business colleagues?'

'A few,' Sophie admitted.

'And what did you think of them?'

'They seemed charming, if a little old-fashioned.'

'Correct. And old-fashioned charm has its place, but not in the cut-throat world of making money.'

'Leonard isn't some young twenty-something whipper-snapper,' Sophie said sharply. 'He's an elderly man with health problems.'

'Then he should have come to me the minute he discovered the mess his company was in.'

'He's in awe of you.'

Alessio stared at her with open incredulity, and then he laughed shortly. 'I think your choice of words might be a little off target. My father has never been in awe of me or anything I have done.'

Alessio vaulted to his feet, taking his plate to the sink with him, but not doing anything with it. Certainly not washing it. Or putting it in the dishwasher.

Sophie assumed that a guy who had a personal chef on speed dial wasn't even going to know what a dishwasher was.

In the recent absence of the housekeeper, Sophie had to do all the kitchen chores herself, which she didn't begrudge, but why on earth should she do chores for Alessio, when he was perfectly capable of doing them for himself? She wasn't paid to cook or clean, but she did it because she loved Leonard and because she now knew that he couldn't afford to get anyone in to do that kind of work for him. But for Alessio…?

She carried the rest of the dishes to the counter, opened the dishwasher and nodded to it. 'You can stack,' she said, 'while I tidy the kitchen. Or else we'll come down here in the morning and it'll look as though a bomb exploded.'

'Stack the dishwasher…?'

'It's easy,' Sophie said, grudgingly amused in spite of

herself and finding it hard not to soften. 'Most people don't need a degree in engineering to do it.'

'I'm being ticked off,' Alessio murmured. 'Is this because you disapprove of me not being able to cook?'

'I'm not ticking you off, and I don't care whether you can cook or not.'

The force of that dark gaze upon her was making her skin prickle, but she remained rooted to the spot, unable to tear her eyes away, distractedly wondering how it was possible for a man to be as sinfully beautiful as this one was. There should be a law against looks like his.

'No?'

His voice was a feathery caress, and had the effect of bringing her back down to earth at speed.

'No,' she denied coolly. 'I'm asking you to help because there's no one to do the daily chores around here and it'll help me out.'

'What happened to the housekeeper?'

'In case you hadn't noticed,' Sophie told him, her voice still cool as she began wiping counters and putting things back into cupboards, all the while bringing more dishes to the sink, 'she hasn't been around for the past eight months.'

'I hadn't noticed,' Alessio said slowly, as he leant against the counter and flung the tea-towel she had handed him earlier over one shoulder. He folded his arms and stared at her with a distracted frown. 'You've been picking up the slack?'

'Who else was going to do it?'

'That hasn't been reflected in a pay rise. I would know.'

'It doesn't matter.' Sophie sighed. She thought of her own childhood. 'Believe me, doing all of this—"picking up the slack", as you call it—is something I'm accustomed to.'

Since Alessio seemed to have forgotten all about the dishwasher as he strolled towards the fridge and fetched a bottle of mineral water, Sophie loaded it herself and then made them both some coffee.

'You were going to tell me how things are going to proceed here,' she encouraged, once they were back at the kitchen table. 'It would be a good idea, so that I can plan my days accordingly.'

'Nothing will change for you,' Alessio said. His dark eyes were thoughtful. 'Except, of course, you may notice that my father's mood goes noticeably downhill while I'm around. Aside from that, you'll do what you usually do.' He looked around him. 'And you can forget about picking up the slack. I'll ensure suitable help is arranged so that you don't have to tidy up this huge pile along with all your other duties.'

'You don't have to do that.'

'Trust me when I tell you that I never do anything because I feel I have to,' Alessio said. 'It will be arranged. As for me? You won't notice I'm here.'

That was true for precisely ten hours the following day. Because Alessio, as Leonard informed her just as soon as she had prepared their breakfast and sat opposite him at the kitchen table, was off to the office, even though it was Sunday and no one would be around.

'Probably getting a head start on laying a few explosives underneath the desks,' he said, and scowled, continuing the theme which had started the second she had entered his bedroom that morning, to find him up and alert and already dressed for the day.

Leonard, now in his late seventies, still had a mane of grey hair, and although age and poor health had slowed him down, he still possessed the demeanour of someone whose entire working life had been spent giving orders he expected to have obeyed.

'Why do you say that?' she asked now.

'Well, you've met him! Now that he's got a bee in his bonnet, he's not going to give up until he's sacked every one of my CEOs! He's there right now, poring through the files and finding out all sorts of who knows what against who knows who!'

Sophie was adept at pouring oil on troubled waters, and in truth she was used to Leonard's cantankerous take on almost everything, from *'young people these days'* to *'all this computer nonsense that's taken over people's lives.'*

She placidly let him rant and rave until he had subsided, and then they had a sensible discussion about Alessio with only a handful of disgruntled expletives thrown in for good measure.

Sunday was meant to be a day of relaxation. It should have been one of her days off. But Sophie rarely took that day to herself, because she knew that it was her employer's loneliest day—the one that seemed to stretch into infinity for him, with no sense of purpose and nothing to do.

It was cold and miserable today, but she drove him to their favourite National Trust house, with its extensive gardens, where they had a light lunch and killed some time, he in the wheelchair he loathed, even though it was only pulled out if he had to cover a lot of distance.

'Your son mentioned something about getting another housekeeper,' Sophie said, as she drove them back to his own country house, the windscreen wipers not quite keeping up with the sudden freezing downpour.

'You told him that Edith had left?'

Sophie sighed and slid her eyes across to Leonard, who was glaring at her, his bushy eyebrows drawn into a black, accusatory frown.

'Don't you think he might have noticed, considering he's going to be around for longer than a handful of hours? Unless he's blind as a bat, he's going to spot that no one's appearing from the woodwork to serve the dinner and clear away the plates.'

'Hmph...'

'You're a crotchety old man, Leonard White.'

'And *you* would try the patience of saint, Miss Court, running around telling tales!' He snorted. 'But I suppose the boy *would* have noticed sooner or later,' he conceded grudgingly. 'Just one more thing to add to the list.'

'What list?'

They were back, and as she slid the car into its usual spot in the grand circular courtyard she glanced across to him to find that he was flushing, his mouth downturned.

'Nothing.'

Leonard began opening the car door and Sophie flew out so that she could unfurl the umbrella always kept on the back seat and help him out on to the drive, where he teetered and then stabilised after a couple of seconds.

'Don't you *nothing* me,' she chided as they made slow progress to the front door. 'What do you mean by that?'

'Just something else I've managed to get wrong,' he muttered, allowing himself to be helped out of his layers of waterproof clothing, which Sophie shook and neatly hung on the row of coat hooks in the cupboard by the front door.

The draught from the cold outside hung around inside the house like a miasma. It felt damp, and she hurried them into the kitchen where the Aga could be relied upon to keep the room warm.

It was later than she thought, so she made them a pot of tea and then started preparing Leonard's early dinner—toast and scrambled eggs. After that they would retire to the sitting room that adjoined his bedroom, and there they would pass an hour or so while Sophie reread some of the stuff he had previously gone through...memories filed away and now brought out and dusted down to be put on paper for the memoirs that were more a labour of love than a plan with a destination.

At the rate at which they were travelling down Leonard's memory lane, he would be two hundred before the task was completed.

She loved Leonard, and wanted to pry further into what he'd meant earlier, but when she thought of Alessio and the disturbing effect he had on her she wondered how far she should allow her curiosity to go.

The equation now wasn't just about her and Leonard. With Alessio physically in the house, it was a picture that was getting wider and broader and more encompassing, and something inside her warned against being swept away and getting too involved. Whatever simmered between father and son wasn't her business.

However, just as she was about to leave him to settle at a little after eight, he said, apropos of nothing in particular, 'He never forgave me.'

'Alessio?' Sophie stopped and walked back to the chair by the bedroom window, where Leonard was finishing the cup of hot chocolate she had brought up.

'The boy hates me.'

'That's not true!'

'I tried. I didn't know how. Now he's here and everything's unravelled for me. He's probably gloating that the old idiot couldn't even run his own company in the end! All the luxuries are gone. Can't even afford to have someone come in to clean the place now. Up to him to hire someone.'

'None of that's true.' Sophie was dismayed. 'And you mustn't stress. You know what your consultant said.'

'Easier said than done, my dear.' He reached out and squeezed her hand. 'Alessio was up at the crack of dawn, bright-eyed and bushy-tailed and raring to tear my company apart.'

'He isn't going to tear your company apart. He's going

to try and sort it out—and isn't that a good thing, Leonard?' Sophie asked gently. 'If your son hated you, wouldn't he have walked away from the responsibility?' She was surprised to find that she meant every word as she added, 'If there's one thing I can tell, it's this, Leonard. Alessio might be tough, but he's fair, and whatever he does to sort the company out and ease your financial problems it will be necessary and done with thought and consideration for the people who might be affected.'

Leonard pursed his lips and harrumphed under his breath, but Sophie had clearly given him something to think about, and he was lightening up and complaining about the usual things by the time she left him fifteen minutes later.

But some of the things he had said had given Sophie pause for thought, and when, an hour and a half later, Alessio strode into the kitchen, where she was nursing a mug of coffee, she had to force herself to appear natural and, more importantly, *neutral*. He was in jeans and a jumper and he was rubbing his hands together, warming himself.

'Bloody awful weather out there. You'll be pleased to hear that there's no need to cook anything for me. I've eaten.' He spared her a passing glance. 'I would have brought you back something, but I assumed you would have powered ahead without me. Tell me what you did today.'

He paced the kitchen, fetching a mug, making himself some coffee, and Sophie watched him and subliminally appreciated the graceful economy of his movements, and the way he somehow managed to own the space in which he moved.

'I didn't realise that you would be heading into the office today,' she countered, her mouth tightening as she recalled Leonard's sadness when he had so briefly confided in her earlier.

'And *I* didn't think I had to run my timetable by you on a minute-by-minute basis,' Alessio said with equal cool as he joined her at the table, sprawling back in the chair, which he somehow managed to dwarf. 'I'm here to get a job done, and how I choose to spend my time doing it isn't really in your remit. Not unless you have a list of responsibilities of which I am unaware?'

'I just thought you might have wanted to spend some time with your dad.' Sophie held her ground, without any rancour in her voice, even though again she couldn't help but marvel that a man so smart and so sexy could also be so impenetrable and so downright loathsome.

'I spent more than sufficient time with him when I popped in before I left for Harrogate,' Alessio said drily. 'I got the distinct impression that he was relieved when I was ready to go.'

'He's scared that you're going to tear his company apart.'

'He has every right to be afraid. It's a mess. I've spent the day reading through a mind-boggling array of numbers and figures and profit and loss columns, half of them filed in metal cabinets, as though the world hasn't changed since those bad old days. I've discovered lots of poor investment decisions and badly thought-out loans, and a total lack of urgency in moving in line with technological progress. Heads will need to roll, I'm afraid.'

'Will you…will you be gentle when you discuss that with him?'

'It's business, Sophie.' Alessio looked at her from under his lashes, his face revealing nothing. 'There's only so much hand-holding I can do when it comes to laying my cards on the table.'

'He's so upset already…'

Alessio frowned. 'Sometimes when you talk about my

father,' he murmured, 'I almost get the impression that you're talking about someone I don't know at all.'

'He's softer than you think!'

'Really? I'm curious to see that side to him, considering it's never been in evidence in the past.'

'Are you?'

Anger twisted inside Sophie at the cool, amused indifference in Alessio's voice. Did he know his father at all? She thought of the acres of emptiness that seemed to separate them. She thought of those articles so lovingly kept, and the wobble in Leonard's voice when he'd told her that he feared his own son hated him.

Sophie had spent a lot of her formative years in situations that she should not have been in—caretaking a bewildered, lost parent and a kid sister who had needed looking after—but not once had she failed to feel overwhelming love for both of them. The very thought of Leonard despairing of his only son's affection brought a sour lump to her throat.

So devastatingly good-looking...so incredibly aloof...

'You only have one father,' she said stiffly.

'You're overstepping your job title, Miss Court.'

'I don't want anything to stress your father. It won't be good for him.'

'Then allow me to handle things my way.'

'You're so...*cold*!'

'I think you've mentioned that before. You should be careful of taking sides in a battle that's not yours.'

'I just want what's best for Leonard, and it doesn't help his health issues for him to think that you hate him...'

CHAPTER FOUR

ALESSIO STILLED.

Had he just heard what he thought he'd heard? Had anyone *ever* overstepped the boundaries as much as the woman sitting opposite him just had? For a few seconds he was quite simply so incredulous that words failed him.

'I'm sorry.' Sophie rushed hurriedly into the lengthening silence. 'I shouldn't have said that. I just…got so frustrated. I'm sorry.'

'I appreciate that you want what's best for my father…' Alessio cleared his throat and tried to wrest back some self-control. But he had taken a direct hit, and for a man who never lost his self-control, far less ever took any direct hits from anyone, he was finding himself on shaky ground.

'I do.' Sophie leant forward, every fibre of her being stretched taut, as if with a sense of urgency for him to understand her outburst.

Their eyes tangled. Alessio wondered how he could ever have described the firebrand leaning towards him as 'background'. She was about as background as a rocket taking off for Mars.

'You do?' he heard himself parrot, still dazed by what she had said. His father thought that he *hated* him? How on earth had things got to where they had?

For ten years he had had a good childhood. Of course his father had, by nature, been the more distant parent. His mother had been the laughter and the exuberance...the one who had flung things into a basket and dragged her husband from his office and dug her heels in until he laughed and agreed to take them to the beach. She had been the one who hugged and kissed and sang in the kitchen and played music, pulling her husband to his feet and twirling him round, teasing him that she would make a dancer out of him if it was the last thing she ever did.

Alessio had adored her. But he had also loved his father and looked up to him. How had that disappeared so completely over the years?

He knew how. The open water between them had grown and swelled with disagreements and nagging differences and harsh judgement calls until an ocean separated them. He had been too young to understand what had been going on with his father after his wife had died, and his lack of forgiveness for his remarrying so soon after her death had solidified into a wall of bitterness that had been cemented into place.

For the first time Alessio felt uncomfortable with the choices he had made and the road he had opted to follow.

He fidgeted and frowned, his dark gaze resting on Sophie's expressive face. Her eyes were blazing with a mixture of determination, sincerity, and regret for what she had said in the heat of the moment. Her short blonde hair was tangled every which way, as natural as it was possible to get. Her mouth was parted.

And as his eyes drifted further down he felt a quickening inside him and a sudden heavy ache in his groin. Because out of nowhere he was imagining more than just a concerned carer. He found himself mentally undressing her, getting to the hot, passionate woman underneath.

It occurred to him that he knew nothing about her personal life. It also occurred to him, hard on the heels of that, that her personal life was none of his business.

'It's very reassuring,' he murmured now, 'to know that the person who is looking after my father is so heavily invested in his well-being.'

'Invested enough to stick up for him against her better judgement?' she asked.

'It's what brought you down to see me in London, isn't it?'

'Yes, it is. I'm very fond of Leonard.'

'Why do you qualify your sticking up for him as going against your better judgement?'

'Because…' Sophie sighed. 'It's not up to me to air anything your father should be saying to you face to face.'

'Do I intimidate you?' Alessio asked softly, his head tilted to one side.

'Of course not! Like I said… I… It's not my place… It just sort of came out… You don't intimidate me…not at all. Why would you?'

'It's been known to happen.' Alessio shrugged. 'I have no idea why, because I am the least forbidding person I know.'

Sophie's eyebrows shot up. 'You can't know very many people, that being the case.'

Alessio smiled and relaxed. He was beginning to think that he really quite enjoyed looking at her. He also really quite enjoyed the way she didn't try to tiptoe around him or suck up to him.

Of course she was perfectly right. She had been totally out of order in saying what she had. But for the moment he decided that he was happy to park that particular irritation to one side.

'So…' he purred. 'Moving on from the topic of my father and his financial woes just for the moment…'

'Okay…'

'Like I said, I feel immensely fortunate that you take such interest in him—but don't you have other things to occupy your time? Other things to worry about? I know we've briefly covered this, but is there no one in your life who takes issue with the amount of time you dedicate to my father?'

'What do you mean?'

'You know what I mean, Sophie. Much as I like the fact that you're devoted to my father, I wouldn't want to think that you're denying yourself the things you should be doing or feel you want to be doing.'

'I'm not.'

'I know very little about you aside from the details of your nursing qualifications.'

'Isn't that all that's relevant?'

Sophie had no idea how they had managed to get to a place where he was quizzing her about her personal life, but perhaps he had a point. Up till now she had been largely invisible, but that time was over.

The situation with Leonard meant that his son was bound to zero in on her, to take more of an interest in the role she played—especially now. Because, whether she liked it or not, he was picking up the tab for her very generous salary.

She had had no idea that Alessio was responsible for her being paid and, that being the case…yes, he might consider it his right to know more about her circumstances than he currently did.

'When my father hired you I of course made sure your qualifications were all in order, but it was up to him to decide who he wanted looking after him.'

'And what's changed now?' Sophie asked quietly.

'When you took on this role, I don't expect you ever thought it would get as complicated as it has, did you? Yes, you signed up for a time-consuming post, but was it supposed to be a full-time residential situation from the start?'

'Less than it's become recently.'

'And then there's the business of having to do all the additional duties which you've undertaken without any increase in pay to compensate. Working around the house.... doing chores you weren't hired to do. I'm assuming that was not something you'd factored in when you accepted the position, however generously it paid?'

'I suppose not.'

'In which case I feel it's only fair that I reassure you straight away that if this mess is impacting in any way, shape or form on your personal life, I will immediately compensate you in whatever manner I deem necessary.'

Alessio knew that he was shamelessly fishing for information without asking any direct questions.

'Does that mean I will have to answer to you?' Sophie queried stiffly.

'It means that I want to make sure that you're still happy with what you do and that all these extra responsibilities aren't being borne with hidden resentment. For instance, the situation regarding a housekeeper should have been brought to my attention a long time ago.'

'It was difficult...'

'I get that. You were under strict instructions to keep me in the dark.'

Because my father thinks I hate him.

Alessio gritted his teeth, but banked down all emotion, focusing instead of the woman sitting opposite him.

In truth, every question he'd asked was a pertinent one, even though his original point of curiosity had been to find out more about the woman behind the profession.

'None of that work should have been part of your job,' he pointed out. 'But I understand that it's difficult to disentangle one thing from another when you get involved on a personal level.'

'I've enjoyed it,' Sophie admitted. 'I haven't been secretly resentful. If I were unhappy, I would have said something. Maybe not to you, but to your father. I'm not some kind of shrinking violet who's content to put up with something she doesn't find acceptable.'

'That may be, but it still brings me right back to my original query. I don't want your absorption with all this to get in the way of your social life.' He paused and looked at her in silence for a couple of seconds. 'It's easy for that to happen. You say your friends all work odd hours… In the nursing profession I suppose that's an inevitable hazard?'

'You get used to it.'

'I assume that your social life dovetails naturally with what you do here. You don't keep traditional hours. But what about family? More importantly, what about a significant…er…*other*?'

Sophie felt the slow creep of heat and colour invade her cheeks. Was it any of his business whether there was someone in her life or not?

No!

But if she were to give him the benefit of the doubt, could he perhaps just be showing a natural concern that she might be overwhelmed by events?

She might have told him that she would never have accepted working conditions she didn't like, but working conditions that changed slowly over time fell into another category, didn't they?

Maybe, now that he was her boss in all but name, he was simply doing what any astute employer would do and making sure that a valued employee didn't have any gripes about the position they were in. The last thing he'd need would be for her to up sticks and decide to hand in her notice.

However, despite her stoic efforts to see the logic in the progression of this conversation, Sophie couldn't help but feel embarrassed to death by her singledom. Her kid sister had had more boyfriends over the years than she had!

She looked at Alessio from under her lashes and shivered. The guy was pure, unadulterated sex on legs. Everything about him was physically compelling. It wasn't simply the arrangement of his features…there was something else there that overpowered. The intelligence, the wit, the shrewdness in those fabulous dark eyes. The suggestion of a complex personality that intrigued.

She would have felt a lot more comfortable having this conversation with someone fatherly and sympathetic.

She knew that he was politely waiting for some kind of response, so eventually she shrugged and said, as nonchalantly as she could, 'There's no one in my life at the moment, so there's no need to worry that I've somehow found myself stuck with duties I hadn't banked on and having to make excuses to a guy, telling him that I'm not going to be around to cook his dinner after all. Not that I would be cooking his dinner.'

'I admit that's something of a relief,' Alessio murmured, lowering his eyes.

'And what about you?'

'Come again?'

'You? Now that you're here, and it's so important that Leonard's affairs are sorted out, is there anyone who might distract you from the task at hand?'

'Are you asking me whether there's a woman in my life?'

Alessio angled his dark head and shot her a slow smile that made her toes curl. It also made her wish that she hadn't risen to the mischievous little voice inside her that had propelled her to ask the question in the first place.

'Women can be demanding,' Sophie muttered vaguely.

'Agreed.'

'And with your father's health issues…the worry…'

'You want to make sure that I've got my mind on the task in hand and don't feel the need to rush between London and Harrogate because I have a woman waiting in the wings, demanding my undivided attention?'

'Naturally no one expects you to devote one hundred per cent of your time and energy to this...'

'I'm afraid it's a big job. Not something I can dip in and out of. I think I may be here longer than the original week I planned, having had a look at the chaos at the company.'

'But how on earth are you going to be able to do that?'

The dynamic in the house had changed with Alessio's arrival, and Sophie was privately alarmed at the prospect of him being around indefinitely. How on earth was her nervous system going to stand it? He did things to her she didn't like. He made her aware of her sexuality, which was something she had put on the back burner to be brought out at some later date.

A lifetime of inherited caution when it came to the opposite sex had ended up being an enemy of adventure when it came to putting herself out there...experimenting with sex and the messy business of relationships. It had been easier to step back completely, to hand herself over to making money so that she could sort out the financial obligations of her family. And then all the stuff with Leonard had made it impossible for her to do anything other than focus on her job.

None of which had prepared her for the effect Alessio was having on her. It was as though his presence in the house and the vitality he radiated in his aggressive masculinity had awakened something in her she had hardly been aware existed.

'The worldwide web,' Alessio said succinctly. 'You'd be surprised how much can be done remotely. The problem here is that it's a hands-on situation. It involves interviewing people and asking questions, identifying the dead wood and extracting it. You can't do any of that from a distance on a computer. But, to get back to your original question, no, there's no one waiting in the wings in London, tapping her watch and asking me when I'll be home…'

'Of course you could always bring your partner here to stay,' Sophie mumbled indistinctly.

'I wouldn't have dreamt of doing that even if I had been dating someone.'

'Why not? It's an enormous house. You could have had your own separate quarters.'

Curiosity dug its claws into her. She had seen pictures of Alessio and the revolving door of gorgeous blondes he dated, and she wondered how it was that none of them ever stayed the course. Did he work so hard that he didn't give any thought to settling down?

'I don't share my space with anyone,' Alessio said abruptly, and Sophie's eyes widened.

'Okay,' she said hurriedly.

'Do you?'

'I beg your pardon?'

'Share your space…?'

Alessio glanced around him just as she had done, putting the same question to her with a single inquisitive look that was tinged with wicked amusement.

'I'm sure my father wouldn't have a problem with you bringing your partner here to live in with you, as long as it didn't distract you from your duties. Or has there been no partner to distract you for the past couple of years?' He grinned and waved his hand in a dismissive manner. 'I sense you're about to make an objection to that line of questioning, so before you can do that I withdraw the question.' He looked at her seriously. 'But we're going to be in one another's company, so perhaps we can have some kind of informal arrangement worked out?'

'Good idea.'

'Tell me how you spend your day and what sort of time my father retires to bed.' He glanced at his watch. 'Very early, you've told me. Would that be every night?'

'Recently, yes. In the past, less so.'

'His health problems leave him tired?'

'And everything that's been on his mind as well,' Sophie said pensively, sliding her eyes away from Alessio's mesmeric stare, which made it easier for her to collate her thoughts. 'It can be exhausting when your brain is churning over things, worrying away at problems. It can keep you up at night, and then insomnia becomes a habit that's difficult to shake.'

'Is that a fact…?' Alessio said softly.

Sophie blinked and reddened.

'Are you speaking from experience?' Alessio asked.

Their eyes met.

Sophie felt the rebuff dry up in her throat, because the eyes that collided with hers were oddly encouraging. How was that possible? How could she disapprove of someone, feel unsettled by them, and yet be drawn to confide, which was how she felt now?

Was it because he was a stranger? Because confidences were more easily shared with someone you didn't personally know?

Or was it just part of his enormous magnetism that he fascinated, attracted and repelled in equal measure…?

Her mouth was dry and her breathing shallow as she was pinned into silence by his eyes.

'Well? Tell me…'

'I… I've had my fair share of problems,' Sophie heard herself admit shakily. 'My father died when I was young, and my mother fell apart. I have a kid sister… Adelaide. And for a little while—well, quite a long while, as it happens—I had to look after both of them because my mum couldn't cope. I had to deal with…a lot. Social workers…

the council... I grew up fast, and it was a very anxious time, so, yes, I know what it's like to lose sleep. And once you've lost it, it's very difficult to find it again.'

She offered a watery, apologetic smile, but Alessio didn't smile back. His dark eyes were serious and concerned.

'You took this job because it paid so well, didn't you?'

'What makes you say that?'

'Nursing in a hospital is a busy job. You're surrounded by people and there's a lot going on. That's a far cry from what you have here.'

'I love working for your father.'

'I'm not disputing that, but I'm guessing the money played a part. If life has been tough for you, perhaps, along with having to deal with a parent who couldn't cope, you've also had to deal with financial problems that kept you awake at night?'

Sophie shrugged and then nodded.

The distance between them seemed to have closed. Had he dragged his chair closer to hers? Had she somehow edged hers closer to his? Their knees were almost touching. When she glanced down she could see the strain of his jeans, pulled taut over his muscular thighs.

This was where a lack of experience got a girl. One minute she had been happily plodding along, content in her own inertia, and then just like that along came Alessio and everything was suddenly tossed into the air.

Her head was suddenly filled with should-haves, and she felt tears prick the back of her eyes.

She was horrified. She never cried. She wasn't a crier—because what was the point of crying over stuff that couldn't be changed? And the past could never be changed.

She stood up and shambled towards the sink with her mug. She began washing it, just for something to do. With her back to him, she was unaware of him behind her until she felt his hands on her shoulders, drawing her round to look at him.

'I've upset you,' he said roughly.

'No!'

'If I had had any idea of what was going on I would have been here in a hurry, whether my father wanted it or not.'

'Of course.'

'You're not being paid to carry someone else's stress on your shoulders. Even if it's something you've been accustomed to doing. How is your mother now? Your sister? Time must have moved on for all of you. But is there anything I can do to help financially?'

The utter kindness of his gesture was too much.

Overwhelmed and wrong-footed by the very fact that she had opened up to someone about her past, Sophie felt one treacherous tear slip down her cheek. Mortified, she tried to shake her head free, but his grip tightened.

'You can cry,' he said gruffly.

She shot him a wobbly smile. 'Is that an order from my new boss?'

'I'm not your new boss.'

'You…you've just said…'

'You will always only ever answer to my father. And… off the record…there's no need for the old man to think that anything's changed on that front.'

Sophie nodded jerkily and drew in a deep breath to steady her nerves.

'Your mother and sister?' Alessio went back to what he had asked her before they were side-tracked. 'Anything I can do?'

'Thank you, but everything is under control. Thanks to the pay I've been receiving here,' Sophie admitted, letting another confidence slip through the net. 'My mother is settled in a little place by the coast, where she's made some friends and got a life for herself. After everything was sorted and the bills and debts paid I managed to get the mortgage there right down. And my sister... I can help her too. She's an aspiring actress.'

'An actress and a nurse?' Alessio mused. 'I'm getting the picture.'

Sophie brushed the tear from her cheek, and this time her smile was rueful but genuine. She stepped back, and was relieved when he released her and also stepped back. But the atmosphere had shifted, and when their eyes met there was a charge in the air that hadn't been there before. It slithered, electric and dangerous, barely visible but *there*. She knew that her heart had picked up pace and she couldn't tear her eyes away from his dark, intent stare.

Alessio couldn't remember the last time any woman had had this effect on him. In truth, he had encouraged confidences in a way he was not accustomed to doing. He was a man who didn't rush into caveman protective mode at the sight of tears. In fact a crying woman had the effect of making his teeth snap together with impatience, and it wasn't because he was hard-hearted. It was because female tears were usually, in his experience, a prelude to pleading for a relationship Alessio had always made sure to warn against from the beginning.

He could understand how Sophie had learned life lessons from what she had described of her childhood and adolescence.

He had learned his own.

The past was a country Alessio tried his best not to revisit. What was the point? But being here, back in the house in which he had grown up, which he was now tasked to save, was bringing back memories of the past.

Memories of happier times before his mother had died. Times before the shutters had come down, separating him from his father with a wall that had ended up too solid to climb.

And now memories of his stepmother, a greedy gold-digger who had married his father with clearly only one thing in mind and that was his money.

Young as he had been at the time, he had disliked the woman instinctively, and what had followed—the acrimonious divorce and the long-winded proceedings during which she had done her utmost to get hold of whatever assets she could—had taught a youthful Alessio that when it came to the opposite sex it paid to be careful. If you took your eye off the ball you were always going to be the one who paid the price.

His father's divorce had taken over six years to reach a conclusion, and during that time those walls between them had grown higher and more impregnable.

He frowned now, a little thrown by the way the past was making itself felt. He raked his fingers through his hair and sought to get the conversation back on track, because just for a second he'd wanted to step back towards the woman in front of him, whose eyes were still glistening with unshed tears.

He gritted his teeth and shifted, but his feet refused to walk away.

'What picture is that?' she asked.

Alessio sensed her desire to break the silence. He breathed in deep. 'You the older, sensible one, allowing your kid sister to live the life you denied yourself?'

'Maybe...'

'It must have been tough.'

'I managed.'

'Everyone can *manage*,' Alessio mused, considering how he had done the same, and probably at a very similar age. 'But it's good to go beyond that.'

His hands itched to touch her. He clenched his fists.

But then he did what he'd sworn not to do and reached to brush the side of her face with his fingers.

It was a light, barely-there touch.

Sophie froze. She couldn't breathe, couldn't move, could barely get her brain to work at all.

He'd touched her.

And the touch hadn't been brotherly and empathetic. The touch had carried the pulsing feel of something sexual…something else.

Or was that all in her fevered imagination?

She wanted to close her eyes and pull him closer.

She wanted his mouth to go where his fingers still were, stroking her cheek.

The klaxon bells warning of danger were muted as she took a trembling step towards him, and when she looked at him, lips parted, her whole body alive with sudden craving, she could see the very same thing mirrored in his dark eyes.

Desire…

She heard her own soft exhalation and felt her eyelids flutter on a gasp as his fingers traced the contours of her mouth, one finger dipping inside. She sucked on that finger, drawing it in, pulling them closer.

His kiss was shattering.

She had expected it, had wanted it, had *feared* it.

His mouth crushed hers even as he drew her against his hard, muscular body. His tongue was a sweet invasion and turned her world upside down.

Never, ever had Sophie experienced anything like this. She'd never even imagined it possible to be so overwhelmed by sheer physical need for someone.

She wound her hands around his neck, stretching up, her breasts sensitive and tingling as they rasped against the cotton of her bra.

It was a moment of complete surrender.

But then common sense kicked in, swiftly followed by horror. Had she felt something similar in him? She imagined she had as she pulled away, devastated by what had just happened.

She looked at him, a hand over her mouth. 'I...'

'Me too.' Alessio stepped back, his fabulous dark eyes shuttered. 'This never happened.' One more step back. 'A moment in time. Nothing more. Tomorrow my work begins in earnest, and you will see next to nothing of me.'

'Good,' Sophie said curtly.

She looked away, down to her trembling fingers, which she curled into a steady fist.

His 'moment in time' had been a shattering awakening for her. He was more than dangerous, so seeing nothing of him while he was here was what she needed. And wanted.

She turned her back on him, waited, and when she eventually turned around the kitchen was empty.

CHAPTER FIVE

SOPHIE APPROACHED THE dining room with apprehension. It had been two days since she had laid eyes on Alessio, and during that time there had not been a single minute when he hadn't been in her head.

That kiss...that moment in time...to be forgotten...

It was seared into her consciousness with the red-hot intensity of a branding iron. Yes, of course it would never happen again, but neither, for her, would it ever be forgotten.

For him...yes, it *would* be forgotten—had probably been forgotten already. Because he was a man of the world to whom a kiss was just a kiss, and it hadn't even been a kiss with a woman he was really attracted to. It had been a kiss born of sudden shared confidences and a moment during which the walls between them had been temporarily dislodged.

A matter of seconds...

Fundamentally, nothing had changed. He was still the sort of man of whom she disapproved, from the way he treated his own father to his casual approach to relationships with women. For all his sharp intelligence and complex light and shade personality, he was still not the sort of upfront, honest, straightforward kind of man she had always imagined herself eventually going for.

She had no plans ever to be knocked for six, made vulnerable. Because she couldn't cope with the love of her life being taken from her, either through death or divorce. She would never be helpless. The kind of man who could give her what she wanted in life would be someone who appealed intellectually, who was kind, and allowed her space, who was thoughtful and undemanding…someone calming, with whom she would feel comfortable. No highs or lows.

Alessio was a raging volcano, and she had no time for those. However powerful the pull to gaze into the seething red-hot lava.

And for him?

Well, how many times had he mocked her for being 'background'? What did that imply? It implied that he found her dull and unexciting…the sort of girl who was always be the wallflower, standing at the back of the room, watching everyone else have fun, waiting for her turn to arrive.

Not that far from the truth, as it happened.

She knew the sort of women Alessio liked and dated. Outgoing, sexy little blondes who paraded their assets and were as 'background' as a firework display on New Year's Eve.

And yet for all her common-sense reasoning he still remained embedded in her head like a burr.

And now, as she hesitated in front of the dining room door, she could feel her heart accelerate.

So much had been accomplished in the space of a couple of days.

A housekeeper had been hired. Leonard had announced that only the morning before.

'Just when I had become perfectly accustomed to the two of us in the house, what does the boy go and do? Another housekeeper! She'll have to work around me, my girl, that's for sure!'

Sophie had been quietly relieved, and she knew that

Leonard had been as well. He was fastidious, and over the months had insisted on many of the rooms being closed so that they wouldn't become cluttered, wouldn't need cleaning. He'd used to entertain his friends in the grand sitting room, with dinner served by Edith in the dining room, but things had become a lot more informal. Gatherings had been smaller, and held in the kitchen, where Sophie had been only too happy to tease his elderly friends and join them as they ate at the kitchen table.

The company overhaul had also begun. This too she'd learnt from Leonard, who had grudgingly admitted that Alessio was not playing the tough taskmaster and flinging all his CEOs out of their offices by the seat of their trousers.

'He was never going to do that,' Sophie had soothed, smiling. 'You should know that, of all people. You've got all those cuttings and clippings stashed in folders. You admire him. You would never admire someone cruel enough to get rid of your friends and colleagues at the company.'

'The boy's ruthless.'

But Sophie had detected a thread of admiration in Leonard's voice. Yes, Alessio was ruthless, because she guessed that was what you had to be to climb the greasy pole to success, but ruthless didn't necessarily mean cruel or unfair, and Alessio was neither.

She'd shrugged and then reddened when Leonard had looked at her with narrowed, thoughtful eyes. 'Plays the field as well,' he had said slyly, and Sophie had gone a deeper shade of beetroot.

'So it would seem,' she'd murmured.

'Women fall for him. Has his mother's striking looks, that boy. Isabella was a beauty. Wouldn't want you to get swept away, my girl.'

'That would never happen.'

'He's going to be here for a couple of weeks, he says...'

'I'm immune to men like your son, Leonard.'

She had vigorously begun fluffing cushions on the sofa where he'd been relaxing in the small sitting room that adjoined his bedroom.

'Good, because you're my gentle little thing, Sophie. Wouldn't want to see you hurt by that son of mine.'

Sophie had brushed that off with a quip about him making her sound about as assertive as a bowl of jelly, but she had been embarrassed, and she was embarrassed now as she pushed open the dining room door and paused for a few seconds to take in the scene.

The dining room table was a highly polished affair that could comfortably seat twelve. At one end sat Alessio, at the other was Leonard, and roughly in the middle a setting had been laid for her.

Alessio's computer was on the table next to him, and next to Leonard. was a stack of paperwork, and both men were paying a lot more attention to the files and the computer than they were paying to one another.

'I'm sorry, but I think I'll have my dinner in the kitchen,' Sophie said with impatient frustration, at which point both men looked at her with such identical frowns that it would have been funny if it had been a different situation.

'This is ridiculous,' she burst out.

'What is, my dear?' Leonard looked startled as he half rose to his feet, frown deepening.

'This…! Sitting around this table as though we're all complete strangers! We're going to have to shout to one another to be heard!'

'Bit of an exaggeration, don't you think?' This cool rejoinder came from Alessio, who was looking at her with one eyebrow raised.

'No, I do *not*!' She glared at Alessio. If this was his way of not stressing his father out, then heaven help them all if he decided that he wasn't going to play ball with the doctor's orders.

She stormed out of the room and returned two seconds later with an amused housekeeper, who tried hard not to grin as she hastily rearranged the seating so that the three of them were huddled up close at one end of the table.

Sophie had no idea where that act of bravado had come from. Perhaps the tension of uninvited feelings had been swirling dangerously inside her and had come to a head at the sight of the man who had put them there by kissing her. The man who had ripped aside her careful self-control and tempted her into doing something that couldn't have been a bigger mistake.

Or maybe Leonard's words of warning had struck home, had made her see how ridiculous the situation was, how absolutely crazy it was that she could be attracted to Alessio. And seeing him here, lounging in all his elegant, sophisticated, *sexy* glory, had rammed home the idiocy of her wayward attraction.

At any rate, with some of the formality removed, computer closed and paperwork shoved to one side, the meal which had been prepared by Sarah, a young student who had taken up the job of housekeeper so that she could study without the pressure of a student loan hanging over her head, was enjoyed.

They talked about food.

It was not a contentious issue. Although Leonard complained about his restrictive diet, and with some attempt at light-hearted banter Alessio wondered aloud how she, Sophie, coped with him.

'She says you're a pussycat,' Alessio drawled, as their plates were removed.

Their eyes met, Sophie's tangling with Alessio's, and for a few taut seconds she felt as though the ground had been whooshed away from under her feet. All she could taste in her mouth was *him*…the wetness of his tongue probing, demanding, questing.

Her voice was croaky when, at last, she broke the silence with a suitably non-committal reply and a jerky laugh.

She could feel Leonard's sharp eyes on her and she knew she was blushing.

'We do get along,' Leonard murmured, with just a hint of smugness. 'She reads me like a book.'

'In that case,' Alessio returned, his voice lazy but laden with silky intent, 'perhaps your soulmate might care to let me know how things will pan out now that I've had a good look around this house. It's in need of a great deal of work.'

'Not going to happen is what she would say! House is perfectly fine as it is!'

'There are cracks in places cracks shouldn't be, and a suspicion of damp in several of the rooms.'

'Not going to happen!' Leonard banged his cutlery on the table and glared.

'I came here to sort things out,' Alessio gritted in a driven undertone.

'That does not include ripping my house apart!'

'I won't be ripping it apart. You were worried that I was going to storm into your offices and chuck everyone out on their ears! Have I done that?'

'If I had known you would start a campaign of home improvement I would never have allowed you to…to… help out.'

'You had no choice, Dad.'

Sophie was fascinated by this back and forth—two powerful personalities at war. She could see both sides, but was quietly impressed that Alessio was going beyond what had been put on the table originally to help out with the business.

'Sorting out the company finances isn't something I begrudge doing,' Alessio muttered. 'And getting this house back on its feet isn't something I'm going to begrudge doing either.'

'You don't understand, son.'

'What don't I understand?'

'I don't want… Your mother…'

He flung his napkin to the table and staggered up, and Sophie raced to his side, stricken.

'Your mother…she's here with me. I don't want that to change. I don't want anything about this house to change. Her soul is here and I don't want it to go away.'

Leonard waved his hands about, and just like that Alessio was standing opposite her.

Their eyes met and there was an urgent request in his as he said, in a low voice over his father's head, 'I'll take it from here.'

Leonard had slumped, a diminished figure, his weakness evident now that the bluster had been blown aside.

'Of course,' Sophie said without hesitation.

'But wait here for me. Apologise to Sarah and tell her that dessert will have to wait until tomorrow.'

'Yes, of course.'

She felt Leonard fumble with her hand, and she squeezed his fingers in return and watched as Alessio walked, supporting him, out of the dining room.

This was what it must feel like to be in the eye of a storm, Sophie thought, sinking into her chair.

She was barely aware of Sarah entering, or even of telling her that there would be no need for dessert and that she could head home. Her mind was all over the place.

'Is everything okay?' asked Sarah. 'I don't mind staying on…'

Sophie looked at the tiny, earnest young girl and smiled. 'Make sure you get a cab back to your parents, Sarah, and I'll see you in the morning.'

It was not yet seven-thirty. Should she remain seated

at the dining table? Sophie had no idea how long Alessio would be, and she could barely keep still because of her anxieties.

Her head all over the place, she went into the kitchen and began clearing away the dishes. She took her time as the minutes ticked past, stretching into an hour...longer.

The routine of the kitchen...the cleaning of the counters and putting things away in their proper places...was soothing, and she was just beginning to relax when she was aware of Alessio in the kitchen with her.

When had he come in?

She didn't know.

She swung round to find him lounging in the doorway, his face paler than usual, fingers hooked over the waistband of his jeans.

In the middle of stacking the dishwasher, Sophie stopped and stared at him with concern. 'How is he?'

'Sit. I'll make us some coffee. Has Sarah gone home?'

Sophie nodded and sidled to one of the chairs, and watched as Alessio strolled into the kitchen, his movements less graceful than usual. He made coffee. Instant. Two mugs. His black, hers white with no sugar. He dragged over a chair so that he was sitting close enough for her to reach out and touch him.

'Well?'

'I've been a long time...'

'I didn't expect you to be back downstairs in five minutes. Leonard was very upset. He would have needed calming. I should have gone...'

'Not your responsibility. What happened was my fault entirely. I never meant to stress my father out...and I'm ashamed that I did. It was unforgivable—as I made clear to him when I took him upstairs.' Alessio looked at her in brooding silence for a few seconds. 'I feel like you're caught in the middle of something you never realised you'd signed up to…'

'What does that mean?'

'I think you know perfectly well what I'm talking about.' Alessio smiled wryly, but his dark eyes remained sharp and deadly serious. 'My father and I have not had the easiest of relationships over the years.' He paused. 'I've already mentioned that. But what you just sat through…'

Sharing confidences? It was a game Alessio didn't play. He had learnt to share only what was necessary. He had never spoken about his fractured relationship with his father to anyone. Even as a young boy, dispatched to boarding school with the memory of his mother's death still fresh in his head, he had learnt how to carry the burden of his misery alone. Let down by his father, he had toughened up and learnt not to trust anyone.

When his father had remarried, Alessio's emotional independence had become total. Now, however, he had to concede that the woman sitting opposite him with the big brown eyes and the cropped blonde hair had a right to know something of the situation into which she had unwittingly been brought.

His father depended on her far more than Alessio had ever suspected—but then there seemed to be an awful lot about his father he knew nothing about. The years had drifted by, and every passing year had placed another row of bricks in the wall separating them.

'You mentioned that you two have had your differences over the years,' Sophie said, then added quickly, 'But there's no need for you to…er…talk about anything you don't want to talk about.'

'That's very generous of you, but considering you've had something against me ever since you first started working for my father—'

'That's not true. Of course I haven't had anything against you.'

'No? Maybe not all the time. When I kissed you, you *definitely* didn't have anything against me. Aside, that is, from your body, which seemed very keen to get a bit more friendly.'

'You said that was never going to be mentioned again!'

'So I did,' Alessio murmured.

He shifted, irritated with himself for having been so easily and swiftly diverted from the matter of hand. This was a serious talk, and yet the nearness of her, that slightly floral smell that tantalised him, the silky smoothness of her skin and the calm intelligence in her eyes...

It was all messing with his head, and to someone who never allowed *anything* to mess with his head, it was frustrating.

Yet, staring at her, he just couldn't resist harking back to that kiss...that five-second, utterly earth-moving kiss that had knocked him for six.

He wanted to see her reaction to that kiss again.

He wanted to have another glimpse behind that smooth, serene mask.

He felt a soaring sense of triumph at the delicate colour that crept into her cheeks, and at the way her eyes suddenly scrupulously avoided his.

Alessio was bewildered by his own reactions.

He had not led a celibate life. He enjoyed women and women enjoyed him. It was a mutually rewarding experience. And the women he had enjoyed over the years had ranged from catwalk beautiful to downright voluptuously sexy.

He had never gone for subtle—always associating that with a woman who'd want more than he would ever be prepared to give. He liked everything upfront, all cards on the table, no mysteries to be explored.

Was he so now arrogant that the pull of the novel and the unexplored was too great to resist?

Sophie Court worked for his father, and she was the last woman on the planet in whom he should be interested.

She was a serious woman who took things seriously, and from what she had told him about herself he suspected that she would only contemplate a relationship if it came with signposts to all sorts of destinations he had no interest in exploring.

In fact, wasn't that partly why she disapproved of him? He was certain of it.

Yet it was so tempting to continue this taboo conversation, he thought. So tempting to court that delicate blushing colour again…to savour her reaction to him.

Serious she might be—but, heck, she was woman enough to have enjoyed a taste of the frivolous.

He liked that.

But he didn't like it enough to play with fire, he told himself shakily.

'My father remarried very soon after my mother died.' Alessio brought himself back down to earth in the most ruthless fashion possible, by launching into a difficult, touchy-feely conversation of the kind he fundamentally loathed and never did.

'Clarissa?' Sophie said.

'You know about her? Of course you do. You know more about my father than I do.'

'We spend a lot of time together.'

'What has he said about her?'

'Does it matter? I shouldn't have let slip that I knew who you were talking about.'

'Why? For the first time, just now, my father and I had something of a conversation that wasn't entirely rooted in the superficial. One thing I found out was just how much he depends on you—and not just for nursing care. Maybe you came here with that as your original intention, but it's clear that your relationship has progressed far beyond that. As he confided to me, you're more of a daughter to him than a nurse.'

'He said that?'

'Yes, he did.' Alessio paused. Then, 'In my absence, I have to concede that his affections have been distributed elsewhere.' He suddenly sat back and flung wide his arms. 'I should have kept my eye on the ball—but there you go. No point dwelling on things that could have been done. Fact is, he's scared of dying, and I bitterly regret stressing him out earlier. But I've managed to at least reassure him on what's happening within the company.'

'He loves you.'

'Let's not go there.'

'I just don't want you to think that because Leonard cares about me somehow you've been pushed to one side.'

'The thought never crossed my mind. And if it had it certainly wouldn't cause me any kind of existential angst. Things are as they are.' He paused and relaxed into the chair, looking at her carefully, his dark head tilted to one side. 'I never forgave my father for remarrying so soon after my mother died,' Alessio said bluntly.

'No… It must have been tough on you.'

'But it would seem that there was a story that had more to it than whatever scenario had been evolving in my head at the time. I was a kid. My father had ceased all lines of communication and I was left at the mercy of my youthful imagination. Clarissa, as he's finally confessed, was just someone he clutched at to try and cope with his grief.'

'It happens…' Sophie murmured gently.

But when she thought about a young, confused Alessio, away from his father, wordlessly thinking the worst and shutting down emotionally because of that, her heart constricted.

She had been guilty of seeing only one side of the story—Leonard's side. She had seen the clippings and the articles, and because she had become so fond of him had been angry at his son for being so cold and dismissive. She had been sure the guy who had seldom shown up was the one at fault.

She was reminded of what he had said to her a while back—that there were always two sides to every story.

'I came here,' Alessio continued heavily, 'to sort out my father's business.'

'And the fact that that's going well will really help Leonard's state of mind,' she told him. 'He might be grumpy, but I know he's relieved that things have been taken out of his hands.'

Their conversation was factual enough now, but there was a thrilling undertow that made Sophie's pulses race. Every nerve in her body was stretched taut and she found it difficult to wrest her eyes away from his.

Confiding didn't come easy to Alessio. She knew that, the situation being what it was, he probably felt cornered into saying more to her than he wanted to. Heck, he had barely noticed her existence for the past couple of years! She could have been a pot plant languishing in the corner of a room for all the attention he had paid her!

But things had changed. Did he think that he had to include her because she had become an important part of his father's life? Or had that kiss shifted the ground underneath them?

It certainly had for her, whether she wanted to admit it or not.

He'd told her that it had been nothing but a blip, a moment to be forgotten, and yet when he had referred to it moments earlier she had felt the feathery brush of lust graze her skin all over again.

She reeled at her treacherous body, which demanded to know what it might feel like to savour that touch of his again, to feel his cool lips on hers. To feel more than that.

'How much…um…longer do you see yourself being here…?' Sophie asked, internally squirming at her private thoughts.

Alessio let that question nestle into the silence as he looked at her thoughtfully. In the space of just a little over an hour—which was how long he had been upstairs with his father—things had changed.

His father had opened up. A crack. Alessio had thought himself beyond having his ideas changed. He had spent a lifetime honing them, after all. But when Leonard had gruffly told him why he had rushed headlong into that catastrophic second marriage he had hung his head and roughly brushed away tears Alessio had never thought he'd witness in a million years…

New possibilities had started to emerge from his cast-iron beliefs.

'Longer than I anticipated,' he said now. 'I hadn't taken into account how fragile my father is. I've always thought of him as…not just tough as nails, but wily with it. Seems in my absence things have changed. I don't want to jeopardise his recovery, and there's plenty more on the way that might push things in that direction.'

'What do you mean?' Sophie asked in alarm.

'I told you I've looked around this house…' Alessio glanced around him briefly. 'I've broached this subject in the past but been knocked back. Now, however, seems a good enough time to broach it again. If the company is being overhauled, then why not do the house?'

'You're really going to overhaul the house? I know you said that at the table…but Leonard seems so against it…'

'Like I said earlier, it needs doing. I've spoken to my father now, told him all the problems he'll be storing up if he puts off having essential work done, and I think he's come round to the idea. Mostly because he doesn't have a choice.'

'He seemed very adamant that that wasn't what he wanted…'

'Well, as you've witnessed, he seems to think that if the bricks and mortar gets bashed about a little, then it's somehow disrespectful to the memories stored inside them. But I've managed to persuade him that the memories are inside *him*. The house is just a house.'

'It's not that easy.'

Sophie remembered how hard it had been for her mother to leave the house she had shared with her husband for so many years. Even though by then she had ploughed her way through her heartache and misery, the final act of saying goodbye to the four walls of that house had still represented a huge change and a frightening one.

Leonard wouldn't be leaving his house, but he would face seeing it knocked about and brought up to date, perhaps remodelled in places. Because Alessio was right—there were structural issues in some of the rooms that would certainly need looking at.

She knew that life had been tough for Leonard in the past few years. He had been forced to walk away from running his company and then he'd had to deal with ill health—which had, in turn, affected his mental health.

'He needed someone to lean on,' she couldn't resist saying, her voice cool. 'He needed *you* to be here.'

'That wasn't what he wanted at the time,' Alessio grated.

'So when is this work going to begin? What is it going to entail?'

'It's going to entail my father moving out for possibly a couple of weeks. There will be workmen in and out of all the rooms, and the dust and noise will be too much for him to endure.'

'And he's *agreed* to this?'

'I've told him that there's not much choice. It's either get it done or watch the place slowly fall apart, until it becomes too difficult to patch it up the way he would like it to be. I'll be keeping as much intact as possible. But there are a lot of historic features that need renovating badly—and quickly. The stained-glass windows on the landing are about to come crashing down because they need urgent re-leading.'

'I'm not following you. Where is he going to move to? London? Leonard has always told me how much he hates London.'

'Not that he's actually been there more than a handful of times,' Alessio returned drily. 'But no. London isn't what I have in mind.'

'Then where?'

'I have a place at Lake Garda in Northern Italy. It's close enough to get there on my private jet in a matter of hours, so the trip shouldn't be too taxing for him.'

'Oh, right… Okay…'

'If we plan on leaving in roughly a week's time, it will give me sufficient time to get the ball rolling with my father's company, so that I can instal some of my own people to tie up the loose ends. I'll also have enough time for my PA to source the best crew available to get the job done here, and of course, there will have to be some time spent packing away anything valuable that needs to be protected. I suggest several of the more robust rooms in the West Wing would be suitable for that.'

'Wait, hang on just a minute… *We*…?'

'You don't think that my father is going to be able to travel without you, do you? I'm assuming you have a passport that's up to date?'

'Yes, but—'

'There aren't really a whole lot of *buts* about it,' Alessio interrupted, before any of her objections could be raised. 'If I'm honest, part of my father's agreement to this—aside from accepting the inevitability of having the house renovated—is based on the assumption that you will provide the continuity of care he needs by being there with him.'

He paused and delivered her a searching look that brought a flame of bright colour to her cheeks.

'Aside from which, what obligations do you have that might be a spoke in the wheel? Naturally, you will be richly compensated for the inconvenience, but it's hardly as though you have compelling personal duties that require your presence here, is it?'

CHAPTER SIX

ALESSIO'S PRIVATE JET landed four days later at a small air-port near Milan. During those four days, Sophie's life had accelerated at supersonic speed.

Alessio had moved three of his top people into Leon-ard's offices in Harrogate, and taken himself back to Lon-don so that he could co-ordinate a crew to—as he had told both Sophie and Leonard before he disappeared—*'throw everything at the estate with no expense spared'*.

He had also arranged for a team of highly experienced house-movers to transfer whatever needed taking from one part of the house to another.

'Leave all the big items,' he had instructed. 'They'll be covered over and protected and it'll be a waste of time to shift them. Just move what you deem necessary.'

Predictably, Leonard had grumbled.

'One minute the boy's barely speaking to me,' he had complained on the evening before the movers had been due to arrive, 'and the next he's giving orders as though he's the master of the house!'

'You've been talking together,' Sophie had pointed out. 'He took you out for lunch before he left for London and you seemed to have a good time.'

'Of course I'm going to be suitably polite when some-one invites me somewhere,' he had huffed. 'Such a thing as good manners, my girl! Not that you'd think they still existed when you look around you nowadays!'

She had done a rapid tour of the house, pushing Leonard in the wheelchair to spare him walking from one room to another, and in the end only very personal possessions had been moved. His computer, his memoirs, and the entire collection of newspaper clippings he had collected over the years, along with photo albums and other mementoes.

She had managed to persuade him that large-scale breakages weren't going to happen. 'These people are experienced,' she had told him, gently but firmly, 'and they'll have Alessio to answer to if they make any mistakes.'

'I suppose the boy does have his head screwed on when it comes to taking charge,' Leonard had said with grudging admiration. 'Gets that from me—not that you'd know it, seeing me in this state now. Isabella, his mother... well, that was a different matter. Depended on me for just about every decision! Could never lose patience with her, though—not with that smile of hers. Could move mountains, that smile.'

Sarah had been asked to check at the end of each day to see what had been done and to make sure that Alessio's rules of tidiness were being strictly obeyed.

Alessio had summoned her before he left, and Sophie had felt sorry for the poor kid, who was so clearly in awe of Alessio that she could barely string a sentence together.

But he had been kind, and patient, and had politely overlooked her beetroot-red face and her self-conscious stammering and gently told her to get in touch with his PA. Her pay would be reviewed and increased accordingly, because of the extra responsibility of keeping an eye on the builders.

'Are they trustworthy? Will they need supervision?' Sophie had asked in alarm, when Sarah had left the room.

At a little after four in the afternoon, Leonard had been

in his sitting room, relaxing, and she had been alone with Alessio, who had wanted to fill her in on arrangements before he returned briefly to London.

They'd been on opposite sofas in one of the sitting rooms. Between them on a small, old-fashioned wooden table had been a pot of tea and some biscuits Sarah had baked earlier.

'Utterly trustworthy and they won't need supervision.'

'But…'

'Sarah's nineteen, a hard worker, and she wants to save money. But I think she would be embarrassed if I were to offer to pay her while we're away for doing nothing. This way, she's doing something, and she'll get compensated for the fact that she's going to have to come here at six every evening and spend an hour or so doing the rounds.'

'That's very…thoughtful,' Sophie had conceded.

And then she had reddened when he had looked at her in silence for a few seconds before saying, with cool amusement, 'I occasionally can be…despite the reputation that seems to have preceded me.'

She had been relieved when he had left for London, and had thrown herself into getting everything in order before they left.

And now here they were.

Travelling on Alessio's private jet had taken Sophie into the realms of ridiculous wealth. Sleek and black, it had waited for them on the tarmac of the airfield like a giant bird of prey, throwing all the other small little hoppers into pitiful shade. People had stared as they had been ushered inside, and she had sucked in her breath and paused just for a moment as she'd glanced around at an interior of cream and beige and dove-grey and walnut.

Breathtaking wealth bred breathtaking respect, and during the flight she and Leonard had been deferred to like royalty.

Leonard had promptly begun dozing, the second they were in the air, but Sophie had been too awestruck to do anything but guiltily revel in the novelty of being flown in spectacular style.

Now, as she disembarked from the obscenely lavish private jet, nerves that had been in abeyance returned with force.

'He told me about this place.' Leonard appeared next to her and they began to descend the metal stairs that had been put in place as soon as the jet had come to a stop. 'He's only had it for a few years. Wish he'd mentioned it sooner.'

'Do you? Why?'

It was very cold, but bright, with blue skies turning indigo because the sun was fading fast.

'Isabella always wanted a villa on Lake Garda. Used to go there when she was a child for the summer holidays.'

Leonard's voice was gruff as they looked around to see someone approaching from a long, sleek black car. The driver they had been told to expect. Alessio was meeting them at the villa.

'I always regretted not buying her what she wanted. She could have bought it herself, but she wanted me on board and, fool that I was, I was too wrapped up in work at the time to contemplate a holiday home. A life of little regrets...' He turned to her, watery-eyed. 'And a number of big ones. If I had known that Alessio had bought a place here... It could have been a bridge between us, maybe...a chance to think about things gone by. But enough of this nonsense. Let's appreciate the scenery, my dear!'

They did.

The lights from a huddle of exquisite houses nestled around the glassy lake twinkled in the fading daylight, disappearing up the slopes of the mountains that rose like stern guardians around them.

They sat in companionable silence in the back seat of the luxury car that drove them quietly and swiftly towards their destination. By the time they got there the mountainous backdrop was a dark, brooding mass, and the colourful houses that dotted the water's edge and clambered up the sides of the mountains were shadowy and indistinct.

Leonard was as good as asleep. It had been a long day. He was jostled awake as the sleek car slowed, and even in the gathering gloom they both fell silent at the spectacle that awaited them.

Wide black gates opened automatically, and the car slowly purred up a winding, uphill avenue bordered with trees. In the distance there were lights, and as the car moved on Sophie could see the outline of a magnificent white turreted villa, spectacularly lit against the dark night skies. Behind it, the mountains looked close enough to touch.

'Oh, my...' she breathed.

'I'm impressed,' Leonard murmured next to her, now alert and wide awake.

The front door was opened as the car swung in an arc to park directly outside and there he was, framed in the doorway, the man who had had her nerves skittering for the past few days.

He was dressed in black. Black long-sleeved polo, black jeans. He looked so sexy and so sophisticated that her heart began to hammer and she could only half focus on Leonard.

'Anybody home?' Leonard asked, nudging her.

When she looked at him, his bushy eyebrows were raised, and his eyes slid across to where Alessio was moving towards the car, then back to her flushed face.

'I was just...just...'

'Why don't you help me out, my dear? It's very rude to stare, and you're staring at my son.'

'Yes! Help you out… Of course!'

Sophie's cheeks were on fire. Leonard could see far too much, and he was nowhere near tactful enough for her liking. He had warned her off his son once, and the last thing she needed was for him to get it into his head that she was bothered by Alessio…that she was attracted to him like one of those blondes he always seemed to be photographed with.

Flustered, she could barely meet Alessio's eyes as he neared them, but she was aware of him with every fibre of her being.

'How was the trip?' he asked.

He moved to stand on the other side of Leonard and took his father's left arm as she hooked his right through hers.

'I'm not a complete invalid yet!' Leonard fussed, but he allowed himself to be led into the magnificent house, and as the door closed behind them they both fell silent and looked around.

It was a vision of pale marble, deep rich wood and white walls. The villa stood solitary in its own grounds, surrounded by an army of tall conifers which gave it a serene, otherworldly atmosphere. It was almost as though they had been transported to another planet. Certainly Sophie had never seen anything quite like it, not even in the pages of the most wildly expensive house magazines she had flicked through in the past.

Her eyes drifted to the broad staircase that wound upwards, drawing the gaze to an uber-modern crystal chandelier that fell in a riot of glass teardrops from the ceiling.

The silence stretched, and when Sophie finally finished her inspection and looked at Alessio it was to find him looking right back at her with amusement.

'The trip was fine, thank you,' she said, belatedly answered his question.

Leonard took over, moving forward at a sprightly pace

and demanding a full tour of their surroundings, while muttering just loudly enough to be heard that he hoped something like *this* wasn't what he would return to when work had been done on his house.

Alessio responded in good humour and his dark eyes held Sophie's briefly in a wry, conspiratorial look that made her flush. 'I think that I've got the message loud and clear about how little you want things changed.'

'Nothing wrong with that, my boy!' Leonard declared, huffing, and moved on to peer into rooms, taking his time with his inspection.

'We all find our perfect moment in time and stick to it,' Alessio murmured, moving to stand behind his father and towering over him, even though Leonard was by no means a short man.

'Quite right...quite right.'

Standing behind them, and to one side, Sophie wondered what Alessio's perfect moment in time was. Judging from the remote splendour of this villa, she wondered whether he had *ever* found his perfect time. There was certainly nothing personal on display here—nothing that would indicate anything other than a house designed and kitted out to suit a man who had money to burn but no time to relax. But, my, it was an impressive place.

She strolled towards the back of the house, in Leonard's nosy wake, and could make out, through a bank of imposing columns, a wide porch, broad enough to house several sitting areas, and then, down a shallow bank of steps, the faraway glimpse of what looked like a swimming pool.

'Who looks after this place when you're not here, son?' Leonard asked. He had shrugged off Sophie's helping hand and was slowly backtracking his way past the winding staircase towards, she assumed, the kitchen.

'I have a couple who check in daily.'

'Damned waste of money,' Leonard growled, and Sophie, glancing across to Alessio, saw a smile tugging the corners of his mouth.

'I have the money,' he said, without batting an eye, 'so it's my choice what I do with it.'

'Your mother used to come here as a girl,' said Leonard, pushing open another door.

Sure enough, they were in a kitchen the size of a football field. There was more splendid white-blonde wood, and a huge range cooker in brushed steel that seemed madly excessive for a guy with no interest in cooking.

'I know,' Alessio said softly. 'I've seen pictures.'

Father and son exchanged mutually cautious looks and the conversation wasn't developed. Watching from the sidelines, Sophie felt a twinge—a stirring of hope—that bridges might be crossed even though what had happened between them was only her concern insofar as it might or might not affect Leonard's stress levels while he was here.

'The couple', it seemed, did more than look after the house in Alessio's absence. One half of the equation—the husband, as it turned out—was an excellent chef, and they were told he would be preparing all their meals. His wife would take care of the laundry and the cleaning.

'Think it's going to be stress-free enough for my father?' Alessio asked later, when dinner had been eaten and dishes cleared and the practically invisible smiling housekeeper had tidied up behind them.

They had remained in the kitchen. It was as impersonal as the rest of the villa, with none of the clutter of Leonard's kitchen on display. The table was a gleaming granite-topped affair, and Sophie was perched at one end and Alessio at the other. With Leonard no longer in the kitchen with them, she was a little flustered when he shifted to move closer to where she was sitting.

'So…?' he drawled, lazing back in the chair and watching her with close attention. 'I was half expecting the pair of you to stay put.'

'What do you mean?'

'The so-called *pussycat* can be a stubborn mule, and I envisaged him digging his heels in and giving you strict instructions to turn away anyone coming to the door with a bag of tools and some tubs of paint.'

'You're so sarcastic…'

Sophie fiddled with the stem of her wine glass, wanting to peel her eyes away but riveted by his magnetic sex appeal. He had shoved the sleeves of his figure-hugging tee to the elbows, and her eyes disobediently drifted to the silky dark hair on his forearms and the flex of muscle visible under the shirt.

Her throat went dry as he hooked his foot under one of the chairs and dragged it closer, so that he could relax with his feet up on it.

'I'm realistic, Sophie. My father doesn't want anything touched in the house. I appreciate that he wants to keep his memories intact, but I've done my best to persuade him that it would be a pointless exercise if the house ended up going to rack and ruin, at which point the renovations needed would be so extreme that he would have to kiss sweet goodbye to anything being left in place. But I still wasn't convinced he wouldn't backtrack the minute I wasn't around.'

'Well, you must have done a good job of convincing him, because there wasn't a moment when he had any doubts that the work would happen.' She paused and tilted her head to one side. 'In fact, he seems quite content at the moment…even if he's grumbling about everything.' She smiled. 'It's funny, but when I look back on the past few months I can see all the signs of someone who was very anxious. Leonard was quiet when he usually isn't, and there were so many times when I had to say something twice before he even realised that I was speaking to him.'

'My father can be difficult,' Alessio murmured.

'That's not being difficult!' Sophie laughed. 'He had stuff on his mind and no one to share it with.'

'Is this leading up to another criticism of my lack of presence on the scene?'

'No!'

Sophie meant that, and her voice registered surprise. Their eyes tangled and she felt something disturbing flutter inside her, like soft butterfly wings, loosening the muscles between her thighs and making her nipples pinch.

It was a physical, sexual reaction, and for a few seconds she was so horrified and shocked by it that she struggled to get her thoughts together.

This was raw. This was different from objectively looking at him and acknowledging that he was stupidly beautiful.

This was *scary*. Because it wreaked havoc with her self-control, and her self-control was something she took great pride in. She refused to be vulnerable to all those things that could hurt, refused to let go. And this squishy sensation rippling through her felt like letting go and she hated it.

'Anyway,' she said hurriedly, 'I would say that he's a lot less stressed that he was even a couple of weeks ago.'

'Most people like to share their burdens with other people or, even better, have someone else take charge in difficult situations. My father might be opinionated, and he may resent the fact that I've taken over, but he's human, and he'll be relieved that I'm picking up the baton and running with it.'

'I guess you're right…'

Sophie's thoughts drifted to her adolescence, and for a few seconds she tried to imagine what it might have been like if someone else had picked up the baton and run with it.

How different would her life have been?

Without the responsibilities she had shouldered, would she have had the chance to enjoy her teenage years free from gnawing anxiety?

Would that have made her a different person?

Or would she still have been the responsible, sensible one? Was that just the legacy of her birth order? She was the older of two siblings...the one who was always destined to be responsible, whatever the circumstances.

'Penny for them.'

'Sorry?'

Sophie surfaced to find Alessio's dark eyes fixed thoughtfully on her. The overhead lights had been dimmed earlier, on Leonard's orders. They were enjoying a very tasty meal indeed, he'd said. Not trying on clothes in a fitting room where you needed fluorescent lighting to spot every crease in a pair of badly made trousers.

Alessio had left them dimmed, and now the shadows and angles of his face seemed even more forbidding and outrageously sexy.

He was as bronzed as she was fair, and she wondered what their bodies would look like next to one another.

With no clothes on.

She so pale and he so much darker.

The very thought brought hectic colour to her cheeks, and for a couple of seconds she completely forgot what she'd been thinking, and what he had said to interrupt her thoughts.

Her heart sped up, pumping hot blood urgently through her veins, and that squishy feeling coalesced into a need that bloomed inside her. She felt her panties dampen and that itch between her thighs...the tingle there that made her want to pass out.

'You're a million miles away. What's going through your head? Negative thoughts about me?'

'It's not all about you,' Sophie said sharply—more sharply than she'd intended. Because her thoughts were all still over the place, making her uncomfortable and defensive with the man who had put them there. 'As a matter of fact I was thinking… I was thinking…'

'Yes? I'm all ears. Tell me what you were thinking.'

He sat forward, and just like that he closed the distance between them, so that she could almost feel the heat emanating from his long, muscular body.

She couldn't escape the suffocating effect he was having on her.

If she kept her eyes on his face she was all too conscious of the depth of his eyes, the lush thickness of eyelashes any woman would have given her eye teeth for, the sensuous mould of his mouth, of the lips that had covered hers…

Looking just a bit lower and the strain of his jeans across his thighs made her feel giddy.

'I was thinking that what you just said…about Leonard being relieved that someone else has taken over…well, you're right. Of course. It's noticeable. It really is. People coping with problems and issues…yes. It's a blessing sometimes when someone steps in…takes over…'

She was stammering, her jerky outpouring of words trying to cover her inner turmoil.

'Not that I would know.'

'You had no one there to help you when you needed help after your father died. Your mother and your sister depended on you and I know you shouldered the burden alone. What about your friends?'

'I don't feel sorry for myself…' she said awkwardly, wishing she had never said anything in the first place.

She focused on what he had said, really giving it consideration. How could she tell him that confiding in anyone about her unhappy situation growing up had felt inappropriate? All her friends had been talking about boys and parties and clothes. Who had wanted to be saddled with her conversation about the cheapest place to buy groceries, or how difficult it sometimes was to deal with her mother when she didn't want to get out of bed? No one.

But Alessio was staring at her, unsmiling, his dark eyes curious, oddly encouraging her to expand on the story she had started.

She thought of the way he had stepped up to the plate. She had been so nervous when she had decided to head to London to see him. She had predetermined that he wasn't going to be obliging, and yet he had put his own life on hold so that he could manage his father's, and he had done so without a single murmur of complaint.

And now here they were, in this stunning villa, and arrangements had been made for Leonard's house to be renovated. And she knew that Alessio had taken a personal interest in finding out just what his father wanted, had allayed all his doubts and fears and done so without resentment.

So...?

As they sat there in the kitchen, Sophie felt the strangest temptation to break all her rules and open herself up in ways she wasn't accustomed to doing.

'Talk to me, Sophie,' Alessio murmured.

He dropped his feet to the ground and leaned towards her, his arms resting loosely on his thighs, his knees almost but not quite touching hers.

'Don't be silly.' Her voice was shaky when she replied, and she was held captive by his calm, unwavering stare. 'Since when are you interested in listening to what I have to say about anything that isn't to do with your father? Besides, I've already told you about...about my mother and my sister. There's no need to pretend any more interest.'

'Now who's being silly…?'

'Alessio…' She threaded her fingers through her spiky fair hair and darted a helpless look at him.

'*Alessio*… I like the way you say my name… You have a husky voice—has anyone ever told you that?'

'Is that a compliment?'

She smiled. Her pulses were racing. There was a simmering, sizzling excitement zigzagging just below the surface that felt dangerous but compelling at the same time. And she didn't know whether she was imagining it or not… didn't quite know what to do with it.

'It is. It makes it sound as though you think carefully about every word that leaves your mouth.'

This time she laughed and relaxed. 'Don't most people think before they speak?'

'You'd be surprised…'

'What do you mean?'

Alessio grinned crookedly and raked his fingers through his hair without taking his eyes off her face for a second.

Sophie's breath caught in her throat and she blinked, because for a moment she could see the boy behind the man, and the humour that made him so much more than an aggressively talented billionaire who was feared and respected in equal measure.

'I *mean*,' Alessio said, 'that most of the women I go out with talk a lot, and in very high, urgent voices. A lot of them seem to feel that their mission should be to cram as many words in as they can before pausing for breath.'

'That's mean.' But she hitched a low laugh.

'I exaggerate. But only slightly.'

'They probably talk a lot because they're trying to impress you.'

'And of course that's the last thing *you* would ever think of doing…'

'The very last thing,' Sophie breathed, lowering her eyes.

'So now we've established that, believe me when I tell you that I'm interested in what you have to say. And I'll tell you something else... You and my dad...' He shook his head, and smiled and shrugged at the same time. 'I never realised how entwined your lives were.'

'I do work for him on a full-time basis...'

Alessio smiled softly. 'My extremely dedicated PA works for me full-time. Our lives are far from entwined.'

Sophie grimaced. 'I suppose to start with, when we were still getting to know one another, it was a more formal arrangement. We had a rigid schedule for pretty much everything. But it wasn't long before...'

'Before my father started pushing the boundaries like a toddler?'

Sophie laughed. 'He *can* be quite mischievous sometimes.'

Their gazes met and held. Was she aware of how exciting she was?

No, she wasn't.

Looking at her, Alessio knew that she had no idea how invigorating it was for him to converse with a woman who wasn't out to impress him. It wasn't just the tenor of her voice that he liked, but the substance behind what she said. She was so different from the women he dated that she could have been from another planet.

There was no name-dropping...no flirting...no thrilling anecdotes about exciting parties where so-and-so had been chatting to so-and-so and you'd never guess who was there...

She was...bloody refreshing.

And he was enjoying more than just their conversation.

He was enjoying the play of emotions that criss-crossed her face and her responses to what he said—some of which he could tell she was trying hard to downplay.

He was enjoying the way she blushed, because he didn't have much experience of women who did that.

Because he only went for a certain type of woman.

That was the thought that registered on the outer edges of his brain as he continued to look at the woman sitting opposite him, admiring the smoothness of her skin, the intelligence in her eyes, the girlish disingenuity and the strength beyond her years that blended into an intriguing mix.

Was it her novelty that he found so captivating all of a sudden?

Of course it was.

What else?

Alessio's work life was high-octane, so he had always liked the predictability of women who didn't stress him. He didn't want to have to deal with shrewish demands or hissy fits. His life might not be free of them completely, but in truth his interactions with the opposite sex were not rollercoaster rides.

After a long hard day at work, who wanted a rollercoaster ride?

In fact, who wanted a rollercoaster ride with anyone? Ever? Certainly not Alessio. As far as he was concerned, emotional rollercoaster rides were for fools who allowed their hearts to dictate their behaviour.

He would never be that person. He would never allow his heart to get in the way of anything. He would never open himself to the pain of loss because he had learnt from a young age that love and loss were entwined. He had loved his mother and he had lost her, and it had driven him half-crazy as a kid.

And he had loved his father and lost him as well. Not in the physical sense, but emotionally. Because his father had withdrawn into a world that had excluded him, Alessio. He had shut the door and that door had never been re-

opened. The lock on it had just grown rustier over time...
harder to break.

So self-control always lay at the heart of Alessio's deal-
ings with women. And if this happened to be one of those
rare instances when his self-control was missing in action, then he knew that there was nothing to worry about.

Why would there be?

Curiosity flared. What sort of guys did Sadie go for
anyway? Tall? Short? Thin? Fat? What fish in the sea took
her fancy? He wanted to find out more about her, and he
liked the novelty of that.

At the receiving end of those dark, speculative, brooding
eyes, Sophie felt the rush of nerves. Her body urged her
to move forward, to let herself be absorbed by his powerful, charismatic personality. But her brain took fright and
she jerked back. Her hand whipped to the side and a wine
glass shattered at the sudden impact.

Was it instinct or distraction that made her reach out to
try and save it at just the wrong moment?

She pulled her hand away with a cry, and when she
looked at her palm she could see a shard of glass caught
there...more than one shard.

Everything had happened in the blink of an eye, but
before she could do anything Alessio had her hand in his
and was staring at the droplets of blood.

'Sit still.'

'I'm fine.'

'I need to get the glass out. The last thing you want is
an infection to set in.'

'Alessio,' Sophie said faintly, 'honestly... I can deal
with this...'

But he was already heading to one of the cupboards,
to return seconds later with a First Aid box and a bottle
of spirit.

She fell silent as he gently took her hand in his and began dealing with the cut. The glass was onlt skin-deep. She hadn't caught it with enough strength for it to have penetrated. He was meticulous, and as he worked he talked to her in a low, melodious voice that was soothing, and relaxing, and knocked back all the barriers that had been in place.

He joked that the First Aid box was about the only thing he could locate fast in the kitchen, because he'd had to sit through a tutorial on how to use the contents when the housekeeper had bought it. He described the lake, which could be accessed from his massive garden down a series of winding steps. He talked about the boat he had which was seldom used because time never seemed to be on his side.

Without her noticing, he had moved to kneel at her feet, and she watched his dark head and the careful delicacy of his fingers as bit by bit he cleaned the tear in her skin.

Sophie wanted to laugh, and make a wisecrack about not knowing that he was a trained doctor along with everything else, but she was mesmerised by him, stilled by the touch of his hand on hers. Her heart was thumping against her ribcage, and she could feel the silence in the kitchen like something weighty and tangible.

He wrapped a bandage around her palm and expertly secured it, but when he finally met her eyes he didn't move away, back to his chair.

He remained where he was, and her mouth parted and her breath hitched in her throat, because there was an intent in his dark eyes that fired something similar in her.

Naked *want*—the very same want she had tried so hard to lock away, where it couldn't do any harm—was out of its cage now and bringing wild colour to her cheeks.

She wasn't surprised when he straightened up to curve

his hand against the side of her flushed face. She angled herself against it and felt her eyelids flutter.

Last time when he had kissed her, sanity had come roaring back at speed.

This time, as she leaned towards him and gently covered his mouth with hers, she wanted to let herself go.

She'd never done that. She had no idea what it felt like to be swept away on a tide of longing and she wanted to find out.

What was wrong with that?

She kissed him.

She was vaguely aware of them shifting positions and wasn't sure how it had happened. But suddenly he had moved from ground to chair, and she had shifted from her chair to his lap, was straddling him and gently rocking as they continued to kiss.

Her panties were wet, soaked, and she rolled her hips so that she could press against him, relieving some of the urgent ache between her legs.

He groaned as she kissed his face, his neck, stroked his shoulders and felt the hard bulge of muscle under his stretchy tee shirt.

She was barely aware of the hindrance of her bandaged hand because her body was on fire.

His hand stole up to cup her breast and then slid underneath her top, and she shuddered and arched her back, urging him to do more than just caress her.

She hissed a sigh and moaned when he shoved the top up, his hand shaking as he unclasped her bra and then pushed that up as well.

Small, perfect breasts.

Alessio had never felt such a loss of his prized self-control in his life before. But the sight of her bare breasts, her blushing pink nipples, fired him up to such a frenzy of response that he was on the brink of losing it completely and ejaculating prematurely.

Unthinkable.

He darted his tongue to flick the stiffened bud of one nipple, and then took it into his mouth and suckled.

Hands on her shoulders, he angled her so that he could enjoy her.

The more he tasted, the more he wanted to taste.

Not just her breasts…not just her nipples.

Alessio wanted to explore every inch of her exquisite body and then, when he'd done that, he wanted to start all over again.

'My bedroom?' he growled, drawing back to look at her.

'Alessio…' Sophie breathed, drowsily meeting his hot stare.

'There's no pressure, Sophie…' he told her.

He contemplated the gut-wrenching disappointment of a long and very cold shower, should she change her mind, but if she did, then that was her right and he would respect it.

'I want this, Alessio…'

'Are you quite sure?' He paused and tangled his fingers in her short, fair hair. 'Is this what you want? I can't offer permanence…'

'I know that.' Sophie smiled. 'For your information, neither can I…'

'So, my bedroom?'

'Your bedroom,' she agreed with pleasurable abandon, as he lost himself in her smile.

CHAPTER SEVEN

SOPHIE GAZED AT ALESSIO, her eyes half closed and feeling greedy with longing. The villa was quiet and in darkness because it was a little after eleven. The couple who worked there had disappeared ages ago, and Leonard was safely tucked away in his bedroom fast asleep.

In front of her Alessio stood, magnificently bare-chested. Low-slung jeans, unbuttoned, rode low on his lean hips. He had tossed his sweater on the ground, and with his hand resting loosely on the zipper of his jeans was ready to complete the job of getting undressed.

Four days...

That was how long these clandestine liaisons had been happening.

They had made love on that first night, after tiptoeing up the stairs, making sure not to wake Leonard, and it had been the most mind-blowing experience Sophie had ever had.

He had touched her in places that had made her melt, had licked and explored with his tongue and his mouth until she had groaned low and deep, barely recognising her own gasps of pleasure.

She had gone from cautious to addicted at supersonic speed, and it had been tacitly and wordlessly decided that their first experience was not going to be their last.

How long it was going to last, Sophie had no idea. Not

beyond this stay at his villa on the lake. She'd assumed that. Relationships didn't last with Alessio, and this one, which was out of the ordinary, would definitely have a cut-off to it that would be shorter than usual.

She was no pliable, dependent, clingy, sexy little blonde thing. She answered back. And she felt he didn't encourage that in the women he dated, even though he'd told her that he liked that trait in her.

She was also trying hard to build on the slender foundations she could see being re-erected between him and his father, and whenever he frowned and looked at her in a way that said *You're going beyond your brief,* she simply stared back at him with feigned innocence and refused to back off.

He never snapped, and she thought that was because he was enjoying himself too much to risk her taking offence and turning her back on him.

'Sex has never felt so good,' he'd told her only the night before.

With Alessio, it was all about the sex. He had a high libido and a hunger for her that was flattering and compulsive.

Only now and again did she feel a twinge of sadness that everything began and ended with the physical—although that was a reaction she didn't stop to think about, because she told herself that it was the same for her.

He was vital and sexy and erotic, and he was opening her up to a world of experience she had been denied.

She wasn't in it for any kind of gooey-eyed, hand-holding relationship. He wasn't her type.

She could never give her heart to anyone who wasn't prepared to look after it, and Alessio wasn't the kind of guy who signed up for looking after a woman's heart.

'Sometimes,' he drawled, now, snapping her out of her thoughts, 'I look at you and you're a thousand miles away.

Where are you? Different place? Different country?' He delivered a wicked smile. 'Just as long as the man you're with there is me, then I don't care…'

He unzipped the trousers and Sophie hitched herself up onto her elbows and watched his smile broaden.

He knew she liked watching him.

She'd told him that it turned her on. Just as it turned him on for her to be naked when she watched, so that he could see her body, waiting in readiness for him to pleasure it.

She was naked now, lying on the king-sized bed in his enormous bedroom, which was a marvel of pale colours, dark wood and lots of hidden cupboards that slid open at the push of a button.

Like in every other room in his magnificent villa, the minimalist paleness of everything made Sophie think that this was a place no one under the age of eighteen should ever be brought—just in case sticky fingers or spillages ruined the pristine perfection. This was an adults-only escape, from the hard beauty of the marble to the bold abstracts hanging on the walls and, outside, the exquisite infinity pool which was surrounded by pruned trees and would doubtless come into its own during the warmer months.

In a playground for the rich and famous, Alessio's villa was right up there with the most dazzling.

The evening before, after Leonard had retired for the night, he had taken her out into the garden, with its lawns clipped to precise perfection, and led her down a bank of stone steps, romantically lit with small twinkling lights. They had led to his very own sprawling deck that accessed the lake. They had stood looking over the glassy dark beauty of the water and it had been magical. Crisp and cold and absolutely perfect.

Was it any wonder that she sometimes felt as helpless as

a moth, dazzled by the force of a flame that shone brighter than anything she could ever have imagined?

She gazed at him, so beautiful in the shadows of darkness. His jeans joined his sweater on the ground, and then the dark boxers, and her breath caught sharply at his proud erection, which he briefly circled with his hand before moving towards her.

Sophie half closed her eyes and touched her breast, then traced the contour of her nipple with her finger. On top of the duvet, completely naked, she let her legs fall apart, encouraging a look of hot desire from Alessio as he joined her on the bed.

'I like what I see,' he murmured, lying next to her on his side, pressed against her so that she could feel the throb of his erection at her thigh.

'What's that?' Sophie curved to face him so that they were eye to eye, her belly touching his.

She lifted her leg to cover his thigh, and then manoeuvred her body so that she could rub her wetness against him. She shuddered and closed her eyes when he gently stroked her nipple with his finger, picking up where she had left off and tracing the outline before homing in on the stiffened bud.

'Are you going to tell me what you were thinking?' he murmured, licking his finger before replacing it on her nipple, so that he could dampen it into even more sensitivity.

'I wasn't thinking anything.'

'Now, why don't I believe you?'

He nuzzled the side of her neck, her jawline, peppering her with the lightest of feathery kisses that made her want to squirm and wriggle against him.

He was the consummate lover.

He knew how to touch her and where... He knew how to get her to fever pitch and then take her even higher. He could make her body feel in ways she had never imagined possible.

Yet Sophie knew the limits of what they had—just as she knew that telling him what was going through her head would be a mistake of biblical proportions.

Because what had got into her that suddenly she was thinking ahead?

Why was she beginning to wonder what it might feel like when this ended amicably?

She'd jumped in, wide eyes open, and hadn't even bothered to think ahead to how they might rub along when they returned to England.

Of course he would go back to London. And she and Leonard would once again resume their daily routine. But how was that going to feel after *this*?

'I have no idea why you don't believe me,' she said, kissing him softly to extinguish a conversation she didn't want to have.

He smiled against her mouth.

'Because you're not a woman whose mind is ever empty of thoughts.'

Their eyes tangled. For a few seconds Alessio was sideswiped by the oddest notion that he *wanted* to find out what she had been thinking…what had put that remote expression in her eyes.

Why?

He *never* felt the slightest temptation to second-guess what was going through any woman's head. That wasn't what he was about.

But for no reason, the compulsion to know what *she* was thinking was overwhelming.

'I'll take that as a compliment,' Sophie murmured.

Having never been given the brush-off before, Alessio took a couple of seconds to actually recognise the sound of it, and when he did he had to force himself to take it on the chin, because the last thing he needed was some kind of deep and meaningful conversation that would end up going nowhere.

Did it matter what she was thinking?

It was almost laughable that he had momentarily been so invested in finding out!

'So you should,' he said. 'But enough talk…'

They made love.

His mind emptied as he touched her. His curiosity to get inside her head fell away as he skimmed her slender body with his hand, pausing to cup her breasts and tease her rosebud nipples.

She arched up, and he knew what she wanted and was happy to oblige. More than happy.

He took one pulsing pink nipple into his mouth and lost himself in the taste and feel of it as he sucked, while he teased her other breast with his hand.

He went slowly.

That first time they had made love he had been so turned on that he'd rushed, hadn't given her the attention she deserved, but he had made up for that since then.

True, the days passed agonisingly slowly, with only the occasional touch, the brush of his fingers accidentally against hers… True, by the time his father was safely asleep he was so keyed up he could barely think straight… But even so he always made sure never to rush when they were finally in bed.

He let his hand drift lazily over her slender body, tracing every inch, feathering over her ribcage, dipping down to her belly button and then edging to the soft downy fluff between her legs.

He parted her thighs, felt the wetness between them, and struggled to hold on to the urge to go faster.

He slipped his finger inside and then trailed his lips

downwards as he played with her, teasing the tightened bud of her clitoris and enjoying the way she squirmed against his finger.

Sophie's eyelids fluttered.

Knowing what he was going to do didn't reduce the thrill of excitement and anticipation that flooded through her.

She tensed, feeling his mouth teasing her, and then groaned, low and soft, when his tongue slid to tickle her clitoris. She let her legs drop, enjoyed him pleasuring her, and then took charge to change the equation.

She heard his full-throated chuckle as she manoeuvred him as expertly as he manoeuvred her, so that she could enjoy and pleasure *him* just exactly as he had been enjoying and pleasuring *her*.

She tasted him as he had tasted her, in a mutual giving to one another that made her feel warm and so fulfilled inside.

Alessio was the first to break their embrace, growling that any more and he would go flying off the edge.

She laughed, and then groaned again when he thrust into her, long and deep, moving slowly at first, then speeding up, his own guttural moans mirroring hers.

Sophie's orgasm ripped through her, stiffening her and then sending her into a spiral of satisfaction that seemed to go on and on until she was finally spent.

They curled into one another, bodies slick with perspiration, and she nuzzled against him.

Alessio felt the warmth of her face pressed against his neck, felt the way she burrowed like a little rabbit, and something very much like peace settled in him, filling every part of him.

He toyed with her hair, asked her whether she'd ever

had it long, smiled when she told him she'd always just liked the ease of short hair.

So like her.

So unfussy.

So suddenly scary.

This was nothing that Alessio had ever felt before. He could have stayed right there...with her so soft against him...for ever.

A perfect moment.

And one that he wasn't going to allow. Letting his body guide him, feeling compelled to touch, was one thing. Lust was instinctive, and even if this felt raw and wild, he knew that it was nothing that could threaten his self-control. In the end, he could put lust right back in its box, close the lid and walk away.

Hadn't he done just that, many, many times before?

So what if this felt different? He had already worked out that it was down to the novelty value. He'd been knocked sideways by an attraction he hadn't seen coming. He'd assumed one thing about the woman snuggled against him, only to find that all his assumptions had been wrong.

Therein lay this weakness now, and it was a weakness that went against every single principle he had ever held dear.

No attachment. No vulnerability. No *caring*.

This felt suspiciously like all three.

No question, he was off target with this, but he'd always been a guy who believed in the motto that it was better to be safe than sorry.

He stiffened, edged himself apart from her—just fractionally, but enough to convey a message. And of course she read that message, loud and clear, and likewise detached herself, with a breathless little laugh that was half awkward, half embarrassed.

Just the sort of laugh he wanted to kiss away.

He clenched his jaw and fought down everything in him that was in danger of softening.

'I'm suddenly thirsty,' he said abruptly. 'Think I'll head downstairs for some water...'

Sophie pulled back as though she'd been stung. She knew what this was about. Just for a second she had utterly relaxed against him, had wrapped herself around him and cuddled him, and he had shot back, his immediate and instinctive response to repel any such intimacy.

Sex was hot and hard and rapturously enjoyable. But cuddles? Tenderness? Those were things that were very different, and he was making sure that she noted the distinction...making sure she didn't get ideas into her head that this was anything more than it actually was.

A time-limited fling between two very different people. *It hurt.*

It hurt because she'd gone and invested more into this non-relationship than she'd dreamt possible. It hurt because she'd clung in a way she'd never planned on clinging. And now he'd sensed it and pulled back because it wasn't what he wanted.

'Sex is thirsty business!'

She injected airiness into her voice and hoicked herself up on her elbows as he swung his beautiful body off the mattress, padding around in the semi-darkness to grab whatever discarded clothes he could put his hands on.

Sophie stared from under lowered lashes, her eyes adjusting to the darkness and making out his silhouette and the grace of his body as he slung on the jeans he had earlier thrown off in his urgency to join her on the bed.

He wasn't looking at her at all.

He spun round but only half turned when his hand was on the doorknob, to ask her if he could bring her anything.

'I think I'll head back to my room,' she said casually.

But really she was waiting for him to leave, suddenly conscious of her nudity.

Alessio didn't say anything, then he nodded and shrugged and turned to open the door, letting in a stream of light that surely shouldn't have been there, because they were always really careful to switch all the lights off in the wide corridor.

Leonard's room was at the end of the corridor, and they had become accustomed to stealth—the trademark of the clandestine affair.

She heard Leonard before she saw him—heard him booming to Alessio that he had heard voices, had been worried that someone might have broken in.

Alessio's voice, in return, was cool and confident and amused as he reassured his father that the house was safer than a bank vault.

'I have so many well-positioned CCTV cameras that not even the Invisible Man could get past them. So there's no need for you to trouble yourself. It's late. Let me escort you back to your bedroom…'

'Hang on just a minute, my boy!'

Sophie cringed in horror as she heard Leonard bang on the door with his walking stick.

Old and in questionable health he might be, but he still had a formidable amount of stamina when it came to making his presence felt.

He pushed the door wide open before Alessio could do anything to stop him and before Sophie could take evasive action.

Although what would that evasive action have been?

Lunging for a cupboard? Ducking underneath the bed? Making a run for the bathroom and locking the door behind her?

Ridiculous.

She drew the covers right up to her chin, pulled her

knees up and watched as Leonard slowly shuffled his way into the bedroom and switched on the overhead light.

'I knew it!' he roared, spinning around to glare at Alessio, who was hovering in the doorway, the very picture of embarrassment.

The fact that he was half naked said it all.

She had never seen him as ill at ease as he was now, indecisive as he leant against the doorframe, raking his fingers through his hair before folding his arms and staring at Leonard, deprived of speech for once.

'How the hell long has this been going on?' Leonard bellowed into the silence.

'Dad…'

'Don't you *Dad* me!'

He tapped his way over to the bed and sat heavily on it while Sophie tried to remember how to breathe.

'I expected better of you,' he told her mournfully, turning his back to Alessio, who was still hovering in the doorway. 'Alessio…' He waved one hand dismissively towards his son without looking around. 'I know that boy and his philandering ways.' He narrowed his eyes on Sophie and looked at her with a shrewd stare. 'Seduced you, did he? Took advantage? I could see you had eyes for him.'

'Leonard…' She felt faint.

'I'm seeing it all clearly now, my dear,' he continued shakily. 'Used his charms on you…turned your head. Seduced you.' At this he cast a baleful glance over his shoulder.

Sophie met Alessio's dark gaze and knew in that instant that he would say nothing in receipt of this slander. He would consider her, consider the relationship she had with his father, which had always been based on fondness, affection and trust, and he would respect it enough to back away from making a stand for himself. He would take the hit.

'It's not like that…' Sophie muttered, beetroot-red.

'Speak up, my dear. I'm old and hard of hearing.'

Sophie knew that Leonard's hearing was as sharp as her own, but he had been confronted with a horror story and he wasn't going to let either her or Alessio off the hook.

In an instant she realised just how deep her affection for this difficult but lovable old man was. The thought of his disappointment cut her to the quick, but there was no way she was going to let his son take the rap for this.

She wished that she was at least having this conversation fully dressed, instead of huddled in mortified nakedness under the duvet.

'It wasn't your son's fault…' She cleared her throat.

'Come again?'

'I said…it just…*happened*, Leonard. Neither of us planned it and Alessio didn't…didn't seduce me…'

Sophie knew how helpless she sounded.

How could falling into bed with a guy who was off-limits *just happen*? Especially when you considered that they'd never had much to do with one another in all the time she'd worked for Leonard.

Was it any wonder that he was now staring at her, open-mouthed? With a look that was a mixture of incredulity and dismay?

That didn't last long, because he immediately stood up, spun on his heel and banged his walking stick on the floor a couple of times.

'You took advantage of her,' he accused.

He tottered towards the chair just beyond the bed and slumped heavily into it. He looked exhausted.

It was late. A combination of weariness and heightened stimulation was gaining momentum, turning his face waxy and ashen.

Alarmed, and with her nursing instincts coming into play, Sophie lunged off the bed, making sure to drag the sheets around her, and staggered to get her balance before retrieving her scattered clothes from the floor, while issuing orders for Alessio to fetch some water.

She went to the ensuite bathroom and flung on her clothes—jeans and a loose tee shirt. No bra. No underwear. No time.

Leonard was still in the chair and barely glanced at her as she moved quickly towards him.

'Leonard…'

'Alessio should have known better!'

'You can't blame your son.'

'I can and I do.'

'Why?'

'Because I *know* you, Sophie. You're not that type of girl.'

'What type of girl is that?'

'You know what type,' Leonard said quietly. 'You don't throw yourself around. You're a homebody. You enjoy being still, not racing through life seeing who you can sleep with.'

'Good Lord, Leonard.' Sophie smiled gently. 'I'm really not sure I like the person you're describing. She sounds very dull.'

'She's not.' Leonard smiled back weakly and reached out to squeeze her hand. 'She's a kind person who's very dear to me, and that's why I blame Alessio for this.'

Leonard rested back into the chair and closed his eyes.

'He's a love 'em and leave 'em man, and that's just fine and dandy. But not when it concerns you, my dear.'

Sophie didn't say anything.

Leonard looked drained.

His doctor had said no stress, and she hadn't seen him this stressed in all the time she had known him.

'We should probably get back to bed.'

Sophie swung round, craning her neck to see Alessio

standing behind her where she had positioned herself on a squat upholstered stool in front of Leonard.

'How the hell do you expect me to sleep, Alessio'

'Here, drink some of this water.'

'Sophie is trying to make me believe that this was some kind of…mutual understanding between the pair of you! But I know you, Alessio, and she's not one of your…your *trollops*!'

'No, she certainly isn't one of those,' Alessio murmured, dragging a chair over so that he and Sophie were now on either side of Leonard.

'You can't have one of those "mutual understandings" with her!'

'Leonard!' Sophie protested. 'Believe it or not, I can have any amount of mutual understandings that I want! I'm a big girl!'

Was she, though?

Uttering those words had brought a wave of confusion. If she really was a big girl, up for 'mutual understandings', then why was she becoming so conflicted about what she and Alessio had started in good faith?

Why had she suddenly found herself wanting *more*?

She was terrified of clinging to him. She knew, and had known from the start, all the limitations that came with this relationship.

If it could even be called a relationship!

Certainly, Leonard would beg to differ!

But common sense was no longer functioning, so how, exactly, did that non-functioning common sense back up what she had said about being a big girl?

'I'd planned on talking to you tomorrow about this,' Alessio was saying softly to his father, at which Leonard seemed to perk up a little.

Sophie frowned at him. 'You had?'

'You've probably forgotten. Yesterday was a busy day.

Walking into town…having lunch by the lake…taking my father out on a boat despite his protests…'

'It was a very busy day,' Sophie said vaguely, trying hard to work out when she and Alessio were supposed to have had this conversation about him having a conversation with his father.

She guessed that it might be possible. Sometimes when she was with him everything seemed to leave her head in a whoosh…every single thought.

Factor in the fact that she was in just about one of the most picturesque places on the planet, and she could surely be forgiven for overlooking the occasional discussion. Who wouldn't forget the odd chat when they were out on a glittering turquoise lake, staring back at colourful houses, an orderly jumble of pastel Lego, as picture-perfect as anything she had ever seen?

Except…

The way he was staring at her now, with his dark eyes warm and…*complicit*…

'Remember I told you that I would be telling my father about us?'

Sophie opened her mouth, because if Alessio had come close to saying anything like that, then there was no question that the conversation would have been lodged at the very top of her mind, picture-perfect scenery or no picture-perfect scenery.

'Telling him that what we have…' Alessio's voice was husky and he reached out and took her fingers in his '…is serious stuff…'

'What are you saying, my boy?' Leonard piped up, temporarily drowning out the clamour of stunned confusion in Sophie's head.

'I'm saying, Dad, that this isn't what you think it is.'

Alessio held up his hand, briefly giving Sophie time to recover from the slow burn his entwined fingers had been arousing in her. He gestured with a mixture of rue-fulness and sincerity.

'Hmph…'

'You think I've been turning Sophie's head…'

'Can you blame me?'

'I don't suppose I can. You've probably seen all the media coverage. Paparazzi always seem to lurk round every corner when I have a woman on my arm…'

'You've never made it a priority to keep a low profile, Alessio,' Leonard said testily, but his mood had changed. His colour was back and there was a brightness in his eyes that hadn't been there before.

Sophie was listening to this exchange in growing be-wilderment. Where was Alessio going with this? Her brain was struggling to join the dots, even though somewhere inside she knew that the dots were easy enough to join.

Leonard had caught them *in flagrante delicto*…

He had become stressed…

His consultant had told them that he shouldn't be stressed because it might lead to a recurrence of his health problems…

And so Alessio had leapt in with a solution he thought would do the trick.

It was easy to figure out, and yet Sophie recoiled from that obvious conclusion—just couldn't make sense of it.

Her heart was racing as she sat in dumbfounded silence. Thankfully, Leonard's attention was riveted on Alessio. If he had glanced in her direction he might have been be-mused by her stunned expression.

She surfaced to hear Alessio reassuring his father that he was a changed man. His hand returned to hold hers in a show of loving unity, and when he gently squeezed it she had no need to glance at his face to know what he was tell-ing her… *Go with me on this.*

She would.

For Leonard's sake…

But she could feel a low-level anger buzzing inside her, growing stronger with every passing second.

'Trust me, Dad,' Alessio murmured, reaching out to pat his father's arm. 'Sophie is different from all the women I've ever dated in the past, and I'm asking you to believe me when I tell you that what we have is nothing like anything I've had in my life before.' Dark eyes slid across to Sophie's face. 'I'm a different man when I'm with her…'

'And this turnaround has all happened in the space of a few days?'

Leonard's attention had shifted to Sophie, who was horrified to be the cynosure of his attention.

He had eagle eyes, and he was as sharp as a tack when it came to ferreting out stuff she might prefer to keep to herself.

'We…er…' Sophie licked her lips and smiled weakly. 'Er…well, you know how it is, Leonard,' she mumbled. 'It just sort of happened…'

She held her breath and waited for a barrage of disbelief. How could someone as switched-on as Leonard, who was so cynical about Alessio, do anything but scoff at the preposterous suggestion that in the space of a few days an inveterate womaniser had changed his spots?

Nothing came.

Sophie nervously looked at him and wondered how else she might expand without giving herself away. But she didn't have to say a word, because he reached forward and covered her hand with his.

His eyes were watery. Was he about to cry because of the horror of the situation?

Sophie opened her mouth to say something, *anything*, but before she could get there he was telling her, softly, that he understood.

'It was the same for me,' he said whimsically. 'One look

at Isabella and she was the one. That mistake that happened afterwards…' He looked at Alessio with a direct stare. 'I was lonely and heartbroken and a fool, and I should have known better.' He reached out and patted Alessio's hand. 'You've made me a very happy man, son.'

He began to heave himself to his feet.

Sophie was numb. She remained where she was as Alessio rushed to help his father. She watched, dimly aware of Leonard still talking as they headed out of the bedroom.

Talking about what?

She shuddered to think.

She would wait for Alessio and then find out what the heck happened next…

CHAPTER EIGHT

ALESSIO REAPPEARED TWENTY minutes later, by which time Sophie had headed down to the kitchen, leaving in her wake a trail of breadcrumbs for him to follow in the form of lights switched on, on the landing, down the grand staircase, and in the broad corridor that led to the kitchen.

Tense as a bowstring, eyes peeled on the door, she straightened when he pushed open the door and entered the room.

'Clear path to follow to find you here,' he said wryly, following her lead and making himself a cup of coffee. 'All the lights on.'

'What's going on, Alessio?' Sophie asked quietly.

She cradled her mug and watched as he took his time making the coffee, helplessly sucked in by his masculine beauty, the economic grace of his movements as he stirred his drink and returned the milk to the fridge, before swinging round to look at her.

He leaned against the kitchen counter in silence for a few seconds, as though marshalling his thoughts. Then, 'You're…taken aback…' he began, at which Sophie gave a dry bark of laughter.

'*Taken aback*, Alessio? *Taken aback* is when something you're expecting in the post arrives a day late! I'm not *taken aback*. I'm…utterly bewildered at what happened just then.'

'You know what happened.'

Alessio padded across to the table where she was sitting and sat on the chair closest to her, adjusting it so that they were directly facing one another.

Sophie's body instantly responded to his proximity, primed to be turned on the second he was within touching distance of her.

She realised, with dismay, just how vulnerable she had let herself become. She had gone from cautious to smitten in record time and she could have kicked herself.

How could she have known Alessio for what he was and still allowed herself to be bowled over by his charm? His wit? His intelligence? His sex appeal?

How could she have moved so swiftly from a position of self-defence to a place where she'd laid down her arms and thrown down a welcome mat?

Leonard had rushed to conclude that his son had been the seducer, but Sophie recognised with painful honesty that she had practically flung herself at him.

She blinked, dragged herself back to the present, and focused on the man sitting so close to her now—close enough for his unique masculine scent to waft over her, making her heart skip a beat.

Disastrously, he reached for her hand and linked his fingers lightly with hers as he proceeded to stare at her with earnest honesty.

'Alessio…'

'I know what happened might have been a little unexpected…'

'To say the least.'

'But when I saw my father on the landing…realised that he had probably woken up and heard a noise from the bedroom when he was on his way to the kitchen for God only knows what reason…well, I had to think on my feet…'

'But how could lying to him have been a good idea?'

'There was no alternative.'

'There's *always* an alternative to lying, Alessio.'

He had the grace to flush, but there was determination in his dark eyes as he held her stare.

'Yes, there is. Of course there is. But let's consider that alternative.'

Sophie stared down at their entwined fingers. If she had spent the past few days on a rollercoaster ride, then it now felt as though that ride had sprouted wings and was flying off into orbit at the speed of light.

In her head, she kept seeing Leonard's face when he had looked at her. She had sensed the disappointment and recoiled from it, but *lying*?

Alessio's voice was low and hypnotic, and she remained silent as he gazed at her. 'The main thing to consider is my father's health. Would you agree?'

'Yes, of course. But all the same…'

'When he clocked what was happening—that you were in my bedroom—his face went ashen. I thought he was going to keel over.'

'He must have been shocked to the core,' Sophie said jerkily, on the verge of tears. 'He might have been big in business, and he might have been through two marriages, but there's a side to him that's very traditional.'

Alessio opened his mouth to contradict that, to point out that however traditional his father might be he was fully aware of the bees and the birds and what happened between a man and a woman when mutual attraction decided to strike.

But then it hit him that Sophie saw a different side to his father, a gentler side, and if she *thought* that he was traditional, then perhaps what she saw was an old man who *was* deeply traditional.

Alessio was one hundred per cent sure that if his father had interrupted him with one of his string of blondes reclining in rumpled disarray in his bed, he would have snorted in resigned disgust and moved on.

But Sophie was different.

He had put her on a pedestal, had formed a bond with her that was paternal and protective—hence his appalled horror at what had been a perfectly natural situation.

More or less…

'He did seem shocked,' Alessio conceded.

'You could have just shut the door firmly behind you.'

'It *was* shut, Sophie. He heard voices. He put two and two together. There's only three of us in this villa, so it really didn't take him long to work out what was going on.'

'We should never have started this,' Sophie whispered.

'It's too late to go down that road. We were caught red-handed, and I knew in that moment that I had to spare my father the stress of thinking that you had become one of my conquests. In case you haven't noticed, his opinion of my love-life leaves a lot to be desired.'

'Yes,' Sophie muttered, thinking back to the many times Leonard had passed caustic remarks about the women his son chose to date and the speed of turnover.

'He… It would have been different if he had interrupted me with another woman…' Alessio raked his fingers through his hair and tilted her chin so that she was forced to look at him. 'But he sees you as his… Well, in some ways as the daughter he never had, and as such he's very protective of you.'

'Yes, but…'

'But nothing, Sophie. He got himself into a state, thinking that I might hurt you…'

'The way you hurt other women?'

'I don't hurt other women. I have fun with them, and they have fun with me, and I treat them very well along the way.' Alessio scowled. 'Besides, we've been over this.

I suppose I could have sat him down and told him that we entered into this from the same starting point, that we're both adults who know what we're doing, but in the heat of the moment the only thing I wanted to do was reassure him.'

'I suppose I can appreciate that.'

She sighed. Was it idealistic to think that telling the truth was always the better idea? And since when could she hold herself up as a paragon of virtue on that front?

When she cast her mind back, wouldn't she think of times when she had bent the truth to spare her mother undue worry? When she'd told her that everything was going to be fine? That the money was all okay? That the teachers were thrilled with Addy's work? That she was working after school now and again for fun, and not because they were desperate for the cash?

That life was just fine and there was nothing to angst about?

So who was she to start preaching now?

Of course when he was presented with the unexpected Alessio was going to do his best to smooth things out. And wasn't that a *good* thing? Didn't it show how far father and son had come that he would do anything to spare his father any undue worry?

'I didn't want him collapsing, Sophie.'

'I understand. But now he thinks…' She shook her head and tried a laugh on for size.

'Is it all such a lie?'

'What do you mean?' Sophie's heart picked up pace.

'We're an item, aren't we?'

'We are while we're here.'

'Let's not get lost in the detail.'

'Isn't it a bit more than a detail?'

Had she hoped for something more? Had she hoped for a declaration that he wanted more than just a passing fling?

She must have been mad… But here they were, stuck in a lie not of her making, and what on earth happened next?

'What happens when we get back to real life, Alessio?' she asked bluntly. 'We can't maintain this fiction. Leonard isn't an idiot. He's going to realise that you made the whole thing up.'

'You tell me that I've made the whole thing up,' Alessio purred, 'but that's not entirely true, is it?'

Without warning he reached to brush the side of her face with his finger, and Sophie shivered at the hot trail left there. Her mouth parted and her eyelids fluttered, and when he placed a butterfly-gentle kiss on her mouth she responded by sighing into his, swept away on a tide of something that was irresistible.

Treacherous fingers laced into his dark hair, tugging him closer, and she felt his smile as he gently drew away—but only a tiny bit. His forehead touched hers, and when he spoke, his breath was warm on her face.

'Who's kidding who, Sophie?' he queried softly. 'This isn't something that's been concocted out of thin air to placate a questioning old man. It isn't an arrangement that we've actively thought up to deceive him into believing in something that doesn't exist.'

'But…'

'Shh…' He briefly placed his finger on her mouth, before removing it, and then he held her head in his hands and looked at her gravely. 'I wouldn't deliver an outright lie to my father, however much it might help towards easing a thorny situation. I would never drag you into pretending something that didn't exist…that was a complete piece of fiction…'

Caught between his hands, Sophie could scarcely breathe, so mesmerised was she by the intensity in his eyes, the warm sincerity in his voice and the urgency of his explanation.

She hated the way her brain seemed to take a holiday when she was near him, and she knew that she should be fighting harder to resist the soft persuasion in his voice. But when she tried to get hold of some vigour, she drew an unhelpful blank.

'We *are* an item, Sophie. We're lovers. And I wasn't lying when I told my father that you're different from all the other women I've ever been out with.'

'You weren't?' Sophie croaked.

Alessio shot her a crooked smile. 'You *are* different. I'd say you're unique…'

Sophie blinked, owl-like, and then recovered sufficiently to get hold of some much-needed common sense.

'So unique that we're not going to prolong this once we return to Planet Earth…' she countered.

For a few seconds Alessio was shaken by the thought that he wasn't entirely sure on that front.

Would they continue what they'd started?

He was so accustomed to having relationships that were defined by the very temporariness of their nature, that he was taken aback to discover that it was different with this one.

At least, it *felt* different.

Maybe he had accepted on some level that they would be destined to meet over time, whether or not they continued what they had.

Maybe in that respect he hadn't got around to mentally predicting the parting of the ways scenario.

At any rate, it was disturbing that he hadn't envisaged ending what they'd begun. At least not in any kind of conscious way. He'd assumed… *What?* What had he assumed? That this would continue indefinitely? Because he wasn't ready to think about her not being there?

Alessio frowned.

'I hadn't thought that far ahead,' he said smoothly. 'Had you?'

'Of course I had,' Sophie answered. 'I'd thought that this was good, but naturally it was going to come to an end. Nothing long term for either of us. A week or two of fun and then we go our separate ways.'

'Well,' Alessio said briskly, 'that line of thinking will have to be put on hold for both of us.'

'How is that going to work, Alessio?'

'It seems relatively straightforward to me.'

'How so?'

'My father is under the impression that this is more than it is...'

He looked at her from under dark, sooty lashes. Her cool agreement with what he'd said should have pleased him. He hated histrionics, and had discovered that women frequently went down that road when it dawned on them that he wasn't for taming. That he hadn't been lying when he'd told them that longevity wasn't in his DNA when it came to relationships.

'That's the problem,' Sophie said, without the slightest inflection in her voice. 'I know you didn't want to stress him out, but I think he would have been okay if we'd been truthful.'

'Not a chance I wanted to take.' He flushed. 'I know what you're thinking, Sophie. You're thinking that I jumped into a lie to protect a father I've barely visited for...for some time.'

There was so much humanity in that admission, from the tone of his voice to the guilty flush that slanted his cheekbones. She felt a wave of tenderness wash through her and her expression softened.

'That's the sound of a guilty conscience talking, Alessio,' she said gently. 'I wasn't thinking any such thing. In fact, I suppose I was rather pleased that you were prepared to go to such lengths to make sure you didn't stress him out unduly...'

'How so?'

Her heart melted further at the quick glance he shot at her, uncertain and questioning. He *wanted* to hear what she had to say. How different was this man from the ice-cold stranger she had confronted not that long ago at his offices in London! A man ruled by his watch, eager to see the back of her and disbelieving of what she'd had to say.

'You've changed. You both have. You and your father.' She gazed at him thoughtfully. 'You might still circle around one another, but the circles are smaller, and there are times when they're not there at all. So I appreciate that you didn't want to jeopardise the bridge that's being built...'

'I'm not sure the situation is really as complex as that—'

'But we're still left with a problem.'

'With one or two upsides.'

'Really?'

'The past few days have stretched me to breaking point, Sophie.'

Alessio shot her a look of pure, wicked charm that made her blood sizzle.

'How so?'

'You know how. Being near you when my father's around...wanting to touch you and not being able to...'

Sophie reddened. Her body began a steady throb. Yes, she knew exactly what he was talking about. Conscious of Leonard's watchful gaze, they had moved around one another, keeping their distance, but those quick glances when their eyes had met had made her blood boil. Sometimes, handing her something or moving towards his father, Alessio would brush against her, and when he did every nerve ending in her body had gone into overdrive.

There hadn't been a single moment during any day when she hadn't been thinking ahead to when Leonard would be safely in bed and she and Alessio could creep into his room like kids playing truant. She'd caught herself drifting off into fantasy land and picturing them together, turned on by images of what they would do once their clothes were off and they were free to touch one another.

The net result?

They'd thrown caution to the winds and taken chances which had landed them in this current mess.

Sophie was ashamed to admit, even to herself, that still, right now, in this concerning situation, what she really wanted to do was strip off all her stupid clothes, straddle the sexy hunk sitting opposite her and feel him plunge into her wet depths. She wanted to fling herself back and feel his tongue laving her nipples.

She drew in a shaky breath and forced herself back into a position of self-control. 'When we return to England, things aren't going to be straightforward,' she muttered.

'The house should be up and running,' Alessio pointed out. 'Largely. There will still be work to do, but nothing that would impede either you or my father from moving around.'

'You've had updates?'

'And I'm keeping my father in the loop. He insists on being involved in every decision taken.'

'Tiring…' Sophie murmured, momentarily distracted.

'Tiring for him. Utterly exhausting for everyone else. I had no idea he could be so insistent on choosing what shade of paint he wants the hall done in.'

'He hasn't mentioned anything to me…'

'At any rate, by the time we return to the UK…'

'You'll be ready to head back down to London?' she finished for him.

'More or less.'

Alessio found that the thought didn't appeal as much as it should have.

'Things will fade between us. It happens. Relationships burn, then sizzle, then gradually stutter until there's nothing left.'

'That's such a sad way of looking at things, Alessio.'

Wake-up call. Alessio stiffened, reminded of why what this woman and many others called sad, he labelled realistic—because it was realistic to protect yourself from the pain of loss, and if loving came with loss then he was happy to discard that fantasy.

'Let's agree to disagree on that one,' he said, his voice cool. 'Trust me on this. We play along for a bit, have some fun in the process, and in a couple of weeks' time you'll find that telling a small white lie to help an old man out will have been worth it...'

The 'old man', Sophie discovered the following morning, had a spring in his step now that he had been given something to live for.

Since when had he ever admitted to her that he'd been longing to see Alessio involved with a suitable woman?

He had scoffed at his son's love-life, jabbing his finger disapprovingly at all the pictures in those articles he had shown her over the years, but he had never banged on about his son settling down, far less framed his own happiness as being something influenced by Alessio's choices. They'd barely been on speaking terms, for heaven's sake!

Yet now he was heaping praise on the newly outed lovebirds, encouraging them to spend time together and leave him to get on with his recovery, happy in the knowledge that his world was a brighter place.

'This isn't going to end well,' Sophie said worriedly now, as she and Alessio were waved from the door by a beaming Leonard, who had declared himself fit to handle the rest of the work on his house remotely.

They had been discussing the possibility of going on a

wine and food tour with a private guide. They would visit the vineyards near one of the lakeside towns and sample the local cuisine, all in five-star luxury. But on hearing of the lovebirds' sudden relationship, Leonard had been only too happy to send them on their way alone. Nothing, it seemed, should stand in the way of their blossoming love affair.

'It'll be fine,' Alessio murmured. 'We have the freedom to enjoy ourselves while we're here. Let's not find ways of downgrading the opportunity.'

He turned to look at her, swivelling her and then holding her in place. In truth, Alessio was happy with the turn of events.

The shock of bumping into his father outside the bedroom door had faded with astonishing speed.

As far as he was concerned, there was nothing not to like about this arrangement.

On every front, it ticked the boxes.

Firstly, he had rescued his father from another possible episode by eliminating a potential source of stress. Hadn't the consultant specifically warned of the dangers of his father worrying to the point where his health would be impacted? Good progress was being made on that front, so why would he jeopardise that?

Secondly, he had legitimised the relationship between him and Sophie. No more sidelong glances…no more hot, fleeting brushing of hand against hand. Now there was positive encouragement to spend time together!

And thirdly, perhaps for the first time in a very long time, he could feel the strength of a bond he had thought perished.

It felt good.

He had relegated his relationship with his father to a

distant holding pen, wherein they co-existed without any real communication.

Things had been changing on that front ever since he'd discovered the whole mess with his father's finances.

And now?

Now things had changed even more—and, yes, that felt good.

'We can do the vineyards another time.' he said. 'Right now, I want to take you to a little village that's not very far from here. The last time I visited was some time ago. I want to show it to you... We'll have lunch. Look at these skies. Bright blue. Cold, yes, but the day is waiting to be explored.'

Sophie could feel all her urgent doubts ebbing away.

Today he looked devastating, in black jeans and a thick black rollneck jumper, over which he wore a tan cashmere coat.

Against the backdrop of colourful houses and majestic mountains he looked every inch the sophisticate. Very expensive...drop-dead gorgeous...and thrillingly *all hers*. Sort of...

Her heartbeat quickened.

They were here, weren't they?

Of course this relationship—if you could even call it that—wasn't going anywhere! But just for the moment Alessio had dumped them in this situation and one thing was clear...

She hadn't stopped fancying him.

Close to him like this, she found her head was filled with images of them making love. She thought of the way his fingers felt when they moved along her body, and she couldn't control the soft tremble that rippled through her.

Who was she kidding?

Was she really going to hold his feet to the fire and labour the point about not liking what they had bought into?

He would laugh out loud! Because here she was, and she just couldn't stop herself from responding to him.

Besides, what would be the point of arguing? Leonard believed what he believed, and to undo that piece of fiction now would be cruel.

Maybe Alessio had a point.

They were both adults and they had entered into this with their eyes wide open. Why not just relax and enjoy what had been brought out into the open?

Once they were back in the UK she could focus on thinking of a way out. They *both* could. Because she was pretty sure that Alessio, with his phobia of anything long-lasting, would be anxious to find the nearest exit and scramble through it as fast as he could.

She could start drip-feeding Leonard, hinting that all might not be right in the land of milk and honey.

Old he might be, but he was no fool. He would follow the thread without too much difficulty.

And why wouldn't he?

Anyone could see that she and Alessio couldn't be worse suited.

She was serious…thoughtful…interested in love and marriage and having kids…

He was casual,…dismissive of love and marriage…and into women who were happy to clear off almost as soon as they'd knocked on his front door.

Bolstered by the thought of her sensible way forward, Sophie smiled at Alessio, and her heart filled as he smiled back.

'So…would you like me to tell you where I'm taking you?' Alessio murmured. 'Or would you rather be surprised?'

He slung his arm over her shoulders and drew her

against him. She rested her head against his arm and felt utterly content.

'I've never liked surprises,' she mused.

'I get it.'

Sophie felt him angle his head to look down at her as he kissed the crown of her head.

'We have more in common than either of us imagines. I'm not a fan of surprises either. Okay. No surprises, in that case...'

He told her where he was taking her—a little village where he had invested in a restaurant that was now world-class...

The driver who had been booked to take them on the now discarded vineyard tour was rerouted to drive them to what turned out to be a truly stunning village, sitting on the very tip of the peninsula. Under the never-ending milky blue skies Sophie gasped at an exquisite thirteenth-century castle that rose in a series of dramatic turrets, around which was clustered a charming array of shops and boutiques and cafés. The reds and ochres and pinks and pale greens of the buildings gave the place an inviting, cosy feel, even though the fabric of every edifice was imbued with its history.

She wondered whether he'd made this enchanting trip in the company of other women, and felt a spurt of jealousy which she squashed because it was inappropriate.

'If you enjoy coming here so much,' she said pensively, as they wound their way through narrow streets, ending up at the promised restaurant, 'why don't you visit more often?'

'Time is money.'

'You're managing to find the time to be here now...'

'My father would expect nothing less.'

'So it's all about your dad? Why you're here?'

Her voice sounded light and teasing, and she wondered

whether she was the only one to register the sting of hurt under the surface.

'There's only so much self-sacrifice a guy is capable of...'

With the restaurant in front of them, and expensively dressed people walking around them, and the bright blue skies reflecting the mirror shine of the lake, he swivelled her to make her look at him.

'Let me tell you in detail about all the other things we're going to get up to... I'm sure you won't be too surprised by any of it...'

There was one surprise.

After a long, lazy lunch, Sophie found that he'd booked them a room at one of the most exclusive hotels in the small town.

'I promised that I'd show you just how signed up I am to our little charade...' he murmured, in a devilishly sexy undertone.

'We can't stay here for the night!' Sophie gasped, walking into a room adorned in sumptuous deep blues and creams and dominated by the most romantic four-poster bed she had ever seen. 'Leonard—'

'Who said anything about spending the night?'

They spent two hours luxuriating in a hotel where one night probably cost the same as a month's worth of her pay.

This was what a woman got when she became the sole focus of this man's attention. She got luxury and opulence on a biblical scale.

She got envious glances from every woman who walked by.

She got the sort of undivided attention that could make her head swim and make her forget the importance of common sense.

She got a guy committed to a charade he would enjoy

while it lasted but discard when the time came without a backward glance.

She got a guy who had the attention span of a toddler when it came to relationships.

She got the one guy in the world she knew she should never have become involved with but, now that she had, could not detach from.

It was a wildly decadent afternoon, with the banks of ivory shutters closed against the world outside.

It was clandestine and sneaky and thrilling.

She feasted on his nakedness, openly admiring the flex of muscle and sinew and the darkness of his olive skin so defined against her much paler English tone.

She gave herself utterly to him as he explored her body. His fingers were magical as they teased her into a complete meltdown, and the world outside was forgotten under the onslaught of their lovemaking.

They surfaced to strewn clothes, into which they both had to climb after luxuriating in a circular bath that was as big as a swimming pool.

'Now, tell me that wasn't fun,' Alessio purred once they were outside, where the blast of cold sunshine was an unpleasant intrusion.

Sophie slipped her arm around his waist, underneath his coat, and could feel the warm vibrancy of his body... the very body that had taken her to the moon and beyond.

It had been fun.

There hadn't been a second in that bed, with the sounds of real life snuffed out for a couple of hours, that she hadn't enjoyed.

Alessio had said that it was a straightforward situation. He'd told her to trust him—that bridges could be crossed later. Living in the moment would be good for Leonard... it was just one small lie, one tiny reworking of the truth...

They hadn't asked for this situation, but it had happened and it would be fine.

So why did she feel uneasy? Was it because she was inherently cautious? Was there such a thing as *too* cautious? Would loosening up a little rub out her unease?

Did it matter? They were where they were, after all.

It was nearly five in the afternoon by the time they made it back to Alessio's villa, and before they could ring the doorbell Leonard was there, pulling open the door to greet them with a broad smile as he hustled them in.

'Nice afternoon?' he asked.

Sophie reddened and looked away, leaving Alessio to move into faultless conversational mode.

'Good, good, good…very nice.'

They ended up in the kitchen, and Leonard turned to them to say, with satisfaction, that it was time for them to return to England.

'Getting a little bored here,' he said, and beamed. 'Might be old, but the brain needs stimulation and there's not much to be had in these parts. Need to get back to my routine! And you kids…your future ahead of you…you'll be wanting to get back to the hustle and bustle…'

'What about the renovations, Leonard?' Sophie frowned. 'The chaos of the builders…?'

Leonard flapped his hand dismissively. 'I can cope. Besides, I have things to do…'

'What things?'

He tapped the side of his nose and winked at her.

'*Things.* No need to trouble yourself, my dear. You just enjoy having fun with this son of mine!'

CHAPTER NINE

IT WAS A wrench, leaving the villa behind. But Leonard, mind made up, would hear nothing from either of them about staying a minute longer, thus leaving the building work more time to reach completion so that he could be spared the nuisance of returning to renovations still in progress.

He was champing at the bit to get going, and within thirty-six hours Alessio was locking the front door and giving instructions to his housekeeper.

'I don't get it,' Sophie said, when finally they were in a chauffeured limousine, heading from the airfield where Alessio's private jet had landed to Leonard's house in Harrogate. 'He made such a fuss about the work being done, and the inconvenience of having people tramping through his house and ripping it apart...'

This was said in low, whispered tones, while in the front seat, which Leonard had demanded, because his stomach was feeling a little sensitive, he slumbered.

'New lease of life,' Alessio murmured wryly, although there was a hint of an edge to his voice that revealed he wasn't quite as laid-back as he wanted her to think.

His hand was resting lightly on hers. Sophie's eyes drifted to it, and she wondered whether he was already regretting the lie he had told. Was it now dawning on him how problematic it might be to extricate himself from an arrangement he hadn't banked on lasting more than a couple of weeks?

Had reality reasserted itself now that they were back on home soil? It was one thing living in a bubble for a while, but bubbles always burst, and she wondered whether Alessio was now getting to grips with that reality.

'Don't say that,' Sophie said, dismayed.

'Why pretend otherwise?'

'If Leonard has a new lease of life because of this…this lie we've told him, then it's going to be so much more difficult untangling the whole mess.'

'Where there's a will, there's a way.'

'That's just a platitude,' Sophie muttered under her breath.

'Platitudes are a bit like homilies and clichés…they're irritating, but often contain an element of truth.'

'When do you plan on returning to London?'

'I haven't given it much thought.'

'I think it should be sooner rather than later.'

'Explain.'

Sophie turned to look at him and their eyes tangled. For a few breathless moments she succumbed to an unsteady drowning sensation that she knew she had to resist.

'If I need to start working on a way out of this…' she broke eye contact with Alessio and stared ahead to where Leonard's head was lolling as he slept '…then it's going to be easier if you aren't around.'

Tempting me…thrilling me…making me want to keep touching you and seeing you and hearing your voice…

'How so? Alessio narrowed his eyes.

She had her profile to him, and he wanted to tilt her head, make her look him in the eyes so that he could read what she was thinking.

The force of his wanting meshed with the force of his needing. Where did one begin and the other end?

It was disconcerting. It drove all his defences into gear. But still…

Around this woman, his defences didn't do what they'd been trained to do.

Around her, he sometimes felt as though his outer armour had been stripped away, leaving him vulnerable to…

To what?

He didn't know. It confused him, and confusion was an emotion that he had no intention of tolerating. Confusion equalled weakness, and Alessio knew what if felt like to be weak, to be helpless. He had been swept away on a tidal wave of grief after his mother's death. Too young to navigate those choppy waters, and faced with a distant father who had withdrawn into himself, he had been carried along on currents over which he had had no control.

Of course he had come through those turbulent times, but he had a very long memory when it came to things like that.

'Well?' he pressed. 'I'm guessing that you have some kind of plan in mind?'

'We're very different people…'

'And?'

'And under any other circumstances there's no way we would have…would have…'

'Say it, Sophie.'

'There's no way we would have ended up in bed together.'

She kept her voice low, although early into the journey Alessio had slid shut the partition separating them from his driver and Leonard still asleep in the passenger seat.

Neither could hear a word, but it still felt weird having this intimate conversation with two other people so close by.

She actually couldn't say the word *lovers*.

She knew that she was bright red, and she guessed that he was probably laughing at her circumspection.

How could you sleep with someone, touch them in the most intimate places imaginable, and then clam up when it came to calling a spade a spade?

Lack of experience.

She'd thought she was tough, having been through a lot growing up, but no amount of toughness had prepared her for a man like Alessio.

She breathed in deeply and held his dark gaze.

'You know that for sure?' he asked.

'Yes.'

'So you think we only ended up being lovers because we happened to be in the same place at the same time?'

'Sort of. More or less.'

'That doesn't say much for the powers of attraction, does it?'

'What do you mean?'

Alessio ignored that question. 'Furthermore, I find it pretty offensive.'

'I don't know what you're talking about!'

Sophie stared at him in dismay. She realised how much she didn't want to hurt him, even though she knew that he was immune to being hurt by anything she said.

His opinion mattered to her.

He mattered to her.

Had her lack of experience brought her to this dangerous point? What was she going to do about it?

Rather, how urgent was the need to do something about it? Just at the moment that need felt pressing.

'How shallow do you think I am?' he asked.

She tried to look down, but Alessio tilted her chin so that she was forced to meet his stare.

'I don't think you're shallow. In fact,' she said with searing honesty, 'you're one of the most complex human beings I've ever met in my entire life.'

Alessio relaxed and half smiled, and Sophie was stupidly pleased that some of the tension had been erased.

'Why did you find what I said...offensive?' she asked.

'I'm not the kind of guy who decides to sleep with a woman just because she happens to be there. I slept with you because you're sexy as hell. You're smart, you're funny, and you're one of the most interesting women I've ever known.'

Sophie smiled back at him. 'Yet, you've known me for a while,' she pointed out gently.

'Have I?'

'I've been working for your father for over two years.'

'You've always been very careful to keep yourself hidden from me.'

'Have I?'

'I've said this before. You've made a point of avoiding me. Why? And don't tell me it was to give me quality time with my father. Things have improved in leaps and bounds between us, but for a very long time, quality time with him wasn't a goal of mine.'

Sophie stilled. They had become close. And as that had happened, as her defences had fallen, he had gained insights into her. He was sharp and he was experienced when it came to the opposite sex. Vague mumbling about avoiding him so that he could bond with his dad no longer held water.

'So, Sophie,' he drawled, 'did you avoid me because I made you nervous? Why would I have made you nervous?' He grinned and brushed his finger across her cheek. 'Maybe even then you were attracted to me...is that it?

Was that why my fiery tigress was once a meek and mild little mouse?'

'You have an ego the size of a continent, Alessio,' she told him. But he was flustering her, and she knew that her colour was bright.

'It's a blessing and a curse.'

'Like I said…' her voice was an insistent hiss '…it was never my place to join you and your dad for dinner…or… or come into the sitting room to have coffee or…or brandy or whatever…'

Alessio tilted his head to one side and looked at her for a while in silence, his dark eyes assessing.

'Maybe I'm just not very confident in myself,' she said, breaking the silence to move the conversation on, because his silence was getting under skin. 'I can't understand why you would be attracted to me.'

'Now you know.'

'Still, there are huge differences between us…' She took a deep breath and ploughed on with reality, rather than giving in to the rush of pleasure which was as powerful as an injection of adrenaline. 'And the reason I asked whether you'd be heading back to London as soon as we get back is that I think I can start dropping hints to your father… you know…about those differences.'

Alessio frowned. He'd been basking in the pleasing satisfaction of wondering whether Sophie had always fancied him. He'd been musing on what he might have done had he been aware of that fact.

What if he had known that she'd been casting hot little sidelong glances in his direction?

The woman had practically made herself invisible every time he had made the trip to Yorkshire to see his father. She'd mastered the art of background dressing.

But if he'd known that she was attracted to him, would

he have seen beyond her deliberate attempts to play herself down? Would he have zeroed in on what was so obvious to him now? The understated allure was so much more powerful than all the flamboyant peacock parading of the women he usually dated?

Or would he have steered clear of something that had the potential to get complicated?

Complicated women encouraged complicated situations, and Sophie was a complicated woman.

Right now, things weren't straightforward, but what would happen if a passing attraction turned into something more now that they were involved in this charade?

That wasn't something he had seriously considered, because as far as he was concerned they had both started from the same ground zero...

An irresistible attraction...

A craving that couldn't be pushed away...

And an environment where one thing had inevitably led to another...

But what if she had been nurturing a secret attraction to him for weeks? Months? Years, even?

It might be flattering, but it might also be dangerous. What if she started taking this pretend situation seriously?

She made all the right noises, but Alessio was very switched on when it came to hearing women making all the right noises and then discovering that their aspirations had been at odds with those right noises all along.

Disquiet filled him as another little voice shattered his easy assumption that now a potential problem had been spotted it would be no trouble to put it right.

What if attachments began forming, ambushing his usual cool control?

He thought about her when she wasn't around...she distracted him...he'd barely done a scrap of work since they'd gone to his villa...

When he was being logical, he knew that she was probably vulnerable. She had had a lousy life—almost as lousy as his. She been forced into taking responsibility at a time when she should have been enjoying her youth.

He had been forced into a similar situation, but he had been cushioned by money. He had had his chance to toughen up, and since then he made sure to be the one who called the shots in everything.

He'd lived life where she had retreated from it.

At least that was what he'd worked out from everything she'd told him, and from her reactions and the way she was.

She was a woman waiting for love to strike, whereas he was a guy who knew it never would.

But what if some of what she felt rubbed off on him?

Could that happen?

Alessio feared nothing except the weakness of being dependent on someone else—either financially, intellectually or emotionally.

And so he said now, more to get a grip on himself than anything else, 'I think that's an excellent idea.'

'I… Yes… It's as well we…er…think about this as early as possible…'

'To avoid unnecessary complications? Agreed.'

'Leonard must know that we're two people who aren't suited.'

'Of course he does! But, as you well know, people will easily believe what they *want* to believe.'

'Yes. They do.'

'He's desperate to believe that I might finally have found a woman who is…' he looked at her with a curling wry smile '…not built along the lines of my usual dates.'

'But it won't be long before he works out that just because I'm the opposite of those doe-eyed, adoring blondes you like to have draped over your arm it doesn't mean I'm the real deal.'

Alessio grinned. 'How you amuse me with your biting choice of words…'

Sophie blushed. His eyes roved over her face and she reddened even more.

She could see a dark, burning intent there that mirrored hers. Whatever her head told her, she still wanted this man more than was good for her.

She needed him to return to London as soon as possible for a number of reasons.

She needed him to be physically away from her so that she could start learning how to think straight again.

Plus she needed him to disappear so that she could start sowing the seeds of their eventual break-up.

She needed him to go.

She longed for him to stay.

'But of course you're right.'

His eyes stayed on her face, in a lazy, thorough inspection that made her quiver and tremble and think about sex.

'So…'

Sophie blinked and was brought back down to earth as he continued, his voice mild and cool and sensible.

'So I'll check the house when we get there. I've been getting twice-daily progress reports, and every member of that team knows better than to slack off, but I'll still need to make sure things are where they should be.'

Alessio paused before taking the plunge. Because it was always better to be safe than sorry, and already he could feel himself lulled into thoughts of hanging around for longer…taking her to bed…enjoying long nights with her sleeping next to him…

It made no sense. In a short space of time he had somehow become accustomed to semi waking in the early hours of the morning and reaching out to feel her warm, naked body next to him. It had been as pleasing just to feel her warmth as any amount of hectic lovemaking.

'On the financial side, things have moved at speed,' he said. 'I've made a point of discussing everything with my father so that he's kept in the loop…'

'He hasn't mentioned anything of that sort to me. In fact, he's barely mentioned the whole business of the company losing money…'

Alessio grinned.

Their eyes met in shared amusement and Sophie shivered.

'He's adapted fast,' she murmured drily, and Alessio's lips twitched further.

'You think so? I'd say the old man has gone from ranting and railing to downright having his say to acquiescence in record time.'

They both burst out laughing and Leonard spun round to look at them. He rapped on the partition, which Alessio obediently slid open.

'What are the pair of you cackling about?'

'We're discussing when Alessio is going to head back down to London.'

Sophie sobered up fast, and shuffled a few inches away from Alessio and his dangerously seductive orbit.

'Why the rush?' Leonard's bushy brows pulled together into a frown.

'An empire to run?' Alessio interjected drily.

'Or is the empire running *you*, my boy? No good if it is! Anyway, you can't leave until the day after tomorrow, earliest.'

'Why's that?'

Leonard tapped the side of his nose and said smugly, 'I want to have a little celebration dinner to mark the turning of the tide.'

'Celebration dinner?'

'Nothing fancy, so no need to start fretting! Sarah is delighted to do the cooking, and I feel with everything that's happened…with my health and all those nights of worrying… I would like to do something a little special to mark a new chapter.'

Sophie's mind drifted. Before he'd had to dispatch his housekeeper, Leonard had been all for formal dinners, even if he was entertaining a party of only one friend. He'd enjoyed that. She was pleased that he was returning to his old form.

She was even more pleased to find, an hour later, that the house had taken shape with such efficiency that any disturbances to Leonard's routine would be minimal.

They'd emerged into bleak cold, with the grey heavy skies wistfully reminding her of what they had left behind, where there had been wall-to-wall blue for a fortnight.

Sarah had been waiting for them, shivering in the open doorway, and the three of them had hurried inside, leaving Alessio's driver to bring up the rear with their bags.

It was freezing outside, but the house was warm. The central heating had been updated.

And inside…

Sophie gasped.

Next to her, Leonard was in an equal state of shock.

This proved just how much could be accomplished when you threw money at something.

Gone was the dated wallpaper and the tired paint and the worn banisters and the flooring which had been lovely once upon a long time ago.

Alessio was running through what had been done, and how the workmen had sectioned off the enormous project so that the basics in the main living areas had been targeted for completion first. His father wouldn't notice much more now, as the remainder of the work could be sealed off from various sections of the sprawling old house.

When Sophie slid a sideways glance at Leonard, she noted how impressed he was by what had been accomplished, and his son's smooth delivery of what he'd promised.

How far they'd come from being those two strangers positioned at opposite ends of the dining table, more engaged in their computers and paperwork than in each other!

When all this was over… This charade for Leonard's benefit…

Suddenly Sophie felt the sting of knowing that she would be superfluous.

Father and son would have one another.

The thought of the loneliness of the life she had put on hold hit her with the force of a sledgehammer and she spun away, pretending to inspect a polished new banister, but she could feel the prickle of tears behind her eyes.

'What's wrong?'

Alessio's voice was gentle behind her, and Sophie breathed in deeply before slowly turning to look at him.

Leonard was vanishing with Sarah, excited to see the remainder of the house, booming that he hoped his colour choices had been respected.

'Well?'

Sophie looked up at Alessio. She lost herself for a few seconds in the deep, dark depths of his gaze. This man had stolen her heart, and she knew that she would have to force herself to contemplate a life without him in it.

How would working for Leonard be tenable if she was on constant edgy alert for Alessio showing up? How would she be able to play the part of wise ex-girlfriend still on good terms with the guy who hadn't worked out for her?

'Well, I shall be relieved when this is over and done with,' she said at last.

'What? The renovations? You'll barely notice the presence of the builders. They've wrapped up most of the areas you and Leonard occupy.'

'I mean,' Sophie said briskly, with a glassy polite smile, 'I'll be pleased when this charade we're spinning for Leonard is over. Seeing him here…so happy to be back in his own territory… Well, it puts into perspective the stupid lie we've both told. And now… Now I wish it was all over and done with.' She gave a heartfelt sigh. 'Then I can get on with my life.'

'Meaning…?'

Sophie shrugged. 'Well, I don't think that my position here will still be tenable once we've "broken up", do you?'

Alessio stilled and stared at her with narrowed intensity. 'That's ridiculous.'

Of course it was—for him, Sophie thought. Because he hadn't invested emotionally. Of course *he* would find it easy to pick up where they had left off. He would expect her to be an amicable ex, happy to have dinner with him and his father when he came to visit—which would be a lot more often, seeing how far their relationship had come.

'I don't think I can play the smiling jilted ex.'

'Then feel free to be the one to jilt *me*.'

'That's not going to work.'

'Why not?' Alessio raked his fingers through his hair and shot her a fulminating look from under his lush, dark lashes. 'I'm very happy to be dumped. At any rate, this wasn't supposed to jeopardise your job, or make your position uncomfortable in any way. Look…' He cast his eye to the doorway, as if in anticipation of Leonard making a sudden stealthy reappearance. 'This isn't the time or the place to have this conversation. Let's park it for the moment. It's late. My father is going to be returning in a minute. But I'm not comfortable with what you're saying. Why don't we wait until this dinner he's having for us tomorrow evening? We can talk after that.'

'I'm not going to change my mind.'

Alessio placed his finger over her mouth and then traced that finger over her lips.

'Shh… Tomorrow…okay? My father eats early. This dinner should be done by eight and we can finish our conversation then.'

Sophie nodded.

Tomorrow evening they would talk, and then she would begin packing her bags in preparation for the long trip back to the life she had left behind.

What difference would a handful of hours make?

Alessio was conspicuous by his absence the following day. He was working and then giving orders to the construction crew, who were busily doing their thing in a completely different part of the house.

And if Leonard seemed a little over excited, what of it?

He had every right to be, with all the stuff happening with Alessio…with the house…with the business.

And when, at five, he disappeared in a flurry of nudge-nudge, wink-wink coyness, Sophie knew that he was simply excited to be entertaining again…with someone preparing his food and dinner formally served in the newly refurbished dining room.

'Be sure to dress up, my dear!' he carolled, before vanishing to his also newly refurbished quarters. 'I've said the same thing to that beau of yours! He's had to go to the office in Harrogate, but he'll be home in time for our little dinner!'

Sophie was putting the finishing touches to her outfit—which was a simple long-sleeved woollen dress and some flat shoes—when there was a knock on the bedroom door.

Alessio.

Tall, commanding…so stupidly good looking…

And deadly serious.

'We have something of a problem,' he opened, stepping into the bedroom and quietly shutting the door behind him. 'Nice dress, by the way,' he murmured, looking at her with rampant appreciation.

Sophie felt a tell-tale dampness spread—the physical manifestation of her arousal—just because he had looked at her.

Her eyelids fluttered and her nostrils flared and she wasn't sure who took a step closer to who. When his arm circled her she breathed him in, and was floored by the warmth of his sexy, familiar body.

She clung.

She didn't want to.

Not when she was trying to grope her way back to the safety of the emotional independence she had abandoned.

But she couldn't help herself.

She felt him back her against the door, tipping her head so that he could kiss her, in a deep, hungry kiss that met her responding passion.

Her hands were all over him, scrabbling to find purchase, pushing under his white shirt which she'd tugged free of his black trousers.

When the first shred of common sense penetrated she let it slip past, because her need for him was unrelenting.

She unzipped his trousers as he shoved up her dress. They were working together, their hands knowing where to go, their mouths melding and crushing any prospect of restraint.

She quivered and moaned very softly as his finger delved between the folds of her soft femininity to find the pulsing bud of her clitoris. She spasmed against his finger, collapsing like a rag doll, as wave after wave of sensuous pleasure rolled over her.

Her fingers dug into his shoulders.

This was good, but she wanted more…needed more. Needed him to push deep inside her so that her whole body exploded.

She tugged him back, and somehow they made their way to the bed, but only barely. She fell back onto the mattress, still fully dressed.

His zipper was still undone and his shirt was flapping, half out, half still tucked into the waistband of the trousers. He eased his trousers off and reached for the thickness of his erection, bulging against his boxers.

There was no teasing…no time for the game of seduction.

No time for getting their clothes off, even.

They fumbled like horny teenagers, and when he sank into her wetness she contracted around him and moved to his tempo, her body bucking, her nails digging into his shirt, her legs wrapped around him even though the dress was still on, hoicked up around her waist.

It was raw and primitive and visceral, and an explosion of mind-bending pleasure that made her want to sob with the joy and satisfaction of it.

'Alessio…'

She looked away as he kissed her neck, and for a few moments they were both lost in the shuddering aftermath of their lovemaking.

Then he heaved himself off her, and turned to look at her before sliding off the bed. His dark eyes were sombre as she shifted and did something to her dress, tugging it down and then retrieving her the knickers, which were hanging off one ankle, kicked aside in those heady moments of lust.

'Sophie… I've just come from downstairs…'

'Why are you looking so serious?' she asked. 'You're freaking me out.'

'We need to go down there, but I'm warning you: this isn't the small celebration we banked on.'

'What do you mean?'

'I mean, Sophie…that he's asked the whole bloody village…'

CHAPTER TEN

SOPHIE HEARD THE babble of voices from the sitting room before they even hit the bottom of the stairs.

She had been galvanised into action the second that contented, utterly ill-advised post-sex lull had passed and Alessio's urgent, serious voice had reminded her that the cold hand of reality didn't include falling back into the sack with him.

There had been no time to shower, but time enough to straighten herself. Still, she felt utterly lacking in composure as she paused to watch Sarah bustling her way towards the sitting room with a tray of appetisers. Behind her an unfamiliar lad in formal black trousers and a white long-sleeved shirt was carrying a similar tray with drinks.

'Leonard's hired *waiting staff*?'

'So it would seem…' Alessio drawled.

'When? Why? He never mentioned a thing… Did he say anything to you?'

'I think he knew better than to let anything slip.' They looked at one another, paused on the staircase, inches apart, their bodies still warm from the ebbing of their lust.

'What's he playing at?' she asked in a high-pitched voice.

But Sophie knew what Leonard was playing at, and she quailed in horror.

When Alessio had said that 'half the bloody village'

had been invited, she'd kept her fingers crossed that he'd exaggerated.

He hadn't.

That much was obvious by the noise levels as they neared the sitting room, which was at the end of long corridor and attached to a huge conservatory, where Leonard was fond of napping in his chair with a view of the garden.

Looking through the open door, Sophie paused to take in the scene in front of her. Sarah and her new assistant, with whom she seemed very familiar, were circulating with nibbles and drinks. On the polished sideboard there was a selection of yet more canapés and buckets filled with bottles of wine and any number of non-alcoholic drinks. Towards the back of the room, perched on a padded chair, Leonard was holding court.

There must have been at least twenty people in the room, and most of them she recognised.

Friends from the village…chums he had worked alongside for years…their other halves…the lady who ran the flower shop…

She paled, and yanked Alessio back before Leonard could spot them, tugging him away from the sitting room and into the snug, which was small and private and set to one side of what Leonard referred to as 'the piano room', even though the piano had long vanished from its pride of place. Sold, she reckoned, to help pay bills.

'This is a nightmare!' she whispered. 'All those people!'

Alessio looked at her…at the patches of colour staining her cheeks and the hectic brightness in her eyes and the look of utter horror on her face.

His body was still coming down from the high of having her touch him.

They hadn't been able keep their hands off one another!

That being the case, he couldn't see why she was suddenly shrieking in the face of this charade they had concocted.

So what if a few people thought that this was more serious than it actually was? They could bide their time, couldn't they? Why the rush to find a way out? Why begin formulating all the reasons why the situation didn't stand a chance in hell of going anywhere? Why not enjoy what they had?

He sighed with a mixture of impatience and frustration and raked his fingers through his hair. He leant against the wall and shoved his hand in his trouser pocket and frowned.

'I admit it's not ideal that he's invited people over to… to celebrate, but they're here, and there's nothing we can do about it.'

'No, I know we can't turf them out. But, Alessio…this is a disaster!'

'Disaster seems a bit overblown, don't you think?'

'No! No, I don't!'

He didn't understand. He just didn't get it. Sophie was sapped by the feeling of utter defeat.

'Sophie, this isn't the end of the world.'

'You looked pretty ashen when you breezed into my bedroom to tell me,' she shot back with asperity.

'I was taken aback.'

But then we fell into each other's arms, Sophie thought, *and you realised that, hey, continuing the charade might be okay, irrespective of other people knowing…*

In a heartbeat, Sophie knew what she had to do.

She knew how the land lay. She'd always known how the land was going to lie, because Alessio was honest when it came to telling it like it was.

No commitment.

No emotional entanglements.

No risk of love.

Just great sex for as long as they both felt the same.

Sophie knew that she had entered into their arrangement with her eyes wide open, and then she had allowed herself to sink further and deeper into something that had now ended up meshing around her like a net, until thrashing her way out felt like a struggle.

But she would have to thrash her way out. And the only way she could do that was by being honest.

As long as Alessio was aware of the power he had over her physically...as long as he knew that she wanted him as much as he wanted her, and that she found him downright *irresistible*...what would be the impetus for anything to change for him?

For a while he had gone along with her urgency to work their way out. Had he thought that a healthy dose of reality would re-establish his parameters?

She felt as though she knew the way his mind worked. How had that happened? How had bristling in his company, armed and ready for a fight with an opponent she scorned, turned into something so profound that it was as if her soul had somehow melded with his?

And how on earth had it been a one-way journey?

With *her* doing the sinking while *he* just enjoyed what was on offer with the safety of shore always within striking distance?

Inexperience.

She had been able to walk tough and talk tough, but deep inside her lack of experience had made her as soft as marshmallow.

Or maybe she had just found the guy she'd never even known she'd been looking for—the only problem being that he happened to be the wrong guy...

Could she keep making excuses about all of this?

Did she have the strength to stay put and manoeuvre her way out? Plant seeds of doubt in Leonard's head?

How long would those seeds take before Leonard began edging towards seeing what she wanted him to realise?

A month? Two months? Six?

When Sophie thought about a month more of being with Alessio…or two months…or, horror of horrors, *six*…she felt weak and scared.

She would never be able to convince him that their sleeping together would be a bad idea. She wouldn't even be able to convince *herself* of that.

He touched her and she melted inside.

He looked at her and she burned for him.

And he knew it.

And here they were now, with a crowd of people waiting for them in the sitting room, and she could hazard a pretty healthy guess as to what they'd been told.

The prodigal son had returned. Having wandered in the wilderness for years, Alessio was back. And he had saved Leonard's company—had rescued him from the nightmare of an uncertain financial future and everything that went with that.

And the icing on the cake?

He was going to settle down with someone of whom Leonard approved.

The whole situation made Sophie feel faint, but she knew that she only had herself to blame because she had gone along with Alessio's idea with only a token show of protest.

She had accepted the wisdom of his 'tiny little white lie' because it had been easier. With a duvet pulled up around her, in the darkness of the bedroom and still warm from Alessio's body, she had heard the sound of Leonard outside and the thought of him being stressed out by finding them together had been too much.

She had been weak when she should have been strong.

Not that there was much point weighing up the pros and cons and beating herself up about it now.

It was what it was.

Reality wasn't thinking in the abstract.

Reality was dealing with Leonard and his friends, who were probably all waiting with the champagne ready to be poured, eager to find out when they should make room in their calendars for the Big Day.

There was only one thing Sophie knew would work when it came to getting out of this scenario.

The truth.

'Because…?' she said.

'Come again?'

'You said you were taken aback. Why?'

'There's a room full of people. Leonard will have been regaling them all with stories of our heady love affair…'

'Yes, I'm sure he will have been.'

'What's wrong?' Alessio looked at her narrowly and then sighed. 'Look, I know you have doubts about this but, as I keep telling you, we just have to enjoy what we have. And when the time comes we probably won't even have to explain anything to my father.'

Sophie frowned. 'Sorry, I don't understand.'

'Well, think about it…'

He drew her further into the room, and his hand lightly resting on hers made the blood rush to her face. She could feel the heat emanating from his body, and his careless power over her senses filled her with the urgency to say what she knew she had to say.

'Tell me how I should be thinking about this,' she said coolly, pulling back slightly, enough to detach herself from his loose grip, and then folding her arms protectively over her chest.

'When things inevitably begin to cool between us, my

father will pick it up. I realise he might try and play ostrich for a while, but he's sharp enough to see when the end comes and by then the process will have been gradual enough for him to deal with it.'

'Because I would have already started warning him of our impending demise as starry-eyed lovers?'

'Something like that. Now, we should go and join the crowd…'

'Not yet.'

'What else is there to say at this point in time?'

Alessio's voice was laced with frustration, and his dark eyes resting on her face were genuinely puzzled. Sophie knew that he had no idea where she was going with her repeated conversations on the same subject.

Alessio was a solution-driven guy. They had jointly agreed on a temporary solution. They had also agreed on the way out they would take and how to deal with damage limitation when the temporary solution was over.

So of course he would wonder why the Spanish Inquisition now? When Leonard and his friends were all lining up to offer their congratulations? When there was a part to be played? Where was the problem when they actually fancied one another so the part was pretty much on point, all told?

For now…

Sophie drew in a shaky breath and managed to look him steadily in the eyes. 'This just doesn't work for me, Alessio.'

'It's not going to last for ever.'

'And that's where the problem lies.'

'I'm not following you.'

But he was very still, and his dark eyes were watchful. He might not be following her, but he was following the tenor of her voice, and he must know that wherever it was leading was not going to be a destination at which he wanted to arrive.

'I don't want this to end.'

Sophie saw his natural inclination was to glance away, so this time it was she who gently placed her finger on his chin so that their eyes met, so that he couldn't obscure his reaction.

'When I first came to see you at your office, Alessio, I knew that I was coming to see someone I disliked…someone I disapproved of.'

'I know.'

'I thought I'd never like you.'

'Again, you're not telling me anything I don't already know.'

He smiled, a slow, wicked smile that sent her pulses racing. From dislike…to the force of passion. She knew that that was what he was thinking.

He was about to be brought very quickly down to earth by the bucket of freezing water she intended to pour on his beautiful head.

If she thought too far ahead—if she let her mind drift to what would happen when she'd left—then she was filled with cold dread, so instead, Sophie focused entirely on the moment.

'But things changed,' she continued carefully. 'I saw the way you related to Leonard… I saw both sides of the coin and I realised that you weren't the man I'd thought you were after all.'

'It pays never to make easy assumptions,' Alessio murmured. 'Although I can understand why you jumped to the conclusions that you did.'

'And then…' Sophie sighed ready to dip her toes into the churning waters that lay ahead.

'And then…?'

'We slept together. And every single thing changed for

me. Not at first. At first, I was just sleeping with a guy I was attracted to. At first, I was doing something I maybe should have done a long time ago.'

'Is this the right time for us to be having this conversation?'

Alessio's voice was rough, a little unsteady, and Sophie wondered whether alarm bells were beginning to ring. *Too bad.*

'It's the *only* time we can have this conversation, Alessio. Don't worry. Your father won't be sending out the search party just yet. You forget—he's under the illusion that we're loved up. He's probably pleased that we didn't bounce down to join the assembled crowd as soon as they started arriving! He probably thinks that you came upstairs to tell me that we had unexpected visitors and then we just couldn't help gazing helplessly into each other's eyes...'

'You're being sarcastic.'

'I apologise. You know that's not like me. But...' She took a deep breath. 'I'll bet you know where I'm going with this,' she said quietly.

'Do I?'

'Of course you do, Alessio. You're the guy who knows the opposite sex inside out. You must surely realise that I've fallen in love with you?'

Of course he knew.

Sophie saw the way he paled. She wondered how fast he would start agreeing with her that the sooner they brought this farce to a close, the better.

'I didn't want to,' she confessed. 'I thought I was immune to a guy like you, because you weren't the sort of man I'd ever had on my list as someone I want to end up spending my life with. And the reason I'm telling you this...'

She waited for a response, but silence greeted her question. For once, Alessio was clearly deprived of the power of speech by the sheer scale of his horror at what he had just been told.

Sophie bit down on the hurt tearing her apart.

'The reason I'm telling you this *now*...' she went on, 'is because I just can't be with you any longer...knowing that what we have is going nowhere. For you, it's all about the hot sex—and believe me, I'm not pointing any fingers, because you never hid the fact that that was the kind of guy you are. But for me...? I want so much more, Alessio. I want to spend the rest of my life with you. I want what your father believes to be true.'

If it wasn't so tragic, it might be funny. His mouth was half open. His eyes were glazed. His fingers, as he raked them through his dark hair, were shaky.

He was a man in the grip of a nightmare.

'So,' she continued briskly, pulling herself together and saving her sadness for when she was on her own, 'here's what I'm going to do, Alessio. I'm going to go in there and, before this all gets even more out of hand, I'm going to tell your father the truth.'

'Sophie...he's...'

'He's going to have to understand what the situation is. I'm going to be honest. But I'm not going to dump you in anything—don't worry. Then, when I've done that, I'm going to head upstairs and I'm going to pack as much stuff as I can. And then, when I've done *that*, I'm going to call a cab and head to the station and pay my mother a little visit. She won't be expecting me. She'll be really pleased.'

'And my father? How is he going to feel in the face of all this truth-telling?'

'Alessio, it's time I thought about how *I* will cope instead of how your father copes. You'll be here for him. That's the main thing.'

Silence drummed between them, alive and throbbing.

'And,' Sophie added with searing honesty, 'of course I'll keep in touch with Leonard. He's a huge part of my life.'

She waited.

What, Alessio thought, did she want him to say?

'If that's what you feel you have to do, then do it,' he said.

His voice had cooled. There was only one way of stopping her and that would be to promise things he could never deliver.

He liked her. He respected her. He fancied her as he'd never fancied any woman in his life before. But that was never going to be enough. Because she wanted him to love her and he would never love her.

Fear tore into him. Fear of what life might look like without her in it.

He rejected it before it had time to take root.

'You want what I will never be able to give you,' he told her, just in case she'd got the wrong idea…just in case she thought that his silence meant something it didn't.

Just in case he was drawn into thinking that this might be more than what it was. Just in case…

He stood back and shoved his hands into his pockets, and then he watched as she spun round on her heel and headed towards the door, pausing for less than a couple of seconds before leaving without looking back.

Alessio stood his ground.

He stayed put with gritted determination, conjuring up in his head a scene the likes of which he could never countenance.

Over-emotional behaviour…hand-wringing and breast-beating and tears.

No. Not for him.

But for it to all be over…

Sophie's confession rang in his ears.

She had fallen in love with him.

He hadn't asked her to! He'd hadn't encouraged her.

Had he? No. Emphatically not! He didn't *do* love. Love was loss, and loss was something he had scrupulously avoided his entire adult life. He would not sign up to the idiocy of being vulnerable to the whims of someone else. How could you have any control over your life if you foolishly handed the reins to someone else?

Yet she was walking away.

He would never see her again.

The space that opened up at his feet when he thought about that made him suck in a sharp breath, and for a few seconds he was queasy.

Would it hurt to see how this played out? There was no point in trying to stop her, and of course he didn't want to do that.

A declaration of love was a gauntlet thrown down...it was an ultimatum he had no intention of meeting.

About to pour himself something stiff, Alessio instead padded out of the room. He hesitated...drawn to where the assembled guests would be hearing... *What?*

He found out soon enough.

He was rooted to the spot by Sophie's ringing, confident voice.

Leonard had obviously imparted the glad tidings to everyone there that a marriage was imminent. That the prodigal son had returned and was to be married to the perfect woman!

And now Sophie was in the process of gently disabusing them of any such understanding, and Alessio was riveted, struck dumb by her sheer courage and the calm in her voice.

He stood, unseen, and listened for a few moments, his breathing thick, his thoughts in disarray.

Sophie had no idea where Alessio was.

She couldn't think about that just at the moment because she was too busy playing to a rapt audience.

She had done her best to wrest Leonard away from his coterie of friends, but he had waved her aside. He'd been far too busy carolling the joys of his son finally settling down and saying it was *'about time, dammit.'*

And now here she was. She'd cleared her throat and nervously ploughed into a stammering explanation of everything, pushing past the moment when all the excited voices had fallen silent—including Leonard's.

She looked around her.

She could barely meet Leonard's eyes, but she did it because he was really the one she was talking to and she was going to be firm but gentle.

'We did it with the best of intentions,' she said softly, motioning for him to come closer to her…close enough for her to reach out and hold his hand in hers.

Even so, everyone else clustered around her too, and she knew she was also addressing them—like it or not.

'I don't understand…' Leonard blustered.

'I was a coward,' she told him. 'You surprised us, and we rushed into an explanation we thought you would accept because we didn't want to stress you out.'

'*You* weren't the coward! Alessio—'

'He did what he thought was best because that's the kind of guy he is, Leonard. He's a good man. What happened wasn't his fault. It was mine.'

'I'm not getting you, my girl. You'll have to stop talking in riddles.'

Sophie could feel the prickle of nervous perspiration breaking out all over her body like a tingling, uncomfortable nettle rash, making her want to fidget even though she remained calm and composed. At least on the surface.

Inside, she was breaking up.

'I made the mistake of falling in love,' she said quietly, 'and before you jump into any accusations, this wasn't

Alessio's fault. He laid his cards on the table from the start. It just so happened that my foolish heart didn't obey the rules of the game.'

'Made the mistake... Falling in love... Wasn't Alessio's fault...'

Alessio had to strain to hear what she was saying, but it was possible because you could have heard a pin drop in the silent room.

He'd imagined an impassioned speech, but he was given instead a quiet, resigned and accepting confession.

And through it all, however she felt after his response to the outpouring of her heart, there was no bitterness in her lowered voice.

Something inside him twisted as the full force of the realisation he'd been hiding from hit him.

It wasn't just a case of her loving *him*.

It was a case of him loving *her* right back.

How had that happened?

And how had he not realised earlier?

The signs had been there. The need to see her…the peace and contentment he felt when he was with her… the way everything inside him took flight at the sound of her voice… The way she made him laugh and he thought about her all the time.

And yet he had pretended to himself that he was immune to the nonsense of love.

Of course Alessio knew just what he had to do.

But would she have him? Would she even believe him? After all, he was the guy who had been happy to launch into a convenient lie.

Would he be rejected?

Just like that, Alessio knew what love was all about. It was about preferring the pain of rejection to the safety of living in an ivory tower. It was about not having a choice when it came to taking a risk with your heart. It was about opening a door that had been kept locked his entire life.

He walked into the room.

All eyes turned in his direction—including his father's.

Alessio had expected condemnation from him. Instead, there was acceptance. They had both come a very long way, he acknowledged. Bridges had been built, and those bridges were now making it possible for them to communicate with trust and affection instead of suspicion and defensiveness.

And he knew that the woman looking at him, her expression guarded, had played a huge role in building those bridges.

His keen eyes noted the way her back straightened. She was ready to defend herself, braced for confrontation.

He remained standing there and looked at everyone. He recognised a few faces. The rest he would get to know over time.

'I'm sorry,' he said slowly, turning to face Sophie and his father.

'There's no need,' Leonard said heavily. 'Life happens. I should be fuming, but I'm touched that you did what you did to try and protect me.'

'Alessio…'

'Sophie…'

He wanted to reach out for her hand, but she had both of them clasped in front of her.

'I've already explained the situation to your father,' Sophie said dully. 'There's no need for you to play back-up guy.'

'That's not why I'm here.' *In for a penny,* he thought, *in for a pound.* 'Gather around, everyone. It's important you all hear what I have to say.'

'What are you doing?' Sophie asked sharply, and he shot her a wry, self-deprecating smile.

'What I would have done a while back if I hadn't been so damned foolish and so damned stubborn and set in my ways.' He paused, and his dark eyes zeroed in on her confused face. 'You told me you loved me,' he said gravely, 'and I heard you and shut the door on you. It was a mistake. That door…the door that safeguarded my heart…was blown open by you a while back, but I was too entrenched in my attitudes to realise it.'

He glanced across to his father, whose eyebrows were raised, and Alessio threw him a sheepish, wry smile.

'No more little white lies, Dad. The truth now, and nothing but the truth.'

His dark gaze rested on Sophie, and he felt a tug of love and need and want that was so powerful it nearly blew him off his feet.

'Sophie, you got under my skin. And I was kidding myself when I thought that didn't pose any danger for my peace of mind, or my tried and tested self-control.' He breathed in, long and deep. 'I'd spent my life protecting myself from being vulnerable. I'd managed to convince myself that that was a state of affairs that would never change because I would never allow it to. The truth is, Sophie, I stopped caring about my precious self-control within seconds of meeting you… You made me laugh and you made me think and you made me *need*.'

The room had disappeared. The only person in it now was the woman he had fallen head over heels in love with.

'Are you just saying that…? Do you mean it, Alessio?'

'Every word. I was a smug, foolish, short-sighted idiot…'

Sophie smiled, heart bursting as she moved towards him to stare up at his dear, perfect face.

'Now I *know* you're going to regret saying that.'

When she reached to stroke his cheek, he captured her hand in his and closed his eyes to kiss it.

'How could I have known?' he asked in a roughened undertone. 'Known that when love struck my defences would all be washed away like a sandcastle in the path of an advancing tide? I'd been a bystander my entire life and I seriously believed that no one could possibly come along to challenge that. But you did, my darling, and I don't want you to ever stop challenging me. You make me the man I want to be.'

He got down on one knee.

'I have no ring, Sophie, so you might not think much of the grand gesture, but it's made from the very bottom of my heart. I love you more than words can say, and in front of everyone here I'm asking…will you marry me?'

As grand gestures went, Sophie didn't think they could come any grander. Their eyes met and she could see heart-felt sincerity burning in the depths of his dark gaze.

Her heart was bursting. She wanted to pinch herself. Because did dreams like this ever come true?

But he was waiting for her answer.

Everyone was waiting for her answer.

She smiled slowly and said, shakily, 'I can't think of anything I would rather do…'

* * * * *

REUNITED BY THE GREEK'S BABY

ANNIE WEST

MILLS & BOON

Dedicated with warm thanks to my reader friends
Elizabeth M, Gill B, Jacqui L and Zeba S,
who were so welcoming on my recent overseas trip.

PROLOGUE

ISLA SAT UPRIGHT in the hard chair, not meeting anybody's eyes. She'd known this would be difficult and had been prepared, but still the place made her shrink within herself.

It wasn't just the curious stares or unwelcoming atmosphere.

She huffed a silent laugh under her breath, tasting a hint of hysteria that she pushed down.

Prisons weren't supposed to be welcoming.

This, her third visit, should have been easier. Yet the cold institutional vibe, the grey walls and hard floors, the even harder stares of the staff and scent of heavy-duty disinfectant, got under her skin. And into her head, bringing memories of another place and time. The walls had been pale green, not grey, but the nose-scratching scent of cleanser and the throat-catching sense of desperation had been the same.

And the desolation.

Isla blinked at her hands, white-knuckled in her lap.

Then she lifted her chin and stared at the guard beside the door opposite until he looked away. It wasn't the past that unsettled her. It was the fact she wasn't wanted here.

For all they'd shared, all Theo had said and everything she'd felt, he didn't *want* her now. Not her help or sympathy or presence. Twice he'd refused to see her. Today would make the third time.

She swallowed, a jagged lump blocking her throat as hurt consumed her.

Theo had more urgent things on his mind than their relationship, like proving his innocence and getting out of here. Being a foreigner, not able to speak more than a few phrases of Greek, she couldn't be much practical help.

Unlike his family and friends.

It was only when news of his arrest became public that Isla had discovered a side to Theo she'd known nothing about. That he was wealthy, well-connected and powerful.

Isla found it impossible to reconcile that Theo Karalis, the one making international headlines, with the passionate, endearing lover who'd swept her off her feet.

There'd been nothing endearing about his terse messages saying he didn't want her to visit.

'Ms Jacobs?'

She looked up to see a slim man in a dark suit standing before her. 'Yes?'

He sat beside her and lowered his voice. 'My name is Petro Skouras. I work for Mr Karalis.'

Isla's heart thumped. A smile cracked the corners of her tight mouth as relief rose. 'Yes?'

Her gaze darted towards the big metal door where the guard stood. Was she going to see Theo at last?

'He asked me to give you this.'

Petro Skouras held out an envelope. It felt flimsy in her hand as she tore it open. Isla read the note, for it was a note, not a letter, in two seconds.

Its meaning was clear but Mr Skouras was taking no chances. His voice was kind but firm as he said, 'Mr Karalis asks that you don't visit again or try to contact him.'

He paused as if awaiting a response but Isla had no words. She scanned the note again, recognising Theo's bold handwriting. Not recognising the cold tone of command. This made it seem like they were strangers and she'd pestered him. Not as if they were in a relationship and shared a special bond.

Maybe they were strangers after all.

The back of her nose prickled as if tears threatened but it was an illusion. She was too shocked for tears. It felt as if everything she'd experienced in the last month, all the excitement and happiness, had been a dream.

'And I have this for you to sign.'

Isla stared at the typed paper he produced. It took a second for her blurry eyes to focus. When they did she gasped.

She'd heard about such things but never moved in circles where they were actually used. She read it again but the words didn't change. It was a non-disclosure agreement. If she signed she'd be barred from telling anyone she'd ever known Theo Karalis, or anything about him or their relationship.

Disbelief hardened into something stronger even than shock as each typewritten word carved itself into her brain.

Theo thought he needed a legal document to stop her blabbing about what they'd shared?

It was impossible. Unthinkable.

But the man she'd known had lied to her by omission about many things.

Obviously she'd been mistaken about so much. She'd believed them soulmates. Yet he didn't understand her at all if he thought she'd sell her story to the press.

Isla took the fountain pen with a surprisingly steady hand and scribbled her name on the dotted line.

Petro Skouras's relief was obvious. 'Would you like me to see you to your hotel?'

'No.' She shot to her feet. 'I'm fine on my own.'

She had been before Theo burst like a bright ray of sunshine into her life. She would be again, given time.

Theo didn't want her. She didn't belong in his life. She'd just been a brief diversion.

Isla held her head high as she walked out into the Athenian afternoon, ignoring the pain in her breaking heart.

CHAPTER ONE

ISLA WRAPPED HER scarf around her neck then shoved her hands in her coat pockets as she walked down the street. Winter bit through her clothes. It was hard to believe that just four months ago she'd been…

Pain scythed through her chest. A reminder she didn't go there any more.

Dragging in a deep breath, she did what she always did when her mood dropped—focus on the positive. Find five things she felt good about. It was a diversion she'd learned as a child and it always helped.

Even if some days it was hard.

Some days it felt like a lie, but she always persevered and eventually, one day, things started to feel a little better.

Okay, five things. To make it easy she wouldn't look too far ahead. It was simpler to focus on the here and now.

One. The sun was shining after a week of English drizzle. The pale blue between the clouds surely invited optimism.

Two. Rebecca had promised chocolate brownies for morning tea, knowing they were Isla's favourite. Her almost empty stomach churned, making her frown, but then it settled and the moment passed.

Three. Rebecca. Her friend and boss was reason enough to feel grateful.

Four. The new wools might be in. It was always fun

unpacking new stock, losing herself in the colours and textures as she restocked the shelves.

Five…

Isla caught the scent of cigarette smoke as she approached a man looking in a shop window. The acrid tang invaded her nostrils and her steps faltered as her sensitive stomach rebelled. He cast her a swift glance, lifted his phone to his ear and turned away to cross the street.

She took another breath, this time scented with wet pavement and the mint she'd automatically popped into her mouth. Thankfully her stomach settled.

Her gaze followed the man. Did she know him? His face, glimpsed in that quick, sideways glance, wasn't familiar. Yet something about the cut of his short, greying hair and nuggety frame rang a bell.

A shiver of disquiet rippled down her spine.

Isla hurried on. She'd cut it fine to open up on time. She couldn't dawdle. Yet as she approached the high street she couldn't banish a tickle of unease, the same feeling she'd had all week, triggered by a feeling someone was watching her.

When she reached the shop she shoved those thoughts aside. She was lucky to have this job and she intended to keep it.

She'd loved her studies and hadn't wanted to give them up but needs must. For now a steady income was more important than pursuing her passion for ancient history and her dream of becoming an archaeologist.

Isla's mouth twisted. Her track record with passions wasn't good. She'd only ever given in to passion with one man. A man who'd used then cruelly rejected her. There was a life lesson in there, but she refused to dwell on that now.

The morning sped by as she served customers, checked deliveries and dealt with online orders. The Friday morning knitting group in the back room finished and Isla got busy tidying up for Rebecca's afternoon patchwork class.

Neither she nor Rebecca had had time for morning tea and her stomach growled as she crawled under the large central table to pick up a stray ball of wool.

'Isla?'

'In here. I'm almost finished.'

She grabbed the grey eight ply and began to back out.

'There's someone to see you.'

That made Isla pause. None of her friends would drop in here during the day.

Plus something in Rebecca's tone jarred. Not disapproval. Caution? Isla frowned. Her boss was a friendly soul, not just welcoming to customers but genuinely warmhearted. She wouldn't object to someone visiting her assistant.

Isla straightened and spun towards the door into the main shop.

Rebecca stood there wearing her velvet patchwork jacket, her grey plait over her shoulder. But instead of her usual smile, her expression was unreadable.

Isla moved closer. 'What is it? Is something wrong?'

Then she saw movement behind her boss. A tall figure moved into view, the shopfront windows in the main room backlighting him. For a moment he seemed more shadow than real, until he stepped into the doorway behind Rebecca.

Isla blinked as the shadow transformed into someone she knew.

Someone you thought you knew.

Isla's eyes widened, her hand clenching the wool like a lifeline.

She opened her mouth but whether to speak or drag in much-needed oxygen, she didn't know. A wave of clammy heat engulfed her and the table tilted as if lifting off the floor. Then the world disappeared.

'Isla. It's time to wake up.'

Rebecca's familiar voice filtered into the blankness, reassuring her. Something damp swiped her cheeks and forehead. The coolness felt good.

'Rebecca. Sorry, I...'

She what? Isla frowned, scrambling to remember what had happened.

She opened her eyes and there was Rebecca, her worried eyes belying her smile. 'There you are. You gave us a shock.'

Us?

Memory exploded and her skin prickled as if an army of ants swarmed there. Her eyes rounded and she turned her head. There was no one else in the room and the door was shut.

'He's in the shop, kicking his heels.' Rebecca watched that sink in, Isla's taut body easing back on the old couch near the wall. 'Not that he wanted to. He seems a man used to getting his own way. I had to threaten him with the police to get you privacy.'

'The police?' Isla stared.

'It wasn't necessary. But after seeing your reaction I wanted to be sure you wanted to see him.' Rebecca lifted a glass to Isla's lips. 'Here, you'll feel better with some water. Dehydration won't help. I should have insisted you stop for morning tea.'

Obediently Isla sipped. 'Rubbish. It's not your job to look after me. I'm a competent adult.' Though she felt like she'd been stuffed full of cotton wool.

She shuffled straighter, swinging her feet to the floor. For a second she felt light-headed but the sensation eased and she let out a relieved breath. 'I feel a lot better now.'

'I'm glad to hear it,' said a deep voice from the doorway.

Isla stiffened, knuckles whitening as she grabbed the velvet-covered couch.

That voice had an appalling impact. It conjured up memories of laughter and magic, moonlit nights by the sea. Of poignant happiness. She was sure that if she'd been standing her knees would have weakened at that deep cadence.

Rebecca, bless her, jumped up, expression militant. 'I must ask you to leave if you can't respect Isla's right to privacy.'

For a woman who barely reached five feet, Rebecca showed no qualms facing down the well-built man who topped her by almost a foot and a half.

Isla's heart swelled. How lucky she was to have such a friend. It was rare, having someone champion her. Orphaned as an infant, never adopted, she'd been alone all her life.

'It's okay.' Isla got to her feet, waiting to see how she felt. 'I'll deal with him.'

Rebecca looked from her to the man whose shoulders filled the doorway. 'I'll put the kettle on.'

'No need, Ms Burridge. I'll do that.' Behind him a bell sounded as the street door opened. 'You have a customer.'

Rebecca surveyed him coolly. Finally she turned to Isla. 'Call if you need me. I won't be far away.'

Isla nodded and turned to the kitchenette in the back corner.

'Sit down, Isla.' His voice came from so close she knew he stood right behind her. 'You need to rest.'

As if he cared about her!

Yet there it was again, sensation coursing from her nape down her spine, like a rolling wave of excitement. Or dismay.

Isla ignored it and flicked the switch on the kettle.

'What I *need* is a cup of tea.'

She turned to reach for some mugs but found herself looking at a firm chin and squared jaw. She blinked, taking in the flat line of a mouth that she knew in repose was carved in sensuous lines. When it curled into a grin it could make her heart stop.

Isla breathed deep, searching for calm. But that indrawn breath tugged in more than oxygen. With it came a subtle scent that reminded her of a seaside grove of pine trees and warm male flesh.

Something turned over inside but she told herself it was her restless stomach.

Yet she wasn't in a hurry to look higher. Her gaze lingered on his crisp white shirt and knotted tie of deep crimson silk, the cashmere coat across straight shoulders. So different to the jeans and short sleeved shirts he'd once worn.

This man oozed wealth and the assurance that went with it.

How had she never seen it before?

Because you had stars in your eyes.

Because you take people at face value.

Because you had no reason to believe he'd lie to you.

Isla stepped back abruptly, heart hammering.

'Fine.' Her voice came from far away but at least it was steady. 'I take milk. Rebecca has milk and one sugar.'

He didn't move. Just stood, waiting.

Inevitably, knowing it was unavoidable, Isla looked up.

Her breath backed up in her lungs. He looked every bit as gorgeous as before. The symmetry and strong planes of his face, the remarkable golden-brown eyes beneath dark brows, the hint of a cleft in one cheek that she knew deepened attractively when he smiled. The burnished olive skin. The dark hair that had flopped over his forehead, now cut short.

It was all familiar, evoking memories of intimacy and dreams, stupid dreams.

Isla clenched her fists against the impulse to reach out and trace those powerful, charismatic features.

'Hello, Isla.'

His voice had a rasping edge that she might, once, have associated with deep affection. Now she knew better.

She narrowed her eyes and that's when she noticed something unfamiliar. A scar near his left eye, ragged and still pink. Obviously recent.

Of course it was recent. It was four months since she'd seen him. The memory of that last morning before his trip to Athens, the laughter and tenderness, undid her.

Because it had been followed by rejection, all the more cruel for being totally unexpected.

Isla stumbled towards the couch, reaching for support.

Instead of touching worn velvet her fingers met flesh. Long fingers closed around hers and she felt the pressure of a warm palm at the small of her back.

'Don't. Touch. Me!'

Isla jerked away, flinging up her other arm to ward him off.

Over her raised hand she read his shock. Good. She'd hate to think she was the only one suffering.

Had he expected her to welcome him with open arms? She might have been naïve once but she'd had a fast-track lesson in reality.

Her knees gave way and she collapsed onto the sofa. 'The kettle's boiled.'

He looked like he was going to speak. Instead he turned away and busied himself with the tea.

It was bittersweet, watching him at such a domestic task, and it took her back to Greece. Except the man she'd known then wasn't this man. He'd been a mirage concocted to seduce a naïve foreigner into a brief romance.

The only thing real between them had been the incredible sexual compulsion that had led, on her side, to impossible fantasies. The affection, connection and understanding—those had been figments of her imagination.

Isla set her jaw and tried to survey him with a clear head. It wasn't just his clothes that had altered. He held himself differently, with rigid shoulders and a guarded expression.

He was uncomfortable? He deserved to be.

He swung around, gaze capturing hers, and she felt it like a blow to her heart. Those leonine eyes glowed molten gold, taking her straight back to the wonder of his lovemaking and the tender acceptance she'd felt in his arms.

Clearly it was a trick of the light.

She blinked. There, the impression was gone. His eyes were brown and unreadable.

'There are brownies.' Isla nodded to the biscuit tin.

He didn't move, just surveyed her in a way that made her feel scraped bare.

In the past she'd revelled in the fact he took his time to see her, understand her, make her feel unique and appreciated. Now she knew it was a clever seduction technique. He'd probably been seducing gullible women for years. It meant nothing.

She'd meant nothing. He'd told her so and backed it up with threats of legal action if she contacted him again.

Her heart dipped. She'd had a lifetime of feeling like an outsider. Theo's rejection had devastated her because she'd finally let down her defences. She'd believed in him, in *them*.

What was he doing here?

Whatever his motivations, this man was trouble. With a huff of feigned impatience she moved to the edge of the couch as if to get the tea herself but he forestalled her.

'Don't move.' He didn't raise his voice but there was no mistaking it as anything other than a command.

Deftly he assembled plates and mugs, poured tea and shared out the food. He put hers on the little table beside the couch, then with a stern look as if warning her from moving, he took a plate and mug through to Rebecca.

As soon as he left the room Isla leaned back, closing her eyes and suppressing a shudder of reaction. Being close to him again made her feel too much. She'd like to pretend it was simply surprise and anger but it was far more. The tell-tale pulse between her legs told its own story, as if her eager body still hadn't got the message that he was trouble.

Her mouth wobbled and she bit hard on her bottom lip, grappling with unresolved feelings she'd tried so hard to conquer.

When she opened her eyes, he was in the doorway but she pretended not to notice. Instead she sipped her tea, clasping the mug in her palms as if its heat could counteract the chill crackling her bones.

The door snicked shut and he strolled closer. With every step the air thickened, making it harder to breathe. She took another sip and wished she'd started with the brownie. Her stomach felt hollow but it was roiling so much she didn't want to test it by eating in front of him.

'When you've had that I'll take you to a doctor.'

'Sorry?'

Her head snapped up and she saw him, stance wide, cashmere coat thrust aside and hands shoved in his pockets, drawing the fabric of his trousers taut over powerful thighs.

'A doctor. You're as white as milk and you've lost weight.' He frowned, his gaze skimming her collarbone. 'You look gaunt.'

Isla clutched her tea close, her heart hammering so fast it couldn't be good for her. She wasn't ready for this. Had never expected to see him again, much less have him deign to talk with her.

'Thanks for your opinion. But I don't need a doctor. I'm perfectly healthy.'

His eyebrows rose. 'Fainting for no reason isn't a sign of good health.'

Deliberately she shrugged. 'I imagine no one reacts well, coming face to face with the single worst mistake of their life.'

He stiffened, streaks of colour slashing those high cheekbones. But instead of retreating he moved closer.

'That doesn't explain the weight loss or the faint.'

Isla flattened her lips. She could tell him. She *should* tell him.

But her one attempt to contact him since returning to England had produced a threat of legal action. That rankled. Yet here he was on her turf, swaggering in as if he had a right to be here, demanding explanations.

Isla felt like she was on a seesaw, swinging wildly as the world tilted and turned upside down. 'Why are you here? Why the sudden concern?'

It couldn't be real.

Something flickered in those eyes and for a second she felt tremulous hope flare. The hope she thought she'd stamped out through the tough months since they'd parted.

'Simon is worried about you.' His words ground low as if dragged from his throat. 'He was stunned you'd rejected his offer of work next season and that you'd dropped out of university.'

Now Isla understood.

Simon was the Greek archaeologist who'd led the dig she'd worked on several months ago. The team, including students from her English university, had explored the remains of an ancient temple complex on a small Aegean island.

Once she'd have leapt at the chance to work there again, delighted that Simon wanted her back. She loved the work and hands-on archaeology was what she dreamed of doing.

But that career was over. Or at least on hold indefinitely.

'He couldn't believe it. He said you were one of the most promising students he's seen.' Once the praise would have delighted her. Now it reinforced all she'd lost. 'A colleague at your university told him you'd left suddenly with no explanation. They were worried you might be seriously ill.' Narrowed eyes surveyed her. 'I can see why.'

When Isla said nothing he went on. 'Simon knew I was coming to the UK on business and asked—'

'Asked you to check on me?' Isla's laugh sounded like a winter wind rushing through an empty corridor. Not surprising as inside she felt hollow and chilled.

Of course *Theo* hadn't been worried. He was acting for his friend. This was second-hand concern.

A sour tang filled Isla's mouth and she put down her barely touched tea. The irony. The man who'd threatened dire consequences should she approach him, checking her wellbeing.

Simon had introduced them one night when the team ate at a small taverna near the dig site. But she'd had no idea the pair were so close he'd ask Theo such a favour.

'Amazing. I can't imagine someone like you being close to someone as nice as Simon.'

His jaw clenched so hard he reminded her of a chiselled marble statue of a warrior, ready for battle.

Except this man's flesh was warm and hot, not cold marble. Her palms tingled at the phantom memory of his silky skin, tight over a body of hard-packed muscle and bone.

It was the final straw. She shot to her feet. 'You can tell Simon I'm fine. I want you to leave.'

She hadn't even finished speaking when he shook his head. 'Not without an explanation.'

A red mist descended, blurring the edges of the room. Vaguely Isla realised this was bad for her blood pressure, but the nerve of the man, pushing into her world and making demands…

Suddenly the energy Isla hadn't felt in weeks was running through her veins. She sparked with indignation and roaring fury. Disillusionment and despair melded with her lifelong sense of abandonment, the knowledge that she was always second best, never important enough to matter to anyone.

She should have known better than to believe she mattered to him, but she hadn't been able to resist building up hopes. She'd let herself believe and the disillusionment was crippling after having let down her guard.

All that hurt erupted in one lava-hot, volcanic burst.

'I don't owe you *anything*, Theo Karalis.' She spat the words so fast it was a wonder she didn't stumble over them. 'If you don't leave immediately I'll call the police and have you charged with harassment.' She drew a deep breath, holding his blazing stare, then spoke slowly so he heard every word. 'I have nothing to say to a murderer.'

CHAPTER TWO

LATE THAT AFTERNOON Theo stared through the gloom at the glowing window of the craft shop. Bright colours beckoned in a display that mimicked a cosy fireside nook.

But it wasn't really the shop he saw. It was Isla's up-tilted chin and crossed arms, rejecting him and signalling her need for protection. From him!

Her glacial stare as she'd warned him off, calling him a murderer...

Outrage pounded through him.

She didn't mean it.

She couldn't.

She knew he wasn't a killer.

Yet he felt the slash to his gut as if she'd plunged a dagger into his belly. He'd assumed she still believed in his innocence. Understood he'd *never* hurt her.

He'd faced many things lately, more dangerous and life-changing than an ex-lover's disdain. Yet Isla's reaction hit him profoundly. She'd turned to ice before him whereas once her blue-grey eyes had danced with warmth when they were together.

Her reaction unnerved him. He, who'd survived a stint in one of Greece's toughest prisons. Who'd taken down one of the place's most feared thugs when the man tried to kill him, no doubt on orders from Theo's enemy, Spiro Stavroulis.

Stavroulis's hatred Theo could understand, even if it was misplaced. But Isla's reaction felt like personal betrayal.

There'd been no mistaking her scathing contempt. She'd looked like a stranger who believed the stories printed about him.

The press had taken Spiro's lead and crucified Theo's character, portraying him as reckless and violent, with a vendetta against Spiro's grandson Costa who they made out to be an innocent. The story was that Theo had deliberately pushed Costa to his death down a flight of stairs. They weren't interested in Theo's innocence. Or that Costa had been deplorable and dangerous. Theo knew that too well from the way Costa had hurt his ex-girlfriend Toula, Theo's stepsister.

A shudder racked him. This reminded him of those long nightmarish nights behind bars when he hadn't let himself sleep properly lest his cellmate try to claim the money Stavroulis had offered to anyone who seriously injured Theo. Or killed him.

Compounding his fear had been the prison rumour that Stavroulis had vowed to get at Theo by harming those closest to him. Desperate, Theo had organised the best possible security for his family. Fortunately *that* rumour at least hadn't been true. Stavroulis had standards and harming women was beyond them. But at the time it had spurred Theo to cut ties with Isla, keeping their connection secret so she wouldn't become a target.

Isla and he hadn't parted well so Theo hadn't expected a warm welcome. Nothing about that time had been as he would have chosen it but he'd needed to protect her. She'd been so persistent, visiting the prison again and again, trying to see him. He'd taken that as proof that she believed him innocent. That had warmed him, despite knowing he couldn't maintain the relationship they'd begun.

Petro, his professionally distrustful lawyer, had suggested her persistence proved only that she'd discovered Theo was rich and stuck by him hoping for largesse.

Theo stifled a bitter laugh. Whatever she felt now it wasn't a desire for closeness.

Through the mayhem of his world disintegrating and the need to cut her loose, Isla's belief in him had given him hope. Especially when the justice system tried to grind him to dust, thanks to Stavroulis's powerful legal and political connections and his media outlets braying for Theo's blood.

Theo had deliberately pushed Isla away, yet her loyalty had been a glowing ember of brightness in a world turned to chaos. For the first time in his adult life he'd felt utterly, terrifyingly helpless.

Theo shoved the limo door open, unable to stand the enclosed space any longer. He told his driver to wait and stepped out. The damp air was better than being confined.

How long before he could stand being in a small space for any length of time?

Theo might be free and beginning to get his life on track but some things would always be different. His perspective on freedom. His gratitude for the simplest pleasures, like eating what he chose, when he chose. Making his own schedule.

But the taint of his arrest and his time locked away would linger until the true killer faced justice.

He raked his hand through his hair, torn between competing impulses. To clear his name fully and to protect the vulnerable. While he didn't *know* who was responsible, he feared it could be someone he cared for, definitely someone who'd been at the house that night. Put like that, his duty was obvious. He had broad shoulders. He was strong enough to weather the gossip and speculation.

The shop door opened and Theo stalked across, stopping a couple of metres away, not crowding her. 'Isla.'

She whipped round, eyes huge.

She couldn't really have thought he'd scurry away with his tail between his legs. 'I said I'd see you later.'

'I thought you were just saving face.'

Because she'd ordered him out? Because she'd threatened to call the police?

'I promised Simon I'd make sure you were all right.'

Theo guessed she'd react better to Simon's concern than to the news *he* was worried for her.

He'd been changed by the events of the last few months. But the alteration he saw in Isla scared him at a visceral level.

She was too pale, too thin. Her bright scarf and bulky winter coat couldn't hide her sharp cheekbones or the hollows in her cheeks, as if her flesh pulled too tight across her bones. He was alarmed at how fragile she'd become, her collarbone more pronounced and her pallor disturbing.

'I'm fine.'

'I don't believe you.'

Eyes bright and hard as diamonds held his. Despite the chill in her gaze, heat detonated in Theo's gut.

For months it had been almost a relief to know what they'd shared was over. It couldn't survive the mayhem that had engulfed him and he'd recoiled from the idea of Isla caught up in that. Yet some things weren't easily extinguished. No mistaking that fire for anything but desire.

Theo suppressed a bitter laugh at the way fate taunted him.

As if on cue the soft drizzle changed to stinging drops of ice.

Isla put up her umbrella. Theo turned up his coat collar but didn't move. A little water wouldn't budge him.

Remarkably he watched her determination waver as she

saw the rain plaster his hair against his head and drips run down his neck. She'd always had a tender heart.

'Look, Isla.' He softened his voice, cajoling. 'This will be easier if you accept the inevitable and agree to talk.'

'The inevitable being you getting what you want? That's what you're used to.'

Her words were accusing. Their relationship had been entirely mutual yet she made it sound as if he'd taken advantage of her. The idea pulled him up short. Or was she referring to his wealth and the power that went with it?

Much good that had done when the police decided they wanted a quick arrest.

'I mean you no harm. You know I'd never hurt you.'

She said nothing and he felt the chasm between them as an ache in his chest, growing sharper with each silent second.

Theo had finally been exonerated but something stronger than pride made him blurt out, 'I didn't kill him.'

He couldn't bear it if she, of all people, believed him capable of such a thing. 'I'm not out on bail,' he continued. 'I'm free, all charges dropped. The authorities know I didn't do it.'

Even if the press hinted he got out of prison on a technicality thanks to clever lawyers. There were stories circulating that he was guilty and that it would yet be proven. Spiro Stavroulis had lost his grandson and wouldn't rest until the culprit responsible faced the full force of the law. Meanwhile Theo was his scapegoat.

He wondered if the old man had even taken in the news that there was proof Theo was elsewhere on the estate when his grandson died, or whether grief blinded him to reason. Maybe Spiro thought that by pressuring Theo he'd move heaven and earth to uncover the identity of the one responsible.

Ice trickled down Theo's spine at the idea of someone

else facing Stavroulis's hatred and all the prejudice he brought to bear, not just in the press but in the legal system.

Anyone weaker than Theo would crack under the pressure. Anyone whose resilience wasn't as strong as his… He had his suspicions about who might be responsible but hadn't been able to confirm them. He just hoped he was wrong.

'That may be so but I don't want to spend time with you, Theo.'

Isla's voice turned husky on his name, evoking memories of her crying his name as she climaxed in his arms. Of them sharing a joke, her voice breathless with laughter.

Of that last morning. He'd woken her at dawn and she'd surveyed him with sleepy eyes that reflected the light on the waves lapping outside the door. Her voice had been husky then too, with a tenderness he'd felt deep inside.

Regret sawed through him, like the swipe of a rusty blade against vulnerable flesh. Regret for how their golden idyll had ended. Regret for what could no longer be. And the pain he'd caused her.

But no matter how much she wished it, he couldn't walk away. He folded his arms, ignoring the weather, and waited.

Finally she nodded, her expression stern as if she already regretted her decision. 'Okay.'

'Excellent.' He gestured to the limo. 'We'll go to my hotel and talk.'

Isla retreated a step. 'Not there.'

Theo frowned. 'We can be private there. That's better than a café.'

Her shoulders rose and fell on a sigh. She glanced towards the shop where her colleague was closing up.

'All right. You can come to mine.'

Relief rushed through Theo. She *did* trust him. Isla wouldn't invite him into her home if she thought him a murderer. The idea of her believing him guilty had been an ache in his belly all day.

Yet his relief was short-lived, outweighed by concern. She looked fragile and unwell. He needed to find out what was wrong and what treatment she needed.

'We'll drive. It will be quicker and drier than walking four blocks in this weather.'

Abruptly Isla retreated under the shop awning. He followed.

'You know where I live?' Her eyes narrowed. 'Of course you do, like you knew how to find me at work. Did you have me followed?'

'Not followed. I paid an investigator to find you.'

'When?'

'This week. Why?'

Isla's expression hardened. 'All week I felt I was being watched. Do you have any idea how frightening that is for a woman? I didn't know if I was imagining things or whether there really was someone keeping tabs on me.' Her chin jutted. 'A woman alone, going home in the dark...'

His belly cramped and Theo swore. He should have assigned one of his own staff to the job rather than hire a local. Someone would pay for this.

'I apologise. That wasn't my intention, far from it. But I take full responsibility. I wouldn't have scared you for the world.'

Silence beat between them, louder than the drumming rain on the awning above.

Finally she nodded but her expression didn't lighten.

It struck him that the change in Isla wasn't just physical. She'd been passionate about archaeology and with him, enthusiastic and giving. Their passion had made him forget his initial sense that she was a little more reserved than her colleagues. Not unfriendly, far from it, but cautious. And sexy, incredibly sexy. Now there was a gravity about her that he'd only seen tiny glimpses of before.

What had changed her? Was it all down to him?

Isla met that hooded stare and felt a rush of all those emotions she'd tried to lock away. Regret, longing, anger, despair.

And happiness. A sneaking burst of happiness that should be impossible but which shimmered in her blood like sunshine on water.

Even with his hair plastered to his head and his expression as dour as a thundercloud, Theo Karalis affected her as no other man did.

She'd told herself he hadn't meant it when he'd said he'd see her after work. But part of her had known he'd be here.

He was no longer the light-hearted lover she'd fallen for. She'd always sensed a core of something solid in Theo, deep and strong. Maybe that was what had drawn her. That and the slow-dawning smile and superb body...

Now that fun-loving gloss had worn thin to reveal another man.

Not surprising given what he'd been through. For a second the impulse to touch him, to reassure herself that he was okay, overwhelmed her. But she overcame it.

He didn't want her sympathy. She should save that for herself. This was going to be tough.

Isla drew a slow breath. 'Shall we go?'

He gestured towards the dark car, its back door held open by a man she didn't know. 'After you.'

The trip was short and silent. Theo introduced her to his driver, a burly man with watchful eyes, then subsided into silence.

Isla had had all day to decide what she'd say if he appeared again and still she didn't know.

It was his fault. He'd rejected her in Athens and her one

attempt to contact him since had made him threaten her with a charge of harassment. She'd given up thinking it possible to talk with Theo Karalis. If his dismissal weren't bad enough, trying to intimidate her with his power was worse.

Isla's mouth tightened as she led the way upstairs and unlocked her flat. She didn't look at him as she hung up her coat and took her umbrella to the bathroom to dry.

When she returned and saw him in her tiny sitting room her heart almost failed.

With the overhead light spilling over his dark, wet hair she had a moment's terrible deja vu. To those glorious days in Greece, swimming in a secluded cove far from both locals and tourists. Theo always found the perfect places for picnics and making love.

Pain zigzagged through her, ripping the paper-thin defences she'd built so laboriously against Theo Karalis. She blinked in horror as her throat thickened and the back of her nose prickled.

She refused to think of those times. Better to remember the cold waiting room at the prison. Signing the paper that had shattered her last hope that he felt anything real for her. Then there was his threat to have her arrested.

'Here.' Her voice was brusque as she shoved a towel at him. 'I'll put the kettle on.'

Theo's hand skimmed hers as he took the towel and sensation shot up her arm, so powerful it verged on pain. It had to be pain. The alternative didn't bear thinking about.

Yet she couldn't prevent her gaze lingering over his impressive form. He'd taken off the cashmere coat to reveal a dark suit. But instead of looking like another city worker, Theo Karalis was in a league of his own. It was more than the superb tailoring of what she guessed was a bespoke suit. It was that tall, athletic body and the casual confidence of a man supremely comfortable in his own skin.

Once she'd found that incredibly attractive, the sense Theo had nothing to prove to anyone. She'd been drawn by his strength as much as his interest in her, so flatteringly intense.

Face it. You were blinded by his charisma and the way he looked at you as if no one else existed.

Now she knew his confidence was the arrogance of an ultra-rich, privileged man, used to getting what he wanted. Including women foolish enough to be taken in by his charm.

Isla turned away, grateful for the routine of making tea. Theo's preferred tipple was Greek coffee, strong and aromatic, but she had none and she wouldn't apologise for that.

She kept her back to the living area, buying time. But she was aware of him moving about the room. Her nape tingled and she knew he watched her as he prowled the small space.

What did he think of her tiny flat with its second-hand furniture? It was quiet, clean and most importantly cheap.

It was bigger than the single room she'd rented near the dig in Greece but smaller than the old house she'd shared with Theo those last weeks.

Her pulse faltered, remembering. That place stood alone, around a rocky point from the village. It had felt like paradise with the aquamarine shallows outside the front door and the gnarled olive trees rising up the slope behind.

She'd fantasised about living there with him, not just during his holiday from work in Athens. That was before she'd found out who Theo Karalis really was.

'Tea's ready.'

Isla turned to find him just behind her, hair rumpled from where he'd towelled it, his jaw shadowed. He didn't look like the wealthy stranger who used limousines and wore coats worth more than she earned in several months.

He looked like Theo, her Theo, eyes glowing golden and beckoning...

She snagged a sharp breath and plonked a mug on the table. It was so small that if they both sat their knees would touch and she'd be caught in his force field.

Isla took the ancient armchair. For a moment he stood as if debating something, then snagged the mug, crossed the room in three long paces and sat facing her.

'What is it, Isla? What's happened to you?'

She bit her lip, shocked at how sincere he sounded. Then, seeing his stare drop to her mouth, she lifted the mug and sipped her peppermint tea, pretending to savour its warmth. But inside she was all jitters.

Tell him. Tell him! It's what you tried to do after all.

Yet she hesitated. She couldn't ignore the way he'd treated her. 'You've changed your tune. In Athens you didn't want to have anything to do with me.'

Sombre eyes held hers. 'I'm sorry if I hurt you, Isla.'

If he'd hurt her! She blinked. Had she known him at all? It seemed not.

'It was for the best, but I realise it may not have felt like it.'

Too right it hadn't felt like it. True, there'd been no promises spoken between them but Isla could have sworn there'd been other sorts of promises made. Trust given and received.

Even if she'd got that wrong and the affection had been all on her side, he'd dumped her so brutally it hadn't just hurt. It had destroyed something she didn't think she could get back. The belief that she really *could* matter to someone. She'd grown up unloved and despite her positive self-talk, that belief had taken a lifetime, and Theo's concentrated attentions, to grow inside her.

Her chin notched up. 'I deserved better.'

Something flared in those leonine eyes. Then it was gone, his face unreadable. 'Yes, you did. I'm sorry.'

Isla sighed. Why rake over the past? He'd implied he'd acted for her sake but the plain truth was she hadn't mattered to him as he had to her. She didn't need to know more. She was simply delaying. Because she shied from telling this man the truth. If it had been the Theo she'd known on the island she wouldn't have hesitated. But this was a cold-eyed stranger, rich, powerful and moving in a social stratosphere that excluded ordinary people like her.

'I'm not sick.'

His dark eyebrows rose but he said nothing, as if the sheer power of his personality would force her to continue.

'And I haven't chucked in my studies. Just withdrawn for now.'

Isla's gaze dropped. Strictly that was true but there was no way she'd be able to return to university later. Even if she had time she wouldn't be able to afford it. Her mouth widened in a crooked smile. Maybe in a few decades.

'Why give up something you love? Something you're good at? Simon says you have a very promising career. It doesn't make sense.'

He paused and eventually Isla couldn't resist looking up at him. Heat trickled down her spine, vertebra by vertebra as she met his stare. How could she be so vulnerable to him after the cruel way he'd treated her?

He leaned forward, narrowing the space between them. 'You say you're not ill but you're clearly not well.'

Isla sighed, expelling the air in her lungs then dragging in a fortifying breath.

'I'm healthy. I'm just not able to eat a lot.' Another breath, another beat of her thundering heart. 'I'm pregnant.'

CHAPTER THREE

THEO COULDN'T TAKE the words in. He watched her watching him, waiting for his reaction, but his brain had seized up.

Isla, pregnant?

One reverberating thud and his heart started again, and with it his brain.

Isla, pregnant!

He couldn't stop his gaze sliding to her abdomen. Heat burned his skin and deep within his chest.

Isla, with another man?

Instant denial turned into revulsion, nausea searing his gut and making him grimace. It wasn't possible.

Of course it's possible. She's a passionate, attractive woman.

Yet Theo was having none of it. As if the sheer force of his willpower could make it untrue.

He breathed deep and slow, forcing himself to think.

It was sixteen weeks and four days since they parted. Theo knew precisely. In prison, counting the days since freedom had become habit. That had to be why he recalled precisely how long since he'd seen Isla.

Plus since then she'd spent at least a week in Athens, trying to see him. Automatically Theo brushed aside the tangle of feelings that memory evoked.

His mind cleared and the terrible weight pressing on

his chest eased. In that time would Isla have taken another lover?

He couldn't believe it.

Theo had been surprised by her sexual inexperience. He'd even wondered if she'd been a virgin the first time they had sex. If not, she'd been close to it, but he hadn't asked, not wanting to embarrass her since she hadn't referred to it.

Whatever her previous experience, Isla was an ardent lover. The memory of intimacy with her still had the power to undo him. Yet a woman didn't reach the age of twenty-four and be sexually inexperienced *and* promiscuous. He'd been honoured that she'd chosen to be with him. It wouldn't be in character for her to leave him and take another lover so soon.

Isla didn't let down her guard easily. When others from the dig partied to excess, she'd enjoyed herself but kept within limits. Despite her animation and warmth, Isla had an underlying reserve. Not coldness, but self-sufficiency. He sensed she participated on her own terms.

When she'd become his lover it hadn't only been sexual satisfaction he'd experienced. He'd felt privileged.

Now this. No other lover had ever caused more than a tiny ripple in the smooth waters of his life. Isla's news was a tsunami.

'You're having my baby?'

Any doubt disintegrated at her expression. Her eyes rounded as if he'd shocked her. There was something in her face too, as if she'd come to terms with something life-changing.

Theo knew that look. He'd seen it in the mirror often lately. 'Isla?'

'You accept my word for it?'

'If you say you're pregnant, I believe you. Why wouldn't I?'

'Not about the pregnancy. About it being yours.'

Her eyes that earlier had been a glacial grey turned misty blue. The same colour as when, a lifetime ago, she'd cuddled into him, breathless from sex and smiling dreamily as if he were some priceless treasure she'd unearthed on her excavation. The sight mesmerised him.

Theo shook his head. This was no time for reminiscence.

If today had taught him one thing it was that Isla was cured of that attraction. The knowledge was a lead weight in his gut, but he ignored it. He'd done what he had to do.

'The baby *is* mine.' It emerged as a statement. Definite, almost possessive.

That's how he felt. Possessive.

Of Isla.

And, as his gaze dropped again to her belly, of the child she carried. *His* child.

It would take time to absorb all the implications, but Theo felt no doubt about his feelings. His child. His responsibility.

His chest tightened on an upswing of emotion. Wonder. Excitement. Fear.

These feelings were so tremendous, he wondered briefly if his biological father had felt such exhilaration when he'd received similar news. But only for a second.

Of course he hadn't. There hadn't been a paternal bone in that man's body. To abandon the woman he'd got pregnant... Theo would *never* do that.

'But something's wrong.' Theo knew little about pregnancy but Isla looked nothing like the rosy-cheeked women he'd seen with their baby bumps. 'You say you're not ill...'

Which, frankly, he doubted. She looked wrung out, as if sheer determination kept her upright. It was all he could do not to pull her close, reassure himself that she couldn't be as fragile as she seemed.

Wouldn't that go down well?

'Tell me the truth. Is something wrong with the baby?' His throat thickened as if his body rejected the notion. He'd known about the child for just minutes yet he couldn't bear the thought of something happening to it. 'Aren't pregnant women supposed to glow?'

'Glow? I wish.' Isla's mouth twisted. Then, meeting his eyes, her expression changed, turning slightly less martial. 'Maybe I'll glow later. I've had severe morning sickness for too long to look the picture of health. But,' she hurried on, 'I'm assured the baby is absolutely fine. Once we get through this stage I'll put on weight.'

Relief seared through him that the baby was safe. Yet that wasn't enough. The sight of Isla worried him.

'Surely you shouldn't be so drained? If—'

Isla raised her palm, stopping his question. 'There's no need for a show of concern. It's unnecessary.' She paused. 'In fact, it's insulting. Don't play the worried ex.'

Her tone was cold. The way she said *ex*, like referring to something malodorous she'd picked up on the bottom of her shoe, made his hackles rise and his conscience sting.

Hadn't they been good together? More than good?

They'd been together only a short time, but he'd felt as if Isla had come to know him better than anyone outside his family. It had unnerved him even as he revelled in the way it intensified their every interaction.

'I *am* concerned.'

Surely that was obvious? She knew him well enough to understand that. Theo didn't lie.

'Really? That's very hard to believe. Especially as you threatened to have me arrested.'

Theo's head snapped back like he'd been slapped.

Logic had warned him not to come to England. He'd severed their liaison and it was a mistake to look back, no matter how tempting. Things were complicated enough without stirring the embers of a dead relationship. But he hadn't been able to resist and now found himself stepping off a precipice to somersault endlessly, reality turning on its head while he struggled to get his bearings.

'Sorry?'

Isla shook her head, eyes never leaving his. The scorn in them unfamiliar. 'Don't play the innocent, Theo. You know what I'm talking about. You threatened me.'

He leaned forward, hands on his splayed thighs. 'I've never threatened you. I never would.'

Her answer was a derisive snort as she lifted her mug. 'Isla?'

She didn't look up, as if her tea were more interesting than the father of the child she carried.

Theo's molars ground together. Indignation was a blistering rush of heat. Until recently he'd never imagined anyone would view him as anything other than a man of honour. Events in Athens had flayed his pride and now, unbelievably, Isla accused him...

'You need to explain. I deserve an answer.'

'*You* deserve? You *deserve*?'

Her eyes blazed, sharp as polished blades.

His skin pricked as if pierced. He'd never seen her so upset. He could understand ill feeling over how they'd parted. But not this.

'Yes, deserve. You're overwrought. You're not making sense.'

'Overwrought!' Liquid spilled from her mug as she slammed it down. Her face turned from pale to flushed. 'Next you'll tell me I imagined that letter.'

Theo paused. One of them had to stay calm. Briefly he wondered if her mood swing was bad for the baby. It couldn't be good for her. This was unlike the Isla he knew. He was both fascinated and horrified.

And reluctantly admiring.

In a perverse way her prickly aggressiveness appealed

to a man used to fawning sycophants. But it was more than that. The glitter in her eyes, the sharp rise of her breasts as she tugged in air, her intense focus and vibrancy made him aware of her as a woman. A woman with whom he'd shared so many intimacies, such secret pleasure that even her concentrated fury was a reminder of the passion that had ensnared him.

What sort of man was he to be excited by a woman's fury? To prefer it to her steely attempts to blank out all emotion as if blocking him from her life?

He was like a kid taunting a pretty girl because any attention was better than none. Shocked at himself, Theo leaned back, away from her.

'I don't know about a letter. There's obviously some misunderstanding.'

'I suppose you don't know Petro Skouras either?'

'Petro? He's my lawyer.' One of them, and one of his oldest friends. 'What has he to do with this?' Though Theo had a sinking feeling he began to understand.

'He wrote to me on your behalf. Said that if I tried to contact you again the police would arrest me.'

Theo's breath hissed. Horror prickled his scalp as he met Isla's needle-sharp stare.

How could Petro have done that to her? So many acquaintances and so-called friends had turned away from Theo when he was arrested. His reputation had been sullied with an avalanche of lies and innuendoes. But this woman had stood by him. Until he'd done what was needed and pushed her away.

It made Theo ashamed.

He swore softly and comprehensively.

He'd asked Petro to find a way to stop her visiting. Their relationship couldn't go on. At the time he'd feared old man Stavroulis might target her. Plus he'd needed to focus on fighting the case against him and dealing with the fallout. He had responsibilities that had to take priority over a budding relationship with a pretty Englishwoman.

Petro had suggested the non-disclosure agreement and Theo had reluctantly agreed. It was brutal and offensive but it meant she'd leave and he wouldn't have to worry about her as well as everything else in the fiasco his life had become.

'You're talking about the non-disclosure agreement?'

Her eyes narrowed. 'No, that was bad enough. As insults went it was pretty low. But I meant the threat of arrest for harassment.'

'Harassment? You?' Isla blinked as if his tone took her by surprise. 'When was this?'

Her throat worked. 'Does it really matter?'

'*When*, Isla?'

'When I was back in England. When I found I was pregnant.'

Gone was the strident fury, in its place a weariness that seemed to weigh her down. Her shoulders slumped and she sagged back in the ugly chair as if drained of energy.

Theo's heart hammered. He hated seeing her like this. He exhaled slowly, searching for calm. 'You tried to contact me?'

It was something he hadn't allowed himself to think about, but after doing what was needed and pushing her away, Theo had missed her. Missed the comfort of her on his side, ready to visit and support him. Ready to believe in him.

'I emailed your office. I'd tried calling but your phone number didn't work.'

'I got a new one.'

Because the press had got it and shared it. What use was a phone that rang nonstop twenty-four hours a day with abusive calls and texts? Some were from civic-minded citizens but he guessed most were from people paid by Spiro Stavroulis to make his life hell.

Theo pinched the bridge of his nose. He could imagine the situation. Petro being efficient and instructing staff to monitor personal messages. Had he red-flagged Isla's name?

Friend Petro might be, and well-intentioned, but tonight his ears would blister when Theo rang him to discuss the difference between help and unwanted interference.

'You sent an email and got a reply from Petro? He threatened to report you to the police for harassment?'

Dull eyes held his. She shrugged. 'Yes. An email with a letter as follow-up, in case I didn't understand the first time.'

Theo erupted from his seat, crossing the small room in three paces. Why hadn't Petro told him? Why take it upon himself?

The answer was simple. Petro was one of the few people who understood the full enormity of what he faced. Not only proving his innocence so charges would be dropped and he could be free. But protecting his family through the aftermath of that dreadful night in Athens, and again taking up the reins of a multibillion-dollar business that had suffered from the fallout.

Theo had come to London for one day only, all he could spare. He was needed in Greece as deals suddenly turned sour and negotiations stopped because people didn't want to deal with a company run by a social pariah. What hurt most was the way his previous good reputation and the company's name for excellence counted for so little.

He swung around to find Isla watching him. No wonder she'd been furious.

'I apologise. I didn't know.' He shoved his hands in his pockets, ignoring the urgent desire to take her hands in his.

'I had no idea you were treated that way, but I take full responsibility. Petro works for me. His actions reflect on me.'

Nothing had prepared Theo for the shock of being accused of murder. Yet the writhing feeling of discomfort and shame was stronger now as he took in Isla's drawn features.

What was she thinking? He couldn't read her. That was another disturbing change. Once there'd been such affinity between them.

Theo cut off that line of thought. It was fruitless. He paced closer and her gaze tracked the movement.

'Do you believe me?'

'Maybe.' Her head tilted. Then finally, 'Yes.'

She didn't sound happy or relieved. Theo opened his mouth then snapped it shut. He couldn't expect her to welcome him with open arms.

'And you believe that I wasn't responsible for the death of Spiro Stavroulis's grandson?'

When she hesitated, something inside him died a little. His chest tightened. He'd weathered doubt and suspicion from the press, business colleagues and acquaintances. Yet this woman's doubt, the negation of her previous trust, affected him deeply.

'I can give you proof. A document from the prosecutor.'

Finally, when every taut muscle screamed at breaking point, Isla nodded. 'I believe you.' Then she ruined it by adding, 'After all, it's easy enough to check.'

Theo rocked back on his feet as if she'd punched him in the gut.

He stared down at her as if he'd never seen her before. Certainly she wasn't the woman he'd known.

Her rich, chestnut hair was pulled back in a low ponytail. His fingers twitched at the sense memory of those silky waves caressing his skin. Of burying his face in rosemary-scented hair. Her heart-shaped face was flushed yet still looked too delicate. As he watched she deliberately lifted it to look down her neat nose at him from eyes that gave nothing away. Her generous mouth was held tight and flat.

Didn't she *want* to believe him innocent?

For several heartbeats shock held him still. Then he realised what he was doing, brooding over how he was perceived when the most urgent issue was Isla's health.

He pulled out his phone.

'Who are you calling?'

'My assistant. It's not late. I'm sure with some persuasion we can see a top specialist here in London tonight.'

Isla was on her feet. 'There's no need. I *have* a doctor.'

'They're not doing a very good job.'

'Who do you think you are, coming here and making judgements?'

Theo stared down into those brilliant eyes, relieved to see that for now at least, Isla was sparkling with energy.

'I'm the father of the baby you're carrying.' He paused, watching her eyes widen. 'That's *our* baby. That gives me the right.'

His words reverberated into silence, penetrating deep, marking his very bones and burrowing into his soul.

He was going to be a father. *They* were going to be parents.

Theo felt a frisson of anxiety and wondered if he'd be up to that, especially given his biological father's appalling behaviour. But already his feelings about Isla and their baby proved him to be unlike the father he'd never known. At least he knew something about positive parenting from his beloved stepfather.

'This changes everything. You know that, don't you, Isla?'

'Of course. Why do you think I tried to contact you? But that doesn't give you the right to ride roughshod over me. I may be carrying *our* child…' Did her voice wobble on the word *our*? 'But it's *my* body and I make the decisions about my healthcare.'

'Ride roughshod?' He scowled. 'Because I try to get you the best medical care? You're exaggerating. You really think it's okay to be this exhausted, this sick? Are you absolutely sure that your condition isn't harming the baby?'

Isla said nothing but he almost heard her thoughts chasing each other. Her gaze shifted as if something beyond his shoulder suddenly took all her attention. Was she worried and putting on a brave face? It wasn't normal to be so unwell.

Theo shoved his hands deep into his pockets. 'I'm trying to do the right thing, Isla, to look after you both. Is that a crime?'

CHAPTER FOUR

THEO'S WORDS STILL echoed in Isla's head an hour later.

Doing the right thing. Is that such a crime?

Of course it wasn't a crime. In fact, the idea of getting a second opinion on her severe morning sickness was a relief. She'd been worried when it hadn't abated and she'd continued to feel so run-down and ill, despite the reassurances she'd received at her last check-up.

It was just the way Theo had taken charge without so much as a by your leave.

And that he spoke of doing the *right thing*.

Isla grimaced. Theo made it clear that he acted out of duty. Not worry because he cared for her in the way she'd once believed. His rejection had been brutal proof that what she'd believed a grand love affair had been, for him, a holiday diversion. When his life turned upside down he'd had no time for her, not even for her support. She simply didn't fit into his real life.

Now he was concerned to do the responsible thing. But his emotions weren't engaged.

Not with her at any rate. Yet, she recalled, there'd been one moment when he claimed the baby as his without question and a frisson of something powerful had trembled through her. He'd worn an expression she'd never seen before, one that made her heart roll over in her chest.

And she'd felt excluded.

Because in that instant it seemed that Theo's emotions *were* engaged. For the baby, not her.

Was that why she was so angry? Because she secretly craved Theo's attention?

The idea made a mockery of everything she'd told herself these last weeks about how she was better off without him. That it was a good thing she'd learned what he was really like now rather than later.

Not that there'd have been a later. She was sure their affair would have ended soon even without his arrest. It wasn't as if he'd fallen in love with her.

Isla bent her legs, tucking them up so she lay in a foetal position on the coverlet.

Determined, she yanked her thoughts in another direction. She'd had her whole life to get used to being on her own, never loved or wanted. Isla swallowed hard, ignoring the familiar hurt. Because it was an old truth, known since childhood, even if for a short time in Greece she'd forgotten.

Anyway, that was about to change. Her lips curved in a smile. There *would* be love. She had so much to give her child, and surely it would love her in return.

Believing in Theo might have been a mistake but this pregnancy felt like the most wonderful, miraculous thing in her life. Despite the sickness. Despite even the need to give up her dream of archaeology. Maybe one day she could go back to that. Isla deliberately ignored the pragmatic voice in her head that told her that wasn't going to be possible.

Had she imagined the flash of emotion on Theo's face that made her think he really did care about the baby? What about earlier, when he'd first heard about the pregnancy? He'd frowned, his mouth drawing back in a grimace of disapproval. She hadn't imagined *that*.

Far from looking like a man excited by the prospect

of a child, he'd looked like someone who'd received distasteful news. It had cut her to the heart. She'd taken it as confirmation of what she'd known, that he didn't want to have any more to do with her.

And yet...

Face it. You have no idea what's going on in his head. You never did. What you took for the beginnings of true love was just a vacation seduction.

Isla slid her hand over her flat abdomen, still stunned after all this time at the reality of her pregnancy. If it weren't for the sickness, it wouldn't seem real.

She stared at the bedroom curtains in swirling shades of blue. How often had she lain here, concentrating on that pattern as she fought down morning sickness?

But this time it was different. She heard a muffled noise from the other room and her heart lurched at just how different.

She wasn't resting because she was nauseous, though she did still feel a little light-headed. She was here because Theo insisted she rest before dinner arrived. The dinner he'd arranged so they could talk some more. And she, feeling hollowed out by the impact of one too many surprises, had finally agreed.

That still surprised her. She told herself it was because it had been a long day in a tough week in a difficult few months. It couldn't be because it was a relief, just once, to let someone else organise practicalities, like a meal she probably wouldn't be able to keep down.

Instead of being alone in her tiny flat, Theo was in the next room, so close her skin still tingled from the electric charge that had sparked between them.

A spark she'd told herself had been a figment of an overactive imagination.

He'd touched her and it had been like lightning dancing across her skin. Worse, she'd been shocked at how much she wanted more. Even his scent, of pines, sunshine and the sea, had threatened to undo her.

A knock sounded on the door.

'Wait!' She scrambled up, swinging her legs off the bed. She didn't want Theo in here. It was hard enough sometimes, trying to sleep with memories of the past tormenting her. She didn't need images of him here in her bedroom.

Theo had taken off his jacket when she emerged. That stopped her in the doorway, her heart tripping to a faster beat as she took in his broad-shouldered, narrow-hipped frame.

He had his back to her as he laid out food on her small table.

His sleeves were rolled up and those strong, sinewy forearms, dusted with dark hair, made her breath catch. Isla remembered the feel of his skin against hers, the surprisingly silky softness of that hair tickling her body and the heat his muscle-hardened frame exuded.

The deft, knowing touch of those capable hands as Theo explored her body and took her to places she'd never been before.

Setting her mouth, Isla told herself it was no wonder he'd haunted her thoughts and dreams. No other man had given her such experiences. One day they'd be memories to treasure, once she was over the heartbreak he'd created.

He turned and she saw his tie was gone, the top few buttons of his shirt open to reveal a V of golden skin. Deliberately she averted her gaze. He looked almost too masculine. Too strong and charismatic.

Their affair was over. Neither of them wanted to revive it. Theo because he'd never been serious about her and she because she needed to protect herself.

It's a little too late for that.

'Feel better?'

His gaze snared hers. She tried to read it and failed.

What was new? She'd never really understood him, until it was too late.

'A little.'

Which surprised her. She'd been so wound up she hadn't thought she'd be able to relax with Theo Karalis prowling around her home.

She moved closer to the table, frowning. There were containers everywhere, not just on the table but filling all the counter space.

'What's all this?'

He shrugged and she looked away, not wanting to watch the play of his powerful muscles through the fine material of his shirt.

'Dinner. I didn't know what you felt like so I got a selection.' He paused. 'I know you like spicy food but I thought it might be better to avoid that with your morning sickness.'

Isla nodded and took a seat. 'Good idea. But you're right, I'm hungry.'

It surprised her. Her nausea wasn't confined to mornings and sometimes just the thought of preparing food, even cheese on toast, was almost too much. She only persevered because she knew the baby needed sustenance.

'Excellent.'

He flashed a spontaneous smile and for a moment she was transported back to that tiny dot of land in the Aegean that held one small village, an archaeological site, some olive and pistachio groves, and the secluded little house they'd shared for a short time. When life had seemed glorious with happiness and possibility. Because of Theo.

Heat suffused her, the warmth of wellbeing and excitement. But only for a second, until her brain kicked into gear and reality crashed down.

She scowled and looked away, reaching for a carafe of

water and pouring a glass. From her peripheral vision she saw his face settle into stark lines.

Had he expected to win her over with a smile? Fat chance.

'Are you eating too?'

'When you've decided what you want.'

Like a waiter, he ran through the menu, lifting off lid after lid so the room filled with tantalising aromas. To her amazement, Isla found herself salivating. It all looked and smelled wonderful.

There were no local takeaway outlets that served food like this. Each dish looked exquisite. 'Where did this come from?'

Theo named a luxury hotel in central London, known the world over. The sort of place Isla would never even consider entering. Startled, she looked up to meet his unreadable stare. Was she supposed to be impressed that he'd spent so much? But then he was one of the richest men in Europe.

Her jaw clenched as she recalled how he'd kept that little fact from her in Greece.

Had he been afraid that if she found out she'd have expected expensive gifts? Or was it that he'd preferred to play a role, slumming it with the naïve foreign student for a few weeks before returning to his pampered, privileged life?

'I thought, with an upset stomach, you wouldn't appreciate a greasy takeaway. That's all that was on offer locally.'

His words cut through her bitter thoughts, and he was right. This food actually tempted her to eat. His thoughtfulness and the trouble he'd gone to surprised her. Until she remembered his words about doing the right thing. That he no doubt saw it as his duty to ensure the woman carrying his baby ate.

It wouldn't be a good look if she collapsed from malnutrition.

'What's so funny?'

Isla shook her head. 'Nothing.' She paused. 'Thank you. This was very kind of you.'

She caught him watching her but chose not to meet his eyes. Instead she scooped up some fragrant lemony chicken and a selection of glistening chargrilled vegetables. Only as she began to eat did he help himself to a rich casserole of beef and mushrooms.

Isla swallowed a mouthful then paused, waiting. The feast before her was like a sensual overload, all looking delicious, all smelling fantastic. But she'd learned to be cautious and see if her stomach rebelled.

'What's the matter? It's not to your taste?'

That sounded like genuine concern. 'No, it's lovely.' She swallowed another forkful.

The other kitchen chair creaked as Theo leaned back. 'Good, I'm glad.'

It was more than good, it was delicious. The tastiest thing she'd eaten in she couldn't remember how long. Her lips quirked in a rueful smile as she surveyed her emptying plate. Clearly there was something to be said for having a fortune to spend on meals you didn't feel like preparing yourself.

They ate in silence and Isla felt herself gradually relaxing with each slow mouthful. If she didn't look at the big, handsome man across from her, she could almost enjoy herself. The glorious food which for once she was able to keep down. The end of the day with no more chores to be done. The cosy sense of warmth and comfort.

She blinked and stiffened. No, it couldn't be that she felt that way because Theo was here in her home. Because, despite knowing he wasn't for her, part of her still longed for him.

The idea appalled her and she hurried into speech. 'I

don't understand how you can accept this as your child so easily.'

Theo's cutlery clattered onto his plate. 'You don't? You'd prefer it if I accused you of lying?'

There was an edge to his voice, as if she'd annoyed him.

Isla finished chewing and swallowing before meeting his stare. Sure enough the gleam in his eyes showed he wasn't as sanguine as he'd appeared earlier.

'Of course not. But it seems so unlikely. Remember I know the type of man you are and the sort of world you live in.' Frowning, he opened his mouth as if to take issue and she hurried on. 'Don't forget your lawyer had me sign away my right to tell anyone that we knew each other. Not that that was a loss. It's a period in my life I definitely won't be sharing with anyone.'

'Isla, it was for the best. I was protecting you—'

'No!' She raised her hand. 'I'm not interested in explanations. It's over. Like our relationship.' She didn't need excuses. She knew where she stood. Had known when he refused to see her in prison.

'My point is you inhabit a world where it seems normal, maybe even reasonable, to threaten people into silence. That non-disclosure agreement I signed is an example. If you'd known me as well as you pretended, you'd have known there was no need for a legal document. That tells me something about the people you mix with and how you see yourself. You think you're so important that everyone is eager to take advantage of a connection to you.'

Theo's eyebrows scrunched together in almighty scowl and his jaw clenched in a hard line. He leaned back, arms crossed over his chest.

He looked powerful and forbidding, and to her horror, still appallingly attractive. What would it take to kill this weakness she harboured for him?

'As for threatening me with the charge of harassment—'

He put his hands on the edge of the table as he leaned towards her. 'I told you I didn't know about that.'

'It doesn't matter whether you did. The fact is that your lawyer thought it necessary, he thought it reasonable to take such drastic action without checking. Clearly he believed you'd approve. That tells me that you and he expect the worst from people.'

Isla lifted her chin, holding his glowing gaze, challenging him to disagree. Of course he didn't.

Finally he spoke, his voice soft. 'Don't forget I was in prison at the time. Things weren't exactly normal and people were spreading untrue stories about me.'

A tremor passed through her. Regret? Sympathy? She'd tried for so long to blank this man from her mind and her heart because she felt too much for him. At one time she'd been frantic with worry for him. Now, hearing that hard, almost blank tone as he talked about being locked up and slandered publicly, Isla couldn't help but feel sorry for all he'd gone through.

She looked from her hands, knotted in her lap, back to those remarkable eyes of dark amber flecked with gold. 'I'm sorry. It must have been a nightmare.'

His gaze softened, or did she imagine it? His mouth rucked up at one corner, driving a cleft down his cheek and making him look far, far too appealing.

'Thank you. It was…memorable. But it's over now.' He paused and she tried to read the expression lurking in his eyes. Surely not amusement? 'Go on, you were saying?'

Isla blinked. How had the scandal and the wrongful arrest affected him?

The lazy way he leaned back in his chair, the rueful half smile and the vaguely bored look on his face almost had her believing he'd shrugged off the horrific experience. But she knew it wasn't true. She might not know Theo Karalis as well as she'd once thought she did, but he couldn't fool her completely. This was a man masking strong emotion.

Isla felt the snap and sizzle of his repressed feelings, the iron hard clamp of control. It both reassured, because it reminded her of the man she'd fallen for, and scared her.

She took another sip of water. 'My point is that, since you expect people to try to take advantage of you, it's out of character for you to accept my word that this is your baby.'

His eyes darkened as they dropped to her hand, now resting protectively across her belly. Isla felt heat flood her cheeks but refused to tug her hand away. The issue here wasn't her but Theo.

'Surely you want a paternity test?'

It was the sort of thing that went with non-disclosure agreements, surely? Like prenuptial agreements and the other legalities the mega rich used to protect their wealth.

'You're saying you left Athens and took up with another man?'

'No!'

He was being deliberately obtuse. Isla was thankful he had no idea how totally unrealistic such an idea was. She couldn't imagine any man ever affecting her the way Theo had.

Wasn't that the saddest thing out of all this? Lots of women had their hearts broken. How many continued to hold a soft spot for the callous manipulator who'd dumped them?

'Then I don't see the problem.'

Isla narrowed her eyes and crossed her arms. It was a gesture of obstinacy, and of vulnerability, emphasising her too-slender frame and fragility.

Once again Theo felt a tremor deep beneath his carefully cultivated calm. As if with a simple gesture, she unsettled the sturdy foundations of his life.

No other woman did that to him. Just Isla. He hadn't realised at first and by the time he did he couldn't work out what to do about it. Except tell himself it was temporary. That it would fade once they went their separate ways.

But here they were face to face after months of separation and every accusation, every expression of hurt, felt like the rake of nails drawing blood.

Surely she shouldn't still have the power to affect him?

He wanted to explain why he'd pushed her away but it wasn't just about protecting her from the press or Stavroulis. He shrank from trying to put into words the terrible taint he felt from his prison experience and the way the world branded him guilty. Besides, the damage was done. He'd ensured she was safe, but at such a cost.

Once she'd left Greece his priority hadn't been her but getting free to support his mother and ensure Toula, who'd fallen apart the night of Costa's death, got the care she needed. And making sure the family company didn't fail.

'I need a simple answer to a simple question. Why don't you ask for a paternity test?'

Had Isla always been this obstinate? Why did she have to pursue this?

Because you treated her badly and she's no fool.

Theo exhaled. 'You want the truth? It's simple. I know you, Isla. You don't lie.'

Her eyes rounded and her tightly folded arms dropped. As if he were one of her precious pottery sherds or an ancient coin that had jumped up and started talking to her.

Finally she spoke. Her voice was so husky it grated across every nerve ending. 'You think you know me so well?'

Oh, he knew her all right. Almost from the start she'd felt unaccountably familiar to him, her attitudes, her reactions, even her humour. As if they were old friends. Even in the early days when all he'd really understood was that lightning bolt of attraction, the sense of connection had been as real is it was surprising.

'You're the woman who noticed the waiter at the taverna had accidentally undercharged the dig team for dinner and went back to pay the difference out of her own money. The woman who, with a colleague, first discovered the ancient helmet which turned out to be the most exciting find of the season's dig. When everyone saw how significant it was and your colleague was too shy to claim some of the credit, you made sure she was acknowledged.'

Theo had been there that day and seen for himself. In fact, it looked to him as if Isla had first spotted the gleam of metal and moved away slightly so her companion could make the actual find. He'd discovered later that the other woman hadn't been particularly useful on the project earlier but the find had boosted her confidence and enthusiasm.

Isla shrugged, her chin rising. 'So? That's a little different to claiming to be pregnant by a billionaire. What's to say I'm not scheming to get my hands on your money? That's what your lawyer will think, isn't it?'

'It doesn't matter what Petro thinks.'

All that mattered was what Theo *knew*. Isla Jacobs was genuine and honest.

How many of his friends and acquaintances could he say that about? True, his closest friends had stuck by him but so many others had proven themselves less than friends and less than honest.

Was that why his belief in her felt unshakeable?

'Of course it's my baby. You didn't have time to start a new relationship.'

Strange how the thought of Isla intimate with another man sent his stomach into free fall.

Though logic told him that hadn't happened, he could picture it in his mind with devastating clarity. More easily than he could imagine Isla's slim body changing to accommodate his baby.

Theo accepted the pregnancy as fact but getting used to the idea of an actual baby, of himself as a father, would take a while. Though, if he really focused, perhaps he *could* imagine Isla's pregnancy. His lungs thickened on a short breath. His palms tickled, as he imagined holding her ripening body against his, her skin silky to the touch.

Isla picked up her fork and took another bite of her meal. Theo barely had time to register satisfaction that his plan to entice her with good food had worked, when she spoke.

'It's been months since we separated. I could have been with any number of men.'

It was sheer bravado, he knew, yet he didn't like it. Maybe that explained the harsh edge to his voice. 'You were a virgin before you met me. Weren't you, Isla?'

'You're making assumptions—'

'It was pretty obvious.'

Not in a bad way. Sex with Isla had been memorable every time. That first night, with her so sweet and ardent, so generous yet so surprised, would always live in his memory. Locked up in his cell, fighting not to lose hope, worried about what was happening to those he cared for, he'd revisited that precious memory again and again.

Theo met her eyes and watched a blush rise up her throat to her cheeks.

'You think you're such a fantastic lover you spoiled me for anyone else?'

Her tone was belligerent and her eyes flashed fire but he read hurt there too and instantly felt like a louse.

'Of course not.' Though some immature part of him would like to think so. 'But after waiting so long to have sex, and being so persistent about trying to see me in Athens…' Her blush turned fiery as if he'd accused her of stalking. 'It wouldn't be in character for you to take another lover so fast.'

She said nothing, just clapped her lips together and put her cutlery down.

He went on. 'We had sex a lot and there was that time when the condom split. Besides, if you really were trying to fit me up for money you wouldn't have let Petro's letter put you off. You'd have written back with your news. You'd have hired your own lawyer. Or fed a story to the press for some astronomical sum and hope I'd agree to settle.'

As he watched, the colour leached from her features, making him wish he'd shut up.

She shook her head. 'You really do live in a different world, don't you?'

Being with Isla again made him understand just how different.

Theo couldn't help regretting how their tentative truce had fractured. He shoved his chair back. 'Would you like a hot drink?'

For the longest time she said nothing. Was she about to demand he leave? Except instead of defiance or anger what he saw was exhaustion. Her shoulders sagged and she leaned forward, supporting her drooping head on her hand and an elbow on the table.

The change in her was so quick it stunned him. 'Isla, are you okay?'

'Sure. Just suddenly very weary.'

The ghost of a smile flitted across her lips but she was frowning. He guessed it was only determination that kept her from laying her head on the table and sleeping.

'Go and get ready for bed. I'll clear this up.'

Her head lifted. 'But we haven't…' She lifted one hand in a half-hearted gesture.

He'd been careful as they ate to avoid mentioning the

future. It had been more important that she get a good meal inside her. Besides, there'd been something innately comfortable, almost satisfying, about sharing a quiet dinner with this woman.

Until, inevitably, it seemed, she'd challenged and argued, as if unable simply to accept his presence.

'Haven't talked about the child?'

Isla sat up at his words, her back ramrod straight, eyes narrow with suspicion. Or was that fear?

Theo digested that, a rusty, metallic taste filling his mouth. Isla, scared of him?

His life had changed dramatically recently. He'd experienced things he'd never expected. But not this. The idea of any woman scared of him was anathema.

'It's late, Isla.' Actually, it was quite early but clearly her body clock said otherwise. How had she managed working and caring for herself, when she had so little energy? Theo made his voice as reassuring as he could. 'We'll talk tomorrow. You're right, we have things to discuss.'

'Tomorrow?' She said it like a foreign, unfamiliar word. 'But you said this was a quick trip to London. I thought you were going back to Athens straightaway.'

'That was before I knew about our child.' The idea still made his pulse quicken. 'I've altered my schedule. I'll return tomorrow. We need to talk.'

CHAPTER FIVE

ISLA STARED IN the mirror, surprised to see colour in her cheeks for the first time in ages.

That's what a good night's sleep will do for you. And not waking to instant nausea.

She couldn't believe she'd slept so long and soundly after all that happened yesterday. It was as if her mind and body had shut down, unable to keep functioning and worrying.

That didn't stop her worrying now.

Whatever she thought of Theo Karalis, it seemed he wasn't a man to walk away from an unplanned pregnancy.

She rubbed her hands up her bare arms and shivered. The question being what *was* he going to do?

Her head whirled with possibilities. He lived a life of privilege and wealth. In a world where people could be made to sign gag orders to protect his privacy. Or threatened with legal action for trying to contact him. Would he aim to buy her silence? Provide financial support so they left him alone?

Or would he *want* their child? Would he demand regular access or even, her breath backed up in her lungs, demand to raise it? Try to buy her off or get sole custody?

Was that even possible?

Isla discovered she was gripping the edge of the bathroom basin with both hands, trembling with something alarmingly like the beginnings of panic.

Deliberately she grabbed her hairbrush and began to sort out her morning tangles, concentrating on long, rhythmic strokes and slow breaths.

She was letting her mind run away with her. Theo had lied to her and rejected her but he wasn't a monster.

He'd surprised her yesterday. He might have been prompted by duty rather than fondness, but he'd looked after her.

He'd sent her to get ready for bed while he tidied up and she'd been too drained to object. When she'd returned to the kitchen it was to find the food packaged up and Theo, sleeves rolled high, wiping down the table.

He'd looked at home, familiar in a way that made her heart squeeze. She'd drunk in the sight, memories of happier days filling her head.

Until he'd turned and seen her. True, she'd been wearing a tatty old dressing gown over her sleep shirt, but there'd been nothing in his expression, nothing at all, to hint that he found her attractive.

Once he hadn't been able to get enough of her. Or she him.

That blank, careful stare had confirmed what she already knew. He had no interest in her any more, except that she carried his baby.

He didn't desire her. That was over.

Isla tugged viciously at a knot till her eyes watered.

When the doorbell rang she reached for her dressing gown, to find she'd left it in the bedroom. The bell rang again, long and insistent. Enough to disturb her neighbours.

She hurried to the door, stopping to look through the peephole. Her breath hissed. Annoyance, she told herself. It wasn't excitement. Not even a little bit.

Setting her mouth, she opened the door. 'Have you looked at the time? It's too early for visiting.'

Theo shrugged, that dimple appearing in his cheek and she silently chastised herself for noticing. He was closely shaved, hair slightly damp, and he looked disturbingly wonderful.

'Not too early for breakfast. You need to keep your strength up if you're going to work.'

He stepped through the open door, nudging it closed with his foot as he offered her a carton. In it were white bakery boxes, fresh fruit and takeaway cups.

The smell hit her, pungent and inescapable. Strong coffee, the rich aromatic sort that Greeks seemed to love. That she used to love.

Isla's insides rebelled, her nose crinkling in dismay as her stomach churned. She spun on her bare foot and raced for the bathroom.

Shocked, Theo stared as Isla ran, all long, gorgeous legs and rippling chestnut hair. Yet it wasn't surprise that tightened his grip on the box but a gut-slamming hit of need.

He'd felt it yesterday too, between the shock of Isla's news and being continually berated.

They weren't lovers any more. He'd had to end that for both their sakes. Going back again... He couldn't do that to either of them. Not with the mess his life still was.

But you want her, don't you? That hasn't changed. It wasn't just the news about the baby that kept you from sleep last night, was it?

The sound of the bathroom door slamming, followed almost instantly by retching, set him into action. A few strides took him to the tiny kitchen where he left the food. Then he was at the bathroom door, debating whether to enter or give her privacy.

The sound of running water made him pause. How

could he help? Unless she needed help standing, she wouldn't welcome him.

His intentions had been good. He'd been buoyed by her appetite last night, seeing her eat what looked like her first proper meal in months. But this morning… He shook his head. He should have thought. Morning sickness was called that for a reason.

By the time the bathroom door opened he'd dumped the box outside her apartment.

Her pallor was marked, the hair around her face damp. The change from the pink-cheeked, attractive woman who'd opened the door shocked him. He had to force himself not to ask if she were okay. He'd learned that with his stepsister, Toula, who was always prickly when she felt weak. Instead he held out the glass of water he'd poured.

'Thank you.'

Isla sipped it gingerly, not seeming to notice that spark of heat as their fingers touched.

One-track mind, Karalis. The woman's ill.

But he wasn't, which was why, despite his concern, he couldn't help noticing that in splashing her face, she'd also splashed her oversized T-shirt. It clung to her skin, lovingly shaping the upper slope of one breast.

Hastily Theo looked away, only to find his attention dropping to her bare legs. The T-shirt preserved her modesty, just, but he had perfect recall of the body now barely covered by thin cotton. Heat saturated him.

'Would you feel better sitting down?'

'Where's the coffee?'

'You want some?'

'Absolutely not!' She shuddered. 'The smell makes me nauseous.'

'In that case it's safe to sit in the kitchen. I took it outside. I wasn't sure what part of what I brought upset you.'

So much for congratulating himself that she'd been able

to enjoy the food he'd brought. He'd undone all the good he'd achieved.

Good one, Karalis!

'Don't look so glum,' she said as she lowered herself slowly onto a kitchen chair. 'You weren't to know.'

But he could have guessed. It was logical that strong smells would disturb someone suffering from nausea. 'What can you have?'

'There are rice crackers in the biscuit tin.'

For the next five minutes Theo waited, leaning against the counter, watching as she nibbled slowly at a thin biscuit then stopped, frowning. After a long pause she took a careful sip of water. Then tried the biscuit again. Then another pause as if waiting to see if she could keep that down.

His mood darkened. If this was how Isla ate it was no wonder she was wasting away. Had last night just been a lucky coincidence? How did she manage to stay on her feet all day in the shop? Surely that drained her as much as the morning sickness?

By the time she was on her third cracker he'd had enough. He collected the food he'd put outside, leaving the cups.

Isla said nothing, just watched as he got out plates, one for the fruit and another for the pastries. The inviting scent of fresh baking filled his nostrils and he paused, shooting a look at Isla. She met his stare, raised her eyebrows and shrugged as if to say she didn't know how she'd react either.

It felt, for a second, as if time reeled back on itself, to those days in Greece when spoken conversation wasn't always necessary and they communicated without words. Their shared understanding had surprised Theo, as if they'd known each other years instead of mere weeks.

Whatever their apparent connection, those days were

gone. He put the plates on the table and sat opposite Isla, watching for signs of returning nausea.

She seemed to wait too, as if unsure of her body's reaction. Then she reached for a plump grape and popped one into her mouth.

A smile lit her face. 'Yum. Thank you.'

Theo nodded but didn't speak. Something about her abrupt transformation, from wan and unsure to beaming, thickened his throat. Because she was grateful for such a small favour as fresh fruit? Because every day, every meal, it seemed, was a battle?

How long had it been this bad? Who had she had to help her?

He kept his queries to himself while she ate a few more grapes, watching her hesitate then reach out again. 'Raspberries! And they look freshly picked.'

Her gaze sought his as if wondering where he'd got such fresh produce out of season. Another reminder of their different worlds. For him money was no object. He guessed, his gaze scanning the small room, that for Isla, every penny mattered.

'Did you drop your degree because you're pregnant?' It was a crime, her not continuing. Simon said she was one of the best junior archaeologists he'd seen.

Isla's smile faded but she nodded. 'I couldn't study and have a baby. I needed to get a job.'

Theo's jaw tightened. He could support her while she finished her degree, but things weren't so simple. For a start, Isla would need other support, not just someone to pay her university fees.

That was assuming she'd let him pay. Her blistering animosity yesterday had left its mark. Theo guessed persuading her to let him help would be uphill work.

Just as well he wasn't easily deterred.

But for now her studies weren't the highest priority. 'I've arranged an appointment with an obstetrician today.'

Her chin lifted. 'Thank you. But I need notice to take time off. Rebecca relies on me.'

'Which is why I made it at lunchtime. I can drive you. I'll have you back in good time.'

Shimmering eyes held his and he sensed Isla sought for another objection. Because she didn't like him interfering? Because she didn't like *him*?

Theo's belly clenched in repudiation. But this wasn't about him. This was about getting Isla to do what was necessary to look after herself and their child.

Their child.

His thoughts slowed even as his pulse quickened.

'I'll talk with Rebecca. If the timing suits then I'll take the appointment.'

Theo nodded, forbearing from saying he'd already contacted her boss and cleared it with her. He didn't want any excuse for Isla to back out.

It had been a useful, if initially frosty, conversation. When the older woman saw he was serious in his concern for Isla she'd been remarkably helpful, even receptive to his other suggestions. But Isla wasn't ready to hear about those. Let her take one step at a time.

His ex-lover was strong-minded. He'd known it before but it was only now, as he saw how she battled valiantly with this daily struggle, that he realised how strong.

Inevitably his thoughts turned to Toula. His stepsister faced different problems, including years of early neglect and, he suspected, abuse. Was it any wonder she suffered with depression and had turned to substance abuse under the influence of Costa Stavroulis? Yet he couldn't help comparing Toula's attempts to avoid things she didn't want to face and Isla's determination to manage her life by confronting reality, not hiding from it.

Instantly he felt ashamed. That was unfair. Toula had demons even he didn't fully understand. She was doing the best she could and at least now she was getting professional help to deal with them.

'Theo? Did you hear me?'

'Sorry.' He found Isla watching him. Her eyes were brighter and she looked more like the woman he remembered. Her shining hair fell in waves below her shoulders, drawing his attention to her puckered nipples against the thin T shirt.

'Don't you want something to eat?'

Theo swallowed and made himself reach for a pastry. He was hungry, but not for baked goods.

But he couldn't sate his real appetite, for Isla Jacobs.

Apart from the fact she was unwell, this was no time to complicate things with sex.

He wasn't her favourite person after the way he'd pushed her away. Plus it would muddy the waters when they had important decisions to make. Theo intended to persuade her into seeing things his way. Ravishing her might bring short-term delight but at the risk of destroying his long-term plans.

Time to start implementing those plans.

He withdrew a folded paper from his jacket and pushed it across the table. 'I brought this for you. To confirm what I told you yesterday.'

Theo didn't want her having second thoughts about spending time with him.

Isla's brow furrowed as she read the official document. It was an English translation and confirmed that the murder charge had been dropped against him and he was a free man.

Theo knew she understood that or she wouldn't have let him into her home. Yet he remembered earlier yesterday, when she'd called him a murderer. He'd been astounded at how appalled he'd been. The world might insinuate such things but *her* accusation had wounded him in a way he hadn't expected.

'I'm sorry, Theo.' Her eyes were too big for her face as she met his gaze. 'I was being bitchy when I called you a murderer.' Her shoulders lifted as she drew a slow breath. 'I knew it wasn't true. I should never have said it. I was just…'

'You don't need to explain.' Neither had been at their best. 'We were both grappling with a lot. I just wanted to clear up any reservations.'

'I *am* sorry though. That you had to go through all that. It must've been terrifying.'

Theo sprawled back in his chair as if the memory of that time didn't still make him tense. 'It's over now.'

'Is it? Have they arrested the killer? I hadn't heard that.'

He sat straighter, no longer able to pretend to insouciance. 'No. Investigations are continuing. They're looking at everyone who attended the party.'

There had been a crowd at the Karalis family home that night. It would take the police ages to investigate them all, now their star suspect's alibi had been proven. Ice trickled down his spine as he considered how that investigation would affect his family. That someone close to him could be arrested.

'It definitely wasn't an accident? He didn't trip and fall down the stairs?'

How much easier if he had.

'Costa Stavroulis was in a foul mood. A witness heard him arguing with someone at the top of the stairs so he wasn't alone.' Theo's dislike of the man had been no secret, especially as he'd previously warned the guy away from Toula. 'Moments later he fell backwards. There were marks on his chest where someone had pushed him.'

The bruising proved he'd been shoved but couldn't provide solid evidence about the size of the person who did it.

Theo shook off thoughts of the crime and focused on Isla. She had to be his priority now. She and the child she carried.

'Why don't you finish your breakfast? When you're ready, I'll take you to work. Then you can check about taking time off to see the doctor.'

The morning went smoothly. More smoothly than any she could remember lately. Her nausea had abated soon after Theo's arrival and she'd kept down not merely some fruit, but a croissant and a cup of tea. Instead of feeling exhausted and empty, she actually had a little energy.

With the prospect of a lift in Theo's car, Isla had plenty of time to shower and dress. Time to dither over what she'd wear. When she found herself debating between a warm, rust-coloured dress or jeans and a blue top that complemented her eyes, she was horrified.

She wasn't interested in impressing Theo.

Was she?

Firming her mouth, she grabbed plain black trousers. She reached for a pullover, but her fingers stalled as she touched the ultra-soft mohair Rebecca had let her take at an enormously discounted price. Isla had only finished knitting it last week into one of the nicest items of clothing she'd ever owned, a snuggly but stylish tunic in jade green.

She should shove it away. Wasn't the point that she *wasn't* dressing up for Theo?

Still she hesitated, then hauled it on and smoothed it over her hips. If wearing something nice made her feel more confident, there was nothing wrong with that.

Being with Theo was tough. He was the man she'd once imagined spending her life with. Now she wasn't sure if he was an ally or an adversary. Her nerves jangled. They still had to discuss plans for the baby. Then there was the obstetrician's appointment. Would it be good news?

When she got to the shop Rebecca had no objections to her scheduled appointment. Isla read relief in the older woman's eyes at the news she was getting another medical opinion.

It was after that when things started to run out of control.

The doctor confirmed that the pregnancy was well on track and discussed treatment for nausea. Fortunately she saw no reason for hospitalisation and after detailed questions, was hopeful Isla's symptoms might ease soon. Isla *did* feel a lot better than she had for ages, possibly because she'd had so much sleep and managed to keep down some food.

The doctor arranged a follow-up appointment but advised Isla to avoid stress and rest as much as possible. She strongly suggested time off work, to allow Isla a chance to regain some strength.

Isla's heart sank. That wasn't easy for a woman who needed to support herself and save for the future.

As if that weren't enough, instead of driving her straight back to the shop, Theo pulled up in front of a small, expensive restaurant, insisting she needed to eat before returning to work.

Isla sat in the luxury car, staring through the plate glass windows at the welcoming scene inside, and felt trapped. By the doctor's orders that she had no capacity to follow. By Theo's insistence that he knew what was best. By her body's weariness and the hollow feeling that said Theo was right and she needed to eat.

It was unreasonable to be annoyed, but she was. In twenty-four hours her world had turned on its head again and she no longer felt like she was running her own life.

It was too far to walk to the shop and she didn't have the

energy to work out the bus route, yet she was tempted to get out and walk away. She'd been essentially alone all her life. Growing up in institutions she'd learned early to take responsibility for herself. The one time she'd begun to feel she belonged with someone had been with Theo and she'd been proved utterly wrong. Maybe she'd allowed herself to be deluded because she'd always secretly sought love.

Now the feeling she was no longer in control unnerved her.

'Shall we?' Theo reached for the car door, sure she'd agree to his plan. He hadn't even asked, just decided for her.

Isla drew a breath and ignored the urge to tell him she wasn't hungry. She needed to be sensible for the baby's sake. 'You go ahead. I need to ring Rebecca.'

He shot her an assessing look then nodded. But instead of entering the restaurant, he waited on the pavement, using his phone. Annoying Theo Karalis might be, but he respected her privacy. He'd left her alone during her medical examination too, only returning to hear the outcome.

Isla rang her boss and explained where she was. For some obscure reason she wished Rebecca would say the shop was busy and she was needed urgently.

'Of course you must take time for a proper meal. And it will give you and Theo time to talk.' Rebecca sounded enthusiastic. Probably because Isla had confided that Theo was her baby's father.

'Only if you're sure…'

'Absolutely! In fact,' Rebecca said, 'I've got someone coming to help this afternoon on a trial basis to see how she works out.'

Isla frowned. 'You're taking on new staff? Is there enough work for three of us?'

There was silence for a moment and when Rebecca spoke it sounded like she chose her words carefully. 'It's good to have backup. There have been days when you were so unwell you shouldn't have been in the store. I feel guilty about that.'

'You shouldn't! It's my job to be there. I'd never let you down.'

'I know you wouldn't, Isla. This is just a precaution. If this new person works out then she can fill in if I need to be away for a few days. And when the baby comes.'

Apprehension scuttled along Isla's spine like spidery fingers. She couldn't fault Rebecca's thinking. She *would* need more staff when Isla gave birth. But if this replacement proved good, and more reliable than a new mum managing on her own, maybe Rebecca would keep her full-time instead of Isla.

And maybe you're getting ahead of yourself.

She forced herself to smile as she spoke. 'It's good to be prepared. I hope she works out okay.'

'She sounded very capable. In fact, why don't you have the afternoon off? Then you can have a proper conversation with Theo. Oops. I've got to go. Enjoy your lunch.'

There it was again, the feeling that Isla's life was unravelling. Surely she was overreacting, yet that brief conversation compelled her to consider facts that previously she'd preferred not to dwell on.

She'd need time off work when the baby came. How long would her savings last? Rebecca was a good friend as well as her employer, but she had a business to run and couldn't leave a position open for her indefinitely.

Then there was childcare. Isla wasn't sure she could afford it and though Rebecca would probably allow her to take an infant into the shop, it wasn't a long-term solution.

And then there was Theo.

'Problems?'

He was at her door, an easy smile on his face but something in his eyes that wasn't at all easy. It struck her again that Theo was a very powerful man, used to getting his own way.

'Nothing I can't handle.'

She *would* handle it. All of it. Somehow she'd find a way to manage. She always had in the past and now she had her child to consider, all the more reason to be strong.

Ten minutes later they were seated in a luxurious booth as a waiter poured sparkling water and took their orders.

'Nice place,' Isla murmured as the waiter left. It was more upmarket than anywhere she'd ever eaten, with an air of understated elegance. Even the occasional clatter of cutlery and the murmur of voices was discreetly muffled.

'I'm told the food's good.'

'It should be, at those prices.'

Glowing brown eyes met hers and she saw a flicker of amusement. Almost like the old days—

Isla looked away. It wasn't the past that mattered, it was the future. 'We need to talk.'

'My thoughts exactly. We have a lot to discuss. Where shall we start?'

Isla turned back and there it was again, deep in those remarkable, leonine eyes. Determination. The look of a man who knew what he wanted and how to get it. Why did it unnerve her?

She sipped her water, feeling the bubbles hit the roof of her mouth. Like the effervescence in her blood when Theo had made love to her.

And wasn't *that* a memory best forgotten?

'Tell me straight, Theo. What do you want?'

His wry grin was far too appealing. 'Apart from lunch?'

'With the baby. You haven't said anything other than to agree that it's yours.' Was it any wonder she was on tenterhooks? 'Do you want to be involved?'

Theo held her gaze as he nodded. 'Absolutely. I want

our child to have the love and support of both parents. All the time.'

Isla blinked. What had she expected? That because he was a billionaire he'd hold aloof from their child?

'When it's old enough to travel we could sort out some arrangement.'

Her voice petered out at the thought of being parted from this baby she hadn't even met. It felt wrong. But she had to be reasonable. Theo was right, she'd do whatever it took to ensure her baby had the love and support of both parents. For she knew exactly how important that was, none better.

'You misunderstand me. That's not what I had in mind.'

'It's not?'

Theo shook his head, his eyes never leaving hers. 'I want our child to have both its parents. Together. As a family.' His mouth curled in one of those trademark smiles that, to her dismay, could still melt a vital part of her. 'I want you to marry me, Isla.'

CHAPTER SIX

THEO HAD NEVER imagined saying those words to any woman. So it was strange that they should settle, low and warm in his belly, feeling like truth.

He saw panic flare in Isla's expressive eyes but felt none himself. Prior to this he hadn't been ready to give up his freedom and tie himself to one woman for life. But he was ready now and when Theo made a commitment he stuck by it.

He'd seen the downside of broken families and wanted none of it for his child. The thought of abandoning a child knotted his belly. He'd *never* turn his back on this baby.

Yet it was more than that. There was something satisfying, almost reassuring, about claiming Isla for himself. Pushing her away had been incredibly difficult. A decision he'd regretted though he knew he had to do it.

Theo wasn't naïve enough to believe marrying Isla would be easy, despite the throb of sexual awareness that underscored every contact with her. In fact that complicated things. He needed to manage the situation and persuade her to his way of thinking. Instead he kept getting distracted by this enticing, infuriating woman.

Their physical attraction was one more thing to build on to convince her. Besides, they'd shared more than that, hadn't they? He hadn't imagined the joy or connection between them.

True, he hadn't told Isla the full truth of who he was, but that was because he'd felt he was sharing his essential self with her. The money, business connections and power weren't all there was to him. There'd been something precious in knowing Isla's response had nothing to do with his money. That she responded to Theo, the man, not the billionaire businessman.

'Marriage. That's a bit excessive, don't you think?'

Theo read amusement in Isla's face, as if she were too sophisticated to take the idea seriously. But she couldn't conceal the throbbing pulse at her throat or the way her hand shook as she reached for her glass.

Because she feared him? Everything within him rebelled at the idea and he forced himself to remember how she'd accepted his innocence. But if Isla wasn't afraid the stories of his guilt were true, what did she fear?

Maybe she's not afraid. Maybe she's decided she really doesn't like you.

Once, she'd *more* than liked him. She'd looked at him as if he'd hung the very stars in the sky and he hadn't been able to get enough of that, and her.

Pain was a black, aching chasm inside at what he'd lost. But even if she hated him now, she'd cared once. If her furtive looks proved anything, she was still attracted. That was a weakness he could exploit, for the sake of their baby.

'Not excessive at all. I've been thinking as I'm sure you have. I want our child to have the best start in life.' He shook his head. 'No, more than that, the best life it can have.'

'You think that's likely if it's raised by two people who don't care for each other?'

Theo surveyed Isla. Her chestnut hair was pulled back in a thick plait and she wore little, if any makeup. Yet that pared-back look emphasised her fine bone structure, the sweet curve of her pale pink lips, the intelligence in her eyes and the determination in the angle of her jaw. Her deep green top complemented her colouring and emphasised an innate air of elegance.

Familiar desire ignited, fiery trails heating his veins. How could the wanting be so sharp when she surveyed him so coolly? When she'd done nothing to entice him?

The first time Theo had seen her, Isla had worn dusty trousers, shirt and disreputable straw hat. He'd taken one look at her serious face as she discussed a fragment of pottery with Simon, then heard her chuckle, the sound like liquid sunshine, and hadn't noticed anyone else.

She'd captivated him though he hadn't been able to put a finger on why, exactly. She was more down-to-earth than his previous lovers. More self-sufficient. More earnest about her work. Yet when she gave herself, it was unstinting, opening her mind and body in a way that made him feel like he'd been given the world.

She was a woman whose beauty and personality transcended clothes. Yet the male in him hungered to see her in satin and lace, beckoning him to her bed.

'I care about you, Isla.'

No matter what he'd let her believe, what he'd told himself in prison, it had never been merely sex between them.

'You've got a strange way of showing it.' Her eyes flashed and it was like summer lightning stabbing out of a blue sky. 'You lied about who you were then you rejected me. That's not caring.'

Theo nodded and sat back as the waiter brought their food. He wasn't used to explaining his motives. In the years since he'd taken control of his father's company, he'd grown accustomed to making decisions, not just for himself but setting the direction for a commercial enterprise worth billions.

Perhaps that was why he felt unsettled. It couldn't be

nerves at the idea Isla wouldn't accept his explanation or his plan to marry.

He waited till she'd begun to eat, wanting to make sure she *could* eat. But she tackled her food with no sign of nausea, as if she preferred to focus on that rather than him.

'You're right. I should have told you who I was from the start. I suppose I was used to being accepted as simply Theo when I came to the village. And Simon doesn't treat me any different because of the money.'

'But the money does make a difference when you're talking about billions.'

'True. Can you understand why it was appealing, connecting with a woman just as Theo? To be accepted for myself and not for status or material things?' He hadn't realised how important that was until he met Isla.

'You mean you're a poor little rich boy?'

Theo grunted with laughter. 'Hardly. I know how lucky I am to have all I do. And I have no trouble identifying people who are genuine and those who aren't. But it's a fact that people who meet me are aware of my wealth. It's not unusual for them to want to make my acquaintance because of what I can do for them. It's why my short breaks on the island feel precious, as if I'm reconnecting.'

Theo frowned. He hadn't thought about it in those terms before but it explained why increasingly he'd gravitated there and why he was considering building a house on the land where his great-grandparents had lived.

Athens didn't hold the appeal it once had, not surprising given recent disastrous events. On the island everyone knew who he was but treated him as an equal. They protected his privacy from outsiders, which was why the rest of the archaeological team hadn't known his identity.

'Reconnecting to what?'

He took his time, chewing a morsel of food while he

collected his thoughts. What, indeed? He hadn't grown up
on the tiny island where he and Isla had met.

'I wasn't born to money, you know.'

He saw her puzzled expression. She must be one of the
few people who hadn't researched his life from the mul-
titude of media reports. Theo didn't know whether to be
pleased or disappointed.

'My mother was born on the island, in that little house
where you and I stayed. She left to work in Athens before
I was born. That's where she met my father and where I
grew up.'

'It must have been a big change for her, from life on a
tiny island to being the wife of such a wealthy man.'

'It was. More than you imagine.' Theo's smile felt tight.
'Constantin Karalis wasn't my biological father.'

It was clear from Isla's expression that she didn't know.

'My mother fell in love with a man who wasn't good
enough for her. He dumped her when he discovered she
was pregnant and she never saw him again. She spent the
next ten years working every hour she could to support
herself and me.'

'She didn't go home?'

Theo shook his head. 'Her father had very traditional
views about children born outside marriage. I think she
wronged him and hope he'd have welcomed her back. But
she's stubborn too.'

'A family trait?'

He smiled. 'Could be. But we were happy together, we
made a great team. I couldn't ask for a better mother. But
believe me,' he leaned across the table towards the woman
who carried his baby, 'I know how tough it can be raising
a child on your own.'

She stiffened. 'You think I'm not up to it?'

'Not at all. I've never met a more determined, self-
sufficient woman. If anyone could do it well, you could.'

Theo watched warm colour suffuse Isla's cheeks. It made her look flustered yet proud and beautiful and his heart plunged into a faster beat.

'But I don't subscribe to the theory that love alone is enough to raise a child successfully. Life is easier when each day isn't a financial struggle.'

'Are you saying that if I don't agree to marriage, you won't provide financial support for the baby?'

Her words stunned him. Instead of looking worried or outraged Isla's expression betrayed something like satisfaction, as if he'd proved her worst imaginings. Theo's patience frayed. He was tired of her expecting the worst, making him out to be some villain.

'I made mistakes, Isla, and I've apologised. But isn't your distrust getting out of hand?'

He shook his head, annoyed at letting it get to him. He was used to being the one people trusted. Whom they turned to for help. The one who solved problems and looked after his family. Isla scored his already battered pride.

'I meant exactly what I said, no more. My mother and I were happy but I remember days during the economic downturn when she lost her job and I went to bed hungry, even though she went without to provide for me. I remember her working for employers who took advantage of her, underpaying her and making her work long hours, but she didn't feel she could leave, because she needed the money for me. I remember how tough it was when I was sick and she couldn't afford babysitting but couldn't afford to take time off work.'

Theo paused, thinking of when they'd lost their apartment and been homeless for a while. Theo had been determined to keep them both safe, though being so young, he'd worried he mightn't be up to the task.

He recalled the gut-wrenching distress of those days.

It was one of the reasons for his discreet support for sub-
sidised housing schemes. No one should have to experience that.

'It wasn't just money. There were times when, I realise
now, she would have loved a shoulder to lean on, to share
the burden of bringing up a rambunctious boy, too full of
energy. And times when I would have loved a male role
model.'

His mother was amazing and he loved her dearly. Yet
he understood in hindsight he'd missed what his friends
had, a man to share with and learn from.

'I remember the day we met Constantin Karalis. We
were walking a couple of kilometres to the bus and this big
car pulled up beside us. The man in the back seat offered
us a lift but my mother refused. She wasn't into charity
and I think she was suspicious of accepting a favour from
someone so obviously well-off.'

'She expected he'd want something in return?'

'Possibly.' He smiled. 'My mother is very attractive.'

'It must run in the family.'

To his surprise an answering smile tugged the corner
of Isla's mouth. Had his revelation softened her view of
him? It wasn't the vivid blaze of delight he recalled from
the past, when her grins had been pure joy, yet even this
muted smile felt like an incredible win.

'I suspect the same is true in your family.'

Her smile faded. 'I've no idea. I never knew my parents.'

Astonished, Theo stared. He remembered her saying
she had no family and had deliberately not prodded for
more information because her tone hadn't invited questions. He'd assumed they'd died recently.

'I'm sorry.' The words were inadequate. He couldn't
imagine never knowing his mother or Constantin or even
Toula. He felt devastated for what she'd missed. 'Who
raised you?'

'Not family.' Her mouth compressed in a tight line that forestalled further questions. How could he not have known about this when in Greece he'd felt he'd known her so well? 'You haven't finished telling me about Constantin Karalis.'

She was trying to divert him. Curiosity seared. Theo wanted to know about Isla's past, not just because it might help him persuade her to his way of thinking but because he wanted to know *everything* about her.

The realisation was profound, another reminder of his powerful feelings for her in Greece. Before his world came undone and he'd made himself push her away.

With an effort he buried his curiosity, for now.

'Every day after that, the big car would stop before we got to the bus stop and he'd offer a lift. My mother kept refusing until the day it poured with rain and her umbrella blew inside out.' Theo laughed. She'd been so haughty and stiff when she accepted the ride, as if *she* were bestowing the favour.

'It was Constantin Karalis in the car?'

'It was. He was an incredibly patient man. It took a lot to win my mother over.'

'What exactly?'

Isla leaned closer, as if caught up in the story. Theo guessed she had no idea how engaged she looked. And how engaging. From the first there'd been something he couldn't name, something deep and true about her that reached out to him at a subliminal level.

A smile broke across his face as he sat back. 'He offered to take me fishing.'

She looked perplexed. 'Fishing?'

Theo nodded. 'At a place on the coast not far from where he lived.' He grinned. 'We had no luck, but it was marvellous. I didn't share my mother's reservations and the experience was new and exciting. Constantin treated me like an adult, not a kid.'

He paused, savouring the memory. 'The next time we fished, we had no better luck, but still it was fun. The third time, he persuaded my mother to let us take his boat out, as a treat for my tenth birthday. Later he confided he hadn't dared take me on his big cruiser earlier because my mother would assume he was trying to impress with his wealth.'

'He took you fishing to get close to your mother?'

Theo shrugged. 'We built up a rapport on those car trips. But yes, he did. Before you label him as ruthless, using a child to get to its mother, you should know he and I remained friends for the rest of his life. Right up until he died we went fishing together and those times were some of the happiest of my life.'

Theo held Isla's gaze. 'I loved the man and he loved me. Until I met him fatherhood had negative connotations for me. The man who fathered me doesn't deserve the name. Being a father is about being there through thick and thin, the tough times as well as the good. About creating a warm, caring home.'

He watched her chest rise then lower on a huge sigh as if she only just understood how determined he was. 'You're telling me that's what you want to do?'

'Absolutely. The only things I have in common with my biological father are the genes I carry. I'm not going to turn my back on you or our child. I intend to be a proper father. Hopefully a good one.'

A spreading warmth filled Theo's chest.

Isla and he might not be in love but they were honest, decent people. They would care for their child and create a good home. The fierce physical attraction between them was a bonus even if at the moment, Isla seemed immune to him. That was something he could work on.

He looked forward to it.

'You look very smug. You're so sure I'll agree?' Isla pursed her lips. 'What if ours was a dysfunctional marriage? That would be no good for anyone, especially the baby.'

Theo kept his voice calm and low, as he did when reassuring Toula on one of her bad days. 'With goodwill on both sides there's no reason it would be dysfunctional.'

'You think you scared me with the tale of how tough it was for your mother as a single parent? That I should marry you so I don't have to worry about making ends meet? Do you really think not having two parents who live together is the worst thing in the world?'

He watched the unconscious lift of Isla's chin. But in her expression was something more than accusation. Something that caught at his gut.

Fear.

A second later it was gone and she looked so calm Theo wondered if he'd imagined it. But her words echoed in his head, making him wonder anew about her upbringing. She'd had neither parent. Who had cared for her?

As for broken families, his own experience hadn't been bad, not like Toula's. Suffice to say he'd seen the terrible effect emotional scars from childhood could have.

'I'm not trying to scare you. I'm explaining how I feel. I believe our child will thrive in a united family. Far better than if we're shuttling him or her between us. Children seem to do best in a stable environment, don't you agree?'

Unwillingly it seemed to him, Isla nodded. 'Stability is important but that doesn't mean we have to marry and live together. Families take lots of forms.' She paused and Theo would have given much to know what was going through her mind. 'If we live separate lives it means we can both pursue our own…interests.'

Interests? Did she mean lovers?

A sour taste filled his mouth. The thought of Isla with

another man was unpalatable. How civilised that sounded when at a deep, visceral level, something hard and primitive exploded at the idea. Theo had never been possessive but Isla was unlike any other lover.

She's the mother of your child. Of course you don't want her going off with anyone else.

Theo considered himself a civilised, reasonable man but, he discovered, he wouldn't stand for another man acting as father to his child. Surely that was at the root of his dismay, not simply the idea of Isla with someone else.

'What interests do you have that you can't pursue if we marry?' He kept his voice easy, concealing his harsh jangle of emotions. 'If you're talking about your career in archaeology, that would be easier if you married me.'

'Because you can pull strings to get me work?' Her tone was cool but her eyes shone brightly. 'I don't like nepotism.'

'Nor do I. I meant that if we were married, you'd have financial support to allow you to continue your studies and a family to help care for our child. You wouldn't have to manage on your own.'

For several seconds Isla said nothing and he wondered if he'd finally convinced her, until she said in a low voice, 'But at what personal cost?'

Theo stiffened. Was the prospect of marrying him so appalling? Despite his determination to woo her carefully, his patience frayed. Until logic overcame ego.

Why would Isla want you after the hurt you caused?

It didn't matter how noble his intentions had been, he'd lost her trust. That's what he had to build again. He needed to find out if she was just set against marrying him or against marriage in general.

The waiter cleared their starter plates, followed by another waiter bringing the main courses. Not that Theo was

hungry, no matter how delicious the food. But the inter-
ruption gave him time to regroup.

After the staff had gone he took a bite of his meal, after
seeing Isla start hers. Even then he waited. She'd barely
touched her first course and he needed to be sure it was
because of their conversation, not sickness. To his relief
she ate slowly, but steadily.

Maybe because it's easier than arguing with you.

But Theo couldn't feel guilty about putting his case. It
was for her benefit as much as the baby's. She'd see that
once she had time to consider.

Meanwhile he needed to tread carefully. If she discovered the lengths he'd gone to in order to get his way on
this, she'd dig her heels in even more. Not that he'd done
anything wrong. Seeing a specialist had been a priority. As
was ensuring she felt free to leave her home and her job.

Isla was loyal. The way she'd stuck by him when he'd
been arrested proved that.

His out-of-hours conversation with Isla's employer had
been carefully considered. He'd been frank about his concerns for Isla and his desire to look after her and the child.
His worry that work and illness was affecting her health.
Fortunately her employer shared his concerns, so when
he spoke about taking Isla to Greece for a rest, Rebecca
had been supportive, while reiterating that it was Isla's
decision.

But Theo knew Isla wouldn't leave if she felt she was
letting Rebecca down. So he'd had his staff busy finding
be perfect replacement for her at the store and the woman
was having a trial this afternoon.

Is that why Isla had looked bereft after talking with
Rebecca? For a moment Theo felt guilty. But he wasn't
forcing her hand, just ensuring there'd be no impediments
when she agreed to his plan.

'You're not eating,' she said. 'Don't you like the food?'

Her concern surprised him. Did she care about him more than she admitted?

For the past twenty-four hours he'd seen a new Isla. That temper was new and though she'd been stubborn about visiting the prison, they'd never been at loggerheads before. Yet he saw both traits as signs of strength. They would have helped her through the last months. And, given her expression when her childhood was mentioned, possibly earlier.

'I've got a lot of my mind,' he murmured.

Her throaty chuckle surprised him. Heat trickled through his veins, pooling in his belly and reminding him of how this woman had once sated his mind and his body.

'Welcome to my world.'

Theo's mouth tugged into an answering smile. 'At least you've had time to get used to it. It still feels a bit unreal.'

It wasn't what he planned to say. Yet maybe it was the right thing to admit for Isla nodded, looking more relaxed than she had since they'd arrived.

She looked rueful, not upset. 'Tell me about it. It's a lot to take in.'

'Did you always want to have children?'

'One day in the future.' Her expression softened. 'I always thought it would be rather nice to have someone…'

Infuriatingly she didn't finish her sentence and he knew better than to badger her for an answer.

Someone what? Some partner to father her baby? Or was she talking about a child? Had she longed to be a mother? Had the people who'd raised her inspired her to want children?

Theo felt a wave of tenderness that had nothing to do with her pregnancy.

'I'm not suggesting we rush into marriage.' Though that would suit him. He watched her head jerk up, her gaze meshing with his. 'Take your time. Consider the implications.' When she did she'd see he was right.

Slowly she nodded yet she didn't look as comfortable as she had a few moments before.

But Theo had a plan to convince her. And it didn't include Isla working herself to the bone in London while he was in Athens. At any other time he'd stay in England to persuade her but he was needed at home, and it was an obligation he couldn't ignore. His family needed him now more than ever.

He leaned across and smiled encouragingly. He wasn't vain but he knew the effect that smile had on women, including Isla.

'What you need is to rest like the doctor said and get your strength back. A break from work. Why not come to Greece with me?'

Her misty blue eyes widened and he hurried on before she could reject the idea out of hand. 'We can discuss my proposal in detail and in the meantime the holiday will do you good.' He paused, making himself take his time so she didn't feel rushed or forced. Deliberately he widened his smile. 'What do you say, Isla? Can I tempt you?'

CHAPTER SEVEN

IT WAS A totally impossible idea, as Isla told Theo.

Going to Greece would be madness when she had no intention of marrying him. Even if the idea of having him remove her money worries was appealing. A billionaire's wife wouldn't have to worry about making ends meet.

But she couldn't raise his expectations.

Besides, she had a strong feeling that giving this man an inch would mean he'd take every future mile.

She understood now, as she hadn't before, what this child meant to Theo Karalis. When he'd spoken with scorn of his biological father, and the tough times he and his mother had endured, she'd seen a man with depth and passion. With strong feelings, not just about duty, which was what she'd imagined drove his need to be involved. Instead she discovered Theo already felt a bond with his unborn child.

He was determined to be a good father.

Isla was simultaneously nervous about the complications that would bring and delighted. Didn't her baby deserve love? Didn't it deserve everything good? All the things she'd never had.

Today she'd seen flashes of the man she'd known and fallen for so precipitately and it had set her battered heart yearning. Marriage would give their child the family she'd never had. Except theirs would be a sham marriage, not based on mutual love. Isla couldn't accept that. Better their child have two loving parents who lived apart.

Though she respected and admired Theo because of his feelings for their child, she now knew him for a powerful man used to having his wishes obeyed.

The idea made her shiver. Because he'd made it clear he wanted her baby.

Not Isla.

He wasn't interested in rekindling their romance, despite suggesting marriage. Far from it. He'd made no attempt to play on the intense attraction they'd shared. The attraction *she* still felt, despite every attempt to stifle it. He wasn't interested in her any more.

Isla was grateful he didn't pretend to feelings that didn't exist. Yet she felt disappointed. He wanted to marry her to get his hands on his child but not enough to try seducing her into compliance.

So how was it that now, this same evening, she found herself in a private jet about to land in Athens?

'Okay, Isla?'

She swung round to see Theo, beside her in another luxuriously padded chair, concern on his face.

'Why shouldn't I be?'

She'd been offered every luxury from heated, delicately scented face cloths to gourmet food and freshly squeezed juice. There'd even been a bed to lie on and a stack of magazines and newspapers, including two specialist archaeology journals that Theo must have ordered in especially.

His ability to make the impossible happen at short notice scared her.

Not for the first time Isla wondered at the coincidental timing of Rebecca finding the perfect substitute to take her place in the shop. And that the newcomer was available without notice. But surely Theo had had nothing to do with that. How could he? Her imagination was running rampant.

'Your jaw is clenched and I thought you might be feeling ill.'

He was right. She felt the ache at the back of her mouth and deliberately relaxed it. 'I'm fine. No nausea.'

In fact, apart from a moment when she got too close to someone smoking outside the airport, there'd been no queasiness since this morning. Maybe the doctor was right and her morning sickness *was* beginning to ease.

'But something's bothering you.'

Isla held his stare. 'It's been an eventful day. I can't help feeling I've been railroaded into this.'

Theo stilled then tilted his head as if intrigued. He looked curious but not in the least guilty. 'No one pressured you, Isla. I offered and you accepted.'

'I know. I'm sorry, that was unfair of me.'

She'd been uncharacteristically short-tempered since he arrived in London, caught in a welter of conflicting emotions that seesawed wildly. Was it pregnancy hormones making her suspicious and ready to anger? More likely the legacy of their past, when he'd let her down so badly.

What he said *was* true. This had been her choice. Yet it didn't feel that way. It felt as if the world conspired to make her fall in with his wishes.

Theo had suggested she fly with him tonight after taking a phone call during lunch. He'd looked at the number then apologised and excused himself. He'd returned looking sombre and saying he was needed urgently in Athens.

His observation that flying back with him would be easier than making her own way to Greece later was nothing but the truth. Flying privately was quicker and simpler than commercial travel. Plus he'd reassured her that he could have her back in London in time for her next doctor's appointment.

He'd even offered to pay her rent for the period she was

away, since she wouldn't be earning. Before she could object, he'd added that she'd be doing him a favour in visiting Greece, allowing them to talk face to face and reach some decisions. The alternative was a series of long-distance calls, because the business crisis he had to deal with in Greece would take time to sort out.

Put like that, his suggestion seemed almost reasonable. Two mature adults determining how to raise their baby.

Still Isla had refused. She didn't like acting on the spur of the moment and she couldn't let Rebecca down.

But when he'd suggested she call her boss to ask about leave, Rebecca had been enthusiastic. Isla knew she'd been worried about her health, but not how much. Her boss had been adamant she take this break, overriding Isla's protests with assurances the replacement worker who'd done a trial that afternoon was excellent.

Isla had rung off feeling that Rebecca would shoo her out the door if she dared front up for work tomorrow.

Even then she might not have agreed, hating this feeling she was being herded in a direction she didn't want to go. Except who could resist the idea of a short break in Greece? Not to work but to rest and relax. Her weary body and even more exhausted brain couldn't withstand that temptation. She put it down to temporary insanity.

So here she was, looking out at the floodlit Parthenon below, the glittering blanket of city lights and beyond that the black velvet of the sea. A shiver kissed her skin. Excitement or warning?

'Maybe it's been too much of a rush.' Theo's voice sounded reflective as if he only just noticed how stressful today had been. 'You'll feel better in the morning. You can sleep in and spend the day relaxing.'

Isla would love to think so, but if she and Theo were under the same roof, she suspected it would be hard to relax. She squeezed her eyes shut.

What had she been thinking, coming here?

Panic welled. That was the problem. She hadn't been thinking, not clearly. It was madness to come here with Theo while her heart was still so bruised.

A warm hand covered hers on the armrest. A hand that was large and capable and shockingly familiar. Gently Theo squeezed and that too tugged the cord of memory in her soul.

'It will be okay, Isla.'

The velvet rumble of his voice caressed her and she swallowed convulsively, hating how badly she wanted to believe him. Was coming here one huge mistake?

'Of course. I'm just tired.'

She opened her eyes and summoned a bright smile that she guessed didn't fool him, for he frowned, the scar at his temple crinkling. He was concerned and every instinct told her he wasn't shamming.

Theo really was worried about her.

More likely worried about his child.

That shattered the moment of tender promise and just as well. Isla couldn't afford to be taken in by his plausible act of concern.

Earlier today he'd said he cared for her. Despite her hard-won defences, hope had shimmered brightly. For a moment she'd imagined his rejection had been a colossal mistake, until she realised she'd misunderstood.

He cared for her in a general, impersonal sense, as the vessel carrying his baby. He hadn't bothered to ask what she felt for him, whether she still cared for him.

His interest began and ended with the baby. His proposal wasn't about *them*. It was window dressing to cement access to the child.

Isla breathed through arrowing pain and drew her hand away.

Everywhere she turned that truth battered her. It was

time she accepted it. She summoned another, brief smile. 'How long till we reach your place?'

Three weeks into Isla's stay in Theo's penthouse her hopes of guarding her heart against him were in tatters.

Instead of haranguing her about marriage he'd left her in peace, reiterating that she needed rest.

They ate breakfast together and when he returned from the office in the evenings, shared dinner in the smaller dining room. To Isla's surprise those meals were companionable, almost as if they'd re-established their lost camaraderie. Probably because they kept to uncontentious topics.

Given how Theo had opened up to her about his family, Isla found herself more in charity with him. Plus his obvious love for them tugged at her heart. It sounded like they were close.

Isla planted her hands on the balustrade of the apartment's landscaped roof terrace. But it wasn't the spectacular view of evening descending over Athens that she saw, it was the light in Theo's face as he talked about his parents.

She bit her lip. What must that feel like? She'd been drawn to him then, as strongly as in the days when she'd thought he was falling in love with her too.

She sighed. Was she still so needy? Just because she'd never had parents. She'd always dreamed of belonging, not out of a conscious act of charity but because she mattered. Because she was loved.

But you're going to have a child.

A bubble of excitement rose. For the first time in her life she'd have someone to love, who'd love her back.

She clung to the railing. The thought rocked her back on her feet, making her feel physically weak for the first time since arriving in Greece.

Every day her stress levels and tiredness were easing. Even her nausea abated.

Maybe the baby likes being in Greece.

Isla scotched that thought. Her physical improvement was more likely because she was ending the morning sickness stage and she'd done nothing but rest. A housekeeper produced gourmet meals and wouldn't let Isla lift a finger, not even make her bed. The shock on the woman's face the first morning when she'd found Isla tidying the bed had been priceless. And had led to Theo stressing again the doctor's orders that she rest.

Now she felt more energised. And more aware of Theo than ever. His smile made her stomach flip. The way he held back from pushing her about his proposal made her think maybe he *did* care, though not in the way she'd once hoped.

On those rare occasions when his hand brushed hers— for he usually kept his distance—Isla felt a tremor through her whole body.

Just thinking about it made her quiver.

'You're cold.' The deep voice came from behind her and sure enough, there it was, that tiny, delicious shudder of recognition. 'What are you doing here without a jacket?'

Isla drew a slow breath, schooling her features so as not to betray the needy woman she became in unguarded moments. His concern added to the illusion of tenderness.

'It's far warmer than London in early spring and the sun shines more.'

She was turning when heat enveloped her. The warmth of his silk-lined suit jacket, imbued with that indefinable seaside pine scent that made her nostrils flare and longing pierce her.

For a second Isla indulged herself, imagining it wasn't his jacket enveloping her but loving arms.

Horror rose. How could she let her guard down like that?

She swung around, shoring up her defences, only to discover in his stern face an expression that made her soften. Isla revelled in it, her heart rising to her throat.

Until she understood what she was doing. Beginning to fall for this man all over again. She reached up to dislodge the jacket.

Adrenaline shot through Theo's blood as he saw Isla's face wearing that dreamy look, the one that had undone him so often.

His heart jolted with an emotion that had nothing to do with her pregnancy. But before he could identify it her expression blanked and she reached up to push his jacket off.

'Don't!' His hand closed on hers. They stilled, gazes locked. Did Isla feel it? The thundering pulse? The coiling, weighted sensation in the groin? The yearning?

Abruptly he stepped out of reach. But his palm tingled from the contact and his breath trapped in his lungs, swelling against his ribs.

'Leave it, Isla.'

She looked like she was going to object then thought better of it. Silence expanded as they stared at each other, a silence filled with his thudding pulse.

One touch had done that. One look.

Such power this woman had. It was unprecedented.

Because there'd been no one since her? Could it be that simple?

He couldn't trust himself to maintain the façade of disinterested concern if he got too close. It had taken all his resolution to leave her behind each day and head for the office even though he was wrangling several crises as other companies thought twice about doing business with him and hungry competitors snapped at his heels. Any thought that being freed from prison would end the nightmare had died as Stavroulis's continuing media hate campaign affected confidence in the company.

Theo was on a knife edge, juggling his concerns about Isla and the baby, his family and the company.

Yet it wasn't the company or his family keeping him awake.

Every night Isla was under his roof sleep eluded Theo. Each morning she looked a little better, a little brighter and he'd been thankful, though he functioned on a bare couple of hours a night.

Every night since she'd arrived, he'd spent hours in the study, working. Or in his home gym. Or in the private rooftop pool, doing laps. The pool had solar heating so even on a wintry night it was inviting. Yesterday he'd turned that heating off, preferring to take an icy dip in hopes of killing libidinous thoughts.

It had worked only until he fell, exhausted, into bed. Then he'd been consumed by memories of them together, moving as one, scaling peaks of fulfilment that surely his imagination exaggerated.

She took a step towards him then paused, frowning. 'You must be cold. You're only wearing a shirt.'

She was worried about him?

'I'm fine.' He was immune to the cold, given the heat searing through his veins at being close to her. He paused, trying to get his brain to focus on something other than sweeping Isla into his arms then into his bed.

'Do you want to go out for dinner?' he said abruptly. 'It would make a change from eating in the apartment.'

It was a spur of the moment idea but tonight Theo didn't trust himself to play nice and keep his distance. Not through an intimate evening alone, just metres from his bed and any number of inviting sofas.

Hell, even the dining table was a danger zone.

'I'd like that,' she said eventually.

Theo tried to read her. But it was no use, she'd retreated behind those walls she erected. He'd give a lot to know what she was thinking.

He had to find a way to get through to her. For their child's sake. And his own.

CHAPTER EIGHT

ISLA ASSUMED HE'D take her to a sophisticated restaurant. Instead the car had wound through increasingly narrow streets until he parked below the towering Acropolis and they walked through tiny lanes. On a summer's day it would be a tourist mecca but on this crisp night it was quiet.

She didn't notice a sign, just lights over the door, then they plunged into a cosy room with small tables, wooden chairs and checked oilcloth tablecloths. The place smelled delicious. Candles in old bottles flickered as they entered but other diners paid them little heed.

Not so the proprietor who hastened across, greeting Theo like a long-lost brother.

Isla knew some basic Greek but had no hope of understanding the machine-gun rapid enthusiasm of their host as he ushered them to a corner table. As they sat Theo introduced her as his friend from England. The owner, Georgio, welcomed her warmly before leaning close and assuring her that Theo was a good man. A very good man, he reiterated, and she was to pay no attention to the lies spread about him.

'It's okay, Georgio. Isla knows me.'

The man smiled and nodded, heading off with promises of food.

'No menus?' Isla queried.

Theo shrugged and grinned and she couldn't help but stare. He was an uncommonly attractive man, but that rare, carefree smile…

'It's easier to let Georgio choose. He knows what's best each day and he never disappoints.'

'You know him well? Obviously he thinks a lot of you.'

'We go back a while.'

He didn't elaborate which left Isla wondering what he'd done to impress Georgio. She caught the direction of her thoughts and felt uncomfortable at her readiness to judge Theo badly. He'd rejected her cruelly but that didn't mean he couldn't behave well to others. Georgio's warmth convinced her it hadn't been just a welcome for a good customer. Had she been too harsh with Theo, always expecting the worst?

'What did he mean by lies about you?'

Theo lifted one dark eyebrow. 'You haven't been following the media?'

'I've had other things on my mind.'

His huff of amusement made her lips curve.

'I can imagine.' He paused. 'There's a lot of finger-pointing about my character and supposed guilt for the death of Costa Stavroulis.'

'But you were cleared. The authorities proved you didn't do it.'

His smile now held little amusement. 'Does something have to be true to make news? Most of them are careful not to accuse me outright but there are plenty of insinuations, gossip, supposed statements from *sources close to the Karalis family…*'

Isla goggled. Once he'd been released from prison she'd stopped following the news.

'But why?'

'The victim was the grandson of Spiro Stavroulis, a media magnate. The old man wants justice for his grandson but until another suspect is identified, he's directing his vitriol at me.'

'That makes no sense if he knows you're innocent.'

'Maybe he didn't believe my alibi was real. Or thinks that in applying pressure, I'll produce the real culprit.'

She shook her head. 'How could you? You're not the police.'

Something shifted in Theo's expression. 'He died in my family home. The night of a farewell party for my mother as she was moving somewhere that suits her needs better. Old Stavroulis probably thinks I've got inside information I'm not sharing.' His jaw tightened. 'He knows I despised his grandson. Costa was a bad influence and I'd warned him away from my stepsister, Toula. I didn't want him hanging around her.'

Theo's tone was harsh and uncompromising. The voice of a man relentless in protecting those he cared for.

Instead of scaring her, Isla was drawn to that. This man would protect his child with the last breath in his body.

She found that impossibly attractive. She wanted that. *For her baby, of course.*

Georgio arrived then with a pile of plates balanced on his arms. The food looked and smelled delicious and her appetite, which had been gradually improving, was suddenly back full force.

The next little while was taken up with eating. She and Theo talked, but only about the food and the location, and with each passing minute she relaxed more.

Maybe it was the warmth of the place and the good food. Maybe because Theo's conversation was easy, as if he wasn't waiting on her decision about his proposal.

Perhaps it was partly because he'd swapped his suit for jeans and a dark green pullover. Even casually dressed Theo had a masculine charisma that couldn't be ignored. Everything about him was attractive. From the hard, compelling lines of his face to that well-defined, sensual mouth and eyes that, when he smiled, reminded her of warm honey. Even the scar near his eye didn't detract from his magnetism.

Worryingly, he looked more like the man she'd fallen in love with than someone who'd destroyed her trust.

Isla sought something to say that would take her mind off him without leading back to the baby and marriage. She didn't want to argue about that tonight.

'Is that pullover hand-knitted? It's a distinctive design.' It had clearly been made to fit his athletic frame. If Theo ever ditched his suits in favour of pullovers, knitwear sales would soar.

Theo's expression softened as he glanced down. 'It is handmade. You've got a good eye.'

'I *do* work in a knitting shop.'

'Does that mean you knit? I don't remember seeing you working with wool.'

When they'd met, she'd had other things to occupy her. Isla's blood quickened at the memories and she hoped that wasn't a blush she felt.

'I've knitted since I was a child.'

One of the carers in the home had taught her one Christmas. It had been a diversion from the fact that their festive season wasn't terribly festive. Isla had been fascinated with the idea of making something from simply a string of wool, plus she'd found it comforting, the steady rhythm of the needles taking the edge off her loneliness. Even surrounded by other orphans there were times when she'd felt utterly separate.

'What are you thinking, Isla? You've gone somewhere else in your head.'

She was about to deny it then stopped herself. Withdrawing from others, even turning away before they had a chance to reject her, had become habit. The exception had been with Theo. Her mouth twisted. Look what had happened then. Yet there was no need to be so defensive. They had to build bridges to sort out their child's future.

She had to trust him more and put aside her wariness.

'I was thinking about how I took to knitting as a kid. I made woollen scarves for everyone I knew.' Someone had donated a lot of wool so she had plenty to work with. 'By the time I was in my teens I was making hats, scarves and other things to sell at a neighbourhood market. Earning my own money was a great incentive.'

'You don't knit for yourself?'

'Sometimes. But there's a good market for quality handmade pieces. I take orders from people who want something unique for themselves or as a special gift. It's not a get-rich-quick scheme because of the work involved. But I find it soothing and any money is welcome when you're a student.'

Not that she was a student now. The reminder dragged the smile off her face.

Theo didn't seem to notice. 'You have a lot in common with my mother.'

'Sorry? How?'

'For a start, she knitted this for me.'

He sat straighter as if to show off the fine work. His patent pride dissolved the restriction she'd placed around her heart. It was sweet that he felt that way about his mother.

Excitement stirred. That's what she hoped for with her child. She hugged the precious idea close.

'Your mother's very talented. I wouldn't mind the pattern.'

'You can ask for it when you see her. She'll be back in Athens soon.' Before Isla could wonder about the possibility of meeting Theo's mother, he went on. 'When I was a kid she knitted my pullovers and sewed my clothes. Every night I'd go to sleep to the sound of her knitting needles clacking. Like you, she made extra money making clothes for other people.'

Isla sat back, stunned, not by the fact his mother had made money that way but by the sudden connection she felt to a woman she'd never met. She too had known hardship, far more than Isla. At least Isla had always had a roof over her head.

Both of them had a soft spot for this man. In his mother's case it was inevitable. In Isla's it was a weakness, yet tonight she couldn't find the determination to thrust him away. The knowledge settled in her with something that felt strangely like relief.

'She'll enjoy meeting you, I know.'

'She knows about me?'

Theo shook his head. 'Not yet. I thought you needed time to rest and acclimatise.' He paused, holding her gaze and when he spoke it was in a deep voice that sounded sincere. 'I didn't want to push you into meeting her too soon. I know I've asked a lot of you, Isla. I know this isn't easy.'

He moved closer and the warmth of his gaze melted another layer of her defences. Soon she'd have none left against him.

She'd done nothing but think about him, yearn for him, even dream about him, since he'd walked back into her life. She'd clung to anger as a defence mechanism but lately, seeing Theo not as an enemy but as someone considerate and patient, it had stopped working. Keeping her distance was increasingly difficult.

'I'm glad you're here, Isla.'

The sincerity in his voice and the look in his gilded eyes reminded her of the intimacies they'd shared. Intimacies she missed so much.

'I'm only here because I'm pregnant. You wouldn't have come after me if not for that.'

Theo didn't respond immediately and she saw something in his expression she didn't understand. A hint of strong emotion. Then he seemed to stiffen, his features setting in hard planes as he lifted his shoulders. 'I was needed here. That had to be my priority.' He paused. 'Would you rather I lied about that?'

'No!' Isla surveyed him, astonished to discover his frankness brought a sense of freedom, though once her bruised ego would have protested his words. She'd rather have brutal truth than deceive herself with lies. 'I only want honesty. I don't want anything else from you.'

'Nothing at all?'

She was about to reiterate that she wasn't interested in wealth or power when his hand covered hers on the table.

Instantly familiar sensations bombarded her. Not merely the warmth and sense of rightness in his touch. But that trembling, eager feeling deep inside.

Of course she wanted more.

Theo Karalis had feet of clay. He wasn't the ideal man she dreamed about. But she wanted him with an abiding need nothing could obliterate. Not disillusionment nor pride nor willpower.

Isla huffed a silent laugh that felt like a groan.

What willpower? She inhaled his scent, drawing in his heat and strength, senses sparking in the newly charged atmosphere between them, and couldn't pull back.

She'd struggled not to be drawn in by his spell. It was a losing battle.

'Isla? Speak to me.'

For the first time she detected real uncertainty in him. Did he too fight not to succumb to the pull between them? She'd told herself Theo was immune and didn't feel that desire any more. But reading his taut features and the slight unsteadiness in his hand, it hit her that she wasn't alone in this.

'To say what?'

His gaze scorched her. 'That you want me. As much as I want you.'

Isla moistened dry lips, knowing how much rode on her answer. She must have hesitated too long for abruptly Theo withdrew, scraping his chair back from the table as if needing to put as much distance between them as possible.

'Sorry. I don't want to pressure you. I keep forgetting you're sick when you look so...' Theo shook his head. 'I'm out of line—'

'You're not out of line.' Caution died with his withdrawal. 'You're right.'

Her breath caught as, instead of triumph in those gleaming eyes, she read relief, crowded out a moment later by excitement. His expression was raw and hungry and it matched exactly what she felt.

'For the record I'm not sick. I feel better than I have in ages.' The enforced rest had restored a lot of her strength.

Something crackled in the air. That lightning spark of sexual connection that had arced between them from the first. The fine hairs on Isla's arms stood on end, her breasts felt fuller and pressed against her bra where her nipples peaked.

Did Theo notice? His nostrils flared as if he scented her arousal. Far from feeling shy about it, Isla experienced an upswell of pride and confidence.

Why shouldn't she admit to desire? Why shouldn't she satisfy it? They both understood the situation. This wasn't about romance. Theo had admitted that she wasn't his first priority. But he *had* admitted to wanting her and suddenly that was all she could think about. Easing the gnawing hunger she carried wherever she went.

Surely she was entitled to that at least?

What had she to lose? She'd learned from disillusionment. She wouldn't expect too much this time, just the physical pleasure Theo could give her.

'You want me.'

It wasn't a question. Theo's tone conveyed satisfaction and something she couldn't identify. But Isla wasn't in the business any more of trying to understand Theo's emotions. This was sex, pure and simple.

As for the baby and Theo's outrageous proposition, those decisions were best left to another day. When she could think straight.

'Yes.'

The smile that unfurled across his face made her light-headed. But not as much as when he scooted his chair forward, reaching out and threading his fingers through hers. The electricity in the air was inside her now and she could barely sit still, so potent was his effect.

'I want you, Isla, you have no idea how much.'

He rose, pulling her to her feet. As they crossed the room Giorgio appeared, all smiles, carrying their jackets. Theo helped her into hers, his hands lingering a moment longer than necessary, before he shrugged into his and passed a credit card to their host. Isla was barely aware of what was said, only that Giorgio invited them back. Then they stepped out into the crisp night, Theo taking her hand as they turned down the lane.

Neither spoke. Every sense was focused on what lay ahead. She stumbled and he wrapped his arm around her, pulling her close and steadying her. She felt the urgency rise in him too yet he kept his pace steady, not rushing her over the uneven surface.

Cool air brushed Isla's cheeks but inside an unquenchable fire had ignited, burning low in her body.

So wrapped up was she in the man beside her that she barely noticed a flash of light across the quiet street as he helped her into the car. She had an impression of movement but turned away to look at Theo's proud profile, her heart rising to her throat in anticipation.

The trip to his apartment was a blur. Isla couldn't say whether it took two minutes or twenty. All that mattered was that finally they were alone, the door closed against the outside world.

Her breasts rose and fell with her choppy breathing as Theo locked the door. In Isla's feverish imagination it felt as if that cut them off from the worries of the world. For this night she was free simply to feel and respond. Tomorrow would be time enough to think about the future and their negotiations.

Theo turned towards her. His face looked different, features pared back, emphasising his magnificent bone structure and that intrinsic, masculine power which she'd always found secretly irresistible. But more important than his charismatic looks was the visceral sensation that being with him was as necessary as breathing.

He reached out his hand and Isla placed hers in it, feeling the inevitable shiver of excitement as his fingers closed around hers.

She'd take tonight and not look back.

CHAPTER NINE

THEO LOOKED AT the woman before him and told himself
to go slow. She was still recuperating. Until a few weeks
ago she'd been ill every day. She was pregnant, carrying
his child in that slim body.

The idea sent a judder of excitement through him, mixed
with incredible tenderness and nerves at the idea of doing
the wrong thing. Of perhaps hurting her or their baby.

*Yet he'd never wanted a woman more than he wanted
Isla Jacobs.*

She stood there, proud as a goddess, head up, shoulders
back, breasts thrust forward against the rich russet of her
dress. Theo's hands prickled with the need to reach out and
touch her. To skim his palms over those delicate curves. To
shape her breasts. To tug her hair free so it spilled around
her shoulders like liquid silk. He remembered the scent of
it, like rosemary, honey and sunshine. Like endless summer days when everything was right in the world.

He wanted her so much he had to take a moment to
gather himself, not simply grab.

Unbidden, memory rose of the moment when they'd
reached his car tonight and a paparazzo had appeared.
Theo had got them away quickly and maybe Isla hadn't
noticed. But it was a reminder that he'd brought her into
his world now and he had to do everything to protect her.

Guilt froze the air in his lungs. Foolish of him to take

her out without a security detail, but he'd worked on the basis that, just once, they could slip under the radar without staff around.

There'd be no turning back the tide of curiosity now about her, about *them*. Isla didn't know it yet but it was another reason for her to accept his proposal. As her husband Theo could protect her better against the inevitable tsunami of press intrusion.

Tonight had proved how important that was. When the photographer had appeared, snapping photos of her, Theo had had to fight down the impulse to march over and rip the camera away. It was something he'd never done despite plenty of provocation.

He could handle anything that was thrown at him, but a possible threat to Isla was a whole new ballgame.

Theo breathed deep, forcing air into cramped lungs.

No time now for worrying about the press. Already his thoughts scattered as he took in the heavy rise and fall of her breasts and the flush of excitement in her sweet face.

He walked towards her, stiff from the way every muscle in his body pulled tight. Plus there was the erection he'd battled all through the journey home.

Her stunning eyes, the colour of early-morning mist over the sea, held his and he recognised the gift she offered. Gone were the recriminations and doubts. She met his stare appraisingly, as an equal.

Need scythed through him, a white-hot blade, taking him right up to her two long strides. 'I'm sorry.'

'About what?'

He was already bending, one arm around her back and the other behind her knees, sweeping her up into his embrace. 'This. You bring out the caveman in me.'

Theo had intended to take her hand and lead her to the bedroom like an urbane, civilised lover but some primitive part of his brain urged him to take control in this most fundamental way. Gather her to him, as if he feared she might disappear like a mirage. As she had all those nights when she'd featured in his dreams, only to vanish, leaving him bereft.

His heart knocked his ribs as he held her close, her face upturned to his.

'Don't apologise. I like it.' Her voice, husky with need, stroked through him, sending his senses into overdrive. She reached up to thread her fingers through his hair then clasp the back of his neck as if she needed to stake her claim.

Adrenaline shot through his bloodstream at the idea and he found himself grinning.

Her soft body nestled against him as he strode to his bedroom. With each step his heartbeat revved faster.

Soon. Soon. Soon.

There was no need to pause and switch on a light. The curtains hadn't been drawn and silvery moonlight spilled across the bed from the huge windows that gave a spectacular view of the city.

Theo stopped beside the king-sized bed and made himself put her down. Of course it wasn't that simple. He was reluctant to release her so he did it slowly, turning the inch-by-inch slide of her body into slow-motion torture and bliss.

A gasp sounded loud in the silence. His or hers, he didn't know. He felt them both stop breathing at that exquisite friction.

Finally she stood between his feet, the bed behind her, but Theo kept his hands on her hips. Not because she was unsteady but because he couldn't seem to release her.

Mine, mine, mine, the greedy voice inside his head chanted. His blood throbbed to the beat of it. His snatched breaths matched it too.

Until his brain began to work. Zips, buttons, shoes. Barriers to what they both wanted. Barriers he wanted to strip instantly, but he made himself pretend he was civilised. A man who understood that tearing his lover's clothes from her body might be scary, even for a woman trembling with a need that matched his.

That tiny sign of Isla's desperation, despite her proud stance, tugged at emotions far deeper than lust. Emotions he'd take time to analyse later. When he could think straight.

'Take your hair down, Isla.'

She didn't hesitate and that was another punch of arousal to his already heightened senses.

Theo watched the glorious waves tumble around her shoulders, her beckoning scent stronger now. Or perhaps he was even more attuned.

'Perfect.' His voice was a rumbling growl that should have scared her. Instead, her lips parted as if she too were so aroused she found it difficult to catch her breath.

Theo's fingers flexed. 'Now the dress.'

Was that a pout? His pulse was a driving beat deep in his groin as she slipped her tongue across her bottom lip and he fought to smother a groan.

'You don't want to take it off me?'

Theo imagined doing it. Not questing for the zip at her side, but fastening his big hands on the delicately draped neckline and tugging to rip it apart from neck to hem, revealing Isla in all her glory.

His throat was lined with sandpaper as he tried to swallow. 'It's better if you do it. Faster.'

Fathomless eyes surveyed him from that uptilted face. 'Only if you take your pullover off.'

Theo lifted his arms and wrenched it up over his head. By the time Isla had found her zip and undone it he was naked from the waist up, the night air a relief against burning skin. Was she deliberately going slow to tease him? More likely his movements were rushed.

He stepped back, giving her space as he removed his shoes and socks. Straightening, he was in time to see her shimmy out of the dark red dress. It dropped to the floor like his plunging stomach as he drank in the sight of her.

'So perfect,' he whispered hoarsely. Despite her recent weight loss she was stunning.

When he looked at her face again Isla held his gaze and even in the moonlight he felt the gut-deep slam of connection. Like the unseen but palpable waves of energy radiating from an explosion. He almost expected to hear the reverberating boom of detonation.

When her hand moved to cover her belly he was surprised. Could she possibly think her pregnancy marred her sensual perfection? Or was it a gesture born of protectiveness?

Either way it pierced his swelling satisfaction.

'You don't believe me?'

'None of us are perfect.'

Finally her hand fell away. There it was, the beginnings of a baby bump. A rush of emotion surged through him. More than desire, more than appreciation.

Theo dropped to his knees, his fingers reaching for the waistband of her tights. He paused, his breath hissing at the delicious shock of her smooth, bare skin against his knuckles as he slipped his fingers inside the stretchy fabric and drew it down her hips.

The scent of her was different here. Earthier, more decidedly feminine, beckoning him with the evidence of her arousal.

He moved quickly, rolling the fabric past the narrow band of her black lace knickers, down her silky thighs, past her knees to her shins, her slender ankles. His heart knocked hard when she planted her fingertips on his shoulders for balance as she lifted first one foot then the other so he could strip the tights away.

Theo skimmed his palms back up to that inviting band of lace. But his patience wore thin and a second later he'd yanked the delicate material down so hard it pooled around her ankles. She shifted her weight, one thigh moving forward a little as if instinctively protecting her modesty.

He shook his head, circling his hand around her thigh and gently tugging it wide. Silently he drank in the treasure revealed. The pale swathe of her abdomen, where a precious new life nestled. The dark V of soft hair guarding her femininity.

The female body, *Isla's body*, was the most wonderful, remarkable thing in the world. And the most arousing. Theo's jaw set hard and aching as he tried to hold on to control.

He looked up, meeting her eyes. 'Now the bra. Take it off.'

Her lips moved, her expression just the right side of mutinous. 'What about the rest of *your* clothes?'

'Soon. First I need you naked.'

His voice was harsh but Isla didn't seem to mind.

Theo had believed he already enjoyed the finest view possible, until she reached back and undid the black lace bra, letting it slide down her arms and freeing her breasts to sway above him.

Was it possible to come just from looking at a woman?

He felt so close, so aroused that for long seconds he couldn't move. Finally, with a shuddering breath he closed the distance between them. Hands gently cradling her bare hips, he kissed her belly. A tiny, fervent yet featherlight kiss right above their baby. Then more kisses, gentle and full of wonderment and desire.

He tightened his grip as she sighed and he felt her wobble as if her knees loosened. He knew the feeling, he was experiencing it right now.

'Easy, *glykia mou*.' His breath feathered her skin and she quivered anew, her hands anchoring on his bare shoulders. Even that simple touch felt like a gift.

As for Isla, she was a miracle. He couldn't imagine wanting another woman the way he did her. Because of the baby she carried? No, it was more than that. Impending motherhood merely added to her potent allure.

Theo skimmed his lips across her abdomen, intrigued by the swell of her pregnancy. Then he kissed his way down to the silky thatch of chestnut hair, nuzzling as he went.

He heard her call his name but because of the rush of blood in his ears he couldn't tell if it was a question or a plea. He slid one hand between her thighs, a grunt of satisfaction escaping as she widened her stance, allowing him access. She was slippery, ready for him, and his erection rose against the confines of his trousers. He was so needy it physically hurt but this wasn't the time for urgent sex.

Theo reminded himself she was pregnant, of the need to be especially gentle. He ignored the ache in his groin, the sense that his lower body had turned leaden, and concentrated on her.

His questing touch reached her clitoris and she stiffened, fingers tightening on his shoulders. As he delved further and deeper, she shuddered and sighed, her pelvis tilting up the way a sunflower follows bright light.

Isla was that light for him, always drawing him. He knew that if he hadn't been locked up in prison, he'd never have been able to keep his distance, even knowing their separation was for the best.

But now there was nothing keeping them apart. His scruples and fears about involving her in his life meant nothing now she carried their child. She belonged with him and he intended to prove it to her.

He smiled as he leaned in and kissed her intimately, drawing in her scent and taste. Slowly he feasted, taking his time, not like the starving man he was, who'd gone without for so long. Instead, he savoured every exquisite sensation and above all Isla's responses.

He knew she had doubts about marriage and them being a family, but he'd win her over. One way or another.

Mouth still on her, he looked up and saw her, head thrown back, breasts thrust forward, looking wild and beautiful. He'd never known a more enthralling woman. Sweet and tender yet determined and with a core of strength that made her all the more alluring.

With or without the baby she was a woman worth winning.

She looked down, their gazes meshing, heat saturated him at their powerful, erotic connection. He drew on her soft flesh and she shuddered. He felt the tiny tremble begin low in her body and did it again.

Her fingers threaded his hair, clamping his skull as she tilted into his caress. His senses were full of her arousal, exacerbating his own need.

'Theo!' It was a cry of exultation and surrender as her body grew taut as a drawn bow, still for just a moment, before completion crashed upon her and he gathered her close as she shivered in ecstasy.

When the shudders stopped he nudged her towards the bed. The backs of her legs touched the mattress and she collapsed onto it. The dreamy bliss on Isla's face told him everything he needed to know. As did her pale arm reaching out for him.

Isla's body had turned to jelly and her soul to radiant light. Theo had given her ecstasy but far more too.

Crazy as it sounded to what was left of her logical mind, it felt as if he'd given back something precious that had been destroyed with his deceit and rejection.

His tenderness made her throat catch. The reverence of his kneeling form before her, his expression of wonder as he'd surveyed her...

She'd known he was thinking of their baby, of the marvel of new life they'd created. Then, when he kissed her there, she'd felt utterly precious. It was a sensation beyond anything she'd experienced and it vanquished her doubts, as surely as if he'd melted an armoury of bristling weapons, turning them into molten gold.

Some men would have been horrified by an unexpected pregnancy. Theo's uninhibited delight in both her news and her body undid every defence. If she hadn't already been impatient for his lovemaking, that would have won her over.

Isla's body floated on the wide bed. But she found the energy to reach out an arm in invitation because, wonderful as that had been, she needed more. She needed Theo.

He stood beside the bed, hands clenched as if resisting the impulse to touch her.

'I should get a condom.'

'It's a bit late for that.' Then she bit her lip. She'd momentarily forgotten that protection wasn't just against pregnancy. 'Unless you...?'

'There's been no one since you, Isla.'

It shouldn't surprise her, after all he'd been locked away for months. Yet he'd been free for some time. A man with Theo's looks, charisma and wealth would have no trouble attracting women and surely he'd been tempted to celebrate his freedom from incarceration.

Yet she believed him. Everything she learned about him told her he was a man who'd protect those he cared for. He might only care for her as the mother of his unborn child but he would keep her safe.

'Then come here. I need you to hold me.'

She'd missed Theo's arms around her, his heart beating against hers and his powerful body sheltering her. Besides, despite the glittering climax he'd bestowed, her body still throbbed eagerly. He'd taken the edge off her need but she wanted him, wanted them together.

The bed dipped as he lay beside her, turning her towards him and surveying her intently. His back was to the window so his face was in shadow, yet Isla *felt* his scrutiny as sure as touch.

She palmed his cheek, feeling his flesh twitch in response. He radiated heat and pent-up tension. When she slid her hand down his neck and across his shoulder she found every inch rigid. His breathing was harsh and uneven.

Everything told her he fought to rein himself in, his need so powerful she wondered if perhaps he didn't trust himself. Otherwise why hold back? There'd never been reticence in their lovemaking and Isla had learned the joys of sexual power and sensual abandon with him as well as the most beguiling tenderness.

'Theo? What is it?'

He breathed deep, the hair on his chest tickling her nipples and sending a shaft of desire straight to her womb.

'I don't want to hurt you or the baby.'

Her breath snared. His concern and hesitation moved her. He didn't act like the uncaring man she'd once painted him, someone who used and discarded people at his convenience.

Isla's heart swelled. 'You're not going to hurt us. I want you.'

I need you.

But she bit her lip so as not to let those words escape.

She shuffled towards him, closing the space between them and a gasp ripped through the night air. His large hand settled on her waist, his knee nudging between her thighs. 'I don't think I can hold back.'

'Good.' Then her breath fractured as his hand moved to her sensitive breast and her eyes rolled back at the perfection of his touch. No other man had ever affected her so.

Yet instead of pushing her onto her back and moving over her, Theo slid his hand around her knee and lifted her leg over his hip, tugging her close until she felt his hard shaft between her legs. They lay on their sides facing each other and she was completely open to him. Even then he didn't move immediately but those seconds of waiting only fuelled her hunger.

He guided himself so she felt the blunt head of his erection against her and couldn't prevent herself moving, seeking all that masculine strength she longed for.

'Isla.' He whispered her name as she planted her palm on his broad chest to feel his heart thrumming as fast as hers.

With one slow, sure thrust Theo brought them together. It had been so long and it felt so utterly perfect that for a second Isla forgot how to breathe. Instantly he stopped, as if trying to gauge if her response was from discomfort. But when she angled her pelvis towards him, hooking her heel harder behind him to bring them together, all hesitancy vanished.

In an instant he was the strong, accomplished lover she remembered. He took command of their rhythm and her body. His guttural words of praise stoked her arousal, as did his ability to find exactly the right spot, deep inside, where she most needed him.

Then, just as she thought this couldn't get any better, he leaned in and kissed her.

Isla had forgotten how flagrantly erotic a kiss could be.

How perfect the sense of communion between two mouths, two bodies moving as one.

Pleasure was a gift equally shared as she gave him back caress for caress, holding him close as if their joined bodies might fly apart unless she held on tight.

His mouth was dark velvet. His body a force of nature, consuming yet revitalising her, making her feel helpless in the face of such power but at the same time stronger and more alive than she'd ever been. As if he stripped her back to bare essentials then revealed something in herself more profound than she'd ever recognised.

Through it all were those threads of pleasure, weaving through her body, unravelling, bunching, but finally coming together in beautiful patterns that presaged bliss and the ultimate mystery between a man and a woman.

Isla felt everything coalesce, every sensation, every emotion and fear was part of it, part of her.

She cried his name as the thundering roar of pleasure bore down on her again. This time, wonderfully, he was there with her, his body urging her on, his mouth swallowing her sob of fulfilment. Wave upon wave of ecstasy broke through her and she clutched him close. Then, just as she found her peak, Theo's powerful body shuddered in her embrace, the hot liquid of his climax pulsing deep.

Incredible tenderness filled her as she gathered him to her. He groaned and called her name, the sound muffled in the sensitive curve between her shoulder and neck.

Finally their breathing eased, their taut bodies slumping together in sated abandon. She didn't have the energy to move even if she wanted to and she knew with a clarity that would have shocked her mere hours before, that there was nowhere in the world she'd rather be than here, like this, with Theo.

It felt as if the world had been shattered and remade by what they'd shared.

As she drifted into sleep Isla told herself it was an illusion. What felt to her like love was merely sex. She couldn't make the mistake of reading too much into it.

All that had changed was her pregnancy. She had to remember that and not fall into the trap of romantic fantasies.

From now on she'd be sensible and pragmatic with Theo. Starting tomorrow.

CHAPTER TEN

SEVERAL HOURS LATER, Isla leaned back, relaxing in the warm water that came up almost to her collarbone. She spread her arms along the edge of the wide bath and felt every muscle in her body soften.

'You look like the cat that got the cream.'

The deep voice burred across her skin. Despite her floating feeling, as if her well-used body couldn't possibly move again, her nipples tightened.

Maybe she wasn't quite as exhausted as she'd thought.

She opened her eyes and there was Theo at the other end of the massive, sunken bath, his eyes glowing like embers as he surveyed her.

'I'm not the only one.' He looked like a man well-satisfied with his lot.

He sat higher than her, the impressive spread of his shoulders and muscled arms evident above the water. His chest, broad and leanly muscled as if from athletic exercise rather than steroids or pumping weights, glistened. The dark hair across his pectorals was wet and Isla remembered how that felt against her skin from the night they'd made love months ago during a moonlit swim.

A coil of heat circled low in her body. Definitely not as tired as she'd imagined. Or maybe she simply responded to this feeling of utter, physical well-being. She'd woken to darkness in Theo's vast bed, alone. Realising he'd left her, the gloss of satisfaction had worn off. Till he appeared in the doorway, naked and compelling, to ask if she felt like a restorative bath.

She'd barely said yes when he hoisted her into his arms and carried her into the most stunning bathroom she'd ever seen. Even here there was a panoramic view of the city. Yet it wasn't that or the luxurious fittings that caught her attention. It was the array of candles set around the room, bathing it in a soft glow, and the vast sunken tub, an invitation to decadence. All evidence that Theo had exerted himself to make this nice for her.

You're going to be sensible and pragmatic, her head reminded her.

Her heart squeezed. She wanted to be anything but sensible. But she owed it to her baby not to be swept away by a romantic gesture.

Her gaze narrowed on Theo's chiselled features, trying to read his thoughts. 'The scar. How did you get that?'

In the heat it looked more livid than usual and she swallowed, registering how close it was to his eye.

He shrugged, sending a ripple of warm water to lap around her bare body. 'A recent altercation.'

Isla frowned. Theo had never revealed a temper or the sort of antagonistic masculinity that sometimes led to fights. She couldn't imagine him provoking violence. Then enlightenment dawned. 'Someone hurt you while you were locked up?'

After a moment he nodded. 'It wasn't a safe place.'

There was something in his tone, irony and understatement, a bitterness she'd never heard from him before. Who wouldn't be bitter, locked up for a crime they hadn't committed?

'I thought the authorities would protect people in a remand centre. After all you hadn't been convicted.'

Another flash of stark emotion in those stormy eyes. 'I

wasn't in a remand centre, I was in a high-security prison. And no matter how good the security, there's always a way around it.'

Isla's heart beat high against her throat. 'How did it happen?' She couldn't imagine him deliberately threatening another prisoner.

Theo shook his head. 'It doesn't matter. It's in the past.'

She slid her arms down and wrapped them around her torso. The image of some hardened criminal attacking him, and by the look of that scar with some sort of weapon, made her feel sick. She knew it would haunt her.

That was why she found herself crossing a boundary she'd vowed not to go near. 'You say you want marriage, yet you won't share that small thing with me. How do you expect me to contemplate marriage if you shut me out? That's not how marriages work, even the sort you're suggesting.'

Not that she was seriously considering marriage, that would be a recipe for disaster, with her craving more than he could give. But Isla wasn't above using his outrageous proposition to satisfy her curiosity. Though it didn't feel like idle curiosity. Her fear when she thought of him being attacked ran too deep.

A vertical line appeared in the centre of his forehead. 'You're right.' He paused. 'I'm used to keeping trouble to myself. But since it's important to you…'

His eyes held hers and Isla felt that powerful tug of connection. Too late she wondered at the wisdom of calling him on this. Weren't there things she didn't want to share, most notably her feelings for him? She was about to tell him it didn't matter when he spoke.

'I had a price on my head in prison and someone decided to claim that reward.'

'What do you mean a price?' Surely he hadn't been there long enough to make enemies.

'It was common knowledge that Spiro Stavroulis would pay handsomely to anyone who injured me badly enough. He's the grandfather of the man I was supposed to have killed.'

Her stomach hollowed. She wanted to object that Theo was innocent, then remembered what he'd said about Stavroulis wanting a scapegoat. What must it have been like for Theo, locked away for something he didn't do, surrounded by violent men, under threat?

Isla drew her knees up and wrapped her arms tight around them, hunching into herself at the thought.

She heard whispered swearing and then there was a wave of water as Theo moved to her end of the bath. He sat beside her, bare hip to bare hip, one arm around her, pulling her against his solid torso. She went willingly, glad for the contact. It was a comfort having him here, so obviously alive and well.

'I *knew* I shouldn't have told you.'

'Of course you should. I'd rather know the truth than be left in the dark.' She lifted her head and met his gaze. 'Was it a knife?'

After a moment he nodded. 'An improvised one with a razor blade.'

Isla blinked, trying to clear the image her mind conjured. 'I'm so sorry.'

'There's nothing to be sorry about. You're right, I need to let you in more if we're to have a future together.'

It was on the tip of Isla's tongue to tell him they didn't have a future, not in the way he wanted, but she didn't say it. For suddenly she found she wasn't as vehemently opposed to marriage as she should be.

Taking comfort in his closeness, reliving the horror of his danger and now feeling a rush of relief, she faced the strength of her feelings for Theo. Despite what she'd told herself in London, those hadn't changed.

Could she really be thinking of marrying him?

Surely not. She cared too much for him while he…

She shivered. This time she couldn't tell if the tremor was from trepidation or something else. What she *did* know was that, despite the past, he was important to her.

She lifted her hand to trace the scar. 'I'm glad you're safe.'

Theo captured her hand and pressed a kiss to her palm, his eyes holding hers. 'So am I. I'd much rather be here with you.'

His crooked smile said volumes about that experience but she'd pressed him enough.

'Thank you for telling me.' It might be a straightforward story but Isla felt his sharing it with her was significant. Like when he'd told her about his childhood, but this time it was something he'd got no benefit from sharing. The information about his family had been part of his plan to persuade her into marriage.

'You're right. We need to understand each other better. In the past we shared a lot but on reflection we never discussed anything truly important.' He grinned. 'Except for the love of your life—archaeology.'

A smile tickled Isla's mouth. 'And the love of yours—football.'

He was right. They'd talked a lot, getting to know each other, but for all those conversations they'd never delved deep. The true sense of connection had come in other ways, when they made love, but also in the mutual understanding that hadn't seemed to need words.

'While we're sharing… There's something I want to ask you.'

Slowly Isla nodded, mentally readying herself for a question about her opposition to marrying him.

'You said you didn't know your parents and that you

were brought up by someone else. Were you adopted or fostered out? Who raised you?'

Isla felt her jaw slacken. Theo had seemed so single-minded, going to so much trouble to persuade her into marriage. Why deviate from that? Knowing about her childhood wouldn't get him closer to that goal and he was a man who focused on achieving his goals.

Her childhood was a cold, disappointing place that she tried not to revisit often. It would be easy to shrug off his question but she didn't. Because what she'd said about Theo not sharing applied to her as well.

Isla had never opened up to Theo about truly personal stuff like her childhood and had steered conversations away from that. It was a habit she'd acquired early, never voluntarily discussing her upbringing. She wasn't ashamed of her past yet was cautious in talking about it. As if by admitting out loud that she'd never been loved, she might invite others to view her as unlovable too.

It was a secret fear she'd hoarded to herself. Perhaps her greatest fear.

Theo felt the tension in her slender body and pulled her closer. He supposed it would be easier to avoid difficult topics and from her reaction earlier he knew this was a difficult topic. But ever since she'd made that dismissive remark about her childhood he'd burned to know more. Not because information was power and the more he knew about Isla the more able he'd be to convince her to marry. His curiosity wasn't strategic. He simply wanted to understand and, he realised, be there for her. Instinct told him that in Isla's case her childhood loss was still very real.

So he didn't retract the question, despite seeing the shutters come down in her eyes and feeling her flinch. Instead he waited.

'Mainly I was brought up in an orphanage.'

'An orphanage?' He'd imagined her as a pretty child, adopted easily. 'I thought you'd have been in a private home.'

'Adoption?' She shook her head. 'It's not always so easy, especially for older children.'

He frowned. Had he misunderstood? 'I thought you lost your parents when you were a baby.'

Instantly he knew he'd said the wrong thing as she stiffened.

'I didn't lose them so much as they lost me.' Her mouth twisted and she turned away, looking towards the window. 'I was abandoned as a newborn. No note, no memento, no name, just me wrapped in a blanket in a box.'

An ache tightened Theo's throat at the idea of a tiny infant left to the mercy of strangers. He pulled Isla fully into his arms to sit sideways on his lap, his arm around her back, another around her knees.

'It's okay, Theo. It was a long time ago. I don't remember it.'

That didn't make it any better. His heart thudded against his ribs as he rocked her to him. He tried to imagine their child left in that way but his mind refused to cooperate.

'What happened? They didn't have enough people interested in adoption?' Easier to ask about that than think of that tiny, deserted baby.

'It wasn't that simple. I'm sure they would have tried adoption but it turned out I was born with a heart defect, which meant surgery. That's daunting for anyone, especially people looking for a perfect little baby to make their own.'

Her voice sounded brittle and who could blame her? Theo's anger built but he kept it in.

He thought of the faded scarring he'd seen on her chest and hadn't asked about. At the time he'd been too busy seducing Isla and later, possibly because it was obviously so old, there'd seemed more important things to concentrate on. He wished he'd asked. Would it have unlocked the story of her past? Or was she telling him now because they'd made a baby together and had to negotiate its future?

'So you stayed in an orphanage? What was it like?'

'Not like a home.' Isla leaned her head against him and nestled closer, and warmth spread through him. 'The other kids and I used to watch TV shows about families and it was nothing like where we grew up. But the people there tried. Some of them were really lovely and others were…okay.'

Theo's muscles tightened as he wondered what okay meant. Better for now to take it at face value.

'Actually, that's where I learned to knit.'

He heard the smile in her voice and responded in kind. 'And where you developed your interest in ancient history?' He could imagine her as an eager child, reading stories of Greek myths and hidden treasures.

She raised her hand, stroking her fingers down his chest and sending a ripple of heat through him. Theo fought not to respond, knowing she wasn't intentionally trying to arouse him, though having her seated on his lap didn't help.

'No. I was fostered with a family for a very short time.'

Her hand stopped, fingers splaying against his chest. Theo covered her hand with his.

'It didn't work out?' He made himself focus on her words.

'Oh, it did. I was happy there. They'd already adopted a boy and we felt like a real family. It was the happiest time of my life.'

Her wistful tone made something still within him, for clearly it hadn't *worked*.

Isla leaned back and looked at him. To his surprise her eyes sparkled. 'Martha was a classics lecturer. She told me wonderful stories about ancient Greece and Rome and gave me a book about the old myths that I loved.'

Now he understood that smile. 'She's the one who lit that spark in you, isn't she? The one who got you interested in ancient history and archaeology.'

'Absolutely. She made it come alive but at the same time spoke about all the mysteries still to be uncovered and treasures to be found. How could I fail to be hooked?'

'She must be very proud of you doing so well with your studies.'

To Theo's dismay Isla's smile faded. 'I'm sure she would be. Unfortunately she died soon after. That's why I wasn't adopted, because Martha was diagnosed with an aggressive cancer. Her husband, Mark, had his hands full with his grief and the son they'd already adopted. The idea of adopting me too...' She shook her head.

'I'm sorry, Isla.' The words weren't sufficient. Even he, who'd never met the family, felt the loss. Isla's smile as she remembered Martha said so much about the woman.

'It was terrible,' she confirmed. 'But I'm so glad I met them. Martha in particular was wonderful...'

And would have made a wonderful mother.

Theo sensed the words she didn't say and his heart twisted in sympathy with the little girl who'd wanted a family of her own. He swallowed, his throat rough as he imagined Isla, abandoned at birth then passed over because of her heart defect, hoping to belong in this family, only to have that hope snatched away.

He remembered how he'd preached to her about the importance of parents, a stable family environment, and cringed.

'It's all right, Theo. It was a long time ago.'

Just because something was in the past didn't mean it couldn't still affect you. Theo couldn't help but think of his stepsister, whose bad choices, especially when it came to men and her recent drug use were, he was sure, linked to her early experiences. Not that there was any evidence of such problems with Isla. On the contrary, she seemed one of the most grounded people he'd met.

'What are you thinking?' She tilted her head to one side, surveying him. 'You have the strangest look on your face.'

'Do I? I was just thinking how remarkable you are.'

The hint of humour in her expression faded. 'Why? We orphans are just like everybody else.'

She'd misinterpreted his sympathy. 'I mean that a lot of people would feel bitter about missing out on a family.' The idea of it made him pause. 'Yet instead of bitterness, you remember that time with fondness and a smile. I think that shows strength of character and I admire it.' He paused. 'I admire *you*.'

He felt terribly sorry for her but knew admitting that wouldn't be welcome. She'd made it clear she didn't want his sympathy and he'd abide by her wishes. And it was true, though she didn't want to know it, that he was impressed with the way she'd put herself through university and gone so far towards achieving her career goals, without the backup and encouragement of family.

'Thank you, Theo. That's…nice.'

Nice? Hardly, not when she was herself remarkable. But he didn't say it, knowing she was wary of what she might see as empty flattery.

Her hand stroked lightly towards his hip and he couldn't help a shiver of response. Guilt bit him. Here she was, sharing her personal history, a history he guessed she rarely talked about, and he was getting a hard-on.

'Is something wrong? You look uncomfortable.'

Theo shifted, trying to conceal the effect she had on him.

'I'm fine. But it's getting late. You need your sleep.'

Though she seemed much better than in England, Isla was still recuperating from months of sickness and exhaustion.

'You're tired?' She drew a deep breath, making Theo too aware off her pink-tipped breasts cresting the water.

Reawakened desire was a bolt of energy, arcing through his body and making his blood pump harder.

Theo was about to make some noncommittal response about needing to work the next day—only too true, given the recent scandal's fallout on his reputation and by extension the company's—when he caught Isla's expression.

Her eyes were knowing, her mouth in an almost-pout that made his grip tighten on her soft flesh.

She was *teasing* him?

It had been so long since they'd shared light-hearted banter and in the interim, life had filled with sombre troubles and responsibilities. Since his arrest, he'd thought of Isla as someone to be protected. His responsibility.

But she was much more, this living, breathing siren.

'I was thinking of you.'

Yet as he spoke, Theo couldn't resist the temptation to trail his hand slowly up her thigh. Satisfaction stabbed as she shivered and leaned into him.

'Do that again.' The words held a throaty edge that rolled through his belly, drawing every nerve tight in anticipation.

Theo splayed his hand across the top of her thigh, his thumb brushing the gossamer-soft hair that hid her feminine core. She shivered again, leaning into his body, her nipples pebbling as if eager for his attention.

Her straying hand moved between them, deft fingers caressing then encircling his erection, and fire scorched every half-formed thought.

'Isla.' It sounded like a warning and a plea, not surprising as he was torn between sexual need and the voice telling him to hold back.

'Theo. You *do* want me, don't you?'

He laughed, the sound abrupt. 'Can't you tell? I thought it was obvious.'

He pushed her thighs apart, sliding his hand down to cup her. Instantly she tilted her hips, seeking his touch and satisfaction blasted through him. Just like before, she couldn't deny the fierce hunger between them. She seemed to revel in it.

He thought of his plan to persuade her into marriage for the sake of their child. But this wasn't a deliberate tactic to win her over. This was simply…essential.

Plans and persuasion could wait. The forces driving him were too elemental.

'You're not too tired?' Was he crazy, trying to talk her out of this? But much as he craved her sweet surrender, a stronger imperative was at work, the need to protect his woman.

'Tired?' Her grip firmed as she stroked his length, eyes shining as she registered his body's response. 'Do I look tired?'

'You look amazing.'

She stared rapt, as if he were something more than an ordinary man. She made him feel ten feet tall.

Her parted lips were an invitation to delight. The damp heat had turned her hair into a sexy tangle of chestnut curls and where they lay, wet against her pale shoulders, they drew his gaze down to her beautiful breasts. Did he imagine they were fuller than before? Was that due to her pregnancy, or was it his imagination?

Theo's hands went to her waist, gripping firmly and lifting her to face him. Her hands went to his shoulders, those lush breasts bobbing before him.

'Sit astride me.' His voice was a gruff command, raw with anticipation, but it didn't matter as she was already setting her knees on either side of his hips.

She rose and he leaned forward, capturing one berry-tipped breast in his mouth. She tasted of summer sunshine and sweet woman. Her moan of pleasure was the best music he'd ever heard as he drew on her, slow and hard, watching her head tilt back as her pelvis circled and her hands clawed at his shoulders.

'Theo. That feels…'

Her words stopped as he pulled her lower body closer, the apex of her thighs against his erection. That connection blasted away any pretence of him being in control. His hands moved to her hips, insistent, as his hips rose, bringing them even closer.

A great shudder ripped through him. It felt like years since he'd had her. Not an hour. The need for her, a potent brew of sensual expectation and primitive compulsion, eclipsed all else.

'Come to me.' Again it wasn't a lover's smooth invitation but a grunted command, all he could manage as his larynx shut down.

She didn't need further urging, positioning herself above him then sinking low just as he rose again, unable to keep still. One urgent slide was all it took and they were joined, so deep and sure it shocked him.

Had it possibly felt so good last time? His hands found Isla's breasts and she jerked against him, making a sound in the back of her throat that would make a grown man weep with excitement if he weren't fully occupied trying to hold himself still. He'd meant to go slower, cautious of the new life she carried.

But Isla destroyed all thought of holding back and taking it easy. Her hips angled and Theo lodged impossibly deep, at the heart of her. The feel of her slick heat so tight around him, the subtle movement of her muscles drawing at him, shot caution and conscious thought to smithereens.

He squeezed her breast, his other hand clamping her

hip as he rose with her. They moved together, finding the primitive rhythm with no effort at all. As if their bodies were totally attuned. Each stroking caress, each breathless coming together was better than the last. His pulse raced harder and faster. The breath sawed from his lungs and the sound of her little gasps of pleasure incited the primitive, desperate man inside him.

They plunged together, riding the surging tide of carnal excitement with growing abandon.

'Come for me, Isla. Let go.'

Because he wanted her to find pleasure, even more than he craved the orgasm he felt bearing down on him like a thundering mountain avalanche.

Once more he bent his head to her breast, closing his mouth around her nipple and sucking till she jerked and cried out, her body clenching hard around him again and again.

Theo wrapped his arms around her, comforting and encouraging her as she came apart, a sense of profound satisfaction blanketing everything else. Until it was too much, the clutching writhe of her body, the way she held his head to her breast, crooning his name over and over as if he'd not only ripped her world apart but put it back together for her.

Whiteout hit. A tsunami of sensation. Heat. Exquisite ecstasy so potent it edged towards pain. Joy so intense it transformed this from sex to something on a new, previously undiscovered plane.

Shudders rocked him and he held Isla close, arms wrapped around her, face buried in the sweet-scented crook of her neck.

He breathed deep, inhaling the tantalising perfume of well-pleasured woman and the tiniest, distinctive trace of rosemary. It was a reminder, not that he needed it, that only with Isla had he ever experienced anything like this.

Because of the baby?

Because of the woman herself?

He'd puzzle it out later. For now all he knew was that Isla belonged with him. He'd do whatever it took to keep her.

CHAPTER ELEVEN

ISLA SLEPT LATE. When she woke, spread-eagled in the centre of Theo's bed, it was to a brilliant blue sky and a sense of wellbeing she hadn't known in forever.

Not since the island, when you were with Theo and wildly in love.

That thought made her breath hitch. She couldn't afford to tumble back into love.

Was it sex that made her feel so good?

From the first Theo had awoken a passionate side of her nature. Yet she felt more than the sated luxury of a blissed-out body.

She thought over last evening, the way they'd connected over their meal out, the barriers they'd broken down as they discussed their lives, each reaching beyond the usual limits to share with the other. That felt significant, as if they really were opening up to each other on a new level as equals.

Was she looking through rose-tinted glasses, seeing what she wanted to see? A cynic would say Theo was motivated by the need to flatten her defences and make her feel they could create a meaningful relationship. Because he wanted marriage, or more specifically, a permanent relationship with his child.

The optimist in her cringed at that view, protesting that last night had been real, both the camaraderie and the joy, and that Theo cared. She'd seen his expression when she'd revealed her past, understanding the sympathy he held in check. His admiration had buoyed her too.

Isla wanted to believe it had all been real but given what had happened before, she needed to be cautious. She couldn't read too much into last night. Theo had only been back in her life a short time. Once before she'd made the error of believing they shared something meaningful and wouldn't make that mistake again.

As for anything more, it was too soon even to consider his suggestion of marriage. Her lips quirked. She couldn't think of it as a proposal, for that implied hearts, flowers and romance. Not something utterly pragmatic.

Besides, she had a sinking feeling she could all too readily fall for Theo again whereas she knew he was focused on practicalities. He was driven by duty and responsibility. Yes, there was caring as well but not the soul-deep adoration she craved.

Was it unrealistic to want that? As long as she could remember she'd yearned for unconditional love. To be the most important person in someone's life, not for pragmatic reasons but just because.

She flung off the sheet and sat up, amazed again that, apart from the tiniest niggle, there was no nausea. She actually felt well. Energised. Fizzing with anticipation.

'Sleep well, *glykia mou*?'

Theo's rich voice curled around her as she entered one of the large sitting rooms. He was sprawled in a large armchair before the huge picture window, phone in hand and computer open nearby. But he wasn't dressed for the office in one of his tailored suits. He wore a dark shirt that somehow emphasised the golden gleam of his eyes, sleeves rolled up casually, and faded jeans.

Isla yanked her gaze back up from those impressive thighs, heat kissing her skin at the memory of Theo's strength. Last night he'd made her feel small and oh-so feminine without in any way diminishing her.

Sexual awareness curled in her belly, the mere sight of him unleashing supercharged, libidinous thoughts.

'Thanks, I did.'

She'd slept a lot since arriving in Athens, though each morning she'd woken knowing her dreams had been uneasy because of her uncertainty about the future. But last night, or rather this morning, her sleep had been deep and restorative.

'You're not going into the office?'

'Not yet. I wanted to be here when you woke.'

Isla had told herself she wasn't disappointed, waking alone in that vast bed. Theo was a busy CEO. No doubt he had teams of people demanding his time. The idea of him letting her sleep in and rescheduling his day to be here for her made her feel special.

'Thank you, Theo.'

Heat flickered in his deep brown eyes, making them glow. Instantly Isla felt an answering heat low in her body. As if it took just one look to bring her to arousal.

But it was true. Isla wanted to snatch his phone away and sink onto Theo's lap, to relive their glorious lovemaking.

She stiffened, horrified at how much she wanted that and how easily he affected her. How could she withstand this single-minded man if she let herself be tempted so easily?

'I looked in on you a while ago and heard the shower running so my housekeeper is preparing your breakfast. I'm expecting a conference call then I'll join you.'

Yet he put his phone down and stood, his expression telling her it wasn't business he had on his mind. He was halfway across the room to her when his phone rang and he stopped, cursing under his breath.

For some reason the sight of Theo stymied of his intentions made Isla smile. He might be rich and privileged but in that moment he seemed endearing.

He swung around and stalked back to collect his phone. Isla hurried after him, grabbing his shoulder and planting a swift kiss on his lips before pulling back.

There was a thud as the phone fell. Strong arms wrapped around her, lifting her almost off her feet as Theo kissed her slowly and thoroughly. She sank into him, holding back nothing as their kiss deepened, desire driving them and the world falling away. Finally they separated just enough to breathe properly. Isla's head spun and she heard bells.

'I'd better take it. It's the third time they've rung back.'

Yet Theo didn't release her straightaway. He held her close, eyes intent on hers, and Isla felt something rise within her as if to meet him. Something big and momentous.

Isla shook her head and pushed his shoulders. 'You need to take the call. They're waiting for you.'

She had to remember that one night's sublime intimacy didn't mend the fractures between them. They wanted different things, even if they both wanted the best for their baby.

Finally Theo released her and reached for his phone. 'You're a bad influence, Isla. This is the first time I've ever been tempted to ignore a meeting. You'd better go before I change my mind.'

Despite telling herself it was only a kiss and that nothing was resolved between them, Isla's heart sang as she left the room.

She was sitting in the sunshine on the roof terrace, the empty breakfast plates cleared away.

Theo paused, taking in the sight of her in a slim-fitting dress of rich blue that enhanced her subtle beauty and intrinsic sexiness. No wonder he'd had trouble concentrating on the call. He wanted to take her straight back to bed.

Since England she'd dominated his thoughts. He had to find a way to combat that. He needed all his faculties to deal not just with the prospect of fatherhood, but the damage to the company and even more urgently, Toula's issues. His stepsister seemed to be recovering well after her breakdown. But she still suffered memory loss of that traumatic night. What would happen when she returned to Athens? She would need all his support. How could he do that with Isla diverting him?

Persuade her into marriage, that was how.

Once he had Isla locked into his plans he could focus on other things again.

Or maybe she'll be a permanent distraction.

It seemed only too likely.

All the more reason to make sure of her as quickly as possible.

That meant bringing forward his plans. The sooner Isla accepted her idea of raising their child alone was unrealistic, the better. This was his child and he had both a right and an obligation to it.

But if she couldn't understand that, she'd soon see that her relationship with a once famous, now infamous billionaire made her public property. Anonymity was impossible, even if she didn't know it yet. When she did, he'd be here, ready to support her.

She'd need him then.

Was it selfish to look forward to her recognising that? He admired her independence yet on another level it rankled. He was continually distracted by this one intransigent woman, while she seemed unimpressed. Except in bed.

He felt a scalding rush to his groin. There it was again, the familiar hunger. But he couldn't give in to it now when there were other matters to settle.

Theo rubbed his hand around the back of his neck, registering tense muscles. Not just because so much rode on getting Isla to marry him. But because he regretted what would come next. She was a private person and she'd feel the intense media attention like a blow.

Guilt swarmed through him. Her life had changed because of him. From now on she'd be a press target, something he knew from experience was difficult. He thought of Toula's experiences and his heart sank.

Isla would have to run the gauntlet of the press every day simply because they were together. Even if they weren't together and she tried to live a *normal* life away from him there'd be paparazzi following her and their child.

He walked onto the terrace.

Instantly she turned, as if sensing his presence. He liked the way she seemed attuned to him. Maybe it was a residue of last night's intimacy. Would it survive what was to come?

'Your meeting went well?'

'As well as could be expected.' Seeing her raised eyebrows, he went on. 'Business hasn't been straightforward since my arrest. The company is sound but my reputation dived and that had a flow-on effect.'

'Surely with your release that's over, even if Spiro Stavroulis is still pestering you.'

Theo went to take a chair beside her then changed his mind. He thought more clearly with some distance. Instead he closed his hands around the balustrade of the glass railing and looked across the city to the shimmering sea.

'Despite its size, Karalis Enterprises is essentially a family company and has been for generations. The name and the family are at the heart of its success. My father and his father before him were good men, sound in business and honest. The character of the CEO plays a huge part in how the company is viewed. Several major contracts and new investments were scheduled for the last couple of months and now...' Theo shrugged.

'That's so unfair.'

Her chair scraped then Isla was beside him. He felt her gaze, just as he did every time she looked at him. It was something he'd experienced with no one else and made him frown.

'Don't worry, I'm working through it. Things will be well in the long term. I'll still be able to provide for you and our baby.'

She turned away, planting her smaller hands on the balustrade and like him, staring out at the view instead of at him. 'That's not what I meant!'

Theo knew it wasn't but it was easier to focus on what needed to be done, instead of carrying her back to bed, if he kept a little distance between them.

His mouth rucked up in a bitter smile. Who was he kidding? Even when she was annoyed with him he had trouble thinking straight around her.

'Of course not. I know you're not here for my money.' A mirthless laugh escaped. He almost wished she were because then it would be easier to bind her and their child to him and a life in Greece.

'But there's something else I need to speak with you about. Something important.' He dragged his phone from his pocket. 'Last night we were photographed returning from the restaurant.'

'I don't understand.'

Of course she didn't. Isla's life was as sheltered from the press as his had been until his mother married into the Karalis family. Even then Theo hadn't been bothered much until he was working in the company and old enough to feature in those stupid lists of sexiest or wealthiest men.

He found the photo that had started this morning's media furore yet he didn't immediately hand her the phone.

Looking into her misty blue eyes Theo felt a pang of regret at how her life changed now because of him. He couldn't prevent that. In fact he was about to escalate it, to get the worst over with as quickly as possible. And show her they needed to be together. Yet part of him wished he could secrete her away in some private paradise and keep her just for himself.

'Theo, what's so bad about a photo?'

He passed the phone to her and watched her eyes grow round.

'But this isn't even a Greek media outlet. This is British.'

'We made the news through Europe, North America, Asia and beyond.'

She bit her lip as she read the speculation about her relationship with the multibillionaire so recently arrested for murder. The piece made him sound dangerous while Isla was portrayed alternatively as an unaware innocent or a gold digger who didn't care about her lover's morals.

'That's libel!' Her horrified face turned to him.

'I suspect they've stayed just this side of libel.'

'What are you going to do? You can't let them print such lies about you.'

Theo blinked then took her hands in his. Her first thought wasn't for her reputation but his. That knowledge was a glowing, precious kernel deep in his chest. Proof that, despite her misgivings, they could move forward to build a strong relationship worthy of their child.

She cares for you.

Just as he'd believed when she visited the prison.

Theo had told himself this was something he could capitalise on to get her to marry. Yet what he felt now had nothing to do with future plans and everything to do with feelings.

'I've got strong shoulders. But if they go too far my

legal team will prosecute. For now my focus has to be on mending the damage done to the company.' He paused. 'And keeping you safe.'

He watched her brow pucker as she thought through the situation. Finally, as he'd known she would, she nodded. 'You have a plan, don't you?'

He inclined his head. She'd always been clever and her relative calm in the face of that outrageous piece boded well. Their baby might have thrown him and Isla together but he knew in that moment she wouldn't just be a necessary wife. He suspected she'd be magnificent.

How would it be to share the burdens he carried? To have someone on his side, apart from his mother, whom he refused to weigh down with more trouble.

'We provide the story they want, but on our terms. The media knows about you now and you won't get any peace until it gets a story. Even then you'll continue to be hounded, especially when your pregnancy becomes news.'

Her hands spasmed in his and he tightened his hold, watching her pupils dilate. It was like watching her innocence being stripped away and it made him feel wrong inside, but he had to go on. She needed the truth.

'Even if you decide not to marry me and opt to bring up our child alone…' As if he'd let that happen! 'The press won't let up. They'll be there whenever you leave your London flat. They'll interview clients at the shop where you work. They'll go through your rubbish to find out what your pregnancy diet is and turn it into some fad diet for their readers or report you're endangering the baby by eating poorly. Later they'll print stories about what you feed our child and if they have no idea, they'll make it up.'

Isla looked so appalled he felt almost guilty spelling it out but she needed to know. 'It's true. The stories they've printed about my stepsister, often without a single word of truth, are legion.' The fact that Toula sometimes behaved erratically hadn't helped.

'They pursued her? I didn't know.'

'Toula has some personal problems but the media loves to portray her as an indulged rich kid, acting out.' Theo paused, reining in anger. He was tempted to explain about his stepsister now but this was enough for Isla to take in at the moment. 'Between their attacks on Toula and on me, I know what to expect. There'll be a media scrum outside any childcare centre you use and as for first day at school—'

'Enough! I get it.'

Reading her distressed expression and pale features he saw she did. He felt the tremor in her hands and vowed to protect her.

'So what's the plan? How do we take back control? And don't say by marrying.'

But they would. Theo was determined on that. Once she understood what he could offer, and how difficult life would be without him at her side, she'd change her mind.

'We dictate the narrative, and we control access to you. I have the resources to provide twenty-four-hour protection wherever you are. It can be so discreet you won't notice it but there will be times when it needs to be up front and obvious to everyone.'

'Bodyguards?' Isla pulled her hands away. 'I'm not sure about that.'

'I am.' Isla was his now, whether she admitted it or not. He couldn't allow anyone to harm her. 'I've lined up an excellent female protection agent.' He read Isla's mutinous look and intervened before she could object. 'She'll be here soon for you to vet. It's important you feel you can trust her.' He waited until finally she nodded. 'And I have plans for our next outing. Next time you're seen it will be in a situation we can control, rather than have photographers mob you in the street.'

It was the casual way Theo mentioned being mobbed in the street that finally convinced Isla. And the pain in his voice when he'd spoken of his stepsister, Toula, being victimised. There'd been something in his voice then that she'd never before heard. A raw ache that made her nape prickle and a slew of questions form on her tongue. But it hadn't been the right time to ask.

So she'd agreed to interview the bodyguard. Fortunately she turned out be someone Isla could imagine spending time with. Of a similar age but with impressive qualifications, she didn't look like a bodyguard and Isla found herself enjoying her understated sense of humour.

That was the first hurdle over. The second was preparing for a gala event Isla would attend with Theo that night. It sounded daunting with formal dress and high-profile attendees. She felt out of place and she hadn't even left the apartment.

Everything had been brought to her here. Racks of amazing designer gowns, shoes in every colour and style, so that even with the help of an expert stylist, choosing what to wear had taken ages. Then there were the masseuse, beautician and hairstylist who spent hours with her.

It was enough to make a woman feel like Cinderella, yet despite the gorgeous clothes and the light but expert makeup that turned her into a sophisticated stranger, it was the massage she loved best. Until then her shoulders had been up near her ears, tension riding her because there was no going back to her old life, even if she wanted to.

But you don't want to, do you? Despite everything you'd rather be here with Theo.

That's what made all this so tough. She fought her own desires when she stood firm against his plan for marriage.

It would be easy to agree and be swept along by the juggernaut that was Theo Karalis, the man who made the impossible happen with ease. She could marry him and know her child would grow up with two caring parents. It would know it was loved. How precious was that?

Life would be easier for Isla too. No money worries. She could continue her studies. Into the bargain she'd have a handsome, attentive lover, for she had no illusions that Theo intended a paper marriage. He was far too passionate for that.

All that held her back was the fear she teetered on the brink of falling for him again. Of wanting too much from a man who thought about duty, not love. And when he tired of sex with her? She didn't think she could bear being married to him when he took other lovers.

So what are you going to do?

A sound behind her made her swing around.

'Theo.' Her voice was breathless, but who wouldn't be, faced with the handsomest man she'd ever seen, tall and resplendent in bespoke formal wear, looking at her as if he wanted to eat her up?

Her insides turned to liquid and a hungry pulse throbbed at that aching, empty place between her legs. They'd made love most of the night but today he'd kept his distance after that single kiss and Isla discovered she missed him.

From the strong planes of his face to the imposing width of his shoulders and the blaze of his eyes as he surveyed her, he was gorgeous.

He could be yours if you just say the word.

Isla knew Theo could arrange a sumptuous wedding celebration just as quickly and effectively as he'd organised her move to Athens and everything else if she let him.

She bit her lip, afraid in that moment that she might yield to temptation and say yes.

Because you want him.

It was shaming but true. She had little pride left where he was concerned and she was afraid that the more she had of him the more she'd want.

'I knew you'd look stunning,' he murmured, pacing across the bedroom towards her, 'but still I wasn't prepared.'

Isla blinked as she registered his hoarse voice and the dark glow of desire in his eyes. These weren't just pretty words. Joy so strong it ached had her pressing her hand to her breastbone.

It wasn't fair when Theo said such things to her. When he looked at her that way. How could she be sensible?

'The press will be out in force tonight, but don't worry about them. Just follow my lead and it will all work out okay. I'll look after you.'

With that reminder, Isla's starry-eyed gaze cleared.

Tonight wasn't about *them*, together because he craved her company and wanted her to meet his friends. It was about public expectations and managing the media.

Isla discovered that after all it wasn't hard to be sensible about their relationship.

CHAPTER TWELVE

THEO HELPED ISLA from the limo under a barrage of flashing lights. Voices called his name, shouting questions. He ignored them. All his attention was on the woman whose hand rested in his.

He felt her shudder at the blare of light and noise surrounding them and wanted to shield her.

'Take your time,' he said softly. 'It'll be okay, I promise. All you have to do is walk inside with me. You don't have to say anything.'

He squeezed her hand as their eyes met and his brain blocked out the hubbub. There was just the two of them.

'Trust me, Isla.'

Finally she nodded and stepped from the car, eyes locked on his, and his breath caught. She was magnificent and her being here felt suddenly like the greatest proof of trust and loyalty.

No matter what he told himself about Isla having no escape from press attention now they knew about her, it took guts to throw her lot in publicly with a man whose once vaunted reputation was now stained. She could have refused to come tonight. Instead she'd risen to the challenge.

She straightened and the din around them eased for real as hardened journalists forgot their questions.

Theo knew the feeling. When he'd first seen her tonight his larynx had frozen while other parts of his body clamoured into eager life.

Her hair was up in an elegant style that left a couple of chestnut curls loose to kiss her neck. Strands of twisted gold threaded through her hair, reminding him of a portrait he'd seen of a beautiful woman from classical times. Isla wore gold, a dress of tiny pleats that burst into life under a renewed barrage of lights as the photographers went wild. The full-length gown was modelled on classical lines, with golden cords around her waist and under her bust, the fine fabric moulding her slim body and beautiful breasts, leaving her pale arms and throat bare. Its clinging fit revealed the tiny curve of her belly, but not obviously proclaiming her pregnancy.

She looked like a goddess. *His* goddess.

Theo was torn between pride as he tucked her arm through his and unfamiliar trepidation, as if no mere man had a right to touch this scintillating, celestial being.

Except Isla was warm flesh and blood. He drew her close and felt that tiny shiver of response that she couldn't quite hide. Her gaze clung to his and as the moment lengthened, he saw her anxiety fade as excitement stirred.

He was tempted to hustle her back into the car and then home where they could be alone.

'Should we move?' she breathed.

He blinked and saw they were still beside the limo. The shouts had reached fever pitch. 'Let them have their photos. They'll bother us less later.'

Except they'd probably clamour even harder for photos of this stunning woman.

Then he noticed the goosebumps on her arms and led her forward, keeping her close for warmth but also in unmistakeable possessiveness. He urged her into the prestigious museum and instantly the decibels dropped.

'I should have insisted you wear a coat.'

'And spoil the impact of the dress?' She shook her head. 'It's the only time I've had a chance to wear anything so gorgeous. I wasn't going to hide it. Besides, it's warm enough in here.'

Not surprising as the huge entry space was filled with the great and the good not only of Athens but from across Europe and beyond. The opening of the new wing was a huge event, years in the planning.

Their arrival caused a ripple of reaction. He saw it like a wave on an otherwise still sea, heads turning, conversations breaking off and beginning again in whispers.

Theo should be used to it yet it still angered him that there were people willing to believe the worst, despite proven facts. Even the evidence that proved he wasn't on the stairs where Spiro Stavroulis had died seemed to have little impact.

Theo stood taller, shoulders back. He sensed Isla glance up at him. This time it was her hand squeezing his. He jerked his gaze away from the crowd, surprised to discover what looked like sympathy in hers. He knew she'd been nervous, even annoyed at finding herself in the eye of a media storm. Now she looked at him with an expression that spoke of warmth and understanding.

'Theo! I'm so glad you could make it.'

He turned to see a familiar smiling face. Not only one but several. There were handshakes and warm greetings as he introduced Isla to the museum's director and his wife, to the head of the nation's archaeology service and the government minister who'd got this major expansion funded.

After that the event went smoothly, though Theo had to reiterate his refusal not to make a speech. Karalis money might have contributed substantially to the project but he wasn't in the mood for public addresses, despite what his PR team advised. He was here tonight for Isla, giving her a taste of what she could expect but limiting her exposure to the prying public. He wouldn't leave her alone to take the limelight on the podium.

Theo set himself to circulate, to introduce her to some of the more interesting guests and make the evening easier for her. They'd met politicians and business leaders, socialites and academics and Isla held her own. Even with a sharp-tongued doyenne of Athenian society who he knew still intimidated his mother. He'd been ready to step in, but Isla handled her perfectly with quiet dignity and honesty. She refused to be bullied, instead responding with questions of her own till the old woman laughed and announced she was a refreshing change from the usual thoughtless girls she met. *That* set people gossiping, but in a good way.

Yet Theo sensed the effort it took for Isla to keep her poise. This wasn't her milieu. But when they met a knot of archaeologists and historians she was in her element, listening avidly as they discussed the exhibits.

They were leaving when disaster threatened. The crowd before them parted and there was Stavroulis, eyes blazing retribution.

Theo's instinct was to lead Isla away before the old man launched another venomous attack. But to turn away would be to insult the grieving man and Theo couldn't do that. Despite the hurt he'd inflicted, Stavroulis suffered.

But Theo did pull her protectively against his side as he approached the other man. The crowd around them hushed and he felt the expectation as a ripple of excitement.

He nodded. 'Stavroulis.' Then he turned. 'Isla, I'd like you to meet Spiro Stavroulis.' When he looked back at the other man it was like looking into a mask, so tightly did he hold in his feelings. 'This is Isla Jacobs, from England.'

Stavroulis's eyes flashed. Would he scream an insult at Theo or storm away without a word? Before he could do either Isla spoke. Not only that but she moved out of Theo's embrace and right up to the old man.

'I heard about your grandson.' The drop of a pin would have been loud in the silence. 'What a terrible thing. I'm so sorry for your loss.'

Theo's heart hammered a staccato beat as he stepped up beside her, muscles tensing, ready to intervene if necessary. He'd visited the man to offer his condolences, only to have them violently spurned. He wouldn't allow Stavroulis to try that with Isla.

But after a pregnant silence during which Theo noticed more than one phone raised to capture the moment, Stavroulis inclined his head in a stiff bow and thanked her. He even added that it was a pleasure to meet her before spinning on his heel and marching away.

Isla was silent on the way home, ignoring the paparazzi and the security team who cleared the way.

No wonder she was preoccupied. The evening hadn't gone as he'd planned. It had backfired, with Isla in the firing line.

'That was awful,' she said as they entered the sitting room, confirming his thoughts.

She shivered and hugged her arms around herself and Theo hated that he'd been responsible for that. He strode across to get them drinks. She wasn't drinking alcohol but he needed something to do, pouring her a soft drink then a brandy for himself that he knocked back in one swallow. It was sacrilege to treat the fine spirit that way, but he welcomed its burn.

'I apologise. I should have checked if he'd be there tonight. He so rarely goes to such events I didn't consider the possibility that he'd confront us. Are you okay?'

'*Me?* It's *you* I'm thinking of. How dare so many of them treat you like that, when you've done nothing wrong?'

Theo stared, his brain playing catch-up with her words. Isla was annoyed on his behalf?

'As for the way they watched you, and that man…' She shook her head. 'It makes me sick.'

He put the soft drink down and moved closer. 'The nausea is back?' Now he really felt guilty. She'd been doing so well lately.

Isla's gaze meshed with his and heat slammed into him as he felt the full force of her fury. Then she gave a lopsided smile. 'Not literally. But the injustice makes me so angry. Treating you both as if you're some sort of public amusement.'

Theo stared. 'You're angry with the guests?'

'Of course! I know there were plenty who were genuinely glad to see you but there were others who enjoyed the drama at your expense. Even after all you've been through.'

His expense not hers. Something shuddered deep inside as her words touched a part of Theo that he'd kept isolated behind his strongest defences.

He couldn't accustom himself to the fact Isla thought of him when *she* was the one pregnant and tired, facing the future in a foreign land, complete with paparazzi and gawking socialites. 'It's you I worry about. I'm okay, I've—'

'Got broad shoulders, so you keep saying.' She shook her head. 'But it's still outrageous.'

She fizzed with energy, like a lit firework about to explode. Theo reached out and took her wrists, gently tugging her arms from around her ribs and pulling her to him, trying to calm her restlessness.

'Don't get worked up about it. It's not good for you or the baby. I'm fine.' It took more than a bit of malicious speculation to get the better of him. 'It's *you* I'm concerned about. Stavroulis is a volatile man. I worried how he'd react when you approached him.'

Isla shook her head. 'That poor man. Imagine losing a family member to violence and not knowing who was responsible.'

Theo's jaw clenched on a familiar spasm of regret. The

whole situation was appalling. If only Toula had never met Costa Stavroulis. If only the guy hadn't gatecrashed the family party.

If only, if only. Were there any more fruitless words?

'Theo?' He looked down to see her bright eyes fixed on him. 'You look…haunted. Is it from seeing Stavroulis again?'

That was the least of it, but the full story wasn't his to tell. He only had suspicions. How could he act on those, knowing the consequences?

'Don't fret about me,' he growled. He was buffeted by frustration at circumstances he couldn't change and the roiling emotions that surfaced every time he was with Isla, or thought about her.

It wasn't the drama of tonight's scene that ripped at him, but that he'd brought this woman into the heart of it all. It would have been easier for her if he'd let her stay in England, out of the limelight. But how could he have? He needed her with him.

Her and their child.

Except when he looked into those silvery-blue eyes it wasn't her pregnancy he thought of. It was her fire, her determination, her stoicism in the face of so many traumas. Her sympathy and warmth.

How he wanted that warmth, that sympathy now.

'Theo?' She licked her lips and swayed closer.

What did she see in his expression? He'd warned himself to keep his distance because she messed with his head and because he'd already let her down. But the words were already in his mouth.

'I want you, Isla.' His voice was rough with a hunger so deep he'd never experienced its like.

He *needed* her so much it made him shake, because he was selfish and losing himself with Isla was the closest he'd come to finding peace in forever. Not that it was peace he wanted now, but the sheer addictive bliss of melding himself with her. Of finding that place where together they touched heaven.

Theo's chest ached and he realised his breath had stopped. Until Isla leaned in, rising on her toes to brush her lips across his.

The air rushed from his lungs like water from a bursting dam. He gathered her to him, lifting her and covering her mouth with his. A storm of sensation hit as their lips met and clung. There was nothing tentative about their kiss now. It was the full-bodied kiss of lovers too long apart, filled with hunger as well as delight and homecoming.

Isla said something, the sound muffled in his mouth, but Theo recognised it as his name. Just as he recognised acute need in the clamp of her fingers against the back of his skull.

No matter the circumstances that had brought them to this point, they were equals in this.

'I need you now, Theo.'

Theo lifted his head. 'The bedroom. I need to take care of you—'

Her fingertips raked his scalp, sending flashes of lightning into his blood and straight to his groin.

'I don't need that. I'm not going to break. *Now*, Theo.' She sculpted herself against him, her softness fitting perfectly against his unyielding body and in her voice he heard his own desperation.

Fighting the shudders of excitement building deep within, he turned with her in his arms and carried her to the nearest upright surface, resting her back against the wall and hitching her higher as he pressed himself close to support her.

The misty blue of her eyes disappeared in a silvery flash and she gasped as their bodies fitted against each other. Theo felt like molten metal poured through his veins, his lungs were bellows, fanning the blaze she ignited in him.

He gathered the fine fabric of her long dress in his hands, bunching it up till her legs were bare. She lifted one slim leg and he grabbed it, settling it over his hip. Someone groaned as their bodies tilted together, then her other leg settled around his waist and he couldn't help that hard thrust that notched his erection against her pelvis. Even through layers of fabric it felt like bliss.

'I didn't plan this well.' He still wore his trousers but he refused to step back to undo them. No power on earth could drag him away from Isla now.

Her gasp of laughter teased him as she scrabbled at his belt while he dragged down the zip. A few long moments of fumbling that tested him to the limit then he was free, his swollen length hard against her heat. Delicate lace scraped his skin and he shuddered as that took him too close to the edge.

Neither laughed now. Their need was too intense.

Theo's normally deft fingers felt clumsy as he slid them under that lace. Isla was slick and hot, pushing eagerly against his touch, her urgency fanning the lit fuse of his desire.

Fabric tore and even that tiny sound made his flesh tighten with anticipation. Then there was only sensation. Heat surrounded him, Isla's legs pulling him close as he guided himself to her centre.

There. A moment to align himself, to catch his own reflection in her shining eyes and he drove home, long and hard, and his eyes threatened to roll back in his head at how exquisite Isla was.

A shudder went through them both, travelling between their bodies as if they weren't separate entities but one being. Theo hefted a breath that turned into another shudder at the friction of her breasts against his chest. He wanted her naked but that would have to be later. He wanted her in so many ways his brain threatened to overload.

No time for that now. There was only the need, blood deep and raw, between them.

He planted his hand on the wall beside her head for support as he withdrew and thrust again, twisting a little and hearing her cry out in delight as he found just the right spot.

Isla's hands ran over him, her mouth working as if to speak, until he slid his other hand between them to find that swollen jewel at her core and she shouted his name, arching her neck and pressing her head back.

Theo kissed her throat, finding that most sensitive spot at the base of her neck as he stroked her with his hand and his body.

The tremors began inside her, harbingers of a crisis so profound he expected it would destroy them both. But there was no stopping now. He lavished all his skill into feeding the fire, giving Isla everything, all the pleasure she deserved, all of himself.

Nails pricked his skin and her encircling legs tightened. They moved together, so attuned that when the fire burst inside Isla, it seared him too.

She cried out, but as her climax filled her, Isla's diamond-bright eyes held his. As if part of her feared the force of what they'd unleashed.

Theo cupped her cheek, seeking to reassure her. She convulsed around him, milking his very essence, drawing him into herself. Then everything broke apart in pleasure so intense it felt like joy and flame together.

Isla called his name, her voice a feather in the midst of an inferno, but he heard it and responded.

Her name on his tongue tasted like the food of the gods, so perfect that he recognised with some arcane, inexplicable instinct that this was far more than sex.

What they shared had the power to stop worlds and change lives.

CHAPTER THIRTEEN

ISLA STEPPED OUT onto the roof terrace the next morning to see Theo powering the length of the pool. The sight stopped her in her tracks.

He really was an extraordinarily charismatic man. Even doing laps it was hard to take her eyes off him. The steady rhythm, the play of sunlight across the sleek muscles of his broad shoulders and back, the kick of those powerful thighs…

She pressed a hand to her abdomen where sensation fluttered. It would be nice to think it was her baby moving but she suspected it was simply a response to Theo.

He looked so…elemental in the water, a study in male strength. She recalled all that energy focused on her last night and her breath backed up in her lungs. The phenomenal focus and vigour, the potency of the man. She'd gone from feeling upset on his behalf to needing him with an intensity that surpassed anything she'd known.

That first coupling, barely inside the apartment, had been urgent and extraordinary. As if he'd taken them both to an unfamiliar plane. Afterwards her legs had been boneless and her heart filled with the extraordinary conviction that being with Theo was the one true, right thing in the world.

Later they'd slept until the early hours when they'd come together again, this time slowly, sweetly and his touch as he stroked her body had been almost reverent. It had been exquisite and had left her marvelling, hoping that perhaps things weren't as simple as she thought. Perhaps this wasn't just about their child.

Maybe Theo felt more for her than she'd imagined.

It was true that duty figured in his thinking. But he felt deeply too. Look at the way he'd treated old Mr Stavroulis last night. The man had made himself into an enemy with his quest for vengeance, yet she'd seen Theo's sympathy. She admired him for not shunning the man and hurrying her way. He understood the grief that drove him.

When Theo had spoken of his stepsister too, she'd *felt* his emotion. He genuinely cared for Toula.

Was it too much to hope that perhaps he cared for her as well? Or was it wishful thinking?

She sighed and crossed the terrace towards the pool. If she'd known he was swimming she'd have come straight here instead of having a shower.

With an effort Isla dragged her gaze from Theo, looking at the spectacular view of Athens and the Aegean beyond. Spring had started and soon the warmer weather would be here.

Where would she be then?

She'd planned to be back in London. But did she want that?

Her breath caught in her chest. What she *wanted* was Theo, but not a Theo who viewed her as an obligation or necessary encumbrance. She wanted to be special in her own right. Was it possible that his feelings might grow over time and that his idea of a practical marriage could transform into the love match she'd always wanted?

Last night he'd made her feel special. Maybe—
'Isla!'

Theo surged from the pool in one lithe movement that drew attention to his innate athleticism. He stood tall, flicking the water from his head, his chest rising with each breath after that intense swim.

Isla's mouth dried and a pulse started up between her thighs as she took in the sight of him wearing nothing but dark swim shorts.

Was it any wonder he'd bowled her over when they first met? He looked like a Greek god. She should know, she'd spent long enough studying images of them. But none moved her the way this flawed, flesh-and-blood man did.

'I didn't know where you were,' she blurted out, then wondered if she'd revealed too much.

Theo didn't seem to think so. He marched across and planted a swift but devastating kiss on her mouth. His lips were cold but his mouth warm and he sparked fire in every secret place. Her knees wobbled as he pulled back. 'Sorry, I'm wet.' Honey-gold eyes framed by spiky black lashes mesmerised her then he turned and reached for a towel.

It was only as Theo dried himself that Isla noticed her shirt was damp. Not damp enough to cool her ardour.

He turned back, rubbing his hair so it stood up in tousled crests. He looked almost boyish except for the knowing light in his eyes and the body that belonged to a male in his absolute prime.

'I wanted to wake you.' His voice hit that husky, tantalising note she couldn't resist. 'But thought I should work off some excess energy in the pool first.'

'Did you succeed?'

Theo shook his head. 'There's only one sure-fire remedy for that.' His gaze was a caress, stroking her libido into thrumming life. 'But last night I wasn't gentle. I thought you might be sore.'

Isla lifted her chin. 'If I'd wanted gentle I would have told you. Besides, we went there later.' She'd loved both. The tenderness they'd shared had been as powerful in its own way as the earlier, almost violent surge of need between them.

His smile, a mix of satisfaction and affection, threatened to undo her. But then his expression turned serious. 'Anyway, we need to talk.'

Isla heard strain in his tone. That stopped her impulsive confession that last night had been the most wonderful experience of her life. She still didn't know for sure where she stood with Theo.

'Shall we?' He gestured to some padded sun loungers.

'You don't want to get dressed?' Isla knew how distracting his glorious body would be. If they were discussing something important she needed to concentrate.

'I've spent too much time cooped up inside. I'd rather enjoy the fresh air. There's no cold wind and I'll dry in the sunshine.'

Isla's heart dipped as his explanation took on a darker cast. He wasn't just talking about hours in business meetings. Theo had been incarcerated. Something he didn't speak of except when she'd made it a test of his ability to trust and share with her. Basically she'd blackmailed him.

Her pulse quickened and she blinked back moisture, distressed for all he'd suffered.

'Isla, are you okay?'

'Of course. What did you want to discuss?'

Theo sat beside her but instead of stretching his legs out, he sat sideways, elbows resting on his knees, facing her. 'It's about my family. Toula and my mother have been away from Athens but my mother just contacted me. She's returning to Athens soon.'

'So I'll get to meet her?' Isla tried to read his expression but failed, as if he deliberately held his feelings in. Did he worry they wouldn't like each other?

She felt that old pang of uncertainty, as if she didn't measure up. It had plagued her through childhood as the girl no one wanted, the girl unworthy of love. Did Theo believe his family would meet her and recognise she was fundamentally lacking?

Isla slammed shut those thoughts. She'd moved beyond such thinking, hadn't she? She had as much right to respect and affection as anyone. It was just the stress of the current situation, throwing up old weaknesses.

'Absolutely. She's already heard about you and is eager to meet you. That's why she's returning.' Theo frowned at his clasped hands.

'You don't want that?' Isla tried not to feel defensive.

Theo shrugged. 'I don't want you feeling pressured. I haven't told her about the baby and I know it's important to you to have time to think things through.'

Relief welled. He was concerned for *her* sake, not because he thought she wasn't good enough for his family.

'I'd like to meet her.' Maybe meeting his family would help Isla with her decision. 'She and Toula have been on holiday together?'

He lifted his head. 'No. My mother's in Corfu with a friend on a short break. It's the first time she's left Athens in months. It took a toll on her, Costa's death, my arrest and all the appalling stories. But she visited me in prison then did what she could to help since my release.'

Isla's heart went out to the woman 'It must have been a trying time for all of you. At least she had Toula with her through the worst of it.'

Theo's mouth twisted. 'Not quite.' Again he paused and it struck her that this assured man was, for the first time to her knowledge, unsure how to proceed.

'It's funny. If you'd been one of those women pursuing me for my money you'd have done your homework and already know at least a version of this from the press.' He saw her stiffen and raised his hand. 'Not that I'm complaining. It's just…difficult, something we don't talk about outside the family.'

Isla jerked back. What was he talking about? She'd known from the news reports that Theo had a sister and widowed mother but her focus had been entirely on his arrest and subsequent release. Maybe the UK press didn't have as much detail about the case either.

'But you *are* family. Even though you haven't agreed to marry me.'

She felt his gaze like a palpable weight, yet this time it didn't feel like a burden, rather like a warm enfolding blanket. Had her feelings altered so much?

'We're linked and always will be, Isla. Whatever happens in our relationship, I want you to know my mother and Toula. They're important to me just as you and our child are.'

She searched for a response but found herself choked up at how he included her with his family. Did he have any idea how appealing that was?

'Sorry, I'm so used to protecting them that this is hard to discuss.' He shook his head. 'Toula wasn't vacationing. She had a severe breakdown and has been in a medical facility since the night of the party when Costa Stavroulis died.'

'Oh, Theo!' Isla rose and sat beside him, reaching for his hand. Despite the heat he always generated, his flesh was chilled.

She grabbed the huge towel he'd discarded and wrapped it around his shoulders. 'Let's go inside where it's warm and you can tell me there.'

His mouth curled up in one corner and her predictable heart skipped a beat at that tiny, enticing smile. 'Even my mother doesn't fuss any more about me catching cold.'

Isla hated seeing him so strained. It wasn't the chill air that affected him but worry for his stepsister. 'See, more proof that I wouldn't make a suitable wife.'

'On the contrary. I like it.'

Safer to ignore that, and the stir of excitement his words evoked. 'You must have been frantic, locked up and not able to go to Toula.'

Theo nodded. 'Prison was already a nightmare but that almost undid me. Not being able to support the people important to me.' His fingers closed around hers, gently squeezing, and Isla could almost believe he included her in that group. His next words made her wonder even more. 'I had to stay close to home when I was released, because Toula needed me.'

Yet he'd trekked to London for a business meeting. That didn't quite ring true but before she could ponder it he spoke again.

'All being well, Toula will come back in a month or so and I wanted to prepare you for meeting her, so you understand that she's fragile.'

'She may prefer not to meet me.'

'She's going to be an aunt. Of course she'll want to meet you! She'll be thrilled that we have something positive to celebrate.' He paused then plunged on. 'My stepsister suffers from depression. She had a difficult childhood and very little stability. My father didn't even know she existed until her mother died, six years ago, not long before his own death.'

'Her mother kept Toula secret from him?'

Even when she'd despised Theo, Isla had tried to tell him about his child. The thought of keeping such a thing secret—

'She did, and seeing the damage she did to Toula…' He shook his head. 'It made me even more determined to help raise our child.'

His blazing scrutiny scorched but Isla didn't turn away. She'd learned to respect his resolve to be a hands-on father.

'What happened?'

'Toula's mother was a singer and very beautiful. She knew my father, my stepfather that is, before he met my mother. The pair had a brief affair then she left the country. From what I've heard, I suspect Toula's mother wasn't even sure of her paternity. She loved excitement, new places and male attention but wasn't good at maternal responsibility.'

His shoulders dropped on a silent sigh. 'Toula had a difficult time, always on the move, but I suspect the real problem was her mother's unreliable parenting. Plus she had male friends on high rotation and some of them shouldn't have been around a vulnerable girl.'

Isla's chest tightened. She understood the dangers for vulnerable children. Some of the kids she'd known had suffered greatly.

'Poor Toula.'

Theo inclined his head. 'She's got a good heart but she finds somethings difficult. When she came to us she was very volatile and hid a lack of confidence with brashness and acting out. It took her some time to believe that we really cared. Then our father died and that was especially tough as they'd just begun to build a special relationship.'

It must have been tough for Theo too but Isla simply nodded.

'She was doing really well until she met Costa Stavroulis.' He scowled. 'He was handsome and charming but quick-tempered and self-indulgent, partying to excess and dragging her with him. It was the worst possible environment. Alcohol and drugs didn't help her mental state and nor did his domineering ways. He went out of his way to undermine her so she was reliant on him. Finally she accepted she didn't like the place she was in and tried to pull back so she could get help. That's when he became aggressive. He wanted her back.'

Isla's stomach hollowed. It was such a sad, familiar story. 'I'm guessing she didn't invite him to the party?'

'She told him she didn't want to see him again plus I'd warned him off, which is one of the reasons I was suspected of assaulting him. Toula was determined to dry out and get her life on track. But he gatecrashed, getting past security when some friends staged a diversion. He was out of control, high on something and aggressive.'

Theo turned to stare across the city. 'He got into an argument with someone and paid with his life. Toula was one of the first to see him lying there and I can still hear the sound of her screams. They just went on and on.' Isla threaded her fingers through his and leaned closer. 'After that she just closed in on herself. She couldn't function, couldn't even talk. She's been in treatment ever since. The one mercy is that her memory of that night is blank, totally erased.'

'Oh, Theo.' Isla turned and hugged him close. How much he and his family had been through. 'I promise I'll be careful with Toula and take our relationship at her pace. I certainly won't press her to become best friends.'

Molten gold showed in his remarkable eyes as he embraced her and lifted her onto his lap. 'Toula's just as likely to insist that you do.' He paused. 'Sorry, now you're damp.' But his arms stayed firm around her, just where she wanted them.

'I don't care about that.' She sounded choked up and didn't care.

'I'm sorry for upsetting you too.'

As if he were to blame for that horrible series of events. 'It's just pregnancy hormones. I'm fine. You don't need to worry about me.'

'But I do, Isla. All the time.'

It wasn't fair that he affected her this way, his tenderness undoing her resolve to keep her distance. Her heart hammered as she heard herself say, 'I've been thinking. About your invitation to stay here.'

Theo stiffened and she saw excitement in his expression.

'I'm not saying I want to marry you.' Though to her consternation just saying the word made her heart tremble with something she could only describe as joy. 'But I'd like to stay in Athens longer. We need to decide about the future and the best way to do that is if we learn to trust each other.'

She realised she'd been the one throwing up barriers. Theo was the one letting her into his life, giving her access to everything that mattered to him. He was serious about making their relationship work. That humbled her, especially since the reason she tried to hold back emotionally wasn't because she feared Theo but herself.

'You don't trust me yet?'

Isla was silent, searching for the right words. This was momentous and she needed to be absolutely honest but not raise impossible expectations. 'I trust you, Theo. I trust you with my body, my well-being, and I know you wouldn't deliberately hurt me.'

'Of course not, I—'

She stopped his words with her fingertips against his lips. 'And I trust you to do your best for our baby. I know you'll be a terrific father.' Whenever she thought of it there was a warm glow in her belly. She knew Theo would be strong but tender and encouraging. 'But that doesn't mean we need to marry. I still have reservations. I need to think through the implications.'

Because she knew now, more than ever, that Theo had the power to hurt her as no one else had. She'd thought parting from him the first time was tough but if she married him it would be because she loved him, even if she didn't say the words. She didn't think she had the capacity to pick up the pieces if he shattered her heart again.

Theo's embrace was gentle as he held her to him. 'You're telling me to be patient.'

Isla felt his broad chest rise and fall against her on a deep breath. What argument would he use next?

Finally he nodded. 'This courtship is going to be excellent for my character.' He bent his head and she caught a twinkle in his eyes. 'But we can enjoy ourselves while I'm being patient, can't we?'

He nuzzled the sensitive skin below her ear then grazed his teeth there, making her shiver.

'Absolutely.'

'Excellent.'

His hand went to the top button of her shirt as his mouth closed over hers and Isla found herself forgetting what it was that had so worried her. When Theo seduced her she felt…cherished. Could it be that she was fretting over phantoms and this would work out after all?

CHAPTER FOURTEEN

AUTOMATIC GATES SLID open and Theo drove in through a surprisingly lush garden and up to a beautiful two-storey home with shutters framing long windows and soft terracotta tiles on the roof. In the turning circle before the door a delicate fountain tinkled soothingly as he switched off the engine.

Isla slid damp hands down her trousers, taking in the elegant charm of the property. Nerves danced down her spine.

'You'll be fine.' Theo squeezed her hand then kissed it. 'She's not scary, just excited. I've never brought a woman home to meet the family before.'

'You've never…!'

His eyes crinkled as he got out of the car and she knew he'd waited to drop that bombshell, knowing it would distract her. Then suddenly they weren't alone. A handsome woman in red hurried towards the car. 'Theo, Isla, you're here at last.'

'Mamma.' Theo bent down to envelop her in a bear hug. Then he turned and reached for Isla's hand. 'I'd like you to meet—'

'Isla. I'm so pleased to see you.' The older woman's voice and brown eyes were warm as she shook Isla's hand. 'It's so kind of you to visit.'

From what Theo had told her Isla had expected a strong-minded woman, kind but a little daunting. She was surprised to feel the other woman's hand tremble as if she too were nervous.

'It's lovely of you to invite me. I don't know anyone in Athens yet, other than Theo.'

Mrs Karalis shook her head. 'We'll remedy that.' Then she leaned in and embraced her warmly. 'Now, that's a better welcome.' Her eyes sparkled and her smile was vivacious as she linked Isla's hand through her arm. 'Come inside, we have so much to talk about.'

And they did. Isla hadn't thought herself particularly loquacious, but that afternoon was full of laughter and conversation. Instead of the interrogation she'd expected they chatted nonstop and easily. Isla felt like she'd been accepted into a circle of warmth and belonging.

At one point Mrs Karalis sent Theo to check the charcoal burner outside while she led Isla into the kitchen.

'Men love to play at being chefs. Give them a fire and something to cook on a skewer and they're happy.' She lifted the lid on a simmering dish and Isla's nose twitched.

'That smells wonderful.'

'It's my beef *stifado*.' She paused then shrugged. 'In the old days we couldn't afford meat often. This was a high treat. It's one of Theo's favourites so I hope you like it.'

'If it tastes like it smells, I'm sure I will.'

'He's…well? He doesn't tell me much, because he doesn't like to worry me, but these last months have been difficult for him.'

Isla met serious brown eyes and saw a depth of affection and worry that made her heart twist.

'He's well.' She stifled the memory of two nights when Theo had tossed and turned, rubbing the scar on his temple and muttering beneath his breath, obviously having a bad dream. Once he'd even shouted out, until she'd whispered soothing words and he'd subsided back into quiet sleep.

She barely knew his mother but didn't want to worry her. She and her family had already been through so much. 'He's busy with the company though and concerned about you and his sister.'

'He told you about Toula?' The other woman's head came up.

'A little. That she hadn't been well and was recuperating.'

Mrs Karalis nodded. 'She's had some difficulties and taking up with Costas Stavroulis was disastrous for her. But I believe she's turned a corner. With luck…'

Theo came in then, saying the first course was ready.

The rest of the day the three of them were together, talking, laughing and eating. There were no more confidences but by the time they left Theo's mother had already arranged a date for her and Isla to meet for lunch and visit her favourite knitting shop. And when they parted the older woman's hug was even warmer than before.

It was early days but Isla couldn't help but imagine what it would be like to be a permanent part of this small, deeply caring family. If she married Theo she and their child would *belong*. It was a heady thought.

Theo's chest was aflame. Each breath felt like burning coals dragged over raw flesh. But the physical pain didn't matter. It was the horror of being here, in this tiny dark place, so small he couldn't even stand. The walls and ceiling were shrinking around him and soon he'd hear his bones crack as he was pulverised into dust.

He shoved the metal door with all his strength, despite knowing it was useless. He'd keep trying until his final breath. He had to get out of here because—he felt the hair rise on his nape—Isla was in the cell next to him. She didn't cry out, she was too stoic for that, but he *knew* she was there. He sensed it in every aching atom of his body. In the terrible thud of his heart against his ribs.

A scream rent the air, high-pitched with fear. Toula.

Theo scrabbled at the door, fingers bleeding. He hammered his shoulder against it. He couldn't let harm come to them. Not Isla. Not—

'Theo!' Isla's voice came, cool running water against his burning body. He gasped, pain searing his chest. 'Open your eyes, Theo.'

Slender fingers shaped his face but he couldn't be distracted. He needed to save—

'Please, Theo.'

Something soft brushed his face and the scent of rosemary filled his nostrils. Rosemary and sweet woman.

He snapped his eyes open. 'Isla!'

'It's all right, Theo. You're safe.'

'You're here.' In the darkness he reached for her, gathering her to his pounding chest, wrapping his arms, his whole body around her, rocking her close. 'You're safe.'

'Of course I'm safe. We both are. You had a nightmare.'

Theo exhaled, his body shuddering with relief. A nightmare. He had them occasionally but usually he managed not to wake Isla.

He swallowed, his throat scratchy. Had he been calling out? What else had he done? 'Did I hurt you?'

'No, I'm fine. I was just worried about you.'

But Theo ran shaking fingers over her, needing to check, discovering silky skin and fragrant curves. The swell where she carried their child. His heart somersaulted. Safe. Isla and the baby were safe.

'I'm sorry. I didn't mean to scare you.'

'You didn't scare me. But you were so distressed I was concerned.'

She moved as if to reach the bedside lamp but he

stopped her, capturing her hand and bringing it to his lips. 'It was just a dream.'

Though his body felt racked with pain from the tension and his belly roiled with remembered fear for Isla and his stepsister.

'They're getting worse, aren't they?'

He stiffened. She *knew* about his dreams? He'd thought he'd concealed them.

When she spoke her voice was soft with a mixture of tenderness and amusement. 'We've shared this bed for almost two months, Theo. It's a very big bed but we always seem to end up in each other's arms. You've been having occasional bad dreams ever since I got here.'

'You never said anything.'

'Nor did you. I thought that, if you wanted to share what's bothering you, you would.'

Theo froze in the act of sliding his fingers through her soft hair. 'There's nothing bothering me.'

Sourness filled his mouth. He hated lying to Isla. But this wasn't his secret to share, no matter that he wanted to. Besides, he only had suspicions that it had been Toula at the top of the stairs that night. Little Toula facing her aggressive ex. She couldn't recall that night at all.

He squeezed his eyes shut, the familiar maelstrom of emotions whirling inside him, so fast he felt light-headed. But what could he do? He couldn't force the issue. He had a duty to protect.

'So it's just the memory of your time in prison bothering you? Nothing else?'

'Isn't that enough?'

Isla stiffened in his hold. She didn't move away yet he sensed her mental withdrawal and silently cursed.

'Of course it is. I think you should see someone, a counsellor, especially as the dreams are getting worse.'

'It's okay. Nothing to worry about.'

Isla said nothing for the longest time and he found himself holding his breath as if awaiting judgement. So many barriers had fallen between them. In every way except Isla's continued refusal to marry, he felt they'd reached a new level of understanding and trust. A trust he broke by not being up-front with her.

But how could he, when it meant a different betrayal? Yet keeping this secret was increasingly hard.

'It's natural the experience would impact on you, Theo.' Her voice was gentle, making him feel even more guilty that he held back one final nugget of truth. 'It doesn't mean you're any less macho.'

Relief stirred. Isla thought his reticence was male ego. That was as good an excuse as any.

'If you don't want to talk about that, there's something else I need to understand.'

'Go on,' he said warily.

'You know I've been seeing Simon at the University?'

'Of course.'

His friend was trying to persuade Isla to continue her studies in Athens. In the meantime he'd offered her some part-time work cataloguing finds and doing a little research. Theo had high hopes that soon she'd accept the inevitable, agreeing to marry him and build a permanent life in Greece. They were good together, more than good. Their relationship was better, stronger and deeper than before, unlike any he'd had or could imagine having with any other woman.

She'd even coped amazingly with the media stampede when they announced her pregnancy. His mother and Isla were firm friends and since Toula's recent return the three had bonded in a way he'd hardly dared hope for.

'Today Simon said something that made it clear he hadn't asked that you check on me in London.' She paused. 'That's what you told me.'

Theo released an easy breath. Was that all? Strange how, at the time, it had seemed vital that Isla believe he'd only looked her up as a favour to a friend. His pride wouldn't let him admit the truth, in case she really had washed her hands of him. At the time he'd convinced himself it was best if he sever their relationship, but he hadn't been able to stay away. They'd moved on so far from that.

He shifted onto his back, pulling her closer into his embrace, her head resting at his collarbone, her rounded belly solid against him. He smiled.

'I was protecting myself.'

'From what?' Her hand spread on his ribs and he covered it with his.

'From the likelihood you hated me for cutting you loose.'

Isla's fingers twitched beneath his. 'Well, that was honest. You're saying you didn't want to admit you wanted to see me but used your friend as an excuse?'

'Put like that it sounds juvenile, doesn't it?' But there hadn't been anything childish about Theo's feelings. 'I believed it for the best that we parted. But even believing that, I kept thinking about you. I couldn't leave it the way I had. I told myself that if I saw you for myself, saw that you'd moved on with your life...'

Even that implied a lie. Isla had become important to him in a short time. He'd told himself in prison it was sentiment and the memory of great sex that kept him thinking of her, but he'd known at a deep, never admitted level it was more than that. He'd needed to see Isla because he felt things for her he'd never experienced before. He wanted her in his life forever and couldn't imagine it without her.

'You wanted to check I was okay so you needn't feel guilty about pushing me away?' Her voice was flat.

'It was more complex than that.' Theo swallowed. 'I cared for you, Isla. I still do, even more so now. When

Simon mentioned he'd heard you'd dropped out and your tutor thought you were sick I had to see for myself.'

'Then, when you discovered I had morning sickness, your sense of responsibility kicked in so you couldn't just leave.'

Theo wished he'd let her turn the light on. He wanted to see her face for her tone made him think she was upset. What was wrong with him feeling responsible for her? He'd thought she'd be happy at his admission he'd visited because he cared about her.

'So the sixty-four-million-dollar question is, why did you push me away in the first place? You never gave me a proper explanation.'

Theo hated the brittle edge to her usually warm voice and the tension he felt in her even as she lay naked against him.

'I'm sorry, Isla. I never wanted to hurt you.' He heard her swift intake of breath and continued. 'But I knew you'd be hurt. The way I ended our relationship wasn't ideal.'

'It was brutal.'

'Yes.' He paused. 'I was in a brutal place at the time.' He didn't have words to describe how terrible it had been, not just living in a cell, but the nightmare of it all, helpless to care for those who needed him.

'I'm sorry, Theo.' Warm lips pressed against his collarbone. 'What I went through was nothing compared with what you suffered.'

'Ah, Isla. Don't apologise. I treated you badly even if it was for the best reasons.'

'Tell me.' She lay her head against him again and he felt the change in her, no longer taut with hurt but supple and receptive.

'I was trying to protect you.'

She made a sound in the back of her throat, somewhere

been a laugh and a snort of derision. 'And I was trying to support *you*. You were the one locked up!'

'And I appreciated it. Many so-called friends melted away once the news of my arrest broke.' Fortunately his real friends hadn't. 'It meant a lot, knowing you believed in me.'

She snuggled closer. 'I'm glad. At the time it didn't seem like it.'

Guilt punched him. 'I was brutal because I had to be. You kept turning up at the prison and it wasn't a place for you.' The thought of Isla, even in the waiting room of such a place, made him sick. 'I *had* to send you away.'

Silence. Didn't she believe him? But then he'd never fully shared this with her. His arms tightened, cradling her, his hand stroking her thick hair.

'I felt tainted,' he admitted at last. 'And I wanted to protect you from that.'

'Theo!' He heard her outrage but ignored it.

'My world caved in the day they arrested me, Isla. I truly hadn't believed it possible they'd do such a thing and I wanted you well clear. I didn't want you embroiled in something so sordid, especially when I wasn't free to protect you. You've seen how fascinated the media is by you. Imagine what it would have been like if they'd learned you were my lover.'

He felt her shudder and knew that at last she began to understand. 'It wasn't just the almighty scandal. There was a dangerous edge to it with emotions running high and Stavroulis whipping up so much negativity. I feared for you. It even seemed possible the old man might take out his hatred on those closest to me.'

Before he hadn't intended to share that with her, but he hated keeping things from her.

'Oh, Theo.' She shook her head, her hair brushing his skin. 'I didn't know how long it would take to clear my name.

If ever. The authorities seemed unwilling to believe the evidence in my favour.' For a while he'd feared he'd never be free. That still haunted his dreams. 'I couldn't allow you to stay in Greece, vulnerable to all that hatred.'

'You pushed me away because you cared?' Her voice was small, as if he'd taken her by surprise.

'Of course. Even when I was released I couldn't go to you. My mother and Toula needed me badly. I had to stay in Athens to support them. Toula was so fragile...'

Yet that had eaten at him. For the first time family obligation had grated, because it had prevented him going to Isla. He'd been falling for her, he realised with a quiver of recognition. He'd been enchanted by her, charmed, and hadn't understood the depth of his feelings until he'd pushed her away.

No wonder he'd felt empty without her. She'd never been simply a romantic fling, had she? Even before her pregnancy, Isla had been important. She...

'I wish you'd explained all that earlier.'

'If I'd explained, would you have done what I wanted and left Greece?'

'Probably not.'

Of course she wouldn't. His woman was brave if reckless.

His woman.

Theo breathed deep, drawing in the truth of that to his very core. Isla *was* his woman. He felt it in his bones, in his head and his gut. He wanted to say it out loud, make her agree. But he couldn't push her. He had to work for it. How was it that he knew, with every atom of his being, that they were meant to be together and Isla still couldn't see it?

Despite the growing understanding between them, she still held back, refusing to accept marriage. It drove him crazy. What more did he need to do to convince her? He could seduce her into agreement. But was that coercion?

Besides, he wanted her thinking clearly and actively deciding to be his wife.

Every time they discussed marriage Isla withdrew, countering every point with some pragmatic, if negligible argument. He had to prove to her that on a practical level it was the most sensible option for them and their child.

'You're a stubborn woman, Isla.'

He felt her smile against his flesh. 'Just as well, since you're the most determined man I know.'

She made it sound like a compliment. 'That's all? Determined?' He moved his hands across her delectable body, slowing as he reached places that made her soften and sigh.

'And sexy,' she sighed, twisting and arching into his touch, her voice suddenly breathless. 'Sexy and sinful.'

Theo nearly told her there was nothing sinful about making love to the only woman he'd ever need. The woman who, he'd discovered, made him whole. But he didn't want to scare her. He'd take it slow, convincing her with his actions and his loving that he was the man for her. Soon, surely, she'd admit it.

He just had to be patient. If it didn't kill him first.

CHAPTER FIFTEEN

'I LIKE THE SWIMSUIT,' Toula said, looking up from her magazine as Isla walked across the roof terrace to the pool, the pavers warm beneath her bare feet. 'I'm glad I persuaded you to buy it. Theo will approve, it's classy but seductive and we all know how sexy he finds you.'

Isla blushed. She'd never had a sister, or anyone really, to talk with frankly about her private life. It took some getting used to but she liked it. She valued her budding friendship with Toula. Theo's mother and stepsister had been so welcoming Isla began to believe she'd found the acceptance, the family, she'd always wanted.

She also adored that Theo found her sexy, even with her now well-rounded curves of obvious pregnancy. Intimacy was more satisfying than ever and even when they weren't making love he usually had his arm around her or her hand in his as if, like her, he felt their growing connection.

'No need to look embarrassed, Isla. It's sweet the way you dote on each other. That's why I always call before coming upstairs to the penthouse, to give you notice.'

Toula's laugh was a rare, lovely sound, making Isla smile.

'I approve. You're good together.' Toula paused, suddenly earnest. Theo's sister was so different to the waif-like woman she'd met weeks ago. More outgoing, more ready to talk. 'He's a good man, you know.'

Isla sank onto a sun lounge next to Toula's. 'I know. He's special.'

She'd seen him with his family and others, both relaxed and under stress. She'd felt his care for her and seen the long hours he worked to get the family business back on track. He was dependable, honest and caring.

They were good together, their trust and affection growing daily. Was it any wonder her doubts disintegrated like water evaporating in the spring sunshine?

Her blood pumped faster. She trusted Theo.

She loved him.

Isla had fought against his logic and her own desires too long. She loved him so much and believed in time he'd learn to love her too. She wanted to be with him and support him.

She was ready to marry him.

'Why don't you put him out of his misery and marry him?'

Isla lifted her head sharply. 'I needed to be sure.'

Toula leaned forward, her magazine falling. 'But you're sure now?'

'That's a discussion for me to have with your brother.'

Eagerness filled her. Maybe tonight before they went out to the black-tie dinner. She'd wear the gold dress he liked so much and tell him her decision. Maybe they'd stay home to celebrate…

Seeing Toula's assessing look, Isla sought a distraction. She glanced at the magazine on the ground and saw it was a university prospectus. 'You're considering study?'

'Perhaps. I don't have a good track record for sticking at things.' Toula shrugged. 'But after all my counselling sessions I've discovered an interest in psychology.'

It was wonderful that Toula was thinking about the future. 'It's not the end of the world if you begin and change your mind. But my experience is that if you find the subject interesting you want to stick at it.'

'You really think I could do it?'

'I don't see why not.'

'Everything is turning out well, isn't it?' Toula gave her a tentative smile. 'I'm feeling better, mamma is happy, Theo has you and he's clearly thriving.'

Isla frowned. 'Well…'

'What?' Isla shifted on the seat, wishing she'd stayed silent. 'Isla? What's wrong?'

Isla bit her lip. She didn't like to dampen Toula's enthusiasm but she knew there was something very wrong, something Theo refused to discuss. But she loved him. Didn't that include an obligation to care for him, despite his belief that he could shoulder every burden?

'Theo is okay,' she said slowly, not wanting to spook Toula. She had her suspicions about the root cause of Theo's trouble but couldn't be sure. 'But he has things on his mind. You should talk to him.'

'You think my brother will open up about something on his mind? He'll clam up. He sees it as his role to protect *me*, though I'm stronger than he thinks.'

Was she? Isla was torn between wanting to see Theo unburdened and caution about Toula's capacity to deal with harsh reality.

'Isla?' Toula's voice was sharp. 'What is it? Tell me.'

She sighed. 'He's had nightmares since prison and they're getting worse.' She met Toula's eyes. 'Do you know some people still think he killed Costa Stavroulis? They gossip about him when he enters a room and it's affected the company's reputation. That's why he works such long hours. Old Mr Stavroulis is making his life hell because he's got no one else to blame.'

Toula paled. 'I had no idea. No one said anything.'

Of course not. Because they worried about her. 'Are you okay, Toula? Maybe I shouldn't have—'

'Of course you should have told me. Mamma and Theo wrap me in cotton wool.' With good reason. But the woman looking back at Isla didn't look panicked. 'Thanks for trusting me with the truth, Isla. It means a lot.'

Isla nodded and hoped she'd done the right thing.

That evening Isla was nervous as she dressed for the reception. Tonight would be special and the Grecian dress gave her confidence. She'd added the gold earrings Theo had given her, beautiful replicas of ancient designs featuring bees feeding from delicate flowers. He'd grumbled about wanting to put a ring on her finger instead but had been mollified at her delight in the gift, precious not just for its monetary value but his thoughtfulness in choosing a design she loved.

It wasn't the reception making her nervous. It was telling Theo she'd marry him, though he didn't love her. Yet. Surely he would one day.

Isla smoothed her hand down her rounded belly and felt the flutter of the baby moving. Anxiety eased as love squeezed her heart. It would be okay. Everything she'd ever wanted was here. A family. A man who lit up her world.

She imagined his delight when she told him. He'd—

The bedroom door swung open and thudded against the wall.

Her heart leapt into her throat. 'Theo?'

Something was wrong. He looked frayed around the edges, something she'd never seen. Usually nothing fazed him. Isla hurried forward as he closed the door carefully. But she stopped as she read his narrowed gaze. She blinked, disbelieving, as she met a furious stare.

'What did you think you were doing?'

'Sorry?'

He shook his head as if trying to clear it. 'Bothering Toula with all that stuff. You *know* how fragile she is.'

Isla's fingers threaded together. 'What's happened? How is she?' Toula had seemed fine, if a bit quiet, when they'd parted two hours ago.

He pinched the bridge of his nose. 'How do you think she is, after you worried her unnecessarily?'

'Theo, is she okay? Does she need someone to be with her?'

'If she does it won't be *you*!' he growled.

Isla stiffened and blinked at his savage tone. 'Tell me, Theo. Does she need company?'

'Apparently not,' he huffed finally. 'We talked in her apartment then she told me to leave because she had things to do.'

Isla took a slow breath. 'Perhaps you should trust Toula to know what's best for her.'

'What would you know about it? You've only known her a short time and suddenly you're an expert?' His chest rose on a mighty breath. 'How *dare* you get her worked up with some sob story about me suffering? And about old man Stavroulis? Were you trying to push her to the edge all over again?'

Isla retreated a step, her hand to her throat, stunned he could say such a thing. He couldn't mean that. It was stress talking. Theo worried about his stepsister, with reason. But Toula's behaviour after their discussion had convinced Isla she'd done the right thing.

'I only—'

'There's no *only* about it. You had *no right*! You don't know what you're stirring up. I don't want you going near Toula or interfering with my family. Keep out of it.'

Her breath was a shocked hiss as his words sank into silence. Ice settled around her heart.

'Yet you want me to marry you and be part of that family.'

'That's not the same thing. That's different.' Theo raked his hand through his hair and turned to pace.

Of course it's different. It was all about the baby.

Isla felt herself crumble inside. All those hopes, all her confidence. A single instant had revealed a truth she'd deliberately avoided facing.

Yet still Isla waited for Theo to apologise, say he didn't mean it.

And waited.

Slowly, reluctantly, she absorbed the truth. Their relationship wasn't real. It was a farce. There was just Theo and his almighty sense of duty, sweetened by physical desire. She'd kidded herself thinking he wanted *her*, spinning fantasies all over again. He wanted their child but she, Isla, was additional baggage.

She'd never *really* belong in that intimate circle he truly cared for. Even if they married she wouldn't belong. She was an outsider and always would be. Second-best. Not worthy of love. Not an equal in his eyes.

Pain lanced her chest and stole her breath.

Isla took a step back and sank onto the bed, knees trembling. How could she have believed there was anything else between them?

Theo stopped pacing near the door as if he couldn't bear to be close to her. 'You've got no idea what you've done. How could you?' His jaw set in a grim line. 'But I can't let you meddle.'

She swallowed a knot of despair and dammed tears. She couldn't get her voice to work so nodded instead.

Theo frowned then stepped forward but she couldn't bear any more. With a sudden, desperate surge of energy she shot to her feet and into the bathroom, locking the door behind her.

Her breaths sounded like sobs as she leaned against the door, scared he'd try to follow. The one thing she had left was pride and she didn't want him to see her undone.

She needn't have worried. Theo didn't follow. Instead she heard a phone ring, then his deep voice, then silence.

How long she stayed there, frozen with distress and misery, she didn't know, but suddenly she felt claustrophobic. She needed air and space to think. Not on the roof terrace where Theo might see her, but out. She had to get out.

Isla didn't remember leaving the apartment or taking the lift. She marched across the marble foyer of the apartment block, catching a flurry of movement from the corner of her eye. Her bodyguard, hurrying to follow.

Isla didn't want company. She needed to be alone.

She picked up her long skirt and hurried onto the street. She'd get a taxi, find somewhere to be alone. In a couple of strides she crossed the pavement, wishing she was wearing flats instead of spindly high heels. Searching the traffic, she stepped onto the street when her heel caught something and out of nowhere the ground came up to meet her.

There was a surge of pain and everything went blank.

CHAPTER SIXTEEN

ISLA'S MOUTH WAS dry and tasted strange. She didn't want to open her eyes. She had a terrible sense of foreboding.

Where was she? Something told her she wasn't in her own bed. She opened her eyes then closed them against the light. Gingerly she reached an arm across the sheet. Her shoulder felt stiff…

'You're awake! Oh, my dear, I'm so happy.' The woman's voice was familiar but Isla couldn't place it. 'Theo will be so relieved. He's been frantic.'

Theo! Theo Karalis.

Isla didn't hear the rest of the words as memory hit like a bombshell. His fury. The revelation of how he really felt about her. Her flight from his apartment. The baby—

Her baby…

Scalding tears leaked from her eyes.

'Please, my baby…' Isla dragged her heavy arm to her abdomen. It was still swollen as if with pregnancy but that mean anything? There was no fluttery movement inside.

She snapped her eyes open, wincing in the glare, and saw Theo's mother rise from a chair near the bed as a nurse entered.

Isla was in hospital. She tried to catch a breath, telling herself they'd look after her baby. But what if…?

The nurse said something she didn't catch and, with a long backwards look, Mrs Karalis left the room.

'It's good to see you awake, Ms Jacobs.' The nurse took her pulse. 'You probably feel strange but you're safe.'

'My baby?'

Did she imagine a slight hesitation? 'You're still pregnant, Ms Jacobs.'

Isla's breath shuddered in a sigh of relief, her eyes closing as tears streamed down her cheeks. The nurse talked about bruising and X-rays but she didn't take it in. Not until she heard that name again and her heart squeezed.

'Mr Karalis has been here all the time. He's only just left but I'm sure he'll be back any minute.'

'No!' Isla opened her eyes and met the nurse's gaze. 'I don't want to see him. Please. I don't want to see anyone.'

Calm brown eyes surveyed her. 'If that's what you want. Now, let me check you over.'

Isla lost track of time in hospital. Was this only the second night here? There'd been more tests and more reassurances. The baby was fine, they said, though Isla fretted when she couldn't feel it move until they used a monitor so she could hear its heartbeat. She cried again then. She cried a lot, as if she'd saved a lifetime's tears and was only now releasing them.

As for her, bruising they said, and a knock to the head that had initially concerned them. But today the consensus was more cheerful. She could leave soon, though she'd have to have someone with her.

That's what kept her from sleep this evening. She'd be released but where would she go? The staff had passed on a message from Theo's mother, inviting Isla to stay with her, but how could she accept?

Wearily, Isla closed her eyes, telling herself it was better for the baby if she slept now and worried tomorrow.

The door opened and footsteps approached. 'Isla.'

Her eyes sprang open. How had he got in? He must have evaded the staff. She opened her mouth to order Theo from the room then stopped, frowning.

He looked like a stranger, gaunt and dishevelled, dark circles under his eyes, that jagged scar livid and grim lines around his mouth. Isla told herself it was an illusion. He couldn't have lost weight in a couple of days and as for dishevelled, his clothes were of finest quality, made for him. Yet he looked haggard, worse than when he'd woken from nightmare.

'I had to see you. To check myself that you were all right.'

'Don't you mean the check on the baby?'

He flinched but didn't deny it. 'Both of you.' Isla was about to challenge that but his words stopped her. 'I love our child already but I don't know it yet, not like I know *you*, Isla. *You're* the one I'm most afraid of losing. I couldn't bear that.'

'Stop that!' Isla pushed herself up against the pillows as he approached. 'Don't lie to me, Theo.'

He shook his head, eyes never leaving hers as he put his hand his heart. 'No lie, Isla. Nothing but the truth.'

Her own heart rolled over. She wasn't ready for this. She'd known she'd have to face him sometime but still felt too raw.

'You're too late, Theo.' Intrigued, she saw his face turn pale but she couldn't afford sympathy just because he wasn't getting what he wanted. 'I can't do this any longer, be what you want me to be. Why should I settle for less than I want just because it suits you?'

If Theo had looked bad before, now he looked stricken. 'I know—'

'You *don't* know.' She loved him and had been ready to accept second-best, just to be with him. To be an unloved wife. 'You did me a favour, actually, spelling out my real place in your life.'

'I'm sorry, Isla. You don't know how sorry. I didn't mean it the way it came out.'

She shook her head, the terrible pain inside blanketed by resignation. Was there any point in more words? She looked him straight in the eye and said, 'I deserve more. More than you can give me, Theo.'

The bedside chair scraped as he collapsed onto it, head bowed. Isla was stunned to see his hand shake as he tunnelled his fingers through his hair.

He didn't look at her as he took a huge breath, then another. Finally he lifted his head. His terrible, stark expression caught her breath in her throat. He looked to be in pain too.

'You deserve everything good, Isla. So does our child.'

She waited for him to try to persuade her to change her mind. Instead he simply looked at her, as if nothing else mattered.

'I apologise for what I said.' He lifted his hand before she could interrupt. 'I'm not making excuses but I owe you the truth.'

'Go on.'

'What I said was terrible and uncalled for and I truly didn't mean it the way it came out. I'm sorry I hurt you.' Theo looked at his hands. 'I was petrified for Toula.'

Isla nodded. 'I know.'

'But you don't. You assumed I was afraid she'd have a relapse if you mentioned the party, and that was true to some extent. But it was far more.' He paused. 'I feared what would happen if she remembered the truth about that night and told the police she was the one who pushed Costa to his death.'

Isla's breath hissed, her eyes popping wide. She'd wondered, given what Theo had said about Toula's ex being aggressive and wanting her back. 'You *knew* she'd done it?'

'No one knew the truth, not even Toula. She couldn't remember anything. But those stairs were a shortcut to a terrace overlooking the gardens and the guest bedroom wing. Toula's room wasn't there but there'd been some problem with the air conditioning in hers and she used one of the guest rooms to get ready.'

He paused. 'It seemed…possible, but Toula was in no state to relive that night.'

Isla remembered all Theo had gone through, both in prison and afterwards. 'You didn't say anything.'

'How could I? I didn't know for sure and I couldn't push Toula. Even if she recovered her memory and it had been her, what would happen? How could I expect her to face what I'd been through, knowing how fragile she is?'

'Oh, Theo.' Isla recalled him saying he had broad shoulders. She hadn't understood just how deep his protective instincts ran.

'I *did* lash out at you and you didn't deserve it. But you needed to know why.'

'You were afraid Toula might collapse again, or maybe face arrest.'

He nodded, his face grim. 'Exactly. I'm sorry.'

Isla shook her head. She wanted to reach out, smooth the worry lines from his forehead. But it wouldn't be right, not when she was determined to keep her distance.

'How is she?'

Theo's mouth hitched up at one side. 'Better than I expected. She really is stronger. And she'll need to be.'

Isla's heart sank. 'She was responsible?'

He nodded. 'She's been getting flashes of memory since returning to Athens but wasn't sure if she could believe them. She's gone to the police.'

Isla sat up, heart pounding. 'She's under arrest?'

'She's got bail. The authorities say it was self-defence. Apparently her arms and torso were covered in bruises that night, all documented when she went into care that same night. I knew Costa was a controlling brute but I hadn't known how badly he'd treated her. He was trying to drag her out of the house and she shoved him away. The fall was an accident, but she'll have to face trial.'

Isla pushed the covers aside.

'Isla, what are you doing?'

She leaned over and closed her hand around Theo's. 'I'm so sorry.'

'Not as much as I am.' He breathed deep and turned his hand to clasp hers, his warmth enfolding her. 'Toula will need all the support she can get but I think my stepsister is stronger than I gave her credit for. My one regret is you. I love you, Isla.'

She blinked, watching his mouth, wondering if she'd misheard.

'I've worked out I fell in love with you right at the beginning. That's why I had to send you away, so you weren't tainted by my degradation. I couldn't bear for you to be caught up in that.' His mouth was a grim line that told its own story. 'Then, when I finally had you back and recognised my feelings, I took it slowly, hoping you'd fall in love with me too, only to destroy my chances the other night.'

Isla's heart squeezed, remembering that awful time. 'That was fear talking.'

'It was, but that's no excuse.'

Isla thought of all he'd been through. The trauma, the attempt on his life, the fear not just for himself but for her, his mother and stepsister. The ridiculous work schedule, trying to save his company from the scandal not of his making. His decency in dealing with the old man who saw him as an enemy. His care for Toula and for her.

She could choose to be offended and carry a grudge or she could choose to believe his sincerity.

'What do you see happening next, Theo?'

He squeezed her hand, his smile sad. 'I'll take my lead from you.'

Isla hated seeing him this way, a proud man humbled. He'd made mistakes but with noble intentions.

'What I'd like is for you to hold me. I've missed you so much.'

His eyes rounded and for a moment she saw disbelief on his features. But her Theo wasn't the passive type. He stood, carefully put his arms around her and lifted her off the bed. Seconds later she was cradled in his lap, his heart thudding against her ear, his arms strong but gentle around her.

'You're not the only one who fell in love right at the beginning. I never stopped loving you, even when you sent me away. Even when I tried to hate you.'

'Sh. Don't say it, *glykia mou*.' Glowing golden eyes held hers. 'You really mean it? You love me?'

'I thought it was obvious.'

Theo's laugh was the best sound in the world. Bright and full of joy. She'd never tire of hearing it.

'*S'agapo*, Isla. I love you so much.' Tenderly he kissed her and she felt the magic weave through her body like sparkling ribbons of flame. 'We're going to be absurdly happy.'

He sounded so sure she had to laugh, but beneath the laughter was an equal certainty. Theo was her dream come true. No, better than some dream lover. He was real— flawed, as she was, but honest and loving, and they were made for each other.

EPILOGUE

THE SCENT OF meat cooking on the charcoal grill filled the balmy evening. Children's laughter drifted over the hum of nearby conversation.

On the shore stood the home where his mother had been born, the place he and Isla had spent those idyllic first weeks. Now renovated, it was guest accommodation, where Simon, as leader of the dig team, had been based the last few months.

'You always were an incredibly lucky guy, Theo. I'm almost jealous,' Simon said.

Theo looked down at the baby sleeping in his arms and felt a rush of tenderness. Niko's dark hair was like his own but his smile was Isla's. As for his determination, he got that from them both.

Theo grinned. 'I'm not going to argue. I know how blessed I am.'

Who'd have thought, six years ago, when it felt like he carried the weight of the world on his shoulders, that life could be so glorious?

'Life's been good to you too, my friend. I know you're eager to get back to Athens to show off your latest finds. And take up your promotion.'

'Well...' Simon shrugged. 'Perhaps a little. But this place is paradise.'

'It is.' Not because of the scenic beauty or sprawling

house he and Isla had built. But because it was *home*, his and Isla's. Their retreat from the capital, close enough for commuting if they chose.

They had a perfect view over the silvery olive trees to the blue Aegean Sea where some of tonight's guests had moored sleek yachts.

Theo turned to survey the crowd around the spit roast on the vast terrace. There were archaeologists celebrating the last day of that season's dig. Locals from the village beyond the headland. Friends from Athens and beyond, including Isla's friend Rebecca from the UK. High-heeled sandals and designer dresses mingled with jeans and T-shirts and everywhere there were smiles.

Two women emerged from the crowd. Toula in lemon yellow and Isla, mouth-wateringly lovely in a halter neck dress of flame red. His pulse quickened at the sight. Two little girls, one five and one three, rushed forward.

'Daddy, Daddy!' They ran over and grabbed at his legs. 'Yiaya says you have to come.'

'You're needed to supervise the grill,' Toula added.

'In a moment. First I have to talk with my wife. Maybe you and Simon can keep an eye on it for now.'

Toula raised an eyebrow at his obvious tactic. She and Simon had been going out for eighteen months, through the end of her community service. The court had ruled she'd acted in self-defence and she hadn't been imprisoned. Since then she'd undergone more counselling and almost completed her university degree. She'd also visited Spiro Stavroulis to apologise for Costa's death. To Theo's amazement, she'd forged an unexpected if careful relationship with the old man, who'd been shocked at the revelations about his grandson.

Theo was proud of his stepsister.

'Come on, kids. Come and help Auntie Toula and

Simon.' His stepsister shot him a knowing look and herded them away.

Instantly Isla moved closer, stroking the head of their sleeping baby and planting a soft kiss on Theo's mouth.

He sighed. 'That's better.' He shifted his hold on Niko so he had an arm free to wrap around Isla.

'Was something wrong?' Misty blue eyes met his.

'Absolutely not. I was thinking how good life is.'

She grinned and leaned close. 'You've been very understanding about me spending so much time on the dig.'

Theo shook his head. 'You understand when I have to work. Besides, it's your passion.'

She kissed him again, this time adding a tiny nip of teeth. 'Not my only passion, *agapi mou*.'

My love. Were there any better words in the world?

'How long before we can sneak away?' he whispered.

Isla's laugh was like sunshine glittering on the sea. 'Too long. But it will be worth the wait.'

Theo held her close, her and their baby, while his gaze roved over his family and friends. Could life get any better?

He kissed Isla full on the mouth, bending her over his arm, enjoying her surprised gasp, and her rising passion.

It was a fact, he decided. He was the luckiest man in the world.

* * * * *

COMING SOON!

We really hope you enjoyed reading this book.
If you're looking for more romance, be sure to
head to the shops when new books are
available on

Thursday 2nd March

To see which titles are coming soon, please visit

millsandboon.co.uk/nextmonth

MILLS & BOON

MILLS & BOON ®

Coming next month

RETURNING FOR HIS RUTHLESS REVENGE
Louise Fuller

As the door closed, the room fell silent, and just like that they were alone.

His heart was suddenly hammering inside his chest. So, this was it. He had imagined this moment so many times inside his head. Had thought of all the clever, caustic things to say, only now his mind was blank.

Not that it mattered, he thought, anger pulsing over his skin. Sooner or later, she was going to realize that he wasn't going to disappear this time.

Not until he'd got what he came for.

Her eyes locked with his. He felt his heart tighten around the shard of ice that had been lodged there ever since Dove had cast him into the wilderness.

She was staring at him in silence, and he waited just as he had waited in that hotel bar. Only this time, she was the one who didn't know what was happening. Didn't know that she was about to be chewed up and spat out. But she would, soon enough.

"What are you doing here, Gabriel?" Her voice was husky but it was hearing her say his name again that made his breathing jerk.

Continue reading
RETURNING FOR HIS RUTHLESS REVENGE
Louise Fuller

Available next month
www.millsandboon.co.uk

MILLS & BOON

THE HEART OF ROMANCE

A ROMANCE FOR EVERY READER

MODERN

Prepare to be swept off your feet by sophisticated, sexy and seductive heroes, in some of the world's most glamourous and romantic locations, where power and passion collide.

HISTORICAL

Escape with historical heroes from time gone by. Whether your passion is for wicked Regency Rakes, muscled Vikings or rugged Highlanders, awake the romance of the past.

MEDICAL

Set your pulse racing with dedicated, delectable doctors in the high-pressure world of medicine, where emotions run high and passion, comfort and love are the best medicine.

True Love

Celebrate true love with tender stories of heartfelt romance, from the rush of falling in love to the joy a new baby can bring, and a focus on the emotional heart of a relationship.

Desire

Indulge in secrets and scandal, intense drama and plenty of sizzling hot action with powerful and passionate heroes who have it all: wealth, status, good looks…everything but the right woman.

HEROES

Experience all the excitement of a gripping thriller, with an intense romance at its heart. Resourceful, true-to-life women and strong, fearless men face danger and desire - a killer combination!

To see which titles are coming soon, please visit

millsandboon.co.uk/nextmonth

JOIN US ON SOCIAL MEDIA!

Stay up to date with our latest releases, author news and gossip, special offers and discounts, and all the behind-the-scenes action from Mills & Boon...

 @millsandboon

 @millsandboonuk

 facebook.com/millsandboon

@millsandboonuk

It might just be true love...